THROWAWAYS™

IMAGE COMICS, INC.

Robert Kirkman — Chief Operating Officer
Erik Larsen — Chief Financial Officer
Todd McFarlane — President
Marc Silvestri — Chief Executive Officer
Jim Valentino — Vice-President

Eric Stephenson — Publisher
Corey Murphy — Director of Sales
Jeff Boison — Director of Publishing Planning & Book Trade Sales
Jeremy Sullivan — Director of Digital Sales
Kat Salazar — Director of PR & Marketing
Branwyn Bigglestone — Controller
Drew Gill — Art Director
Jonathan Chan — Production Manager
Meredith Wallace — Print Manager
Briah Skelly — Publicist
Sasha Head — Sales & Marketing Production Designer
Randy Okamura — Digital Production Designer
David Brothers — Branding Manager
Olivia Ngai — Content Manager
Addison Duke — Production Artist
Vincent Kukua — Production Artist
Tricia Ramos — Production Artist
Jeff Stang — Direct Market Sales Representative
Emilio Bautista — Digital Sales Associate
Leanna Caunter — Accounting Assistant
Chloe Ramos-Peterson — Library Market Sales Representative

IMAGECOMICS.COM

CAITLIN KITTREDGE
Writer

STEVEN SANDERS
Artist

PAUL LITTLE
Colorist

RACHEL DEERING &
STEVE WANDS
Letterers

COVER ARTISTS

MAIKO KUZUNISHI	ROBERTA INGRANATA	JASON BAYS
Issue #1	Issue #1 SDCC Variant	Issue #2-4

FOREWARD

"Pitch whatever you want."

That was the response I got from Eric Stephenson at Image when he asked if I had my next comic lined up, and I told him no; what kind of story was he looking for?

That's a terrifying concept for a writer. An embarrassment of riches, really. I had a file on my computer that had ballooned to 50 pages over the years of concepts and story ideas that hadn't yet found a home.

I thought about playing it safe—I had just launched a successful horror comic at Vertigo, and I was known as the chick who wrote dark, disturbing fantasy stories with both sexy and unsexy monsters as stars.

But none of the monster stories were the ones I most wanted to write. If I stopped overthinking it, I knew which idea I needed to pitch. It was nothing like any of my previous books. It was gritty and real-world based and a thriller, and it starred a bunch of really broken characters grappling with issues I'd never tackled before. Plus, there wasn't a shirtless werewolf in sight.

I screwed up my nerves and pitched to the biggest opportunity of my career thus far a book in a genre I'd never written and was completely untested in.

Fortunately, Image said yes, and THROWAWAYS evolved and grew from a germ of an idea I got one day years ago, while reading articles about extremist groups in America, to a series and now this trade.

I am more than happy and thrilled to have the chance to write this book—I'm honored. I'm grateful and amazed at the reaction to the series when it premiered, and I'm just plain glad so many readers stuck around to follow Abby, Dean and Kimiko through their story.

I took a chance, and it turned out better than I could have hoped. Here's to a dozen more trades just like this one to line up on your shelf. Keep reading, and I'll keep writing.

-Caitlin Kittredge
Massachusetts, September 2016

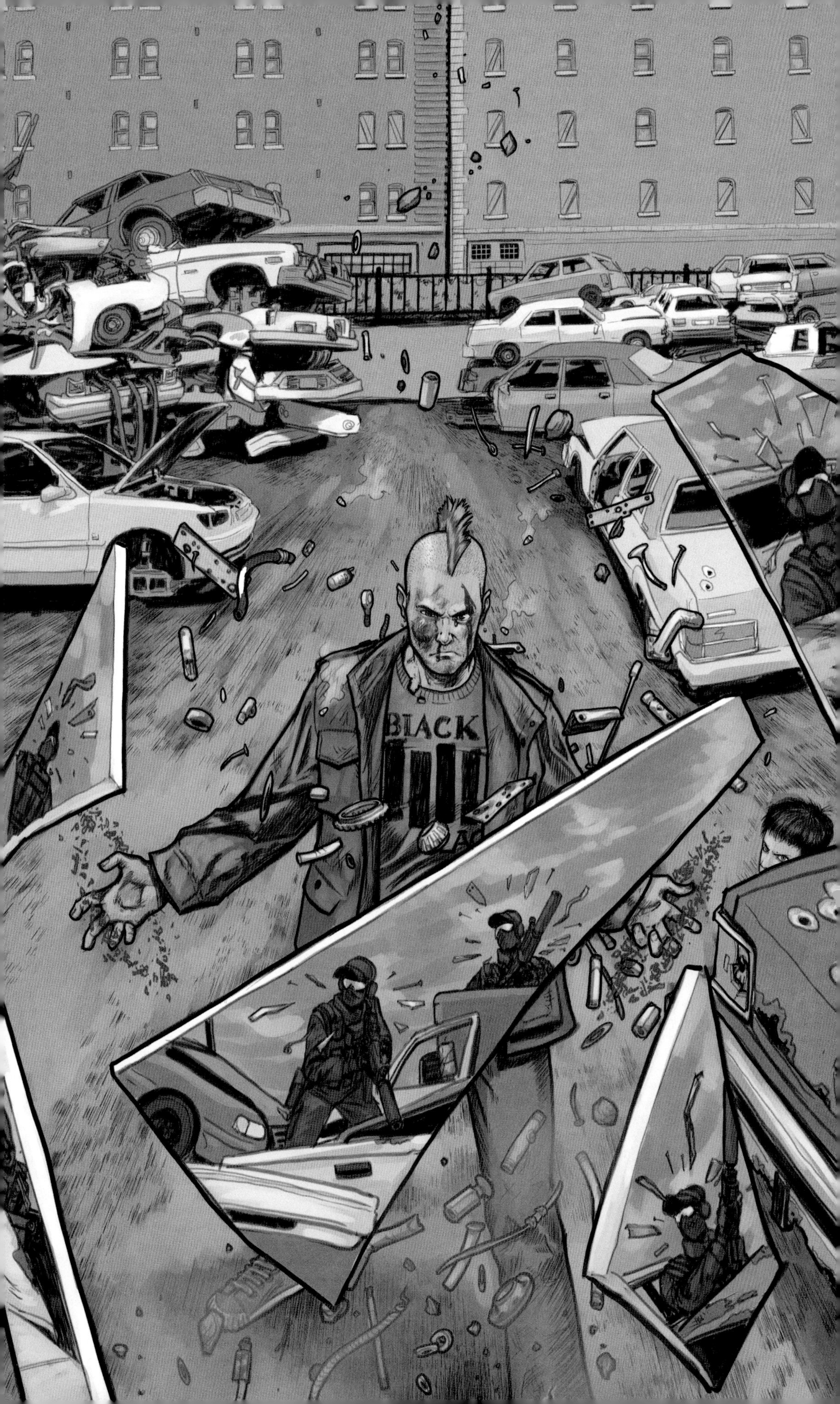
BLACK

CHAPTER ONE

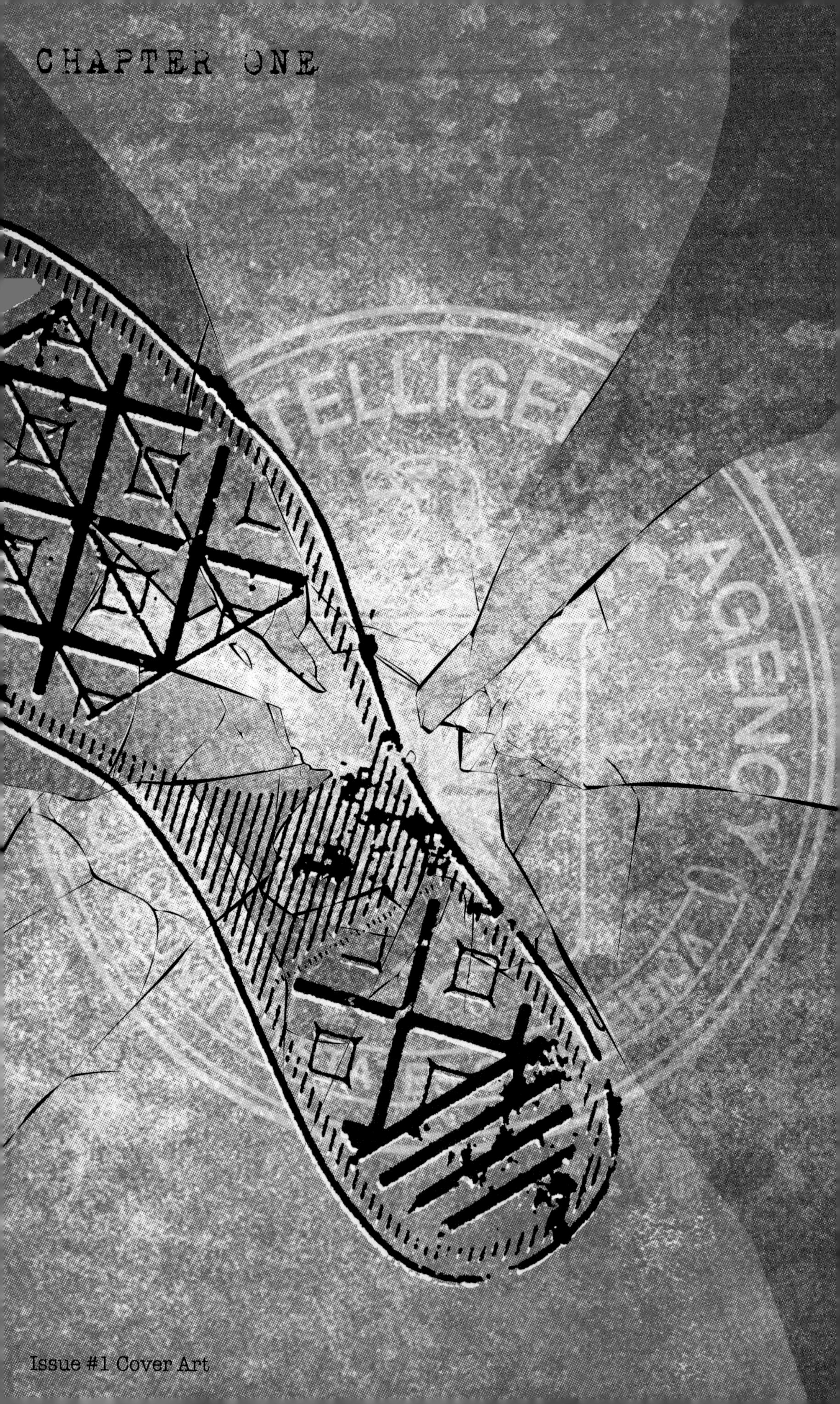

Issue #1 Cover Art

tHROwawAy (n.)

Espionage slang. Used by intelligence handlers.

1. A disposable asset, used for a single mission. 2. A disavowed assassin, meant to die alongside their target.

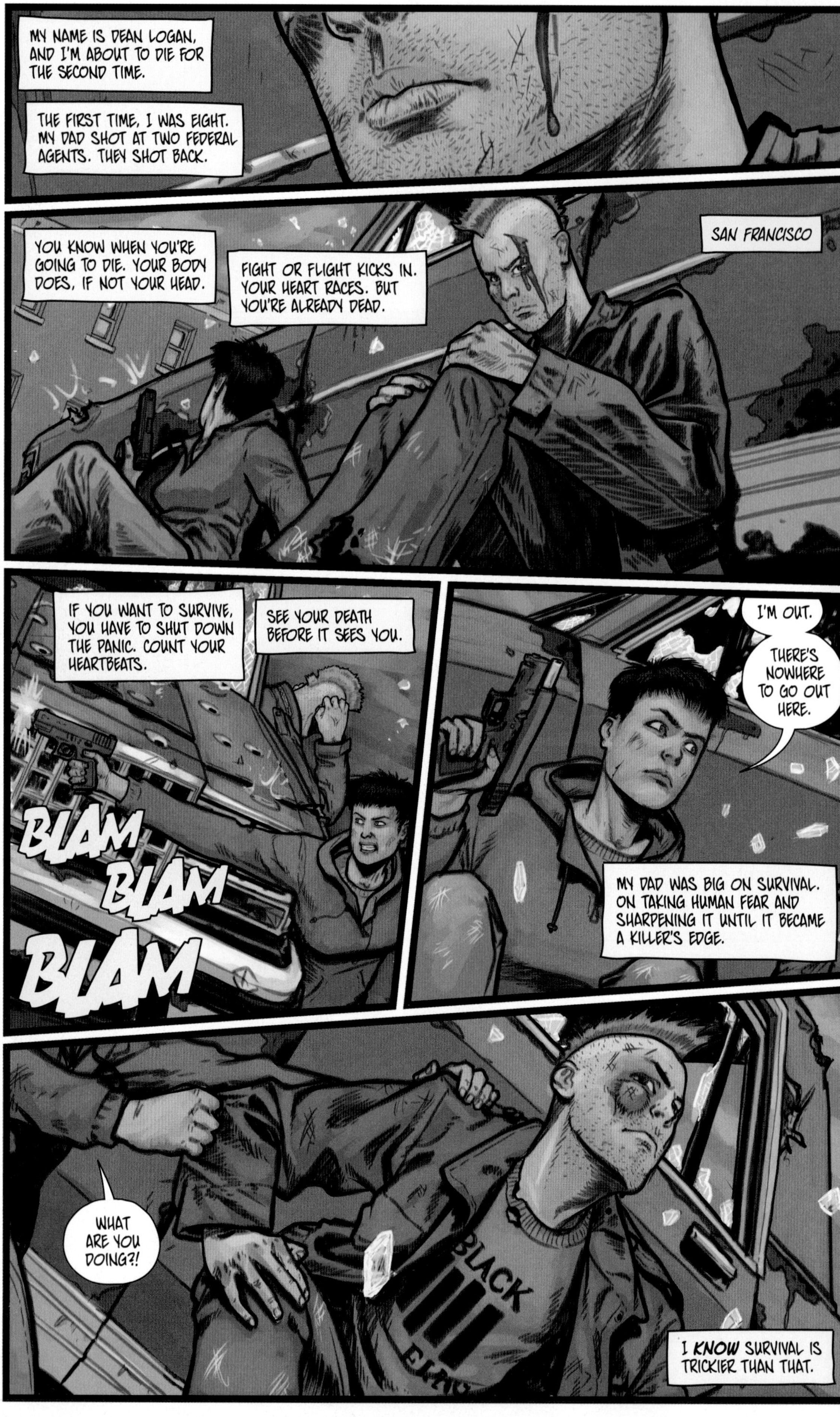
MY NAME IS DEAN LOGAN, AND I'M ABOUT TO DIE FOR THE SECOND TIME.
THE FIRST TIME, I WAS EIGHT. MY DAD SHOT AT TWO FEDERAL AGENTS. THEY SHOT BACK.
SAN FRANCISCO
YOU KNOW WHEN YOU'RE GOING TO DIE. YOUR BODY DOES, IF NOT YOUR HEAD.
FIGHT OR FLIGHT KICKS IN. YOUR HEART RACES. BUT YOU'RE ALREADY DEAD.
IF YOU WANT TO SURVIVE, YOU HAVE TO SHUT DOWN THE PANIC. COUNT YOUR HEARTBEATS.
SEE YOUR DEATH BEFORE IT SEES YOU.
BLAM BLAM BLAM
I'M OUT.
THERE'S NOWHERE TO GO OUT HERE.
MY DAD WAS BIG ON SURVIVAL. ON TAKING HUMAN FEAR AND SHARPENING IT UNTIL IT BECAME A KILLER'S EDGE.
WHAT ARE YOU DOING?!
I KNOW SURVIVAL IS TRICKIER THAN THAT.

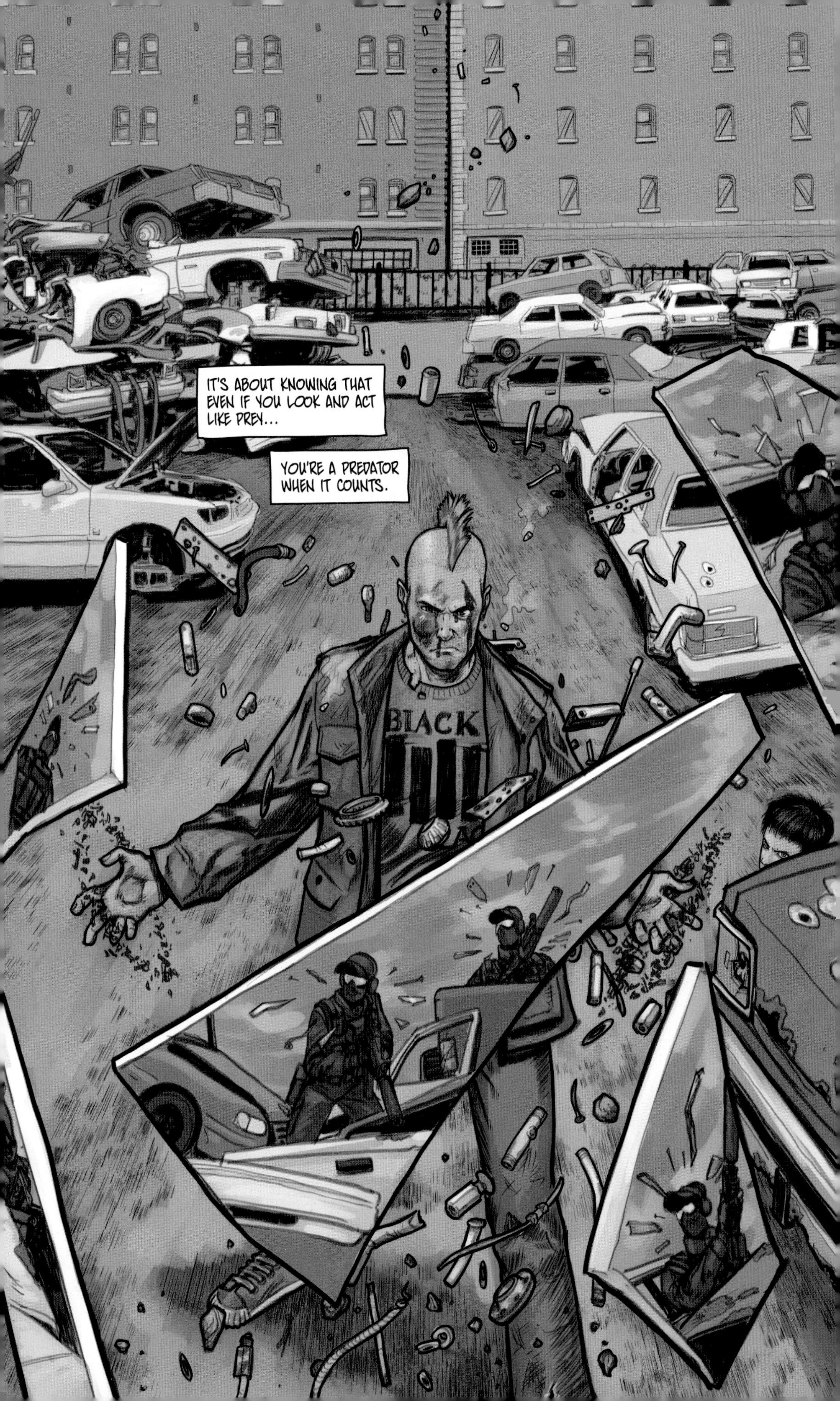
IT'S ABOUT KNOWING THAT EVEN IF YOU LOOK AND ACT LIKE PREY...
YOU'RE A PREDATOR WHEN IT COUNTS.
BLACK

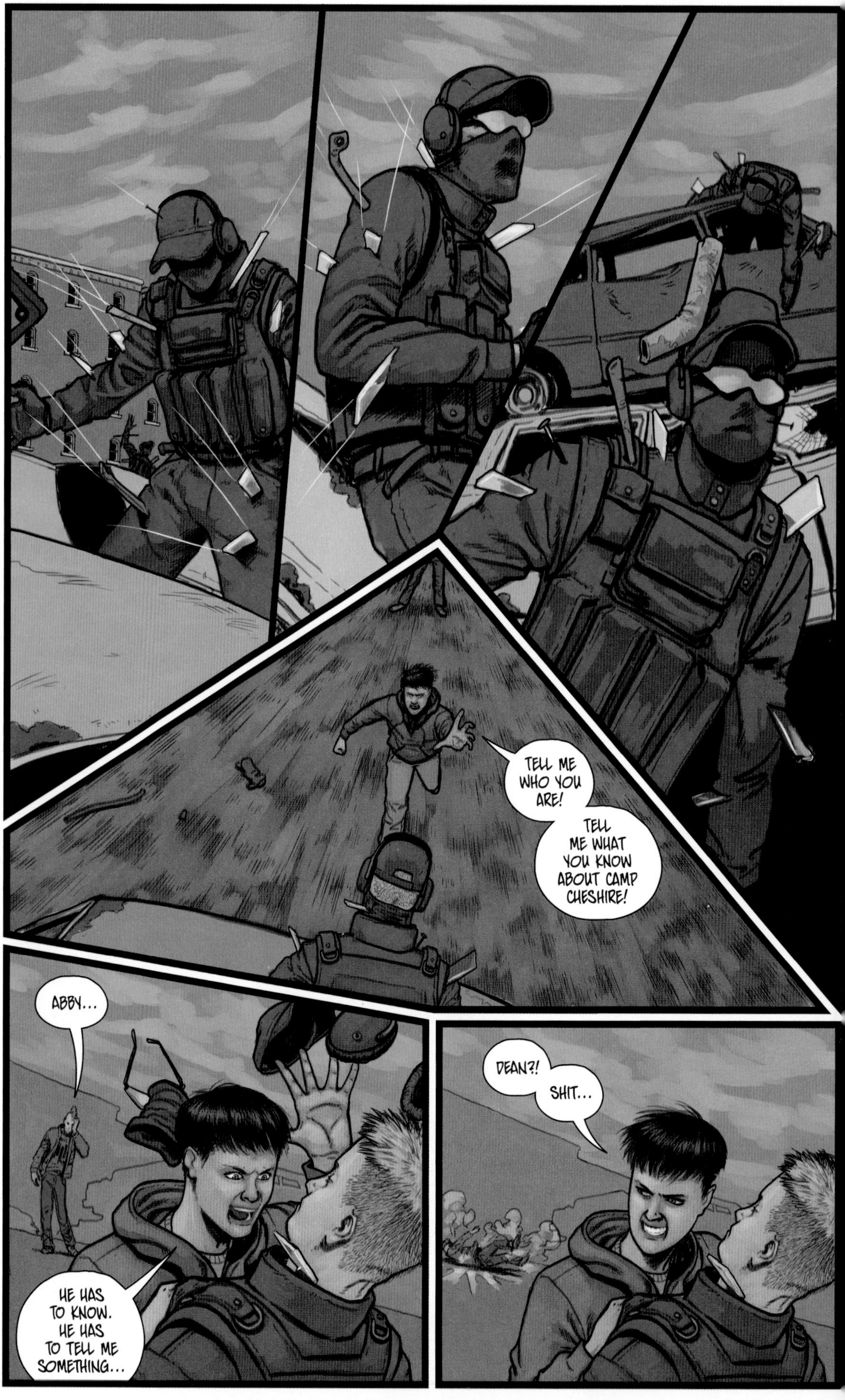

TELL ME WHO YOU ARE!
TELL ME WHAT YOU KNOW ABOUT CAMP CHESHIRE!
ABBY...
HE HAS TO KNOW. HE HAS TO TELL ME SOMETHING...
DEAN?!
SHIT...

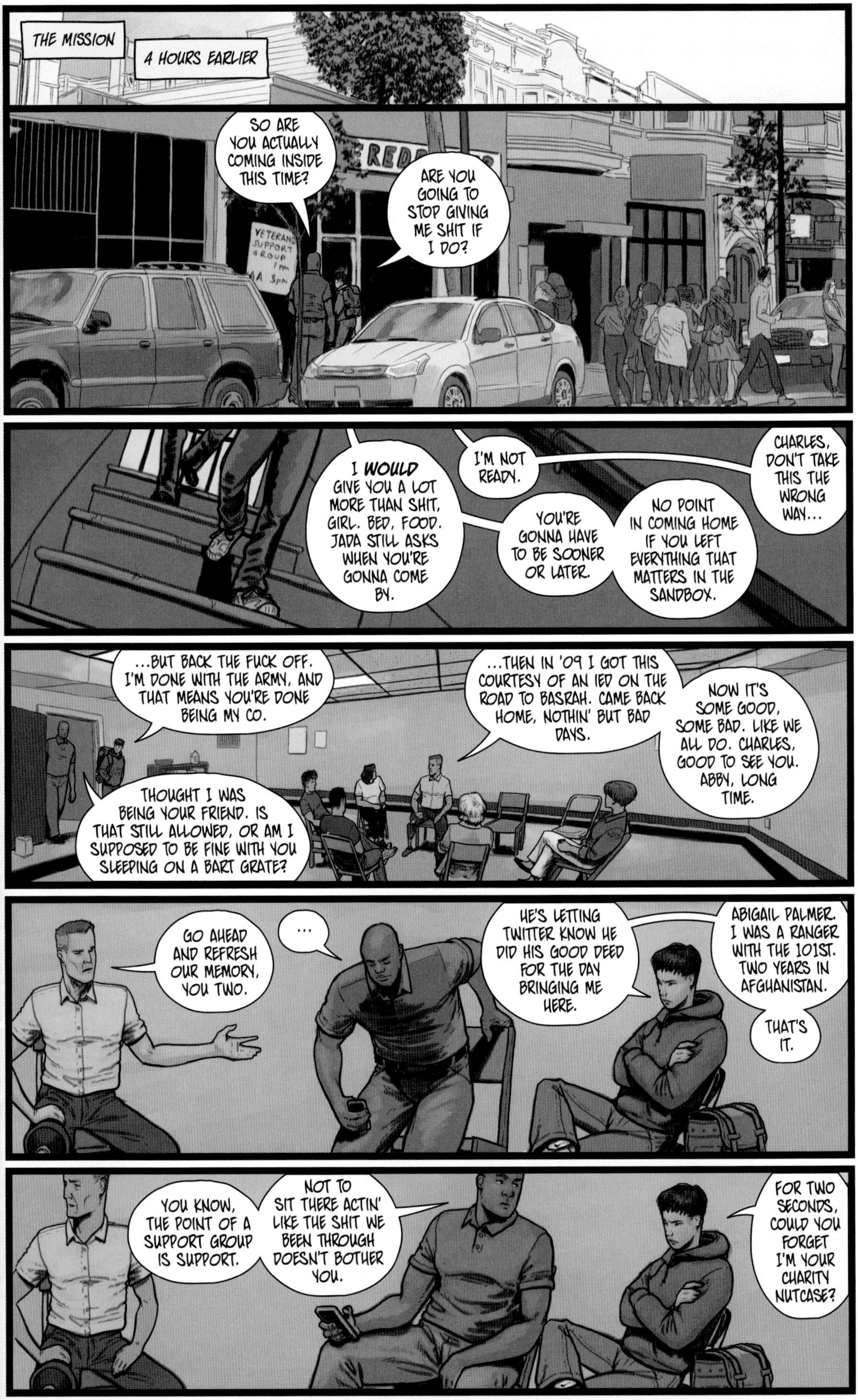
THE MISSION
4 HOURS EARLIER
SO ARE YOU ACTUALLY COMING INSIDE THIS TIME?
VETERANS SUPPORT GROUP
ARE YOU GOING TO STOP GIVING ME SHIT IF I DO?
I **WOULD** GIVE YOU A LOT MORE THAN SHIT, GIRL. BED, FOOD. JADA STILL ASKS WHEN YOU'RE GONNA COME BY.
I'M NOT READY.
CHARLES, DON'T TAKE THIS THE WRONG WAY...
YOU'RE GONNA HAVE TO BE SOONER OR LATER.
NO POINT IN COMING HOME IF YOU LEFT EVERYTHING THAT MATTERS IN THE SANDBOX.
...BUT BACK THE FUCK OFF. I'M DONE WITH THE ARMY, AND THAT MEANS YOU'RE DONE BEING MY CO.
THOUGHT I WAS BEING YOUR FRIEND. IS THAT STILL ALLOWED, OR AM I SUPPOSED TO BE FINE WITH YOU SLEEPING ON A BART GRATE?
...THEN IN '09 I GOT THIS COURTESY OF AN IED ON THE ROAD TO BASRAH. CAME BACK HOME, NOTHIN' BUT BAD DAYS.
NOW IT'S SOME GOOD, SOME BAD. LIKE WE ALL DO. CHARLES, GOOD TO SEE YOU. ABBY, LONG TIME.
GO AHEAD AND REFRESH OUR MEMORY, YOU TWO.
...
HE'S LETTING TWITTER KNOW HE DID HIS GOOD DEED FOR THE DAY BRINGING ME HERE.
ABIGAIL PALMER. I WAS A RANGER WITH THE 101ST. TWO YEARS IN AFGHANISTAN.
THAT'S IT.
YOU KNOW, THE POINT OF A SUPPORT GROUP IS SUPPORT.
NOT TO SIT THERE ACTIN' LIKE THE SHIT WE BEEN THROUGH DOESN'T BOTHER YOU.
FOR TWO SECONDS, COULD YOU FORGET I'M YOUR CHARITY NUTCASE?

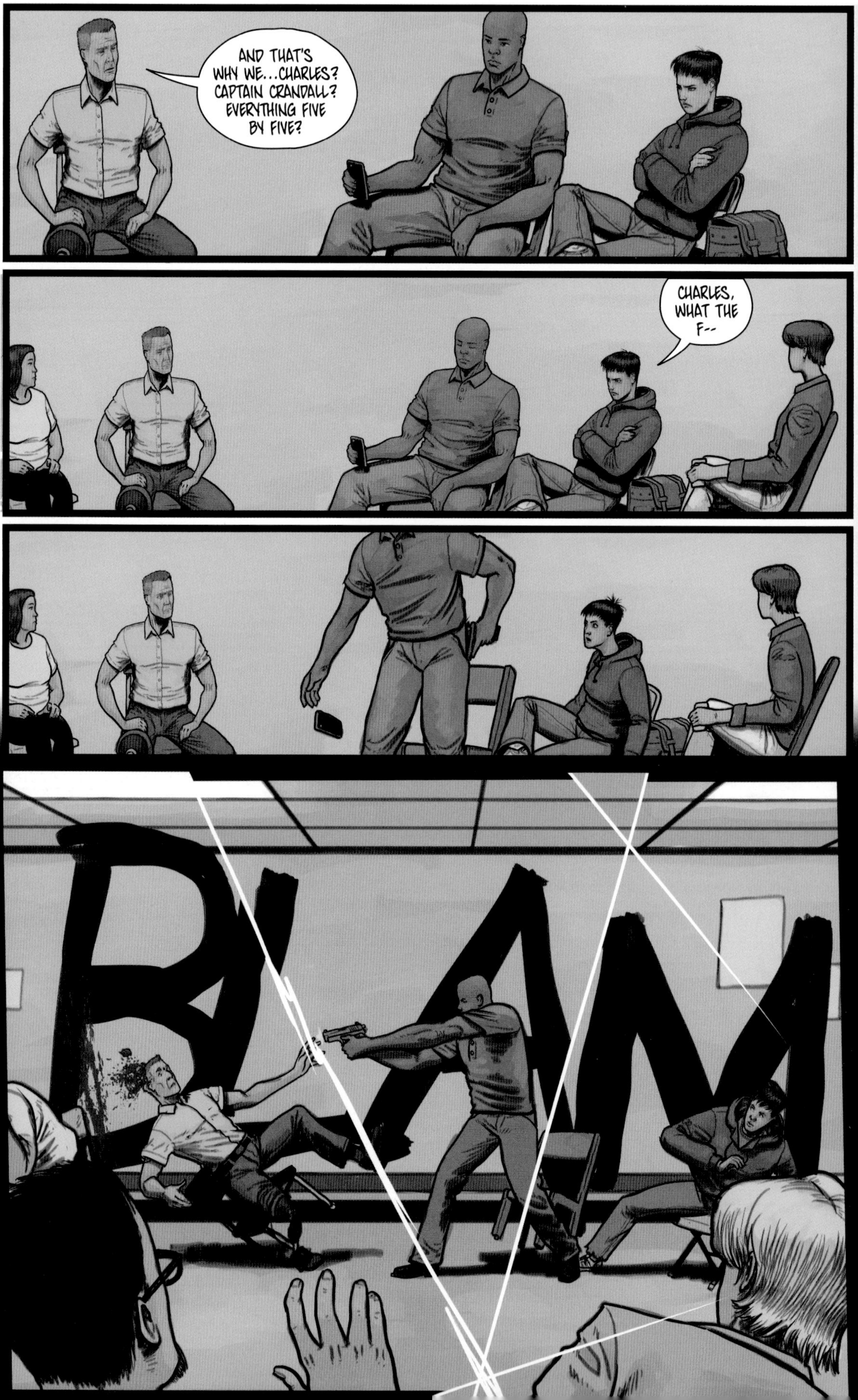
AND THAT'S WHY WE...CHARLES? CAPTAIN CRANDALL? EVERYTHING FIVE BY FIVE?
CHARLES, WHAT THE F--
BLAM

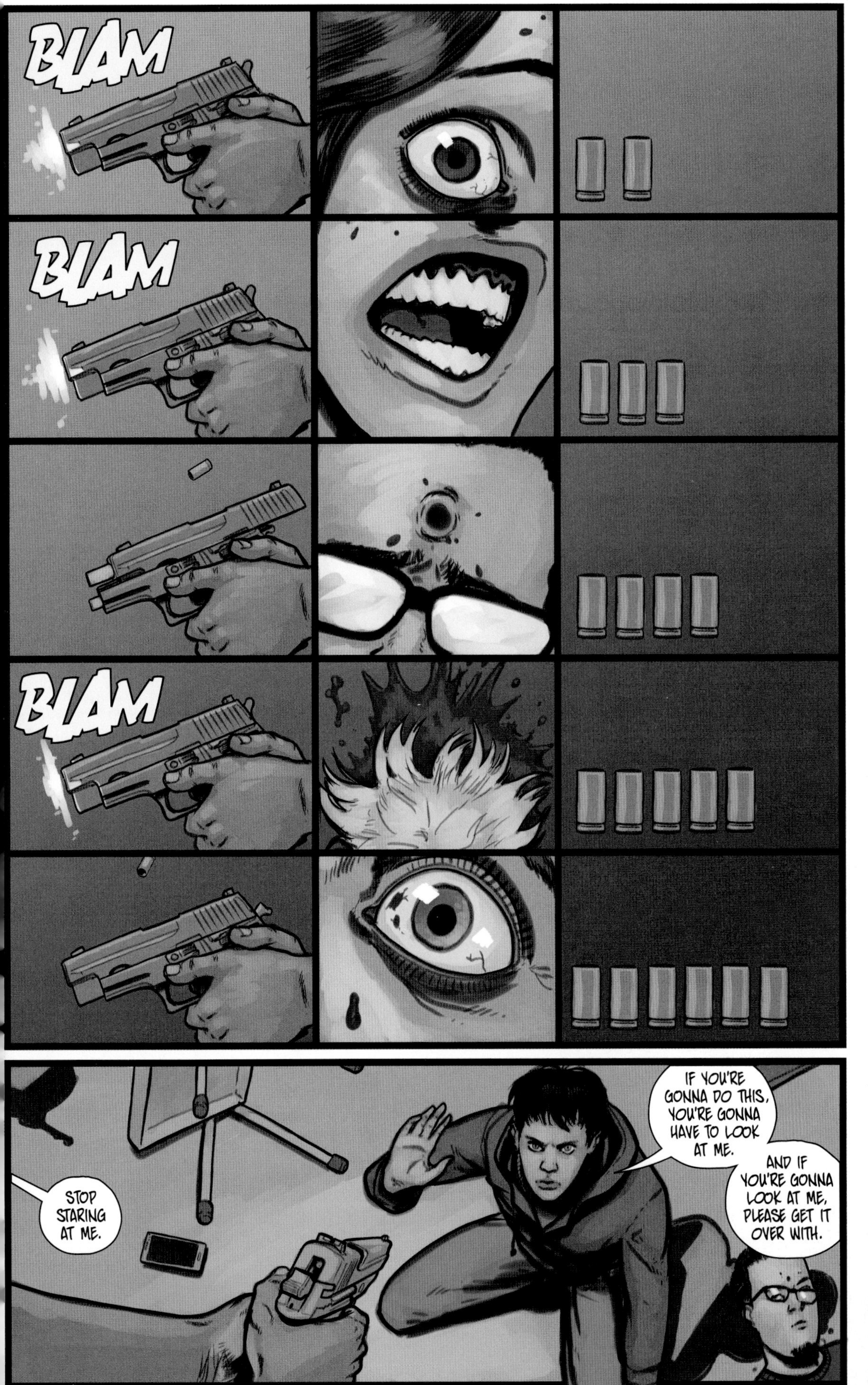
BLAM
BLAM
BLAM
IF YOU'RE GONNA DO THIS, YOU'RE GONNA HAVE TO LOOK AT ME.
AND IF YOU'RE GONNA LOOK AT ME, PLEASE GET IT OVER WITH.
STOP STARING AT ME.

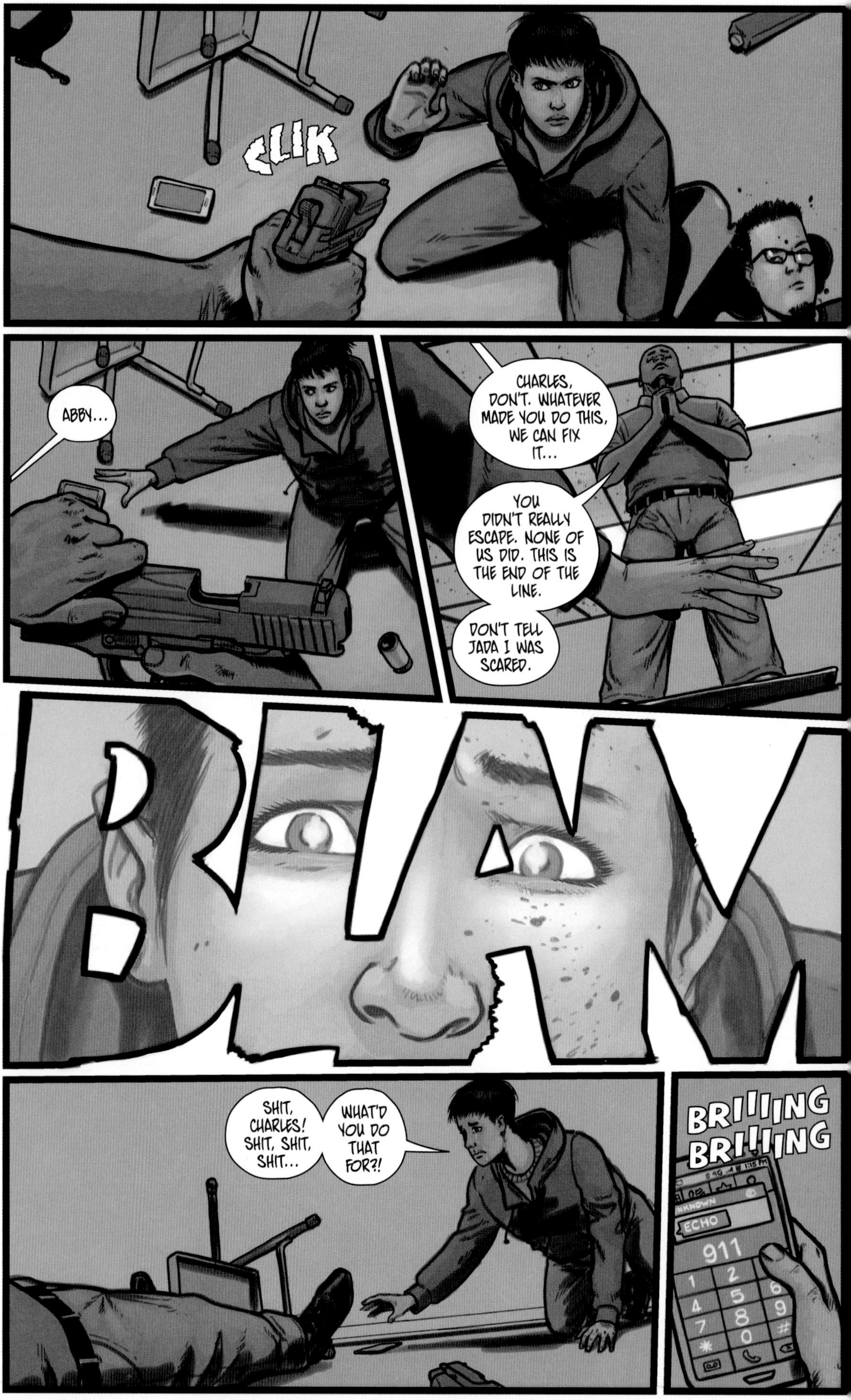
CLIK
ABBY...
CHARLES, DON'T. WHATEVER MADE YOU DO THIS, WE CAN FIX IT...
YOU DIDN'T REALLY ESCAPE. NONE OF US DID. THIS IS THE END OF THE LINE.
DON'T TELL JADA I WAS SCARED.
BLAM
SHIT, CHARLES! SHIT, SHIT, SHIT...
WHAT'D YOU DO THAT FOR?!
BRIIIING
BRIIIING
UNKNOWN
ECHO
911

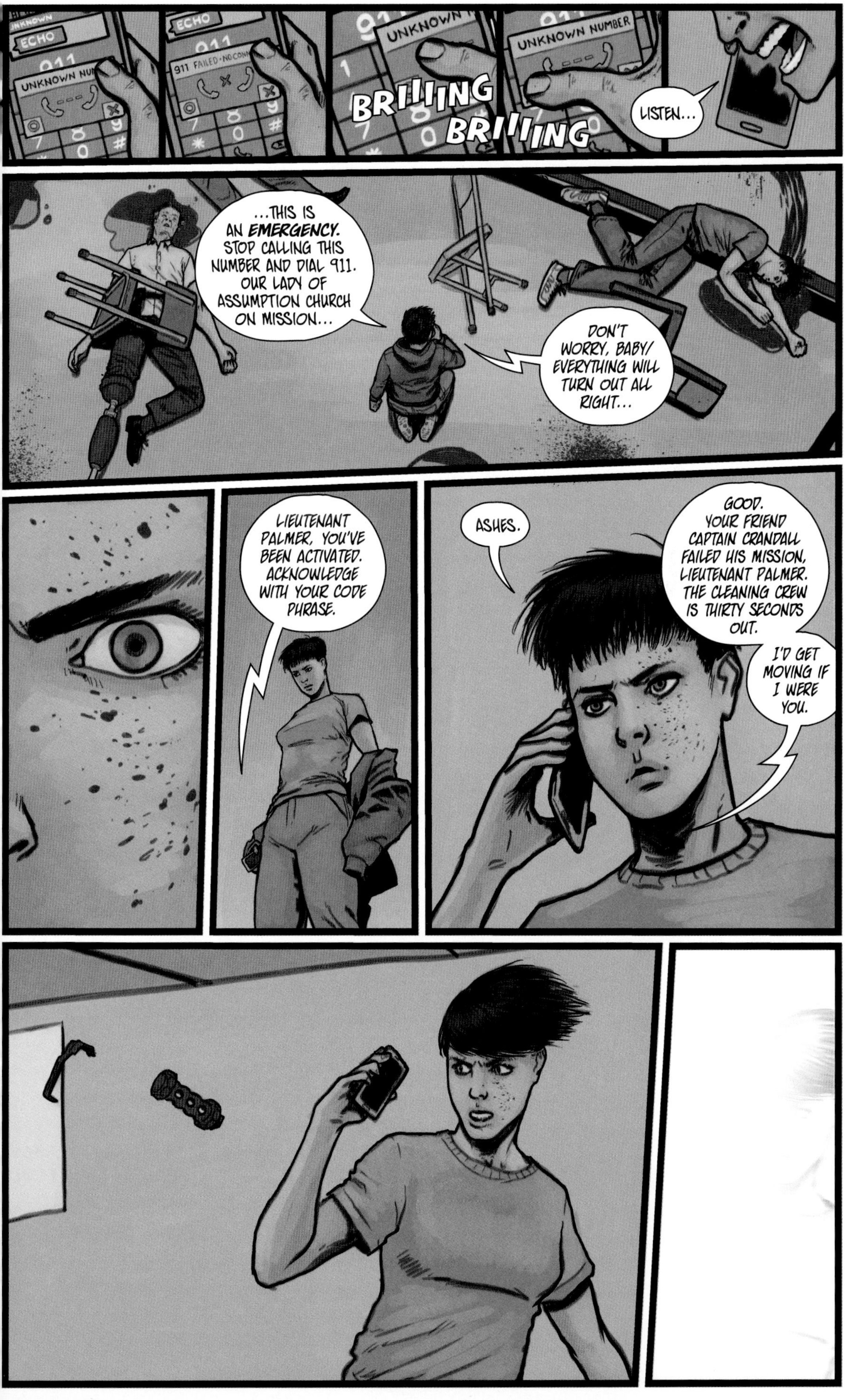
ECHO
UNKNOWN NUMBER
BRIIIING
BRIIIING
LISTEN...
...THIS IS AN **EMERGENCY.** STOP CALLING THIS NUMBER AND DIAL 911. OUR LADY OF ASSUMPTION CHURCH ON MISSION...
DON'T WORRY, BABY/ EVERYTHING WILL TURN OUT ALL RIGHT...
LIEUTENANT PALMER, YOU'VE BEEN ACTIVATED. ACKNOWLEDGE WITH YOUR CODE PHRASE.
ASHES.
GOOD. YOUR FRIEND CAPTAIN CRANDALL FAILED HIS MISSION, LIEUTENANT PALMER. THE CLEANING CREW IS THIRTY SECONDS OUT.
I'D GET MOVING IF I WERE YOU.

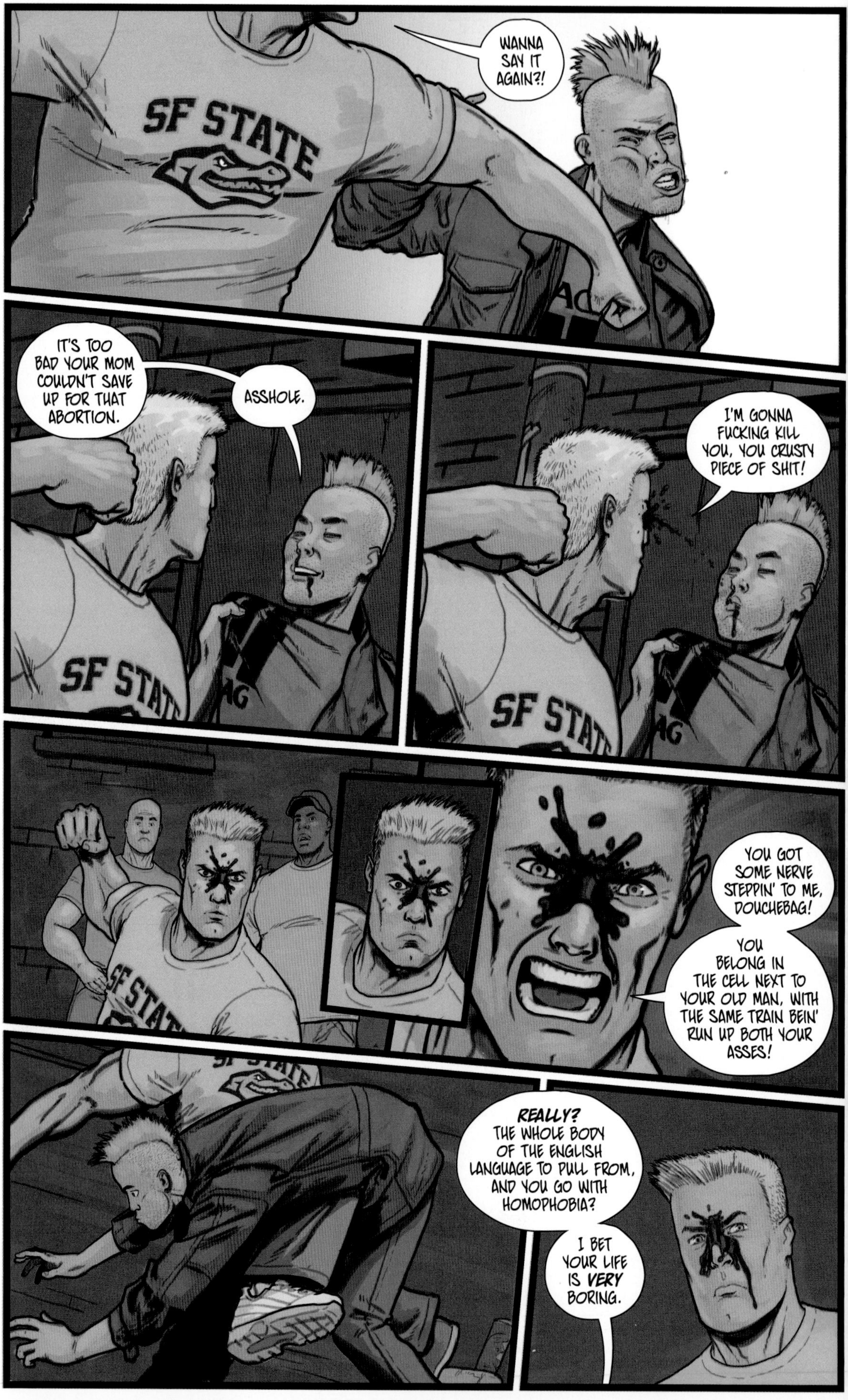
WANNA SAY IT AGAIN?!
SF STATE
IT'S TOO BAD YOUR MOM COULDN'T SAVE UP FOR THAT ABORTION.
ASSHOLE.
SF STATE
I'M GONNA FUCKING KILL YOU, YOU CRUSTY PIECE OF SHIT!
SF STATE
YOU GOT SOME NERVE STEPPIN' TO ME, DOUCHEBAG!
YOU BELONG IN THE CELL NEXT TO YOUR OLD MAN, WITH THE SAME TRAIN BEIN' RUN UP BOTH YOUR ASSES!
SF STATE
REALLY? THE WHOLE BODY OF THE ENGLISH LANGUAGE TO PULL FROM, AND YOU GO WITH HOMOPHOBIA?
I BET YOUR LIFE IS **VERY** BORING.

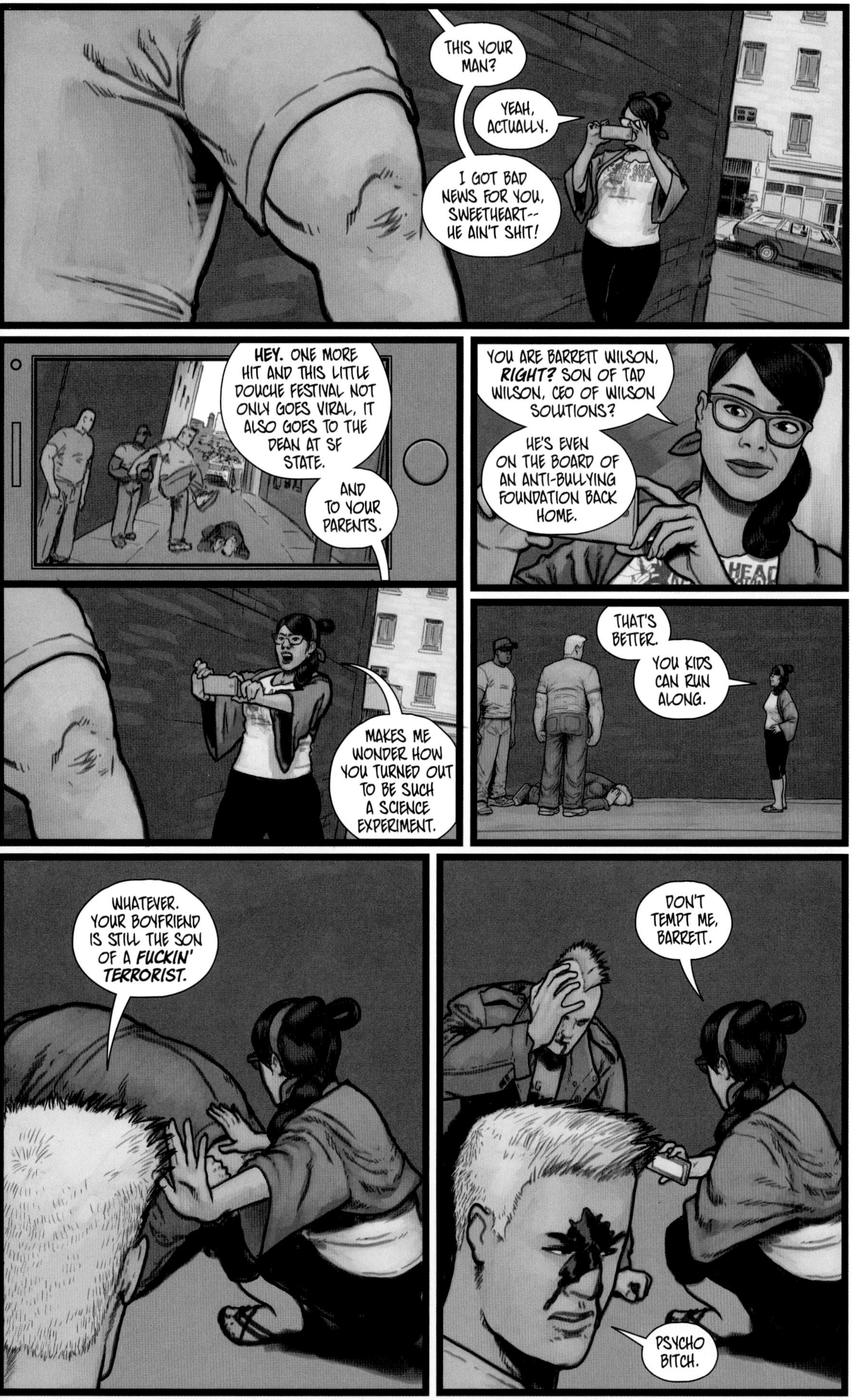
THIS YOUR MAN?
YEAH, ACTUALLY.
I GOT BAD NEWS FOR YOU, SWEETHEART-- HE AIN'T SHIT!
HEY. ONE MORE HIT AND THIS LITTLE DOUCHE FESTIVAL NOT ONLY GOES VIRAL, IT ALSO GOES TO THE DEAN AT SF STATE.
AND TO YOUR PARENTS.
YOU ARE BARRETT WILSON, RIGHT? SON OF TAD WILSON, CEO OF WILSON SOLUTIONS?
HE'S EVEN ON THE BOARD OF AN ANTI-BULLYING FOUNDATION BACK HOME.
MAKES ME WONDER HOW YOU TURNED OUT TO BE SUCH A SCIENCE EXPERIMENT.
THAT'S BETTER.
YOU KIDS CAN RUN ALONG.
WHATEVER. YOUR BOYFRIEND IS STILL THE SON OF A FUCKIN' TERRORIST.
DON'T TEMPT ME, BARRETT.
PSYCHO BITCH.

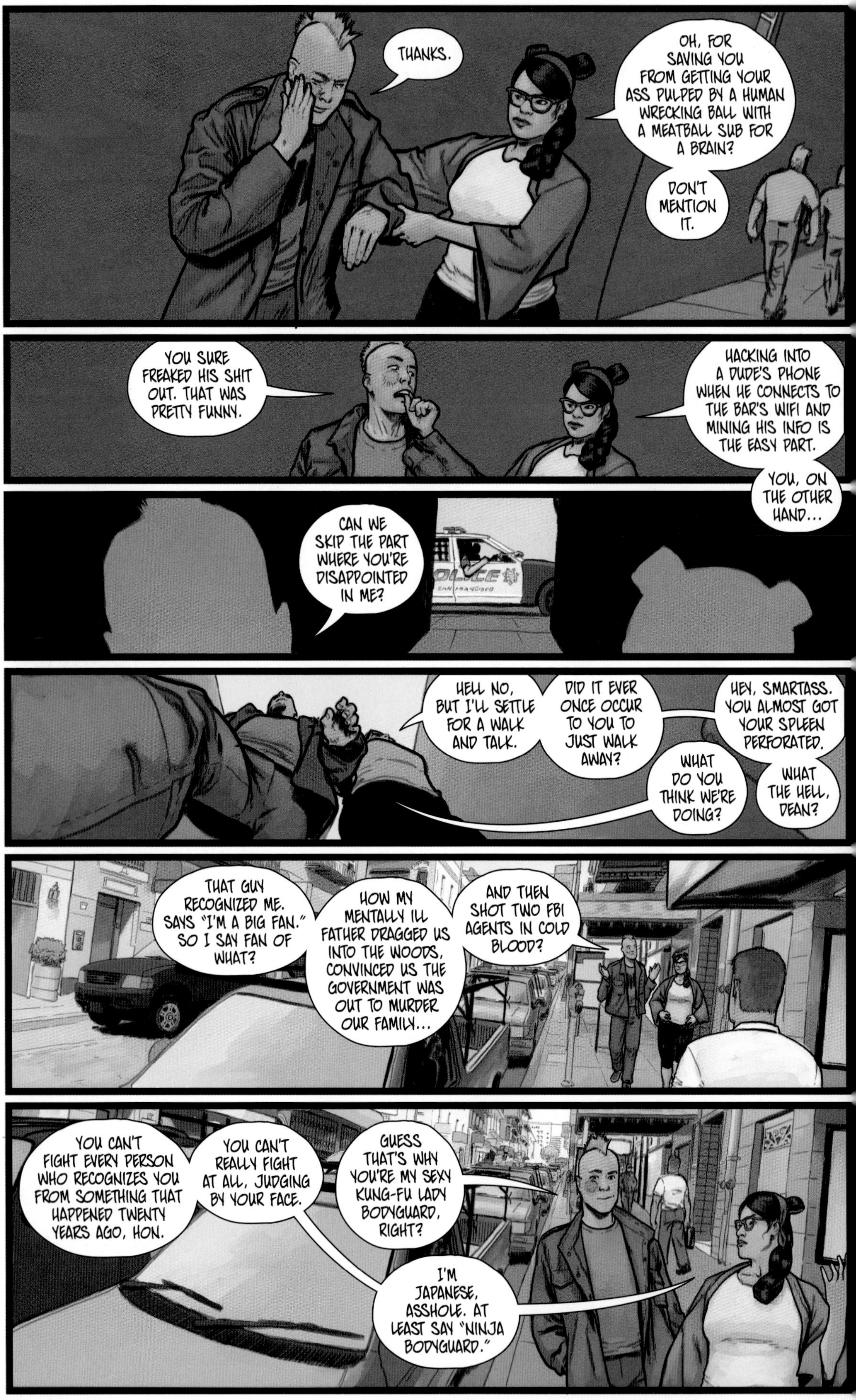
THANKS.
OH, FOR SAVING YOU FROM GETTING YOUR ASS PULPED BY A HUMAN WRECKING BALL WITH A MEATBALL SUB FOR A BRAIN?
DON'T MENTION IT.
YOU SURE FREAKED HIS SHIT OUT. THAT WAS PRETTY FUNNY.
HACKING INTO A DUDE'S PHONE WHEN HE CONNECTS TO THE BAR'S WIFI AND MINING HIS INFO IS THE EASY PART.
YOU, ON THE OTHER HAND...
CAN WE SKIP THE PART WHERE YOU'RE DISAPPOINTED IN ME?
HELL NO, BUT I'LL SETTLE FOR A WALK AND TALK.
DID IT EVER ONCE OCCUR TO YOU TO JUST WALK AWAY?
HEY, SMARTASS. YOU ALMOST GOT YOUR SPLEEN PERFORATED.
WHAT THE HELL, DEAN?
WHAT DO YOU THINK WE'RE DOING?
THAT GUY RECOGNIZED ME. SAYS "I'M A BIG FAN." SO I SAY FAN OF WHAT?
HOW MY MENTALLY ILL FATHER DRAGGED US INTO THE WOODS, CONVINCED US THE GOVERNMENT WAS OUT TO MURDER OUR FAMILY...
AND THEN SHOT TWO FBI AGENTS IN COLD BLOOD?
YOU CAN'T FIGHT EVERY PERSON WHO RECOGNIZES YOU FROM SOMETHING THAT HAPPENED TWENTY YEARS AGO, HON.
YOU CAN'T REALLY FIGHT AT ALL, JUDGING BY YOUR FACE.
GUESS THAT'S WHY YOU'RE MY SEXY KUNG-FU LADY BODYGUARD, RIGHT?
I'M JAPANESE, ASSHOLE. AT LEAST SAY "NINJA BODYGUARD."

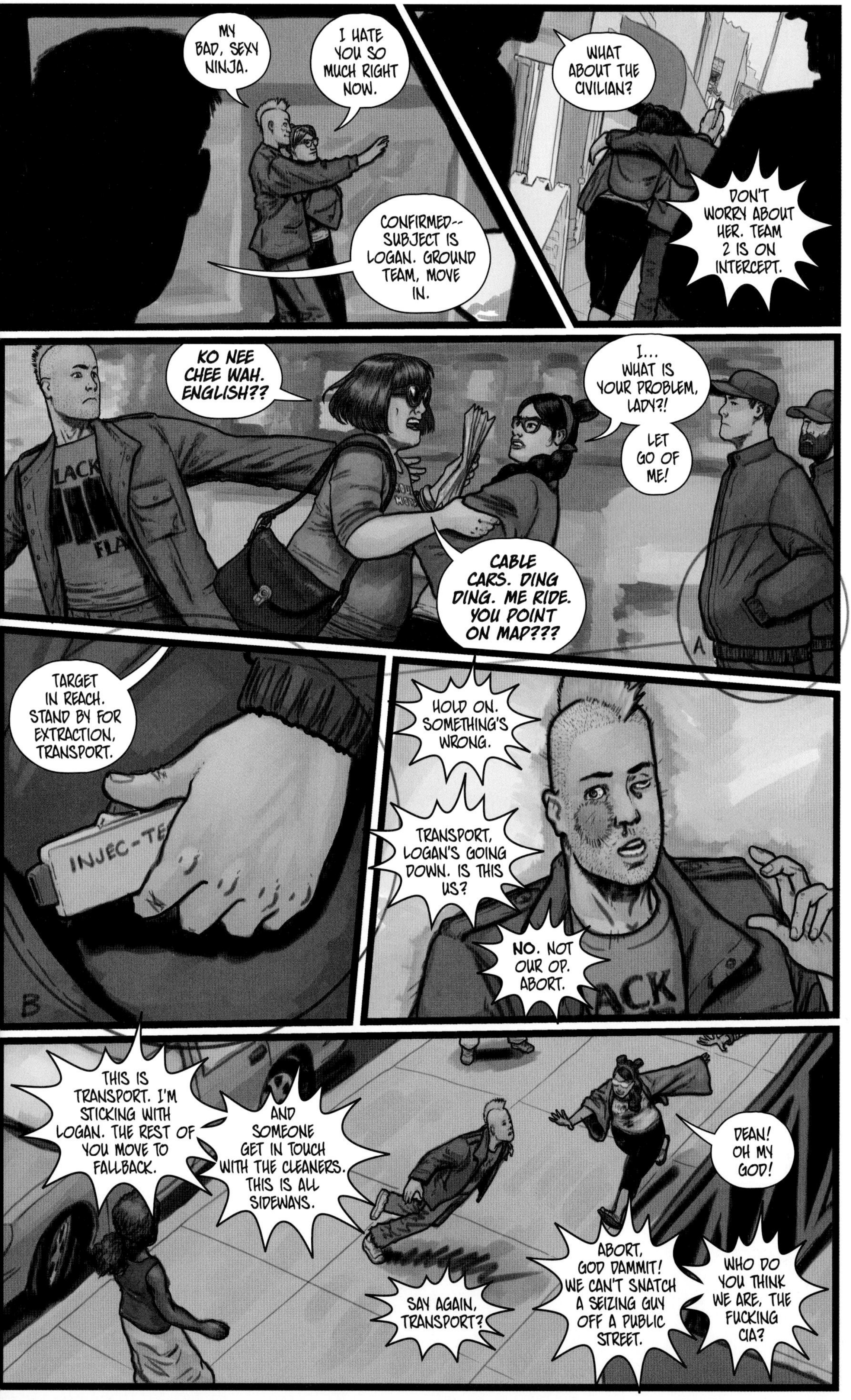
MY BAD, SEXY NINJA.
I HATE YOU SO MUCH RIGHT NOW.
CONFIRMED-- SUBJECT IS LOGAN. GROUND TEAM, MOVE IN.
WHAT ABOUT THE CIVILIAN?
DON'T WORRY ABOUT HER. TEAM 2 IS ON INTERCEPT.
KO NEE CHEE WAH. ENGLISH??
I... WHAT IS YOUR PROBLEM, LADY?!
LET GO OF ME!
CABLE CARS. DING DING. ME RIDE. YOU POINT ON MAP???
A
TARGET IN REACH. STAND BY FOR EXTRACTION, TRANSPORT.
INJEC-TE
B
HOLD ON. SOMETHING'S WRONG.
TRANSPORT, LOGAN'S GOING DOWN. IS THIS US?
NO. NOT OUR OP. ABORT.
THIS IS TRANSPORT. I'M STICKING WITH LOGAN. THE REST OF YOU MOVE TO FALLBACK.
AND SOMEONE GET IN TOUCH WITH THE CLEANERS. THIS IS ALL SIDEWAYS.
DEAN! OH MY GOD!
SAY AGAIN, TRANSPORT?
ABORT, GOD DAMMIT! WE CAN'T SNATCH A SEIZING GUY OFF A PUBLIC STREET.
WHO DO YOU THINK WE ARE, THE FUCKING CIA?

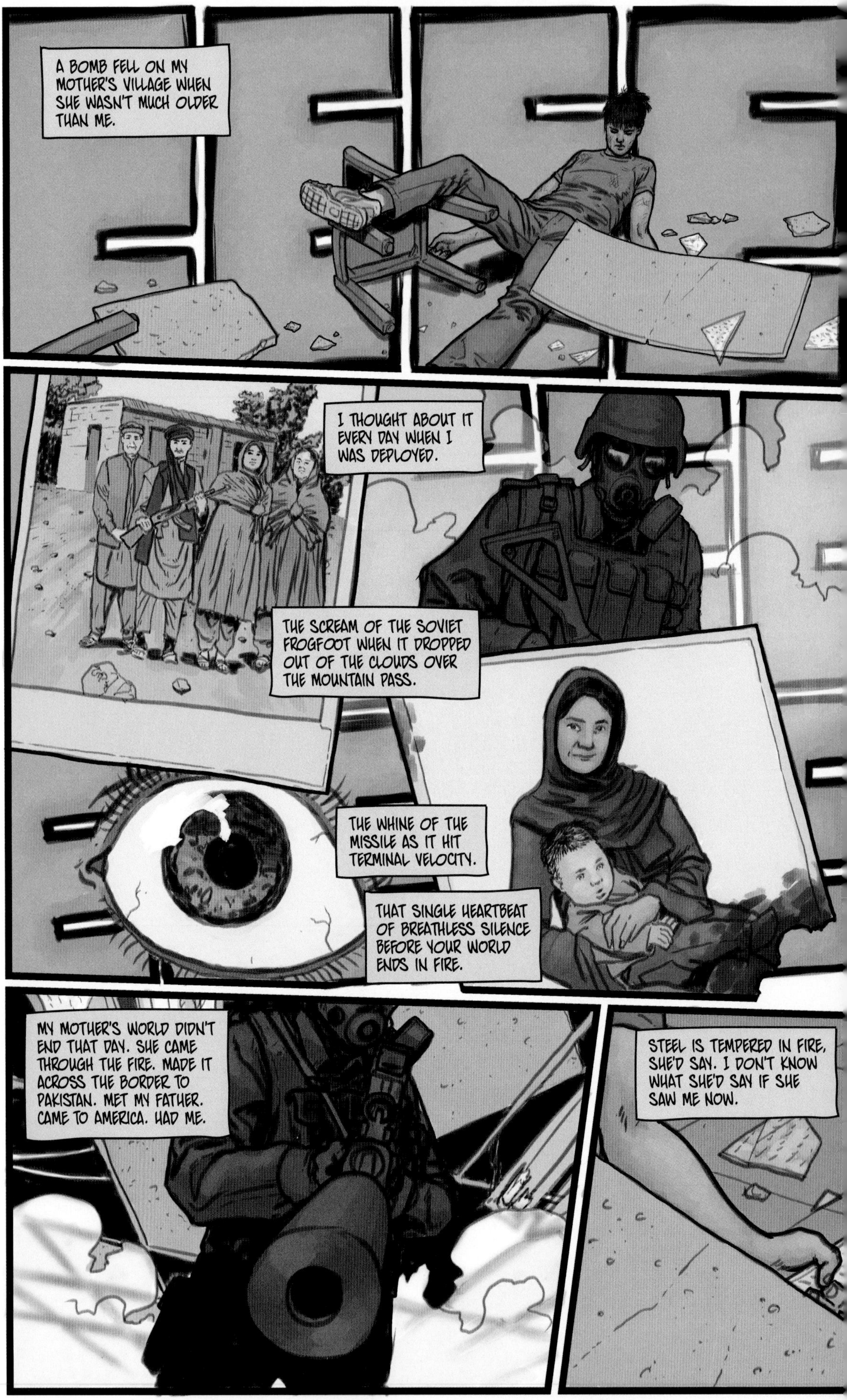
A BOMB FELL ON MY MOTHER'S VILLAGE WHEN SHE WASN'T MUCH OLDER THAN ME.
I THOUGHT ABOUT IT EVERY DAY WHEN I WAS DEPLOYED.
THE SCREAM OF THE SOVIET FROGFOOT WHEN IT DROPPED OUT OF THE CLOUDS OVER THE MOUNTAIN PASS.
THE WHINE OF THE MISSILE AS IT HIT TERMINAL VELOCITY.
THAT SINGLE HEARTBEAT OF BREATHLESS SILENCE BEFORE YOUR WORLD ENDS IN FIRE.
MY MOTHER'S WORLD DIDN'T END THAT DAY. SHE CAME THROUGH THE FIRE. MADE IT ACROSS THE BORDER TO PAKISTAN. MET MY FATHER. CAME TO AMERICA. HAD ME.
STEEL IS TEMPERED IN FIRE, SHE'D SAY. I DON'T KNOW WHAT SHE'D SAY IF SHE SAW ME NOW.

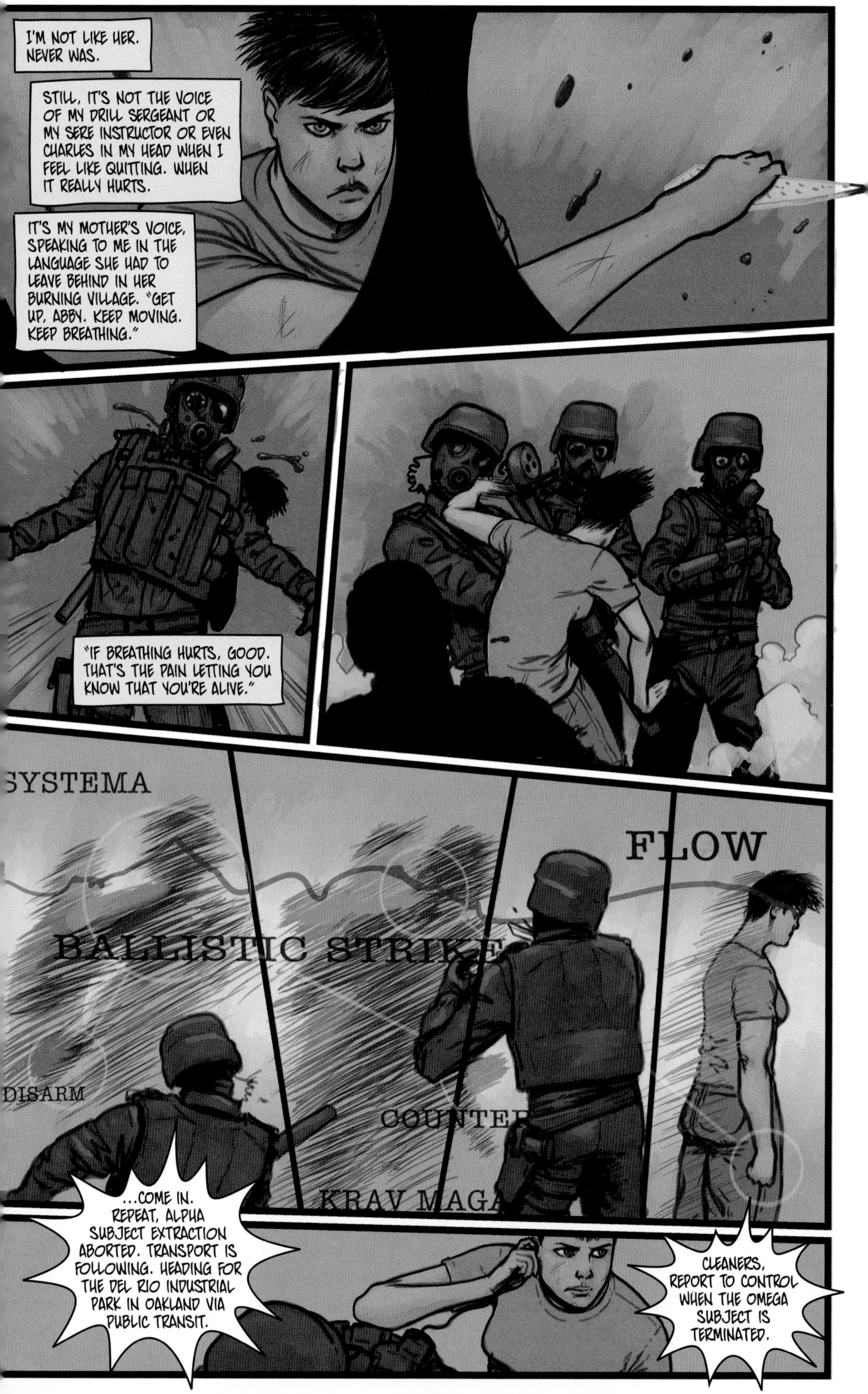
I'M NOT LIKE HER. NEVER WAS.
STILL, IT'S NOT THE VOICE OF MY DRILL SERGEANT OR MY SERE INSTRUCTOR OR EVEN CHARLES IN MY HEAD WHEN I FEEL LIKE QUITTING. WHEN IT REALLY HURTS.
IT'S MY MOTHER'S VOICE, SPEAKING TO ME IN THE LANGUAGE SHE HAD TO LEAVE BEHIND IN HER BURNING VILLAGE. "GET UP, ABBY. KEEP MOVING. KEEP BREATHING."
"IF BREATHING HURTS, GOOD. THAT'S THE PAIN LETTING YOU KNOW THAT YOU'RE ALIVE."
SYSTEMA
BALLISTIC STRIKE
FLOW
DISARM
COUNTER
KRAV MAGA
...COME IN. REPEAT, ALPHA SUBJECT EXTRACTION ABORTED. TRANSPORT IS FOLLOWING. HEADING FOR THE DEL RIO INDUSTRIAL PARK IN OAKLAND VIA PUBLIC TRANSIT.
CLEANERS, REPORT TO CONTROL WHEN THE OMEGA SUBJECT IS TERMINATED.

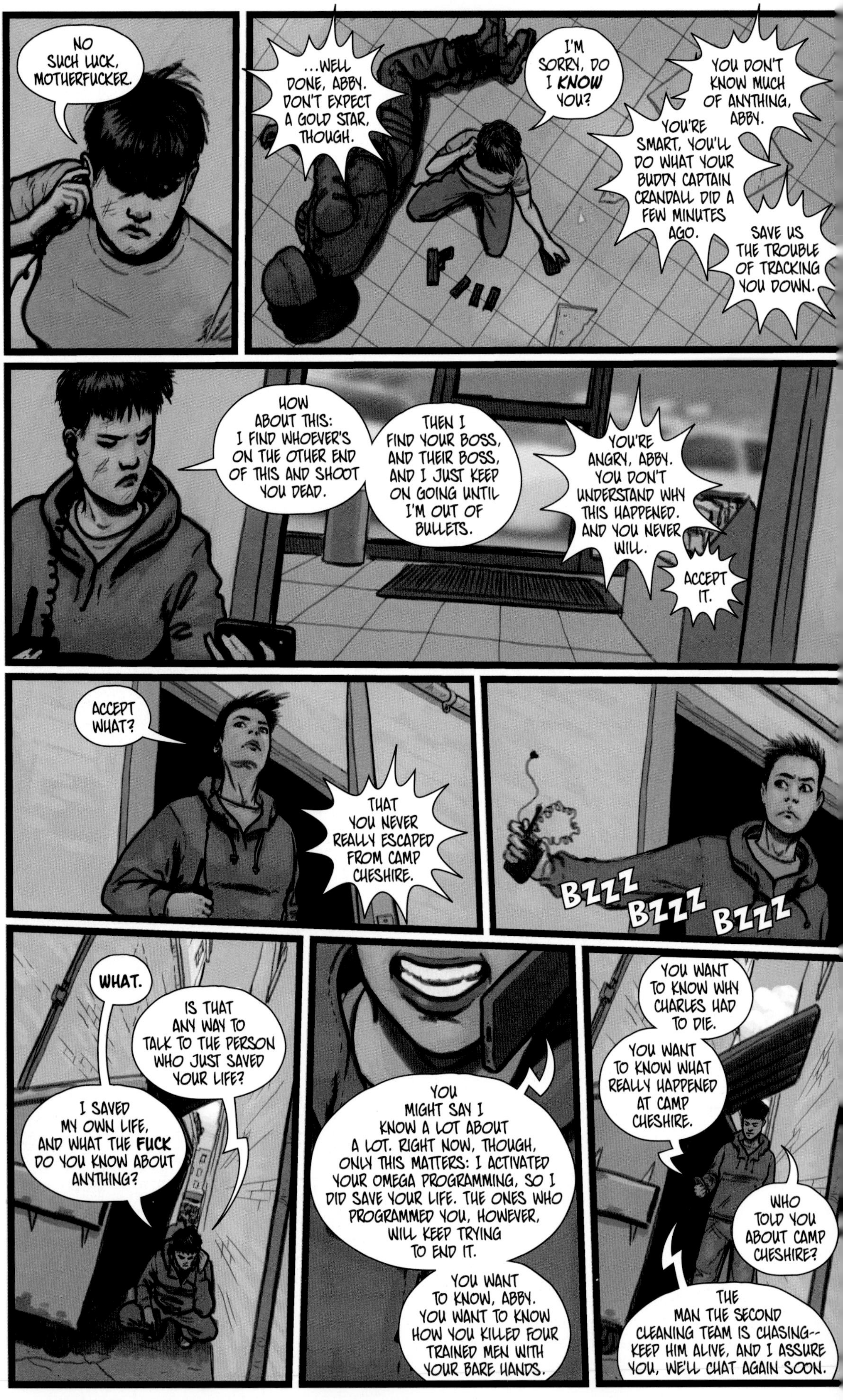

NO SUCH LUCK, MOTHERFUCKER.
...WELL DONE, ABBY. DON'T EXPECT A GOLD STAR, THOUGH.
I'M SORRY, DO I **KNOW** YOU?
YOU DON'T KNOW MUCH OF ANYTHING, ABBY.
YOU'RE SMART, YOU'LL DO WHAT YOUR BUDDY CAPTAIN CRANDALL DID A FEW MINUTES AGO.
SAVE US THE TROUBLE OF TRACKING YOU DOWN.
HOW ABOUT THIS: I FIND WHOEVER'S ON THE OTHER END OF THIS AND SHOOT YOU DEAD.
THEN I FIND YOUR BOSS, AND THEIR BOSS, AND I JUST KEEP ON GOING UNTIL I'M OUT OF BULLETS.
YOU'RE ANGRY, ABBY. YOU DON'T UNDERSTAND WHY THIS HAPPENED. AND YOU NEVER WILL.
ACCEPT IT.
ACCEPT WHAT?
THAT YOU NEVER REALLY ESCAPED FROM CAMP CHESHIRE.
BZZZ BZZZ BZZZ
WHAT.
IS THAT ANY WAY TO TALK TO THE PERSON WHO JUST SAVED YOUR LIFE?
I SAVED MY OWN LIFE, AND WHAT THE **FUCK** DO YOU KNOW ABOUT ANYTHING?
YOU MIGHT SAY I KNOW A LOT ABOUT A LOT. RIGHT NOW, THOUGH, ONLY THIS MATTERS: I ACTIVATED YOUR OMEGA PROGRAMMING, SO I DID SAVE YOUR LIFE. THE ONES WHO PROGRAMMED YOU, HOWEVER, WILL KEEP TRYING TO END IT.
YOU WANT TO KNOW, ABBY. YOU WANT TO KNOW HOW YOU KILLED FOUR TRAINED MEN WITH YOUR BARE HANDS.
YOU WANT TO KNOW WHY CHARLES HAD TO DIE.
YOU WANT TO KNOW WHAT REALLY HAPPENED AT CAMP CHESHIRE.
WHO TOLD YOU ABOUT CAMP CHESHIRE?
THE MAN THE SECOND CLEANING TEAM IS CHASING-- KEEP HIM ALIVE, AND I ASSURE YOU, WE'LL CHAT AGAIN SOON.

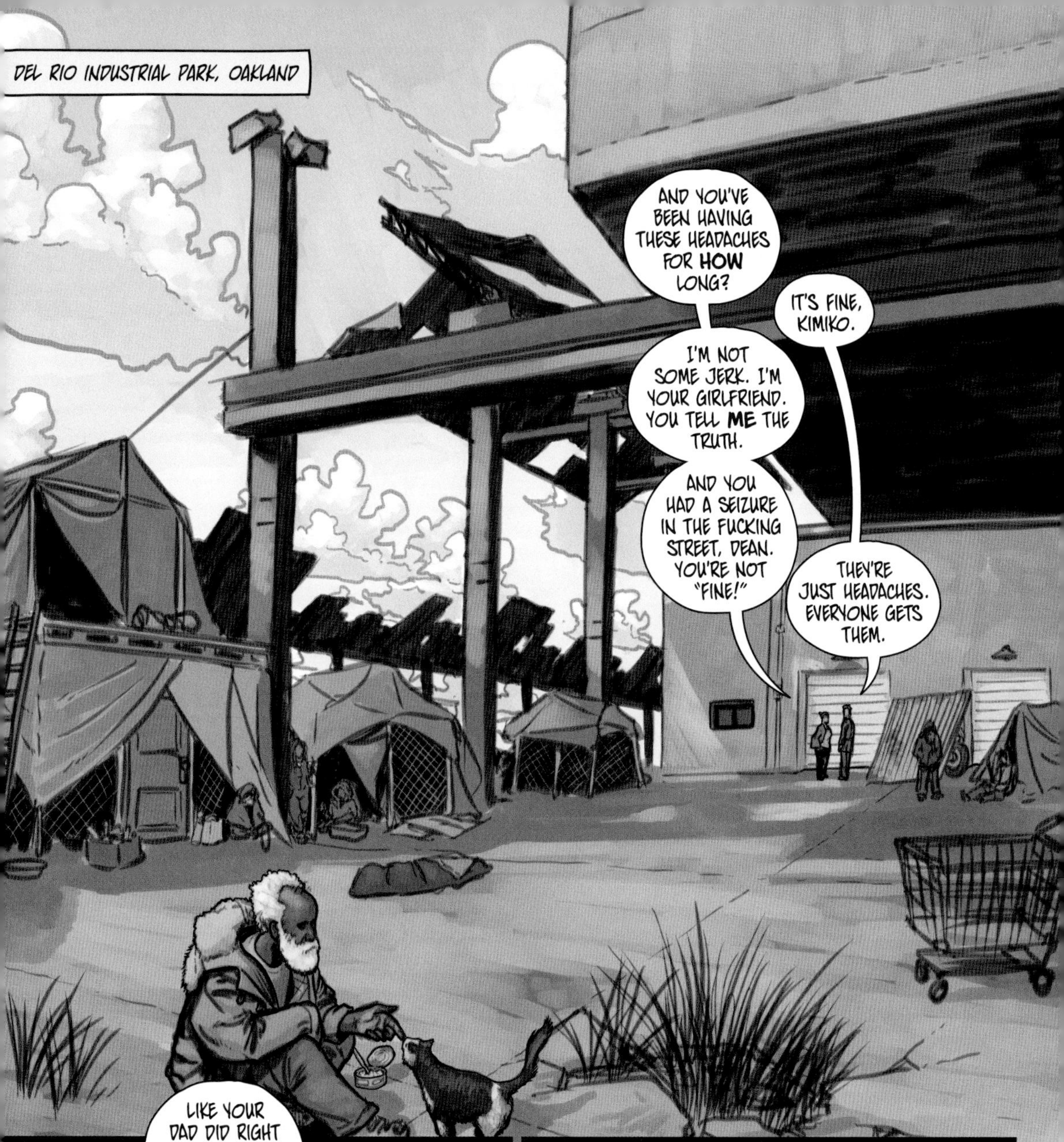
DEL RIO INDUSTRIAL PARK, OAKLAND
AND YOU'VE BEEN HAVING THESE HEADACHES FOR **HOW** LONG?
IT'S FINE, KIMIKO.
I'M NOT SOME JERK. I'M YOUR GIRLFRIEND. YOU TELL **ME** THE TRUTH.
AND YOU HAD A SEIZURE IN THE FUCKING STREET, DEAN. YOU'RE NOT "FINE!"
THEY'RE JUST HEADACHES. EVERYONE GETS THEM.

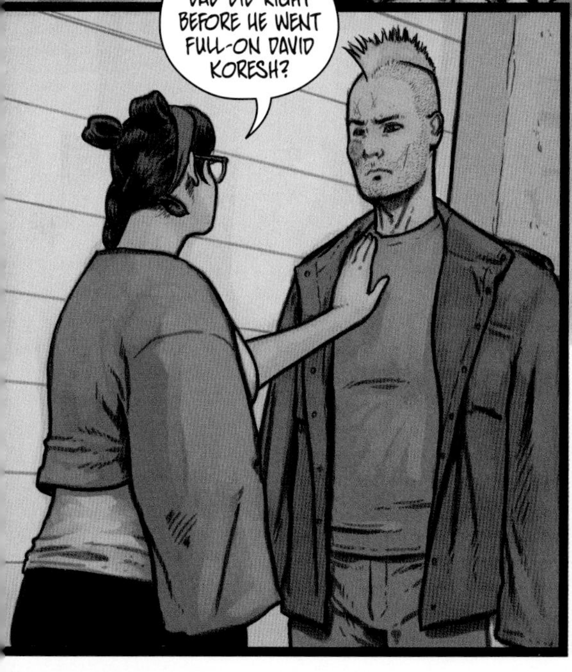
LIKE YOUR DAD DID RIGHT BEFORE HE WENT FULL-ON DAVID KORESH?

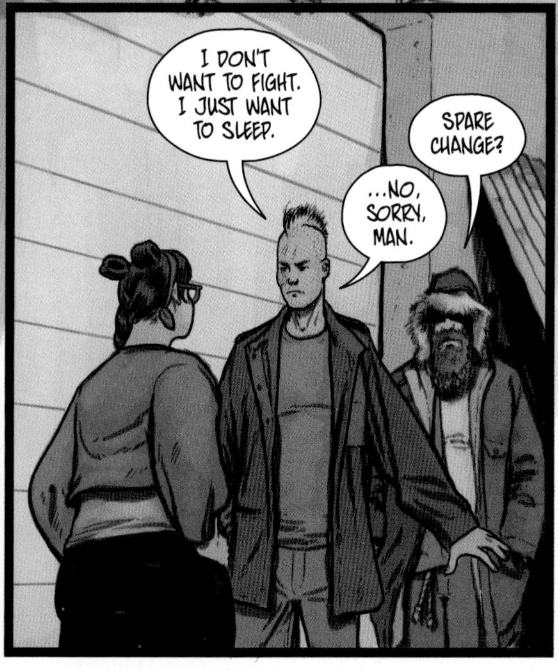
I DON'T WANT TO FIGHT. I JUST WANT TO SLEEP.
SPARE CHANGE?
...NO, SORRY, MAN.

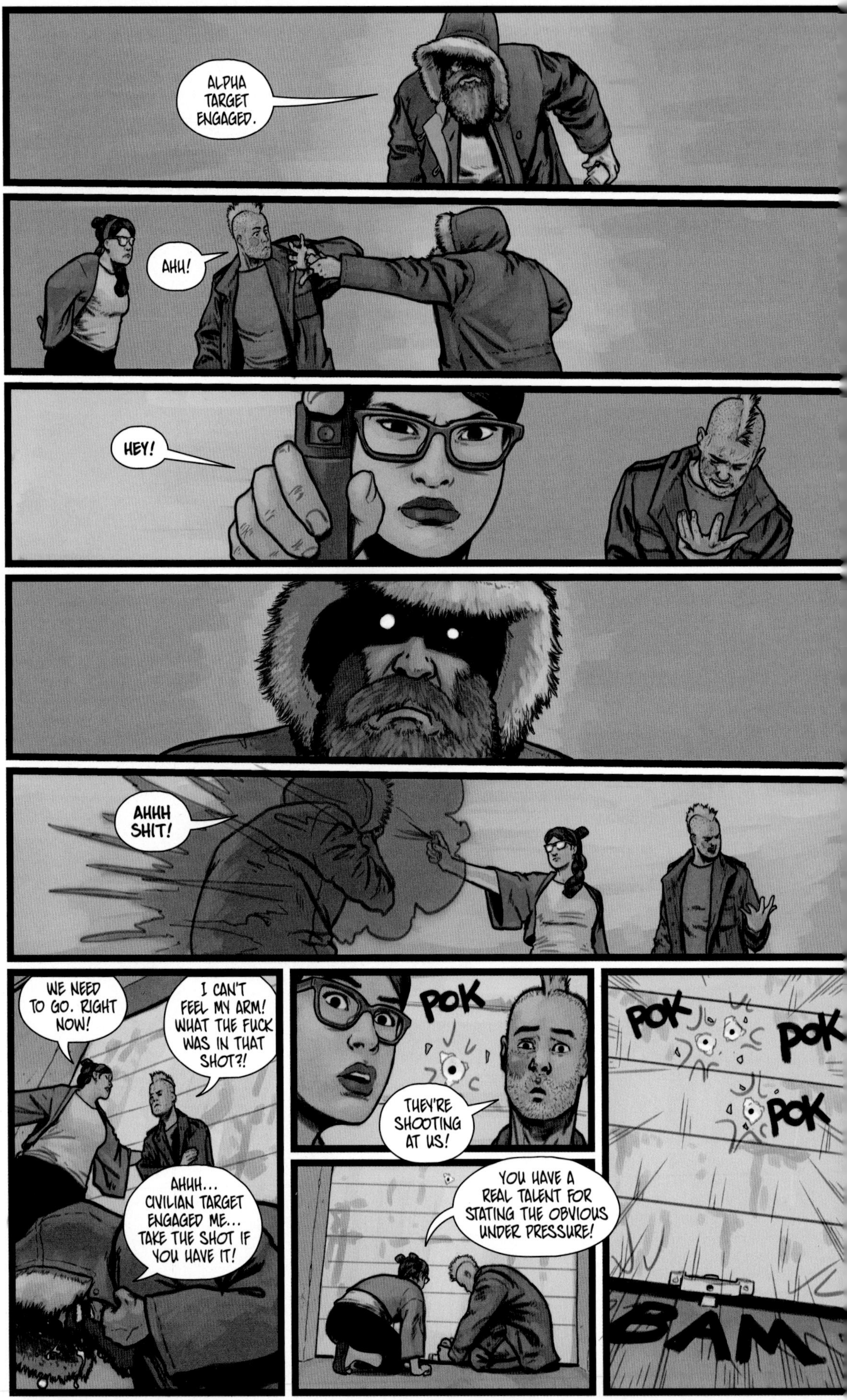
ALPHA TARGET ENGAGED.
AHH!
HEY!
AHHH SHIT!
WE NEED TO GO. RIGHT NOW!
I CAN'T FEEL MY ARM! WHAT THE FUCK WAS IN THAT SHOT?!
AHHH... CIVILIAN TARGET ENGAGED ME... TAKE THE SHOT IF YOU HAVE IT!
POK
THEY'RE SHOOTING AT US!
YOU HAVE A REAL TALENT FOR STATING THE OBVIOUS UNDER PRESSURE!
POK
POK
POK
BAM

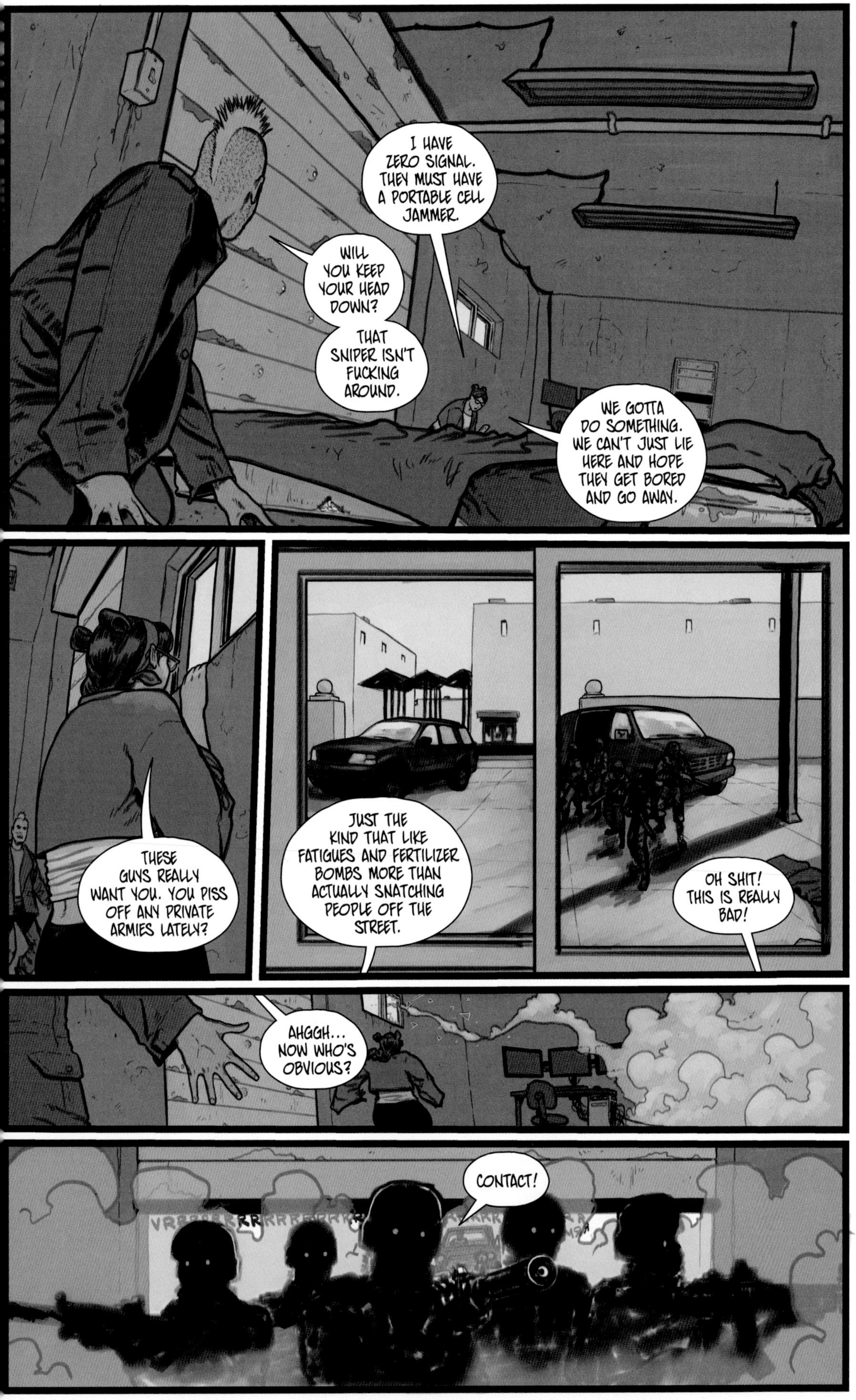
I HAVE ZERO SIGNAL. THEY MUST HAVE A PORTABLE CELL JAMMER.
WILL YOU KEEP YOUR HEAD DOWN?
THAT SNIPER ISN'T FUCKING AROUND.
WE GOTTA DO SOMETHING. WE CAN'T JUST LIE HERE AND HOPE THEY GET BORED AND GO AWAY.
THESE GUYS REALLY WANT YOU. YOU PISS OFF ANY PRIVATE ARMIES LATELY?
JUST THE KIND THAT LIKE FATIGUES AND FERTILIZER BOMBS MORE THAN ACTUALLY SNATCHING PEOPLE OFF THE STREET.
OH SHIT! THIS IS REALLY BAD!
AHGGH... NOW WHO'S OBVIOUS?
CONTACT!

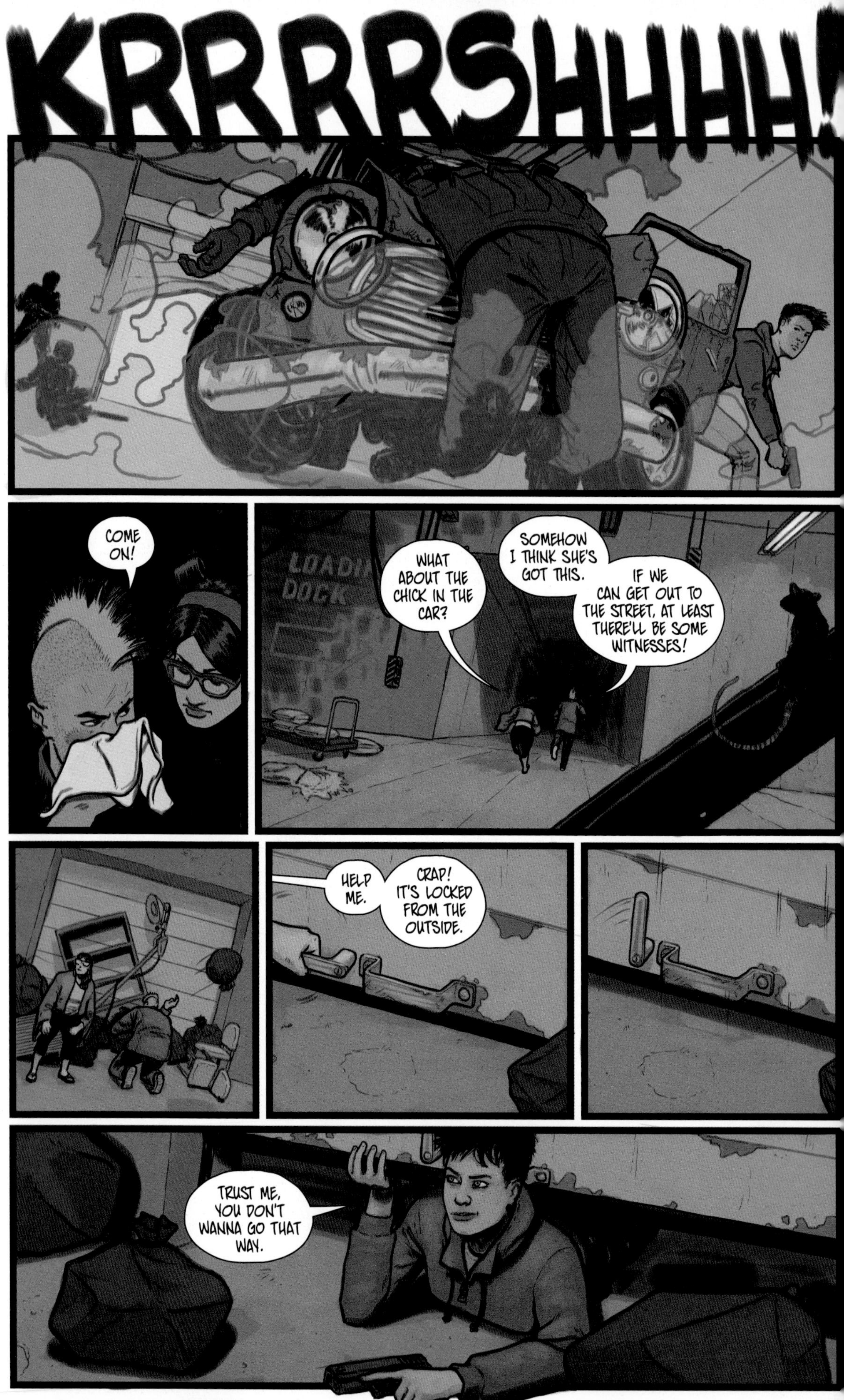
KRRRRSHHHH!
COME ON!
LOADING DOCK
WHAT ABOUT THE CHICK IN THE CAR?
SOMEHOW I THINK SHE'S GOT THIS.
IF WE CAN GET OUT TO THE STREET, AT LEAST THERE'LL BE SOME WITNESSES!
HELP ME.
CRAP! IT'S LOCKED FROM THE OUTSIDE.
TRUST ME, YOU DON'T WANNA GO THAT WAY.

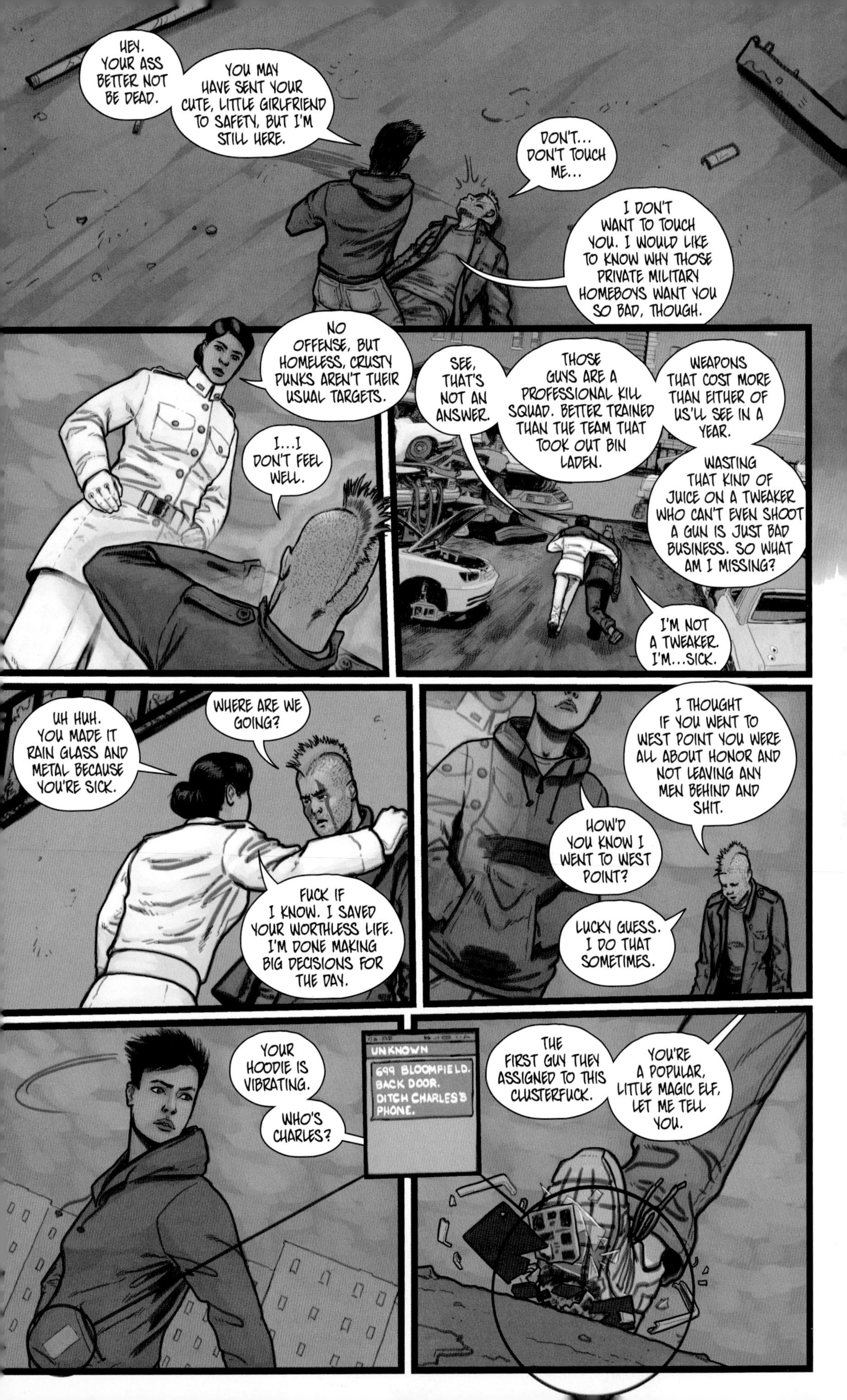
HEY. YOUR ASS BETTER NOT BE DEAD.
YOU MAY HAVE SENT YOUR CUTE, LITTLE GIRLFRIEND TO SAFETY, BUT I'M STILL HERE.
DON'T... DON'T TOUCH ME...
I DON'T WANT TO TOUCH YOU. I WOULD LIKE TO KNOW WHY THOSE PRIVATE MILITARY HOMEBOYS WANT YOU SO BAD, THOUGH.
NO OFFENSE, BUT HOMELESS, CRUSTY PUNKS AREN'T THEIR USUAL TARGETS.
I...I DON'T FEEL WELL.
SEE, THAT'S NOT AN ANSWER.
THOSE GUYS ARE A PROFESSIONAL KILL SQUAD. BETTER TRAINED THAN THE TEAM THAT TOOK OUT BIN LADEN.
WEAPONS THAT COST MORE THAN EITHER OF US'LL SEE IN A YEAR.
WASTING THAT KIND OF JUICE ON A TWEAKER WHO CAN'T EVEN SHOOT A GUN IS JUST BAD BUSINESS. SO WHAT AM I MISSING?
I'M NOT A TWEAKER. I'M...SICK.
UH HUH. YOU MADE IT RAIN GLASS AND METAL BECAUSE YOU'RE SICK.
WHERE ARE WE GOING?
FUCK IF I KNOW. I SAVED YOUR WORTHLESS LIFE. I'M DONE MAKING BIG DECISIONS FOR THE DAY.
I THOUGHT IF YOU WENT TO WEST POINT YOU WERE ALL ABOUT HONOR AND NOT LEAVING ANY MEN BEHIND AND SHIT.
HOW'D YOU KNOW I WENT TO WEST POINT?
LUCKY GUESS. I DO THAT SOMETIMES.
YOUR HOODIE IS VIBRATING.
WHO'S CHARLES?
UNKNOWN
699 BLOOMFIELD. BACK DOOR. DITCH CHARLES'S PHONE.
THE FIRST GUY THEY ASSIGNED TO THIS CLUSTERFUCK.
YOU'RE A POPULAR, LITTLE MAGIC ELF, LET ME TELL YOU.

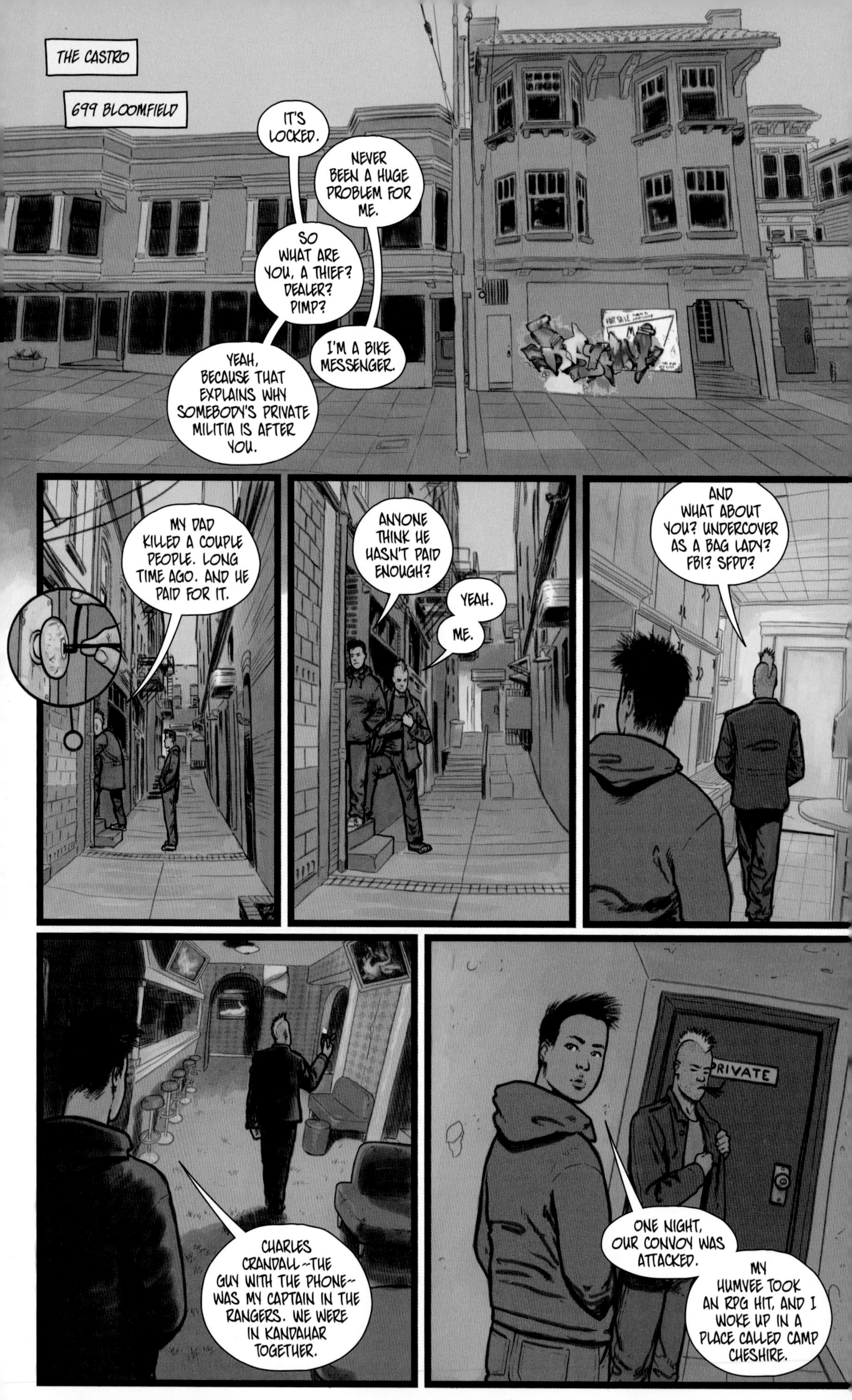

THE CASTRO
699 BLOOMFIELD
IT'S LOCKED.
NEVER BEEN A HUGE PROBLEM FOR ME.
SO WHAT ARE YOU, A THIEF? DEALER? PIMP?
I'M A BIKE MESSENGER.
YEAH, BECAUSE THAT EXPLAINS WHY SOMEBODY'S PRIVATE MILITIA IS AFTER YOU.
MY DAD KILLED A COUPLE PEOPLE. LONG TIME AGO. AND HE PAID FOR IT.
ANYONE THINK HE HASN'T PAID ENOUGH?
YEAH.
ME.
AND WHAT ABOUT YOU? UNDERCOVER AS A BAG LADY? FBI? SFPD?
CHARLES CRANDALL--THE GUY WITH THE PHONE--WAS MY CAPTAIN IN THE RANGERS. WE WERE IN KANDAHAR TOGETHER.
PRIVATE
ONE NIGHT, OUR CONVOY WAS ATTACKED.
MY HUMVEE TOOK AN RPG HIT, AND I WOKE UP IN A PLACE CALLED CAMP CHESHIRE.

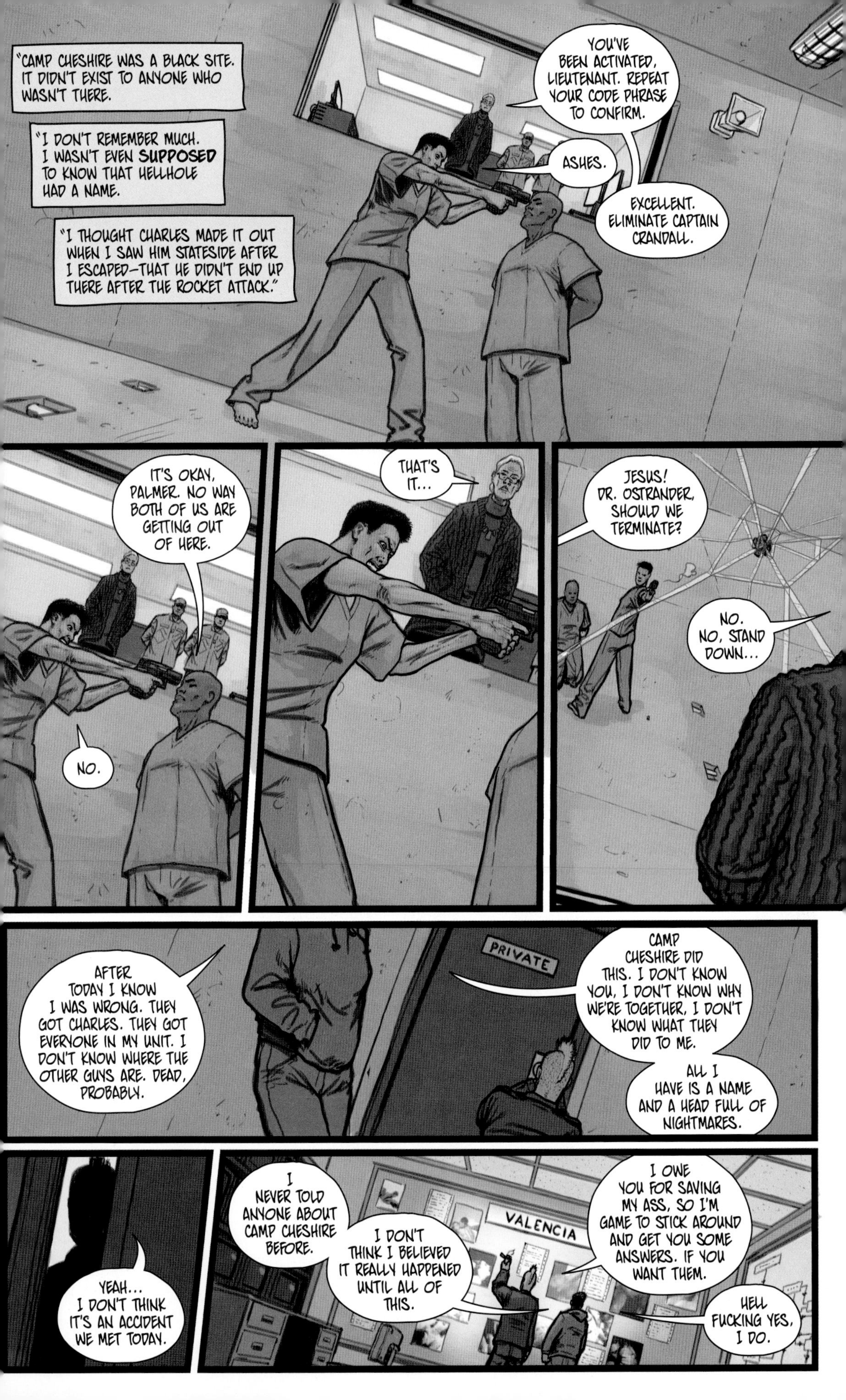
"CAMP CHESHIRE WAS A BLACK SITE. IT DIDN'T EXIST TO ANYONE WHO WASN'T THERE.
"I DON'T REMEMBER MUCH. I WASN'T EVEN **SUPPOSED** TO KNOW THAT HELLHOLE HAD A NAME.
"I THOUGHT CHARLES MADE IT OUT WHEN I SAW HIM STATESIDE AFTER I ESCAPED—THAT HE DIDN'T END UP THERE AFTER THE ROCKET ATTACK."
YOU'VE BEEN ACTIVATED, LIEUTENANT. REPEAT YOUR CODE PHRASE TO CONFIRM.
ASHES.
EXCELLENT. ELIMINATE CAPTAIN CRANDALL.
IT'S OKAY, PALMER. NO WAY BOTH OF US ARE GETTING OUT OF HERE.
NO.
THAT'S IT...
JESUS! DR. OSTRANDER, SHOULD WE TERMINATE?
NO. NO, STAND DOWN...
AFTER TODAY I KNOW I WAS WRONG. THEY GOT CHARLES. THEY GOT EVERYONE IN MY UNIT. I DON'T KNOW WHERE THE OTHER GUYS ARE. DEAD, PROBABLY.
PRIVATE
CAMP CHESHIRE DID THIS. I DON'T KNOW YOU, I DON'T KNOW WHY WE'RE TOGETHER, I DON'T KNOW WHAT THEY DID TO ME.
ALL I HAVE IS A NAME AND A HEAD FULL OF NIGHTMARES.
YEAH... I DON'T THINK IT'S AN ACCIDENT WE MET TODAY.
I NEVER TOLD ANYONE ABOUT CAMP CHESHIRE BEFORE.
I DON'T THINK I BELIEVED IT REALLY HAPPENED UNTIL ALL OF THIS.
VALENCIA
I OWE YOU FOR SAVING MY ASS, SO I'M GAME TO STICK AROUND AND GET YOU SOME ANSWERS. IF YOU WANT THEM.
HELL FUCKING YES, I DO.

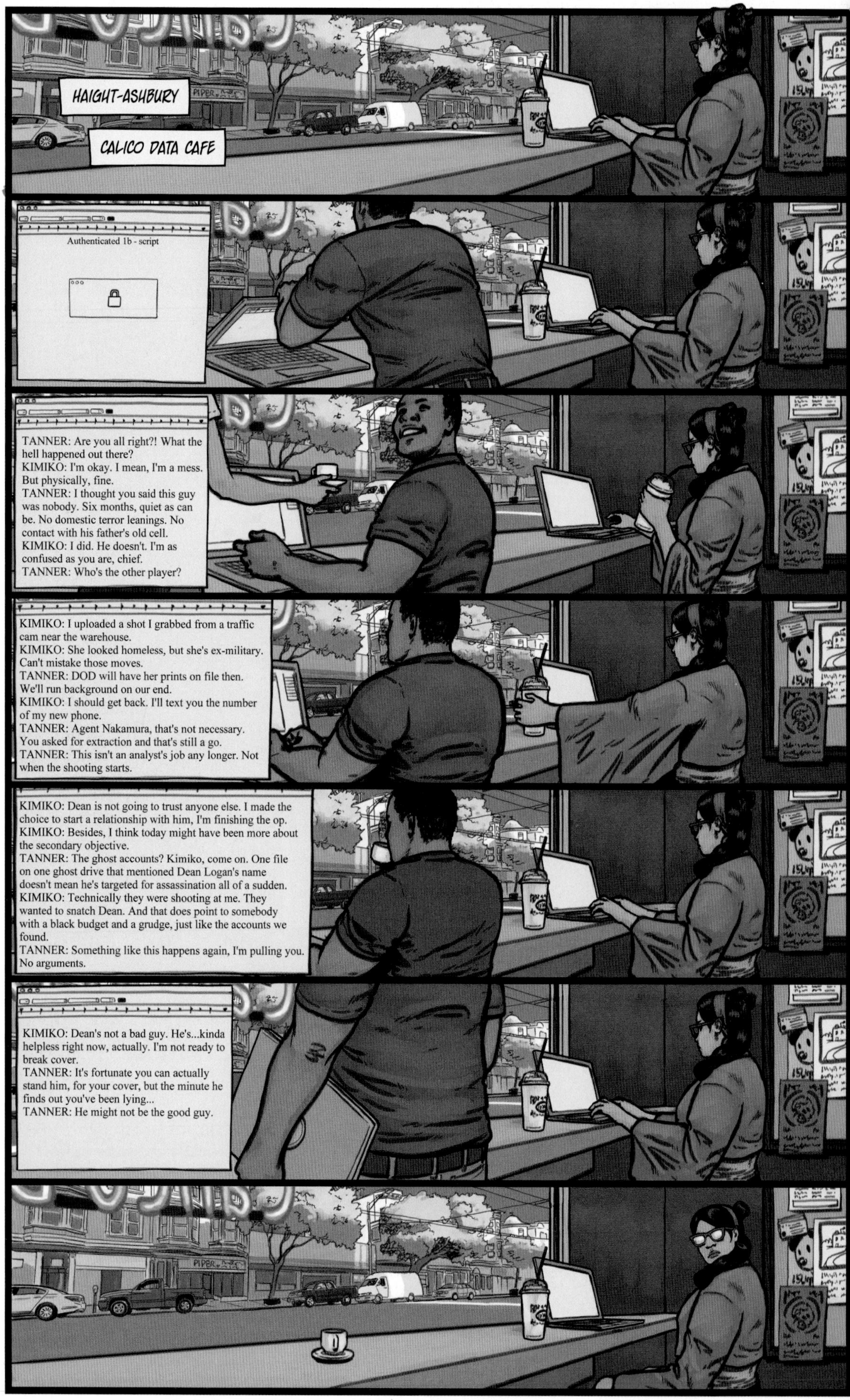
HAIGHT-ASHBURY
CALICO DATA CAFE
Authenticated 1b - script
TANNER: Are you all right?! What the hell happened out there?
KIMIKO: I'm okay. I mean, I'm a mess. But physically, fine.
TANNER: I thought you said this guy was nobody. Six months, quiet as can be. No domestic terror leanings. No contact with his father's old cell.
KIMIKO: I did. He doesn't. I'm as confused as you are, chief.
TANNER: Who's the other player?
KIMIKO: I uploaded a shot I grabbed from a traffic cam near the warehouse.
KIMIKO: She looked homeless, but she's ex-military. Can't mistake those moves.
TANNER: DOD will have her prints on file then. We'll run background on our end.
KIMIKO: I should get back. I'll text you the number of my new phone.
TANNER: Agent Nakamura, that's not necessary. You asked for extraction and that's still a go.
TANNER: This isn't an analyst's job any longer. Not when the shooting starts.
KIMIKO: Dean is not going to trust anyone else. I made the choice to start a relationship with him, I'm finishing the op.
KIMIKO: Besides, I think today might have been more about the secondary objective.
TANNER: The ghost accounts? Kimiko, come on. One file on one ghost drive that mentioned Dean Logan's name doesn't mean he's targeted for assassination all of a sudden.
KIMIKO: Technically they were shooting at me. They wanted to snatch Dean. And that does point to somebody with a black budget and a grudge, just like the accounts we found.
TANNER: Something like this happens again, I'm pulling you. No arguments.
KIMIKO: Dean's not a bad guy. He's...kinda helpless right now, actually. I'm not ready to break cover.
TANNER: It's fortunate you can actually stand him, for your cover, but the minute he finds out you've been lying...
TANNER: He might not be the good guy.

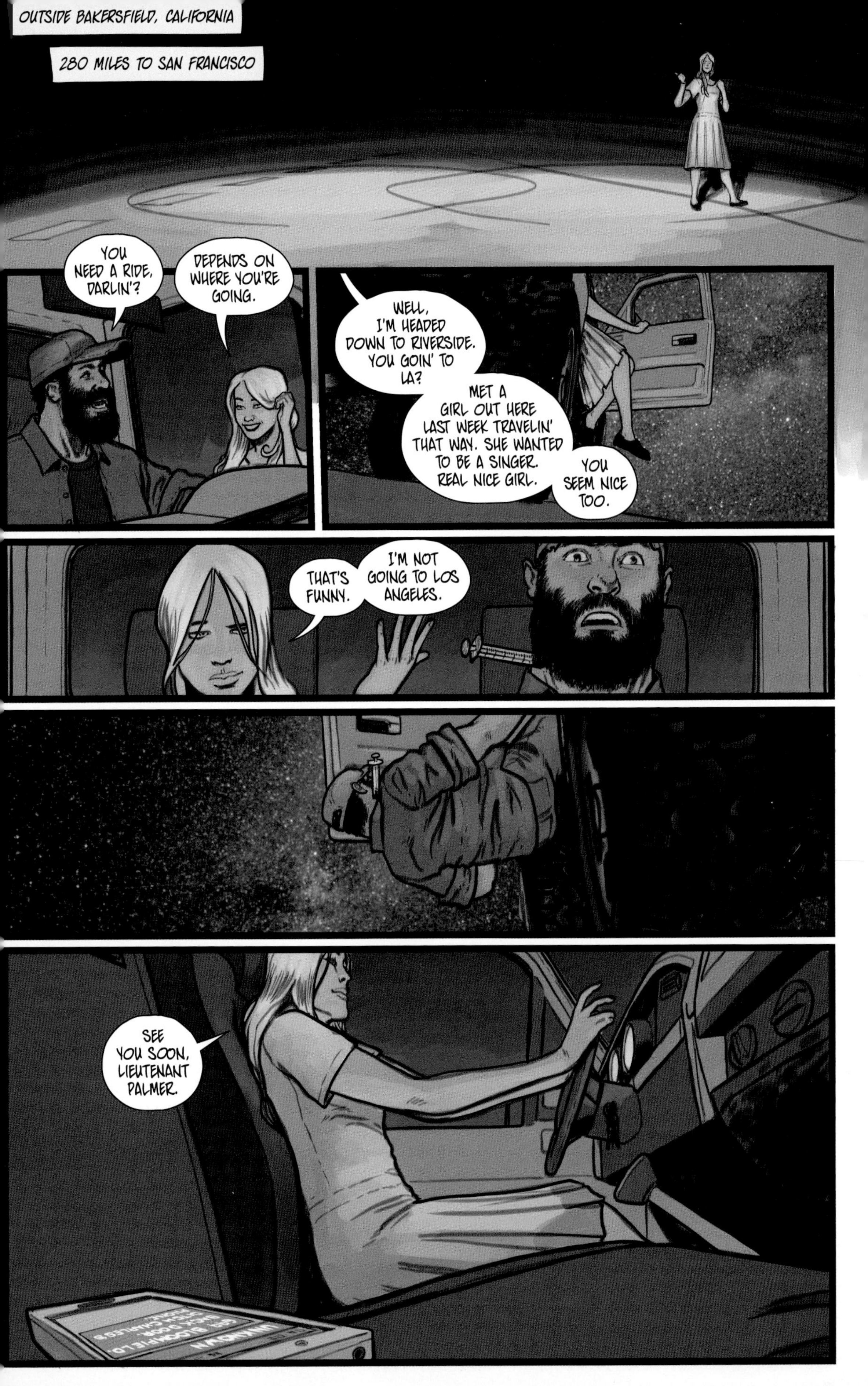
OUTSIDE BAKERSFIELD, CALIFORNIA
280 MILES TO SAN FRANCISCO
YOU NEED A RIDE, DARLIN'?
DEPENDS ON WHERE YOU'RE GOING.
WELL, I'M HEADED DOWN TO RIVERSIDE. YOU GOIN' TO LA?
MET A GIRL OUT HERE LAST WEEK TRAVELIN' THAT WAY. SHE WANTED TO BE A SINGER. REAL NICE GIRL.
YOU SEEM NICE TOO.
THAT'S FUNNY.
I'M NOT GOING TO LOS ANGELES.
SEE YOU SOON, LIEUTENANT PALMER.

CHAPTER TWO

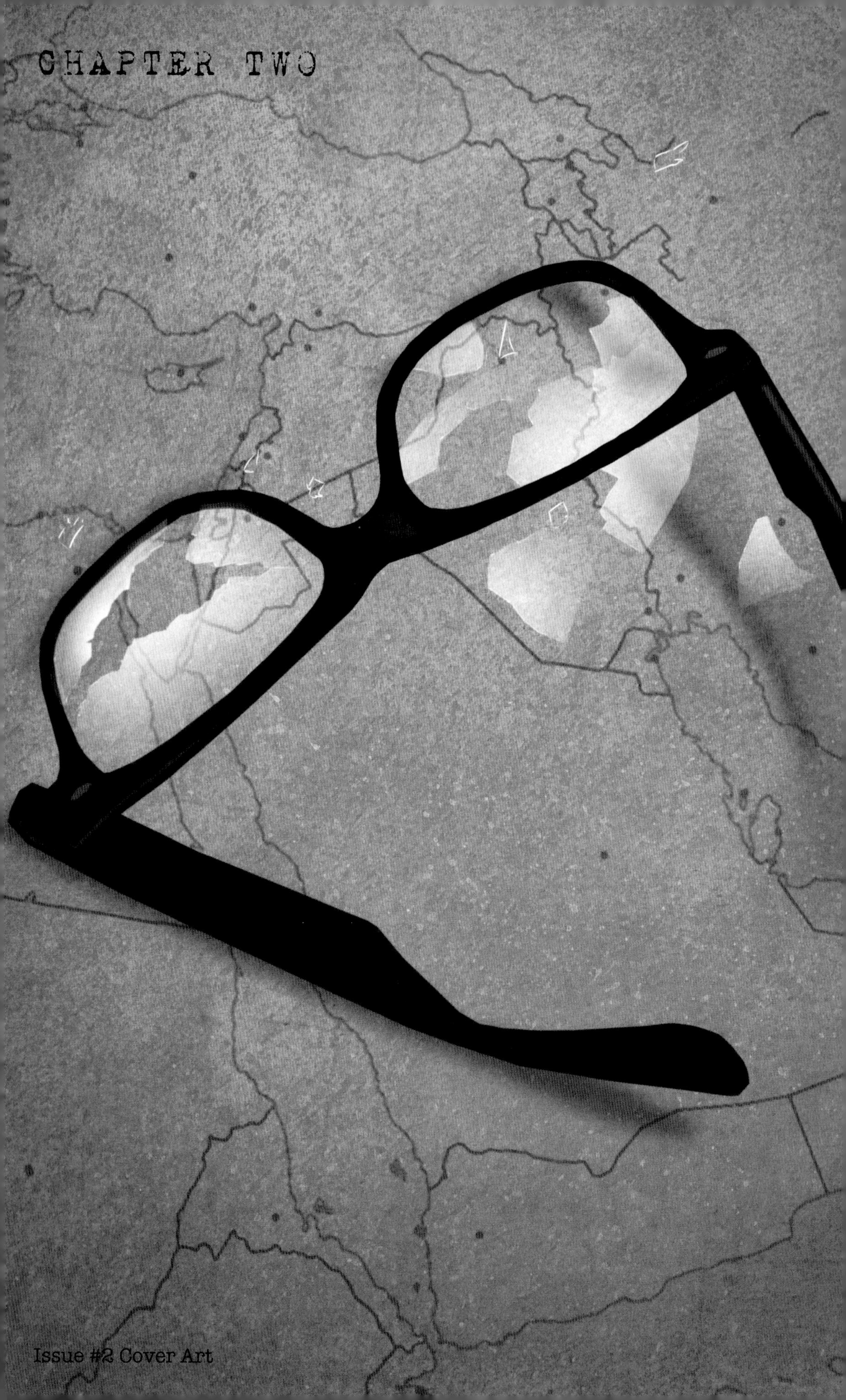

Issue #2 Cover Art

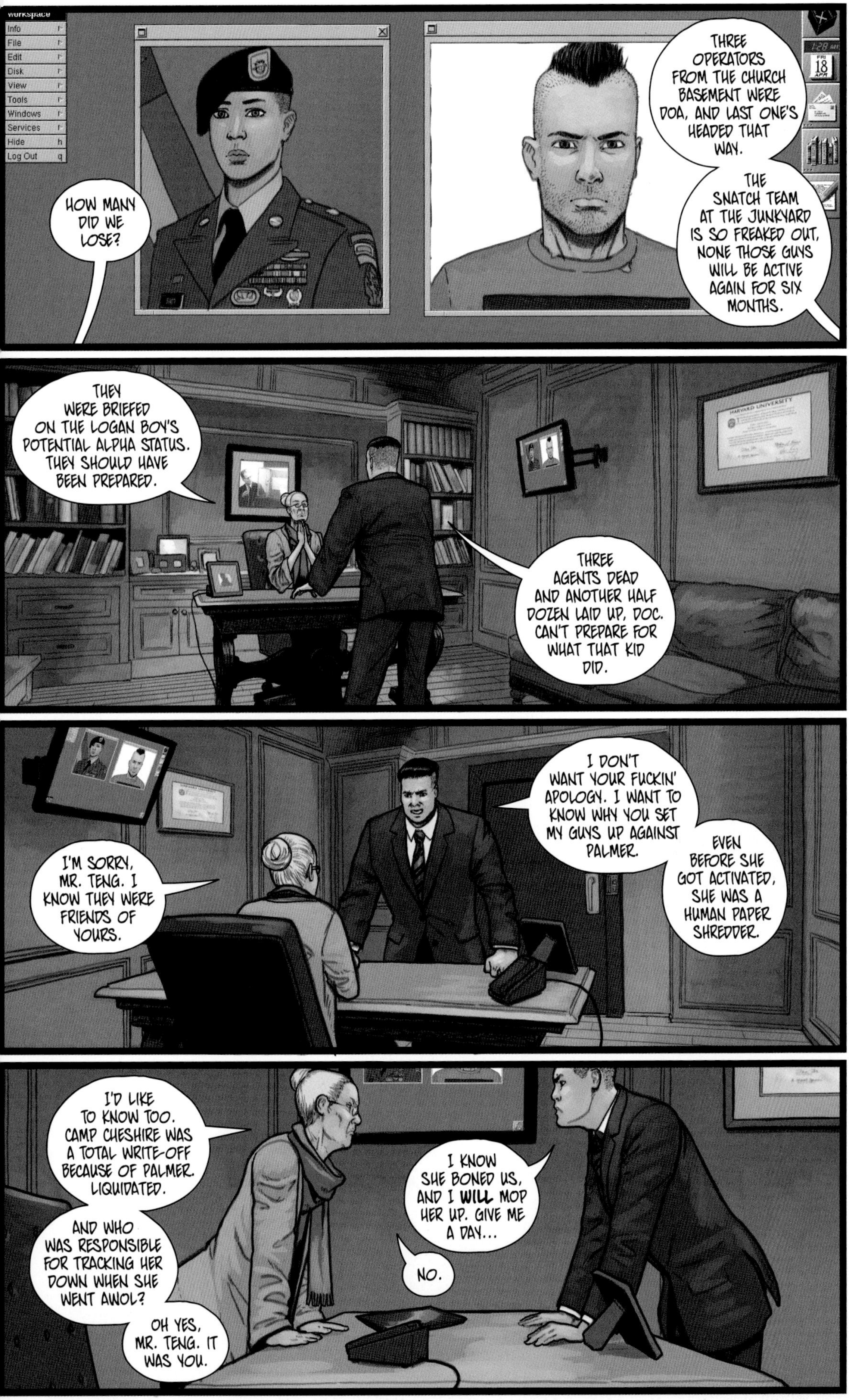
Workspace
Info
File
Edit
Disk
View
Tools
Windows
Services
Hide h
Log Out q
FRI 18 APR
HOW MANY DID WE LOSE?
THREE OPERATORS FROM THE CHURCH BASEMENT WERE DOA, AND LAST ONE'S HEADED THAT WAY.
THE SNATCH TEAM AT THE JUNKYARD IS SO FREAKED OUT, NONE THOSE GUYS WILL BE ACTIVE AGAIN FOR SIX MONTHS.
THEY WERE BRIEFED ON THE LOGAN BOY'S POTENTIAL ALPHA STATUS. THEY SHOULD HAVE BEEN PREPARED.
HARVARD UNIVERSITY
THREE AGENTS DEAD AND ANOTHER HALF DOZEN LAID UP, DOC. CAN'T PREPARE FOR WHAT THAT KID DID.
I'M SORRY, MR. TENG. I KNOW THEY WERE FRIENDS OF YOURS.
I DON'T WANT YOUR FUCKIN' APOLOGY. I WANT TO KNOW WHY YOU SET MY GUYS UP AGAINST PALMER.
EVEN BEFORE SHE GOT ACTIVATED, SHE WAS A HUMAN PAPER SHREDDER.
I'D LIKE TO KNOW TOO. CAMP CHESHIRE WAS A TOTAL WRITE-OFF BECAUSE OF PALMER. LIQUIDATED.
I KNOW SHE BONED US, AND I **WILL** MOP HER UP. GIVE ME A DAY...
AND WHO WAS RESPONSIBLE FOR TRACKING HER DOWN WHEN SHE WENT AWOL?
NO.
OH YES, MR. TENG. IT WAS YOU.

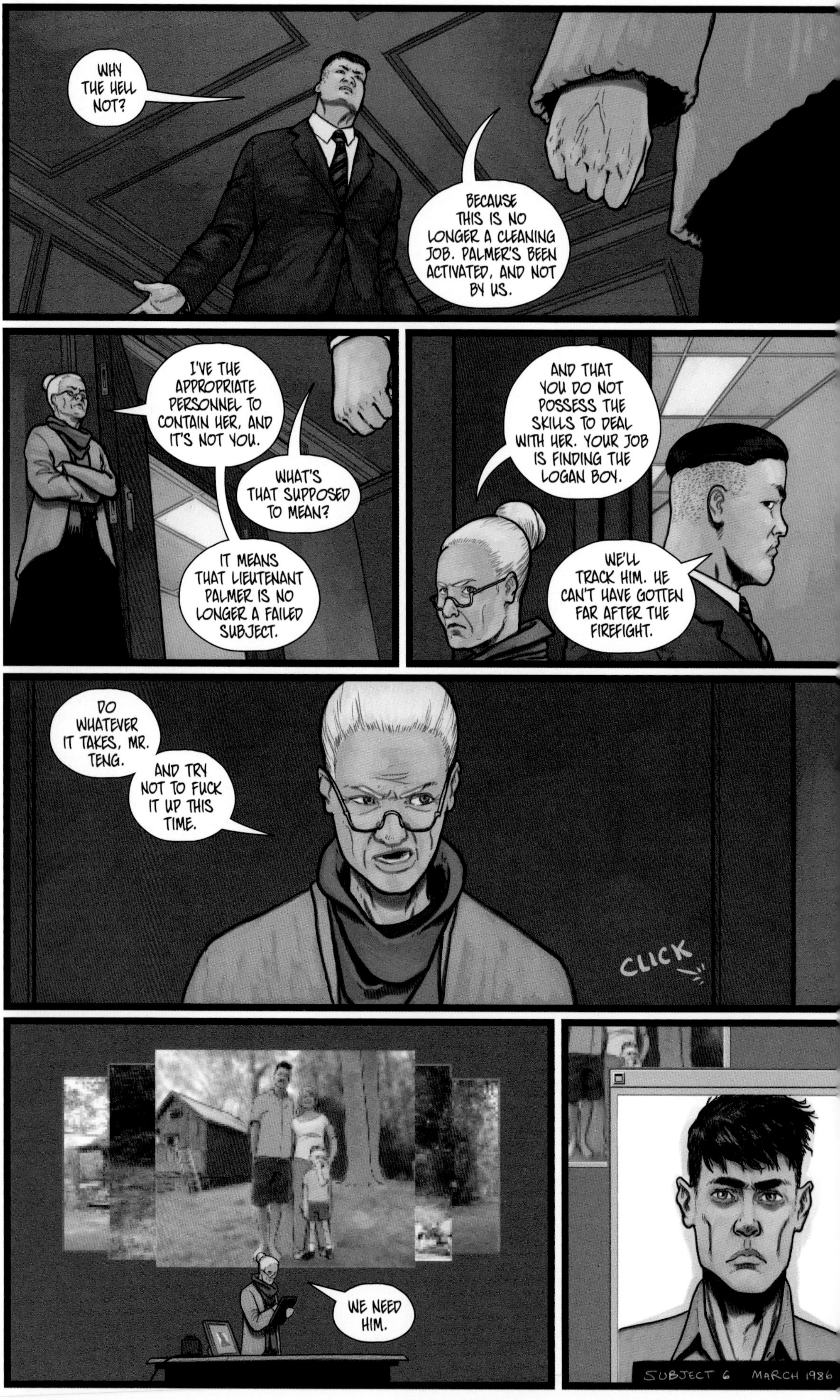
WHY THE HELL NOT?
BECAUSE THIS IS NO LONGER A CLEANING JOB. PALMER'S BEEN ACTIVATED, AND NOT BY US.
I'VE THE APPROPRIATE PERSONNEL TO CONTAIN HER, AND IT'S NOT YOU.
WHAT'S THAT SUPPOSED TO MEAN?
IT MEANS THAT LIEUTENANT PALMER IS NO LONGER A FAILED SUBJECT.
AND THAT YOU DO NOT POSSESS THE SKILLS TO DEAL WITH HER. YOUR JOB IS FINDING THE LOGAN BOY.
WE'LL TRACK HIM. HE CAN'T HAVE GOTTEN FAR AFTER THE FIREFIGHT.
DO WHATEVER IT TAKES, MR. TENG.
AND TRY NOT TO FUCK IT UP THIS TIME.
CLICK
WE NEED HIM.
SUBJECT 6 MARCH 1986

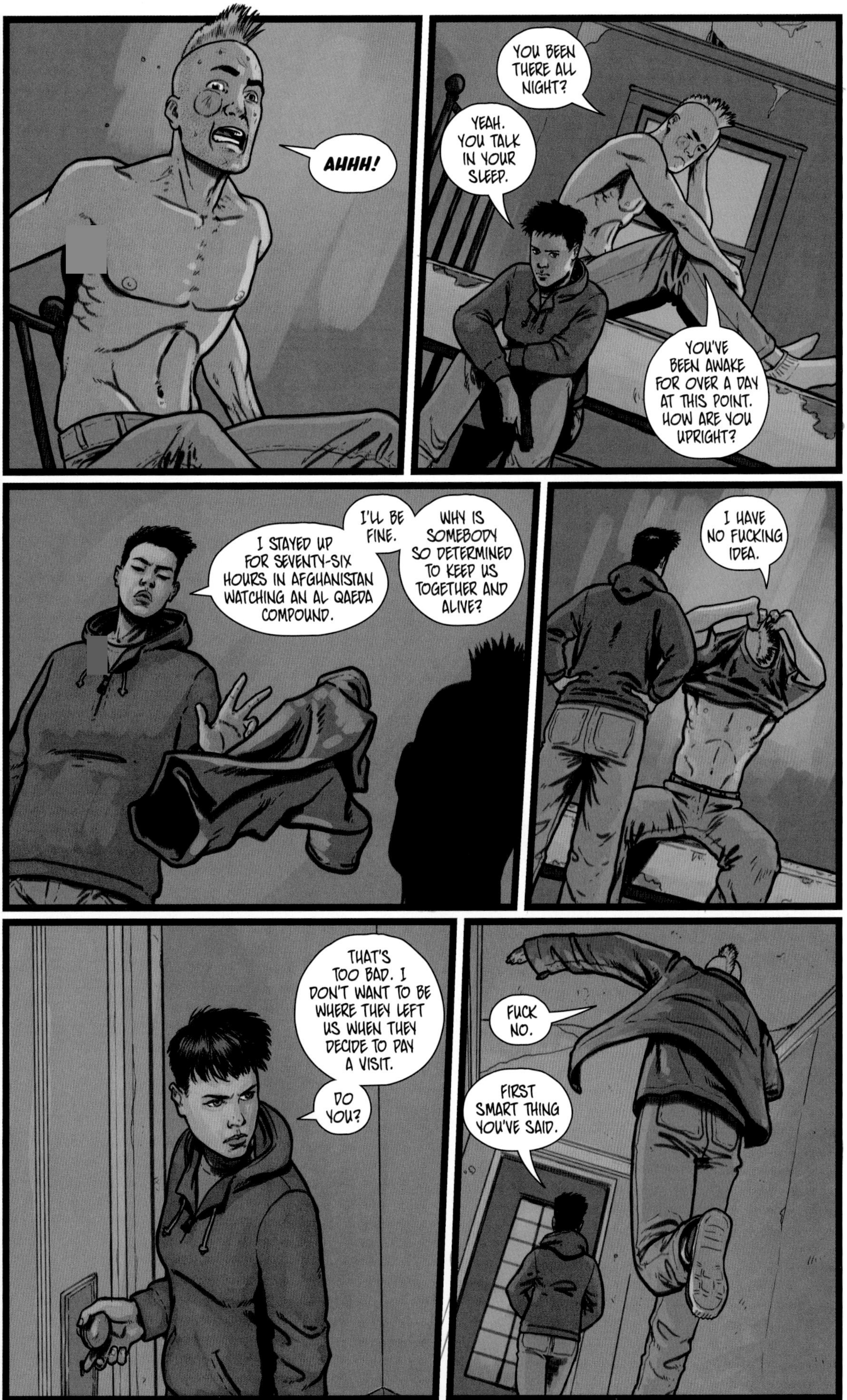
AHHH!
YOU BEEN THERE ALL NIGHT?
YEAH. YOU TALK IN YOUR SLEEP.
YOU'VE BEEN AWAKE FOR OVER A DAY AT THIS POINT. HOW ARE YOU UPRIGHT?
I STAYED UP FOR SEVENTY-SIX HOURS IN AFGHANISTAN WATCHING AN AL QAEDA COMPOUND.
I'LL BE FINE.
WHY IS SOMEBODY SO DETERMINED TO KEEP US TOGETHER AND ALIVE?
I HAVE NO FUCKING IDEA.
THAT'S TOO BAD. I DON'T WANT TO BE WHERE THEY LEFT US WHEN THEY DECIDE TO PAY A VISIT.
DO YOU?
FUCK NO.
FIRST SMART THING YOU'VE SAID.

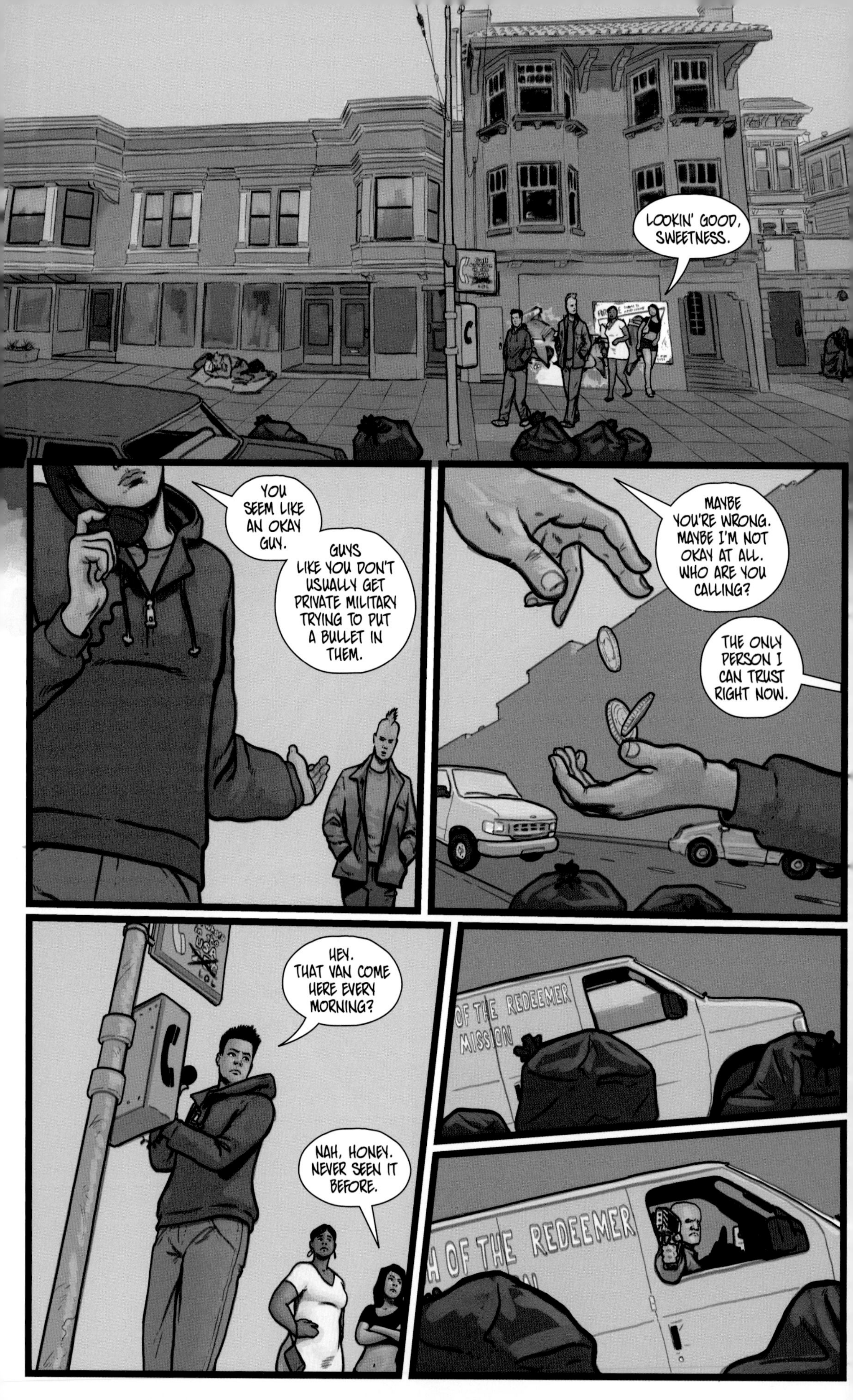
LOOKIN' GOOD, SWEETNESS.
YOU SEEM LIKE AN OKAY GUY.
GUYS LIKE YOU DON'T USUALLY GET PRIVATE MILITARY TRYING TO PUT A BULLET IN THEM.
MAYBE YOU'RE WRONG. MAYBE I'M NOT OKAY AT ALL. WHO ARE YOU CALLING?
THE ONLY PERSON I CAN TRUST RIGHT NOW.
HEY. THAT VAN COME HERE EVERY MORNING?
NAH, HONEY. NEVER SEEN IT BEFORE.
OF THE REDEEMER
MISSION
H OF THE REDEEMER

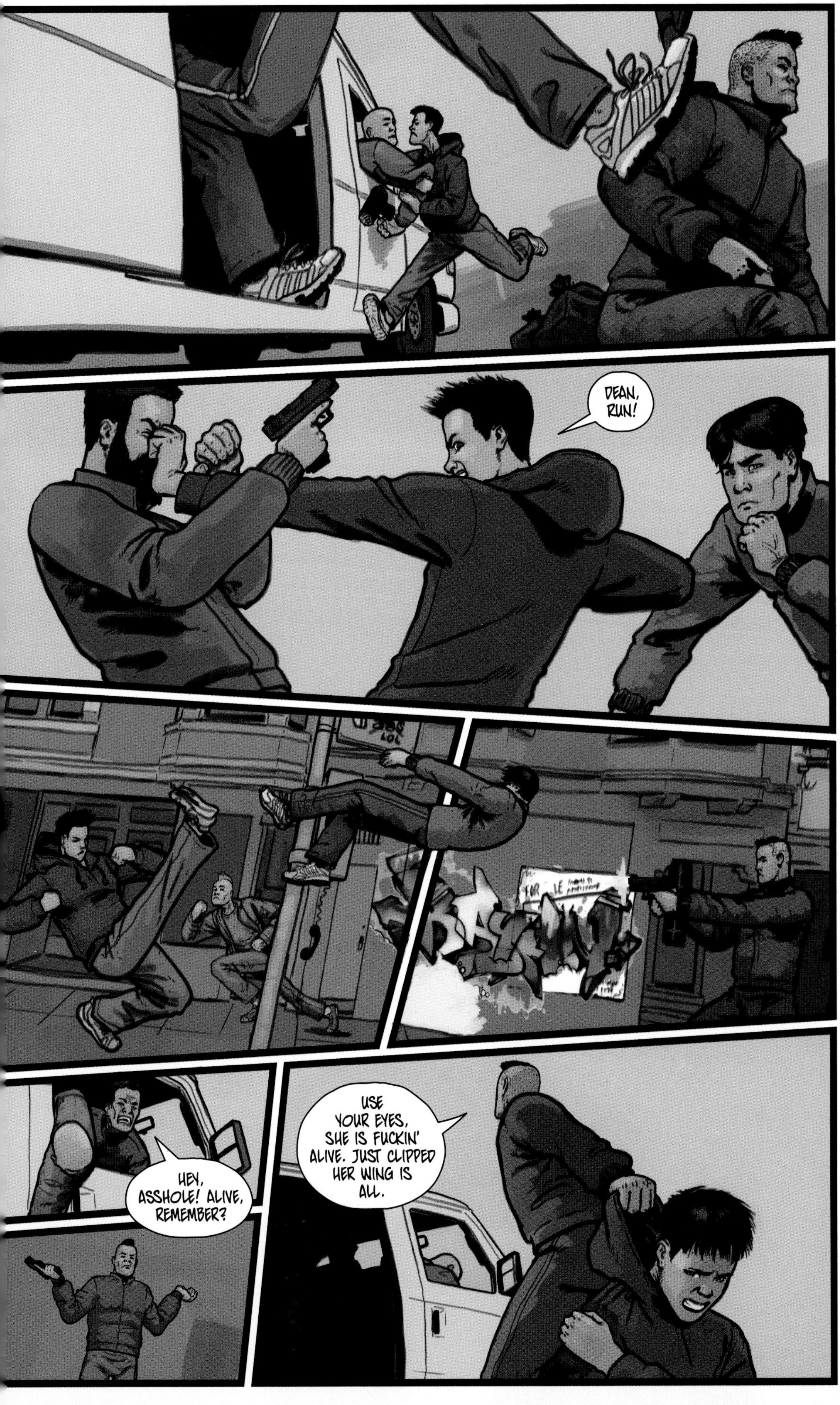
DEAN, RUN!
HEY, ASSHOLE! ALIVE, REMEMBER?
USE YOUR EYES, SHE IS FUCKIN' ALIVE. JUST CLIPPED HER WING IS ALL.

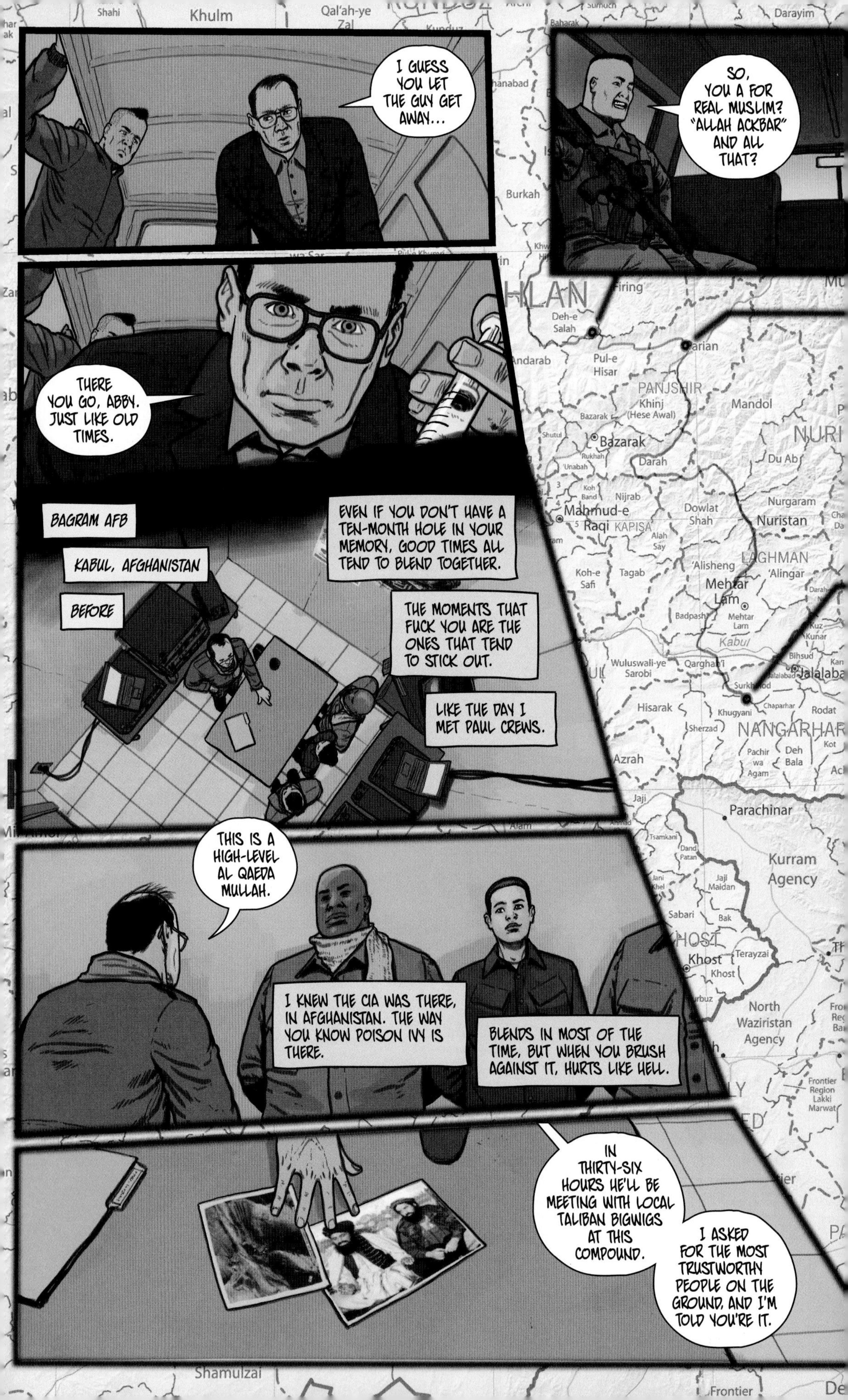

I GUESS YOU LET THE GUY GET AWAY...
SO, YOU A FOR REAL MUSLIM? "ALLAH ACKBAR" AND ALL THAT?
THERE YOU GO, ABBY. JUST LIKE OLD TIMES.
BAGRAM AFB
KABUL, AFGHANISTAN
BEFORE
EVEN IF YOU DON'T HAVE A TEN-MONTH HOLE IN YOUR MEMORY, GOOD TIMES ALL TEND TO BLEND TOGETHER.
THE MOMENTS THAT FUCK YOU ARE THE ONES THAT TEND TO STICK OUT.
LIKE THE DAY I MET PAUL CREWS.
THIS IS A HIGH-LEVEL AL QAEDA MULLAH.
I KNEW THE CIA WAS THERE, IN AFGHANISTAN. THE WAY YOU KNOW POISON IVY IS THERE.
BLENDS IN MOST OF THE TIME, BUT WHEN YOU BRUSH AGAINST IT, HURTS LIKE HELL.
IN THIRTY-SIX HOURS HE'LL BE MEETING WITH LOCAL TALIBAN BIGWIGS AT THIS COMPOUND.
I ASKED FOR THE MOST TRUSTWORTHY PEOPLE ON THE GROUND, AND I'M TOLD YOU'RE IT.

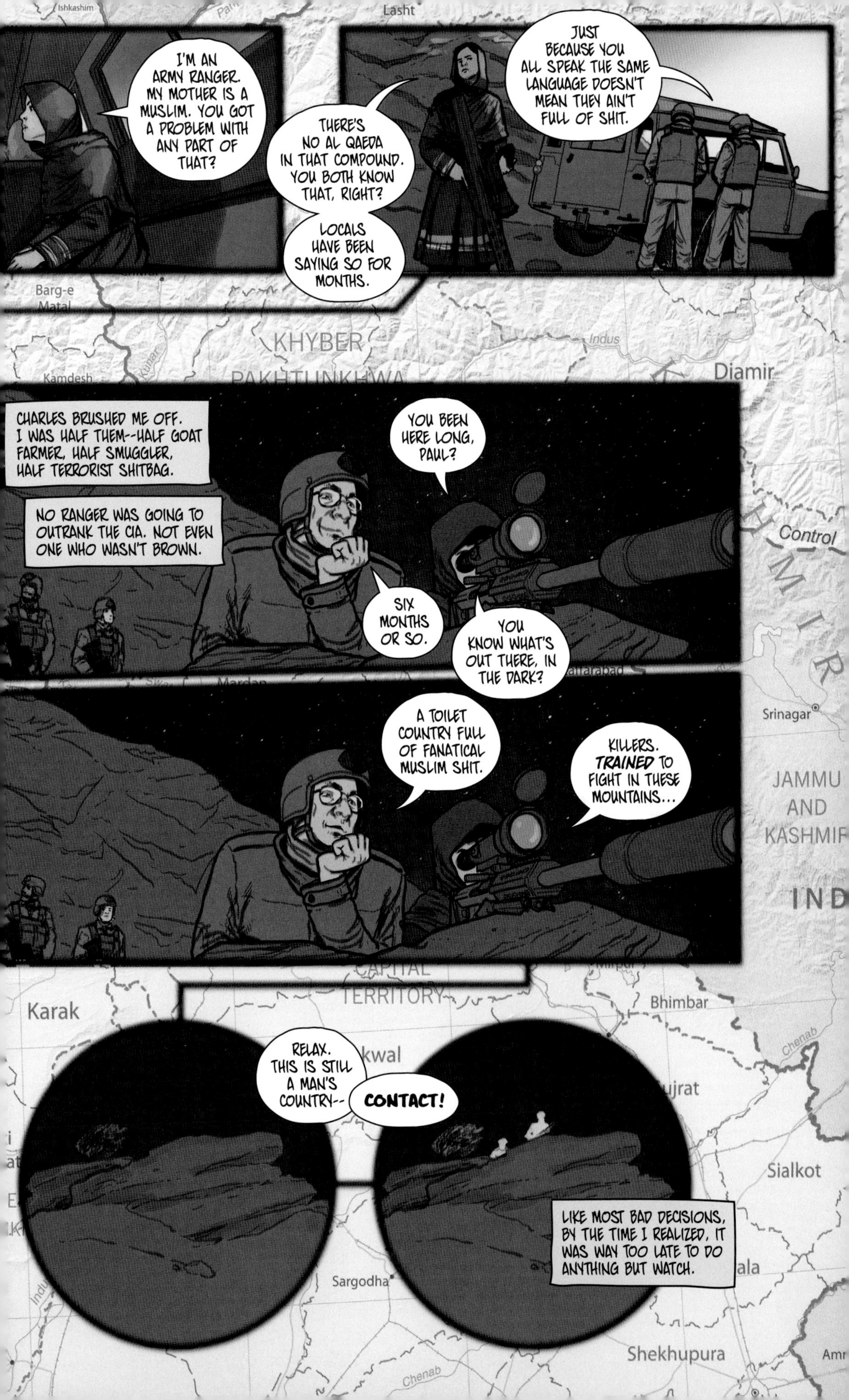
I'M AN ARMY RANGER. MY MOTHER IS A MUSLIM. YOU GOT A PROBLEM WITH ANY PART OF THAT?
THERE'S NO AL QAEDA IN THAT COMPOUND. YOU BOTH KNOW THAT, RIGHT?
LOCALS HAVE BEEN SAYING SO FOR MONTHS.
JUST BECAUSE YOU ALL SPEAK THE SAME LANGUAGE DOESN'T MEAN THEY AIN'T FULL OF SHIT.
CHARLES BRUSHED ME OFF. I WAS HALF THEM--HALF GOAT FARMER, HALF SMUGGLER, HALF TERRORIST SHITBAG.
NO RANGER WAS GOING TO OUTRANK THE CIA. NOT EVEN ONE WHO WASN'T BROWN.
YOU BEEN HERE LONG, PAUL?
SIX MONTHS OR SO.
YOU KNOW WHAT'S OUT THERE, IN THE DARK?
A TOILET COUNTRY FULL OF FANATICAL MUSLIM SHIT.
KILLERS. *TRAINED* TO FIGHT IN THESE MOUNTAINS...
RELAX. THIS IS STILL A MAN'S COUNTRY--
CONTACT!
LIKE MOST BAD DECISIONS, BY THE TIME I REALIZED, IT WAS WAY TOO LATE TO DO ANYTHING BUT WATCH.

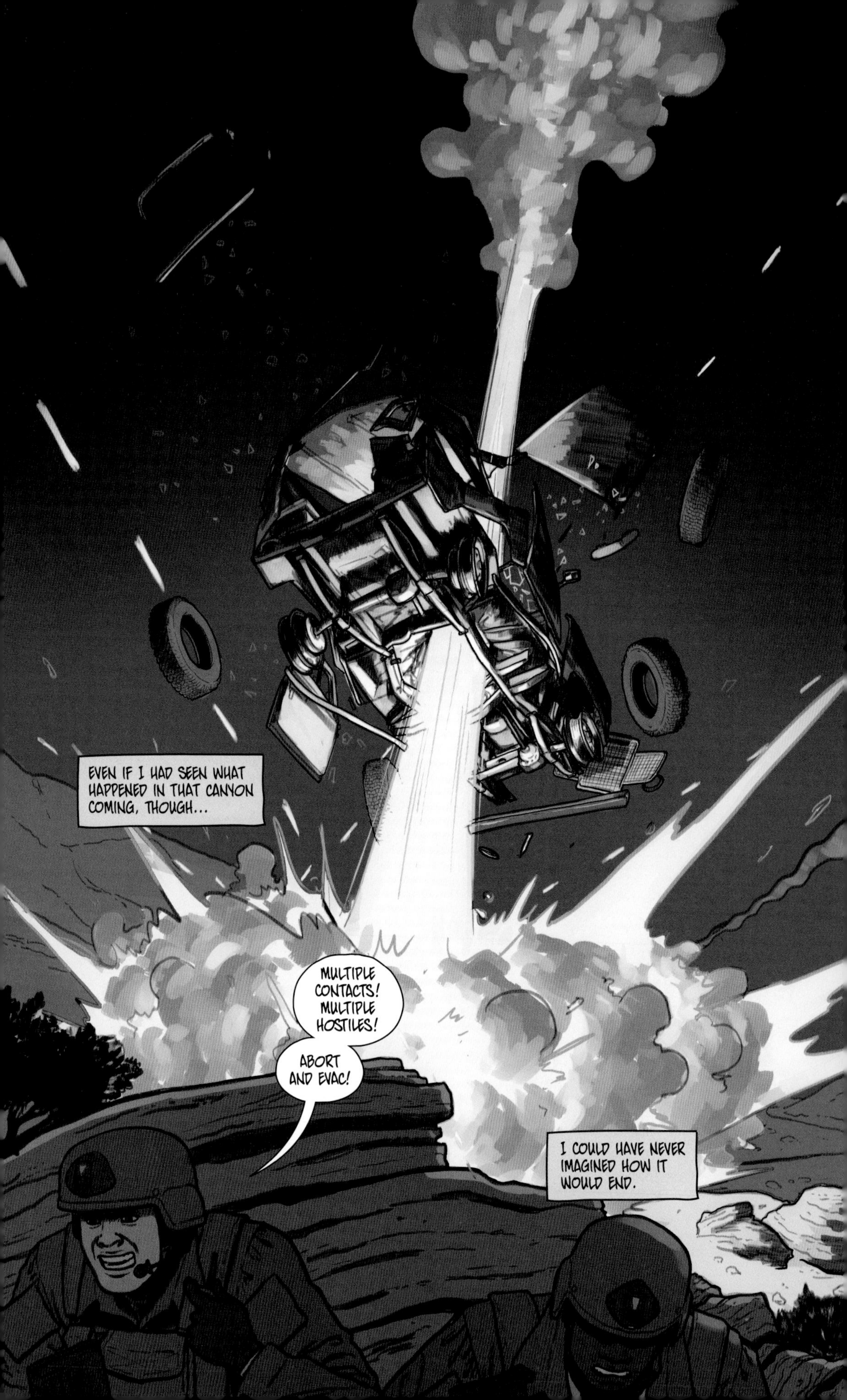
EVEN IF I HAD SEEN WHAT HAPPENED IN THAT CANYON COMING, THOUGH...
MULTIPLE CONTACTS! MULTIPLE HOSTILES!
ABORT AND EVAC!
I COULD HAVE NEVER IMAGINED HOW IT WOULD END.

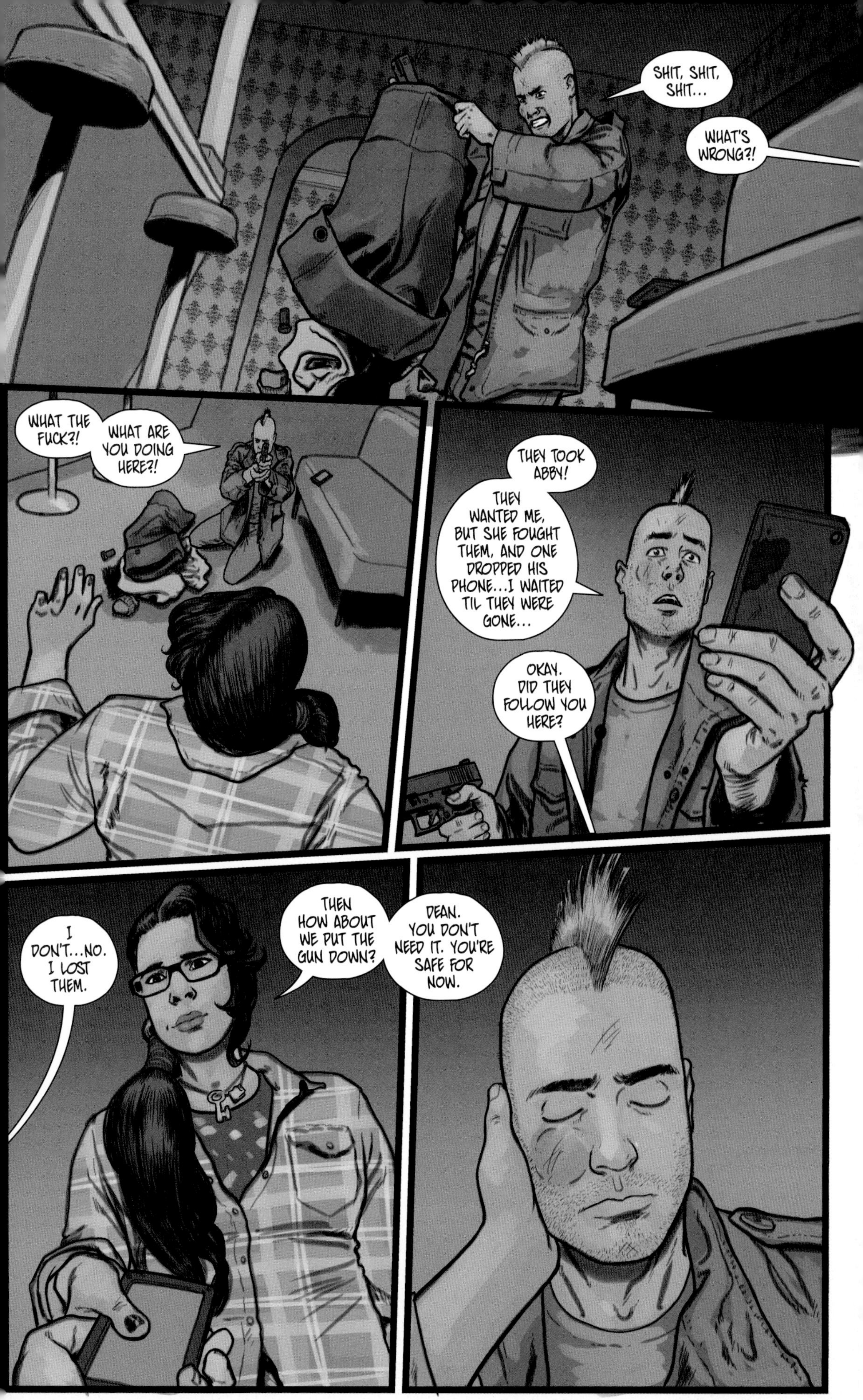
SHIT, SHIT, SHIT...
WHAT'S WRONG?!
WHAT THE FUCK?!
WHAT ARE YOU DOING HERE?!
THEY TOOK ABBY!
THEY WANTED ME, BUT SHE FOUGHT THEM, AND ONE DROPPED HIS PHONE...I WAITED TIL THEY WERE GONE...
OKAY. DID THEY FOLLOW YOU HERE?
I DON'T...NO. I LOST THEM.
THEN HOW ABOUT WE PUT THE GUN DOWN?
DEAN. YOU DON'T NEED IT. YOU'RE SAFE FOR NOW.

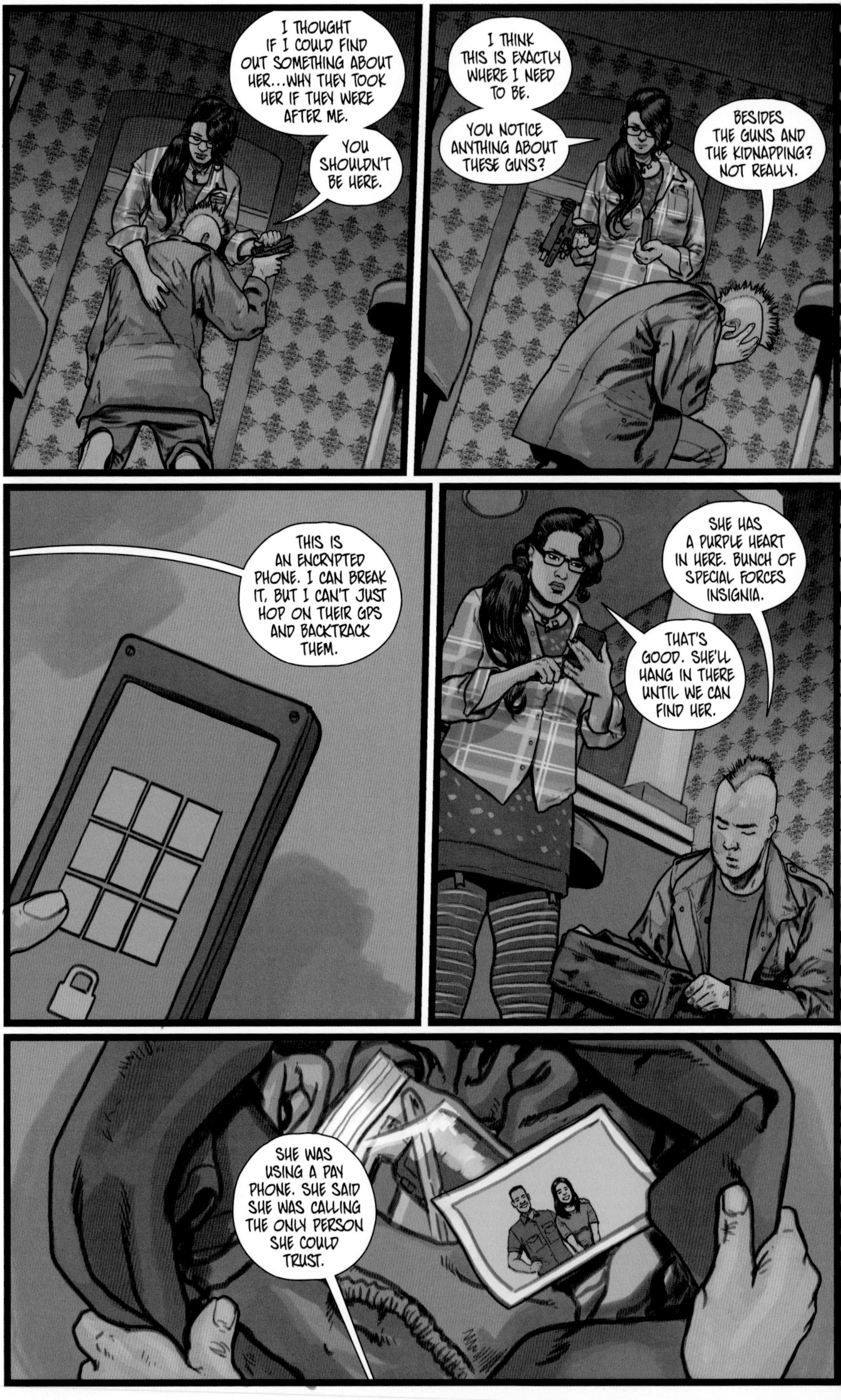
I THOUGHT IF I COULD FIND OUT SOMETHING ABOUT HER...WHY THEY TOOK HER IF THEY WERE AFTER ME.
YOU SHOULDN'T BE HERE.
I THINK THIS IS EXACTLY WHERE I NEED TO BE.
YOU NOTICE ANYTHING ABOUT THESE GUYS?
BESIDES THE GUNS AND THE KIDNAPPING? NOT REALLY.
THIS IS AN ENCRYPTED PHONE. I CAN BREAK IT, BUT I CAN'T JUST HOP ON THEIR GPS AND BACKTRACK THEM.
SHE HAS A PURPLE HEART IN HERE. BUNCH OF SPECIAL FORCES INSIGNIA.
THAT'S GOOD. SHE'LL HANG IN THERE UNTIL WE CAN FIND HER.
SHE WAS USING A PAY PHONE. SHE SAID SHE WAS CALLING THE ONLY PERSON SHE COULD TRUST.

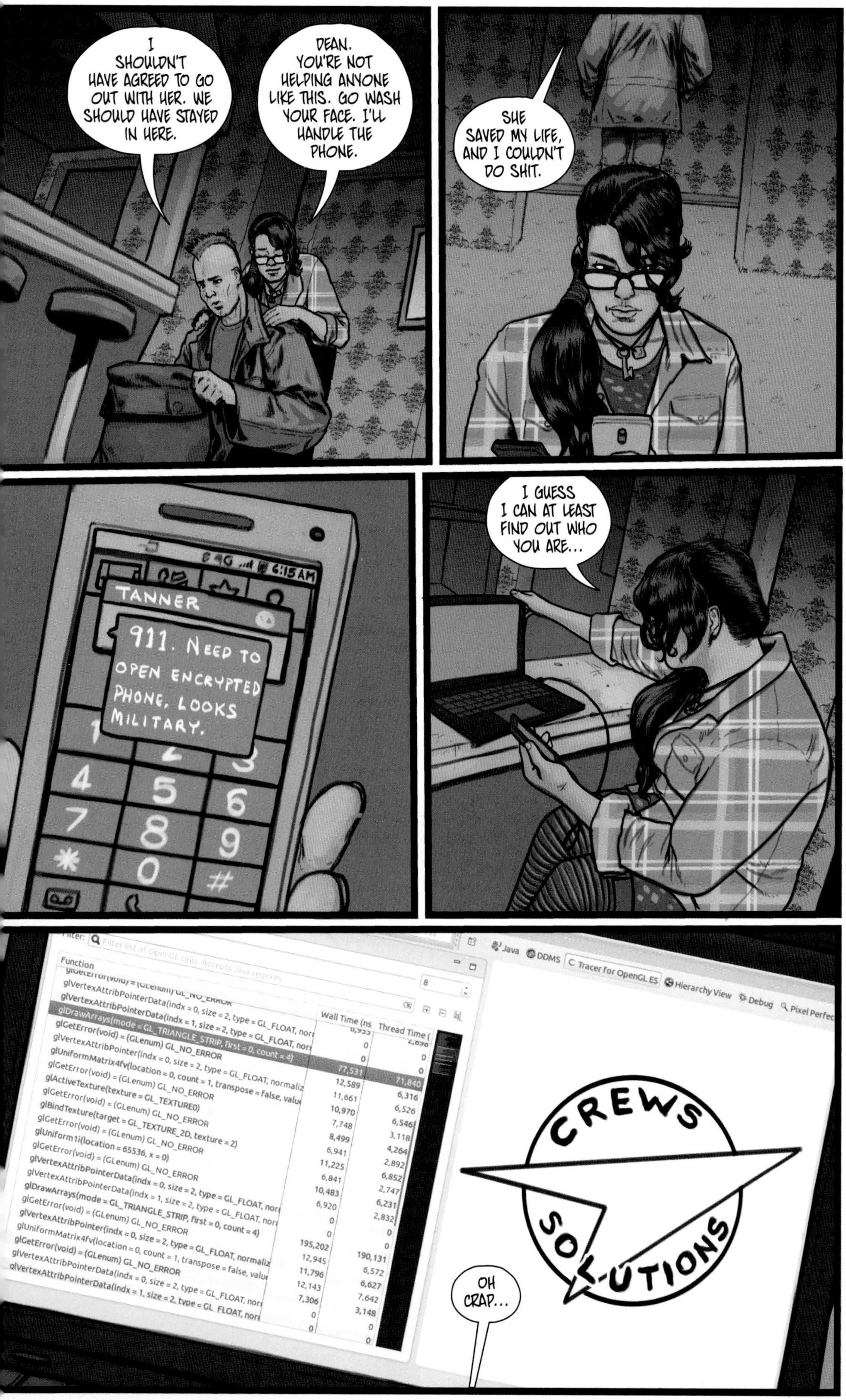
I SHOULDN'T HAVE AGREED TO GO OUT WITH HER. WE SHOULD HAVE STAYED IN HERE.
DEAN. YOU'RE NOT HELPING ANYONE LIKE THIS. GO WASH YOUR FACE. I'LL HANDLE THE PHONE.
SHE SAVED MY LIFE, AND I COULDN'T DO SHIT.
6:15AM
TANNER
911. NEED TO OPEN ENCRYPTED PHONE, LOOKS MILITARY.
I GUESS I CAN AT LEAST FIND OUT WHO YOU ARE...
Function
Wall Time (ns
Thread Time (
Java
DDMS
Tracer for OpenGL ES
Hierarchy View
Debug
CREWS SOLUTIONS
OH CRAP...

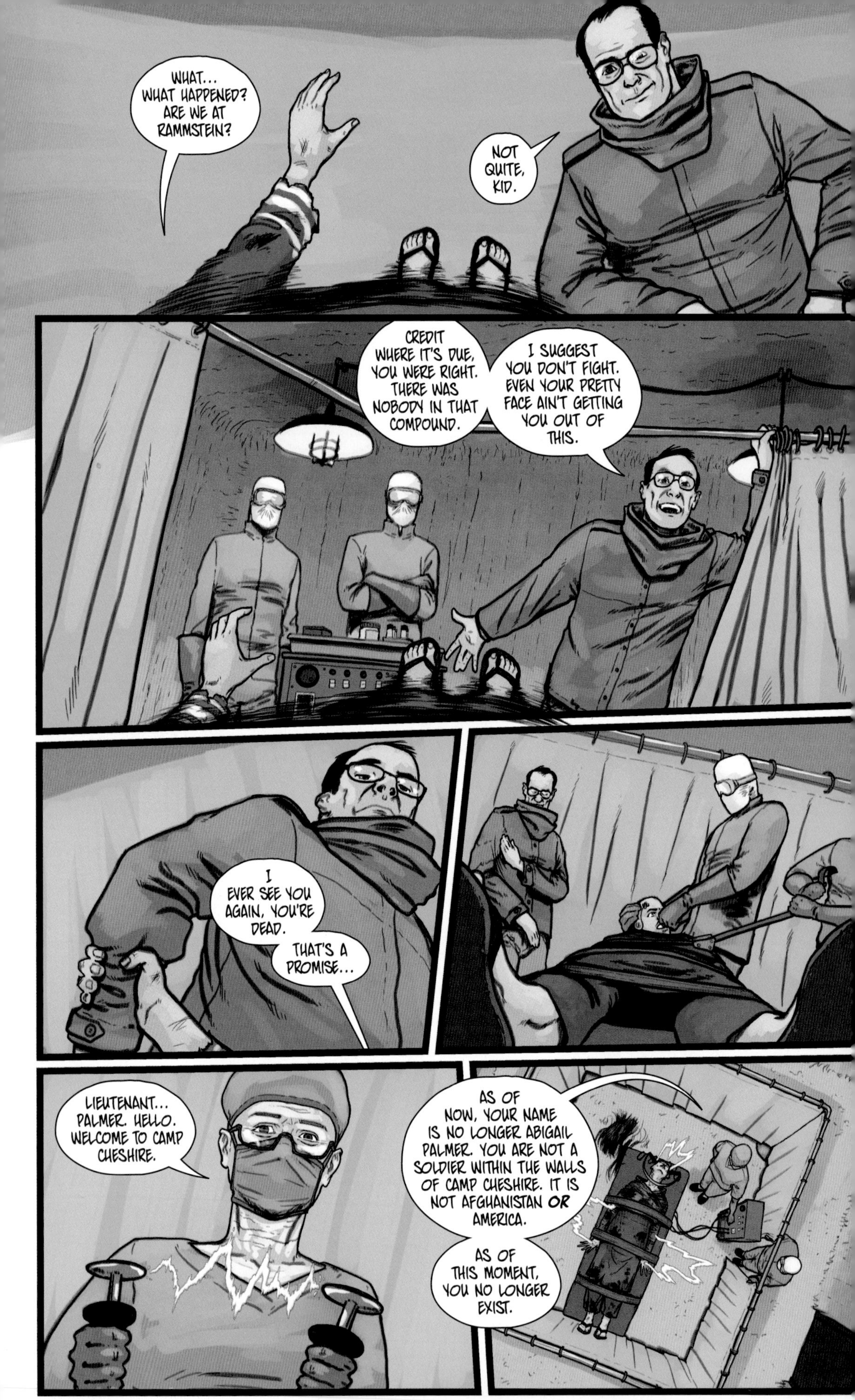
WHAT... WHAT HAPPENED? ARE WE AT RAMMSTEIN?
NOT QUITE, KID.
CREDIT WHERE IT'S DUE, YOU WERE RIGHT. THERE WAS NOBODY IN THAT COMPOUND.
I SUGGEST YOU DON'T FIGHT. EVEN YOUR PRETTY FACE AIN'T GETTING YOU OUT OF THIS.
I EVER SEE YOU AGAIN, YOU'RE DEAD.
THAT'S A PROMISE...
LIEUTENANT... PALMER. HELLO. WELCOME TO CAMP CHESHIRE.
AS OF NOW, YOUR NAME IS NO LONGER ABIGAIL PALMER. YOU ARE NOT A SOLDIER WITHIN THE WALLS OF CAMP CHESHIRE. IT IS NOT AFGHANISTAN **OR** AMERICA.
AS OF THIS MOMENT, YOU NO LONGER EXIST.

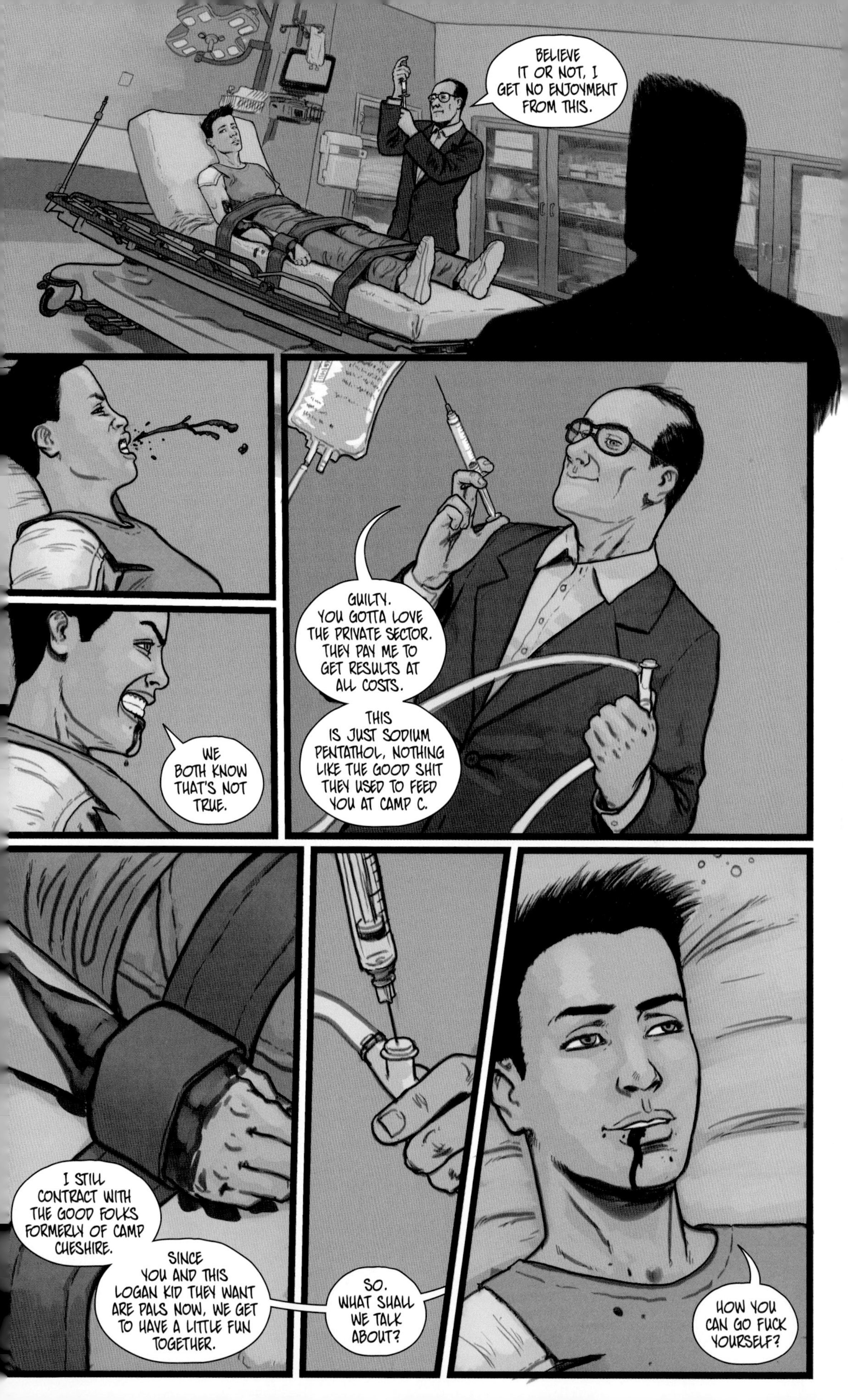
BELIEVE IT OR NOT, I GET NO ENJOYMENT FROM THIS.
GUILTY. YOU GOTTA LOVE THE PRIVATE SECTOR. THEY PAY ME TO GET RESULTS AT ALL COSTS.
WE BOTH KNOW THAT'S NOT TRUE.
THIS IS JUST SODIUM PENTATHOL, NOTHING LIKE THE GOOD SHIT THEY USED TO FEED YOU AT CAMP C.
I STILL CONTRACT WITH THE GOOD FOLKS FORMERLY OF CAMP CHESHIRE.
SINCE YOU AND THIS LOGAN KID THEY WANT ARE PALS NOW, WE GET TO HAVE A LITTLE FUN TOGETHER.
SO. WHAT SHALL WE TALK ABOUT?
HOW YOU CAN GO FUCK YOURSELF?

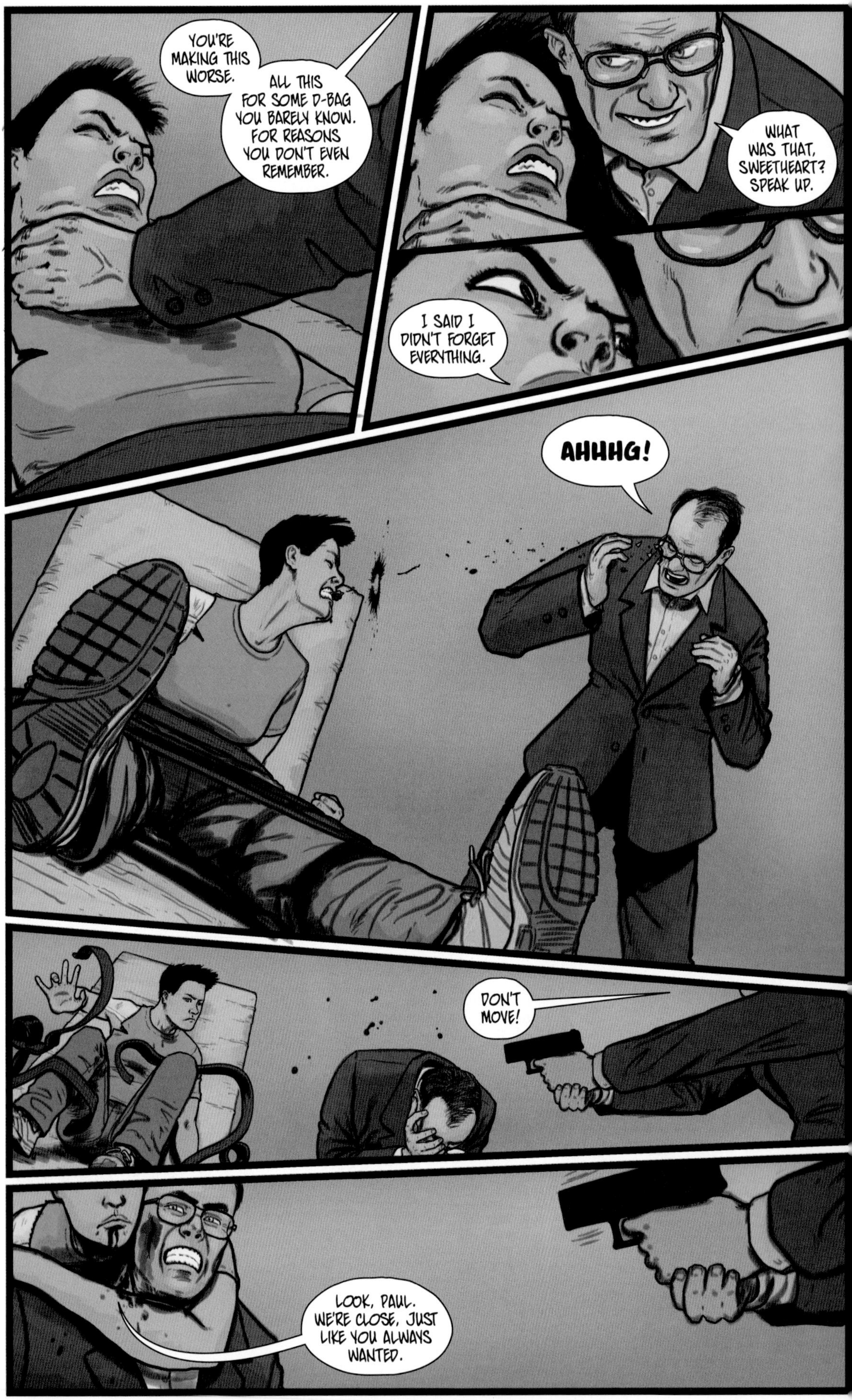
YOU'RE MAKING THIS WORSE.
ALL THIS FOR SOME D-BAG YOU BARELY KNOW. FOR REASONS YOU DON'T EVEN REMEMBER.
WHAT WAS THAT, SWEETHEART? SPEAK UP.
I SAID I DIDN'T FORGET EVERYTHING.
AHHHG!
DON'T MOVE!
LOOK, PAUL. WE'RE CLOSE, JUST LIKE YOU ALWAYS WANTED.

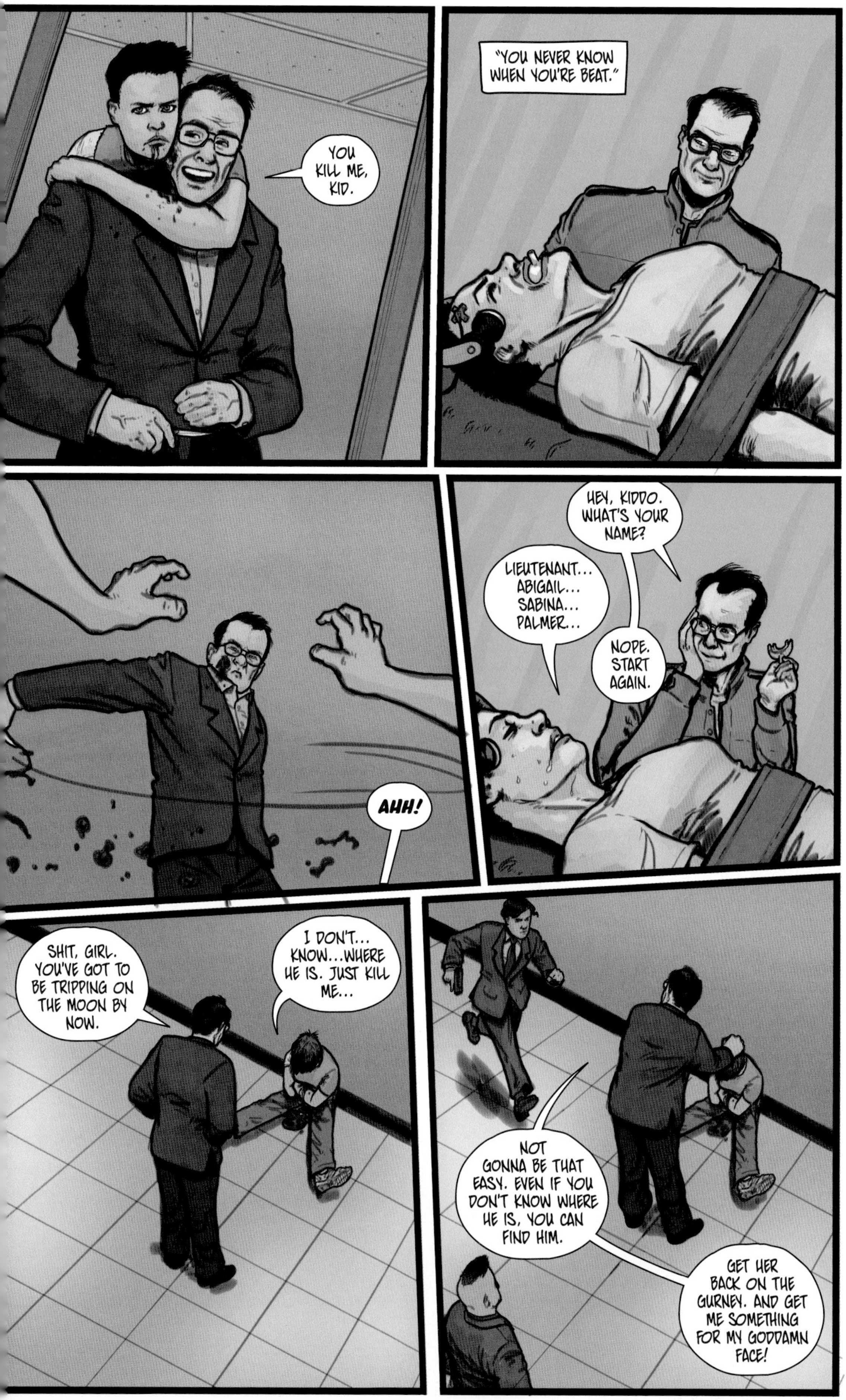
YOU KILL ME, KID.
"YOU NEVER KNOW WHEN YOU'RE BEAT."
AHH!
HEY, KIDDO. WHAT'S YOUR NAME?
LIEUTENANT... ABIGAIL... SABINA... PALMER...
NOPE. START AGAIN.
SHIT, GIRL. YOU'VE GOT TO BE TRIPPING ON THE MOON BY NOW.
I DON'T... KNOW...WHERE HE IS. JUST KILL ME...
NOT GONNA BE THAT EASY. EVEN IF YOU DON'T KNOW WHERE HE IS, YOU CAN FIND HIM.
GET HER BACK ON THE GURNEY. AND GET ME SOMETHING FOR MY GODDAMN FACE!

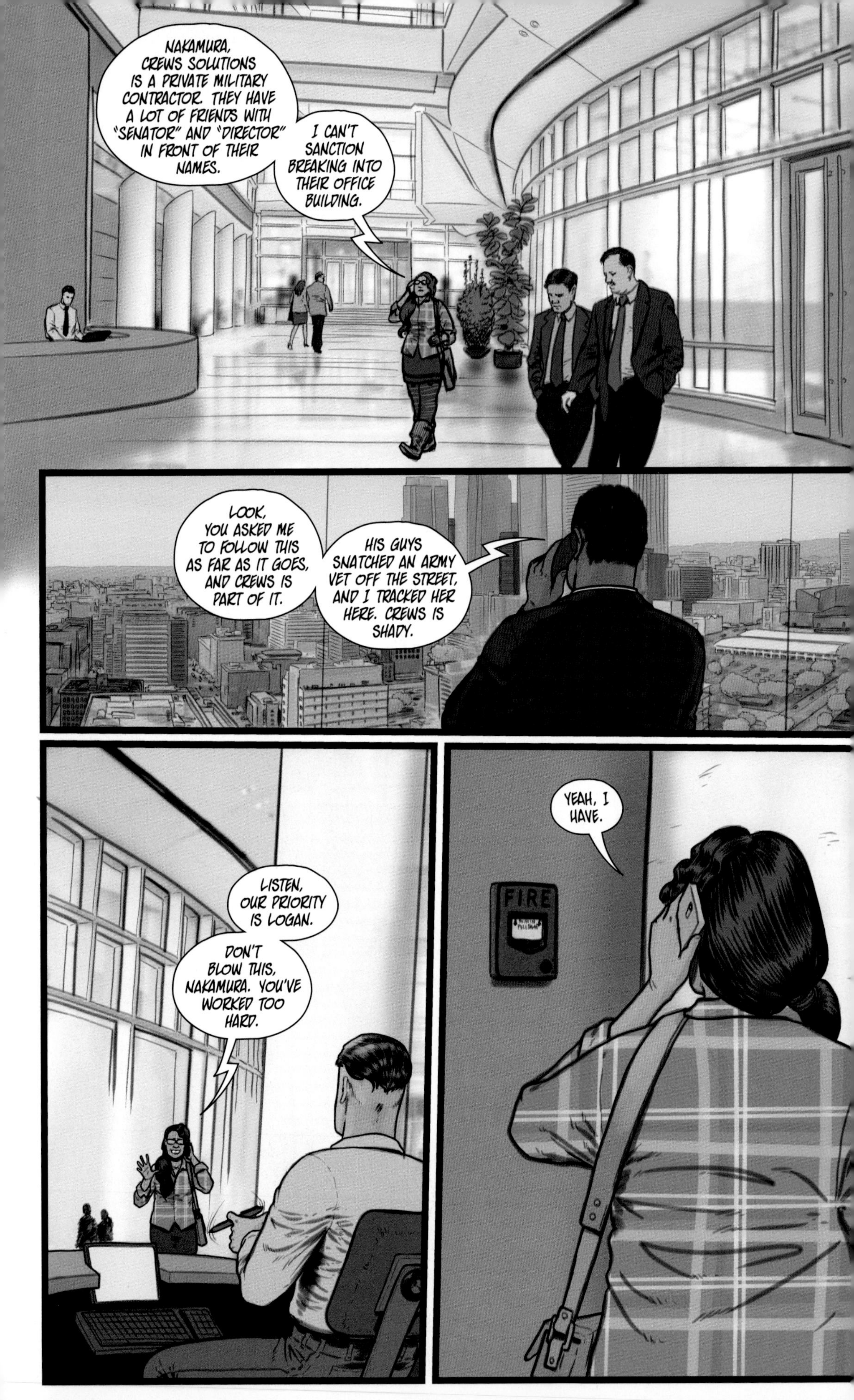
NAKAMURA, CREWS SOLUTIONS IS A PRIVATE MILITARY CONTRACTOR. THEY HAVE A LOT OF FRIENDS WITH "SENATOR" AND "DIRECTOR" IN FRONT OF THEIR NAMES.
I CAN'T SANCTION BREAKING INTO THEIR OFFICE BUILDING.
LOOK, YOU ASKED ME TO FOLLOW THIS AS FAR AS IT GOES, AND CREWS IS PART OF IT.
HIS GUYS SNATCHED AN ARMY VET OFF THE STREET, AND I TRACKED HER HERE. CREWS IS SHADY.
LISTEN, OUR PRIORITY IS LOGAN.
DON'T BLOW THIS, NAKAMURA. YOU'VE WORKED TOO HARD.
YEAH, I HAVE.
FIRE

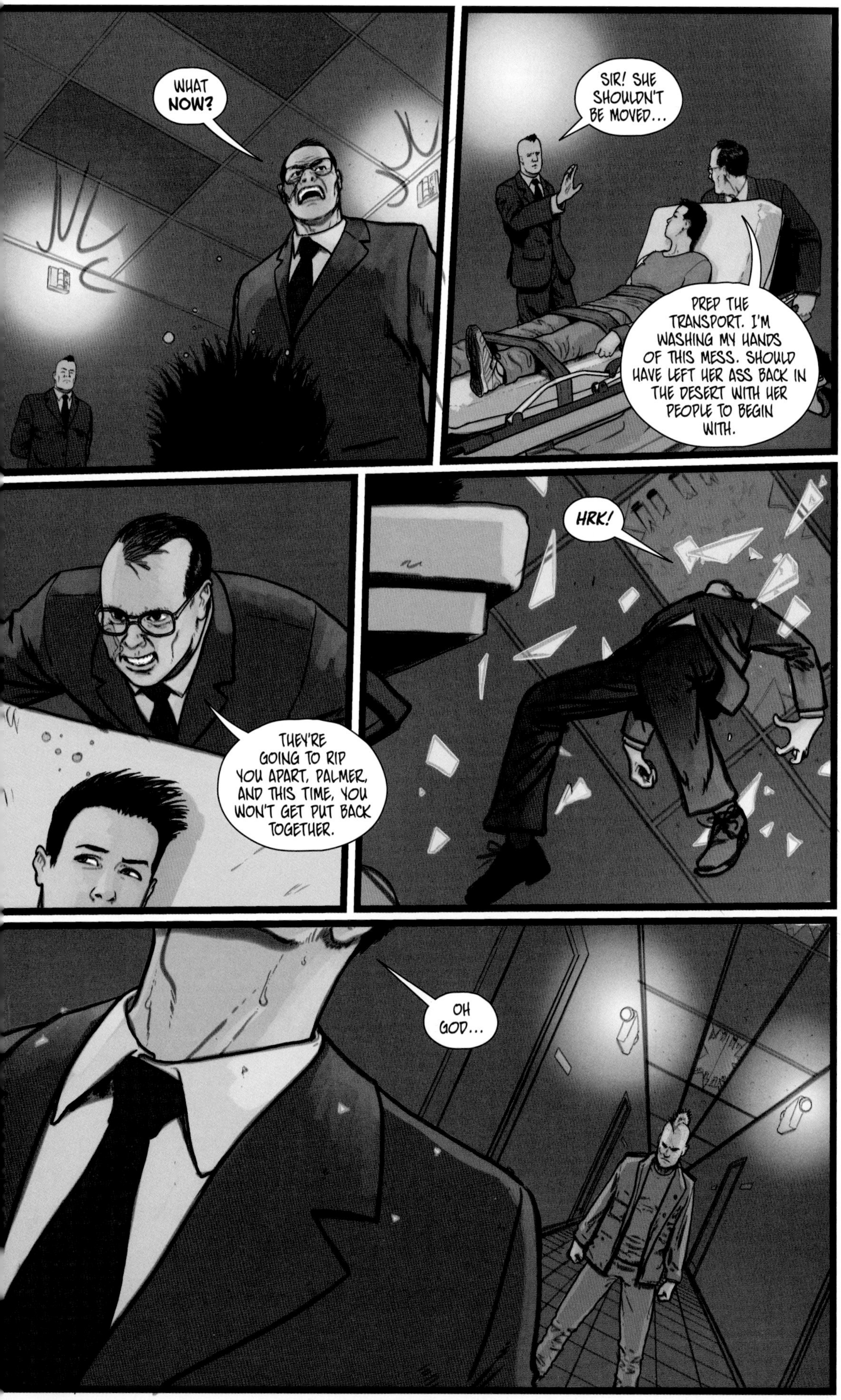
WHAT NOW?
SIR! SHE SHOULDN'T BE MOVED...
PREP THE TRANSPORT. I'M WASHING MY HANDS OF THIS MESS. SHOULD HAVE LEFT HER ASS BACK IN THE DESERT WITH HER PEOPLE TO BEGIN WITH.
THEY'RE GOING TO RIP YOU APART, PALMER, AND THIS TIME, YOU WON'T GET PUT BACK TOGETHER.
HRK!
OH GOD...

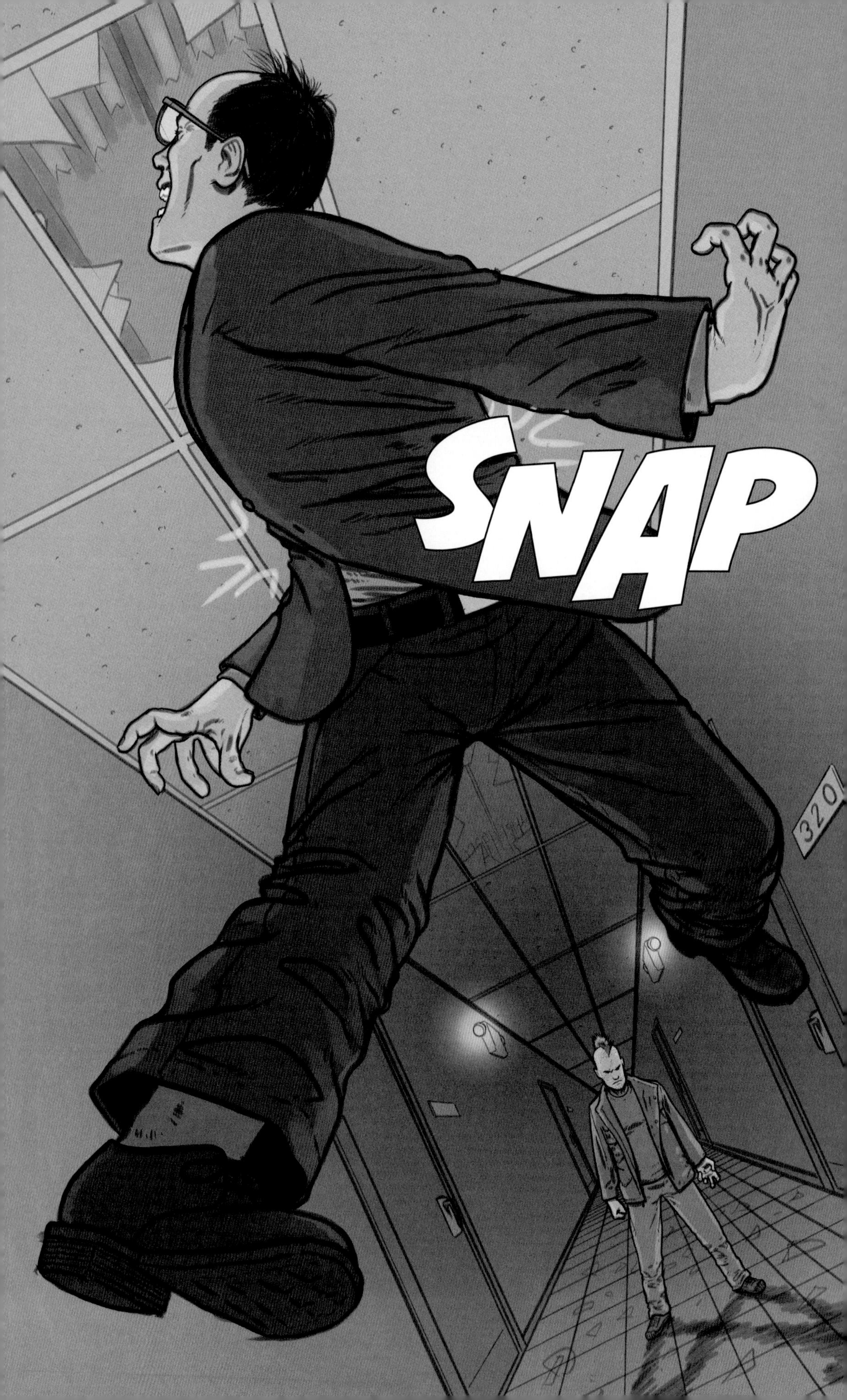
SNAP
320

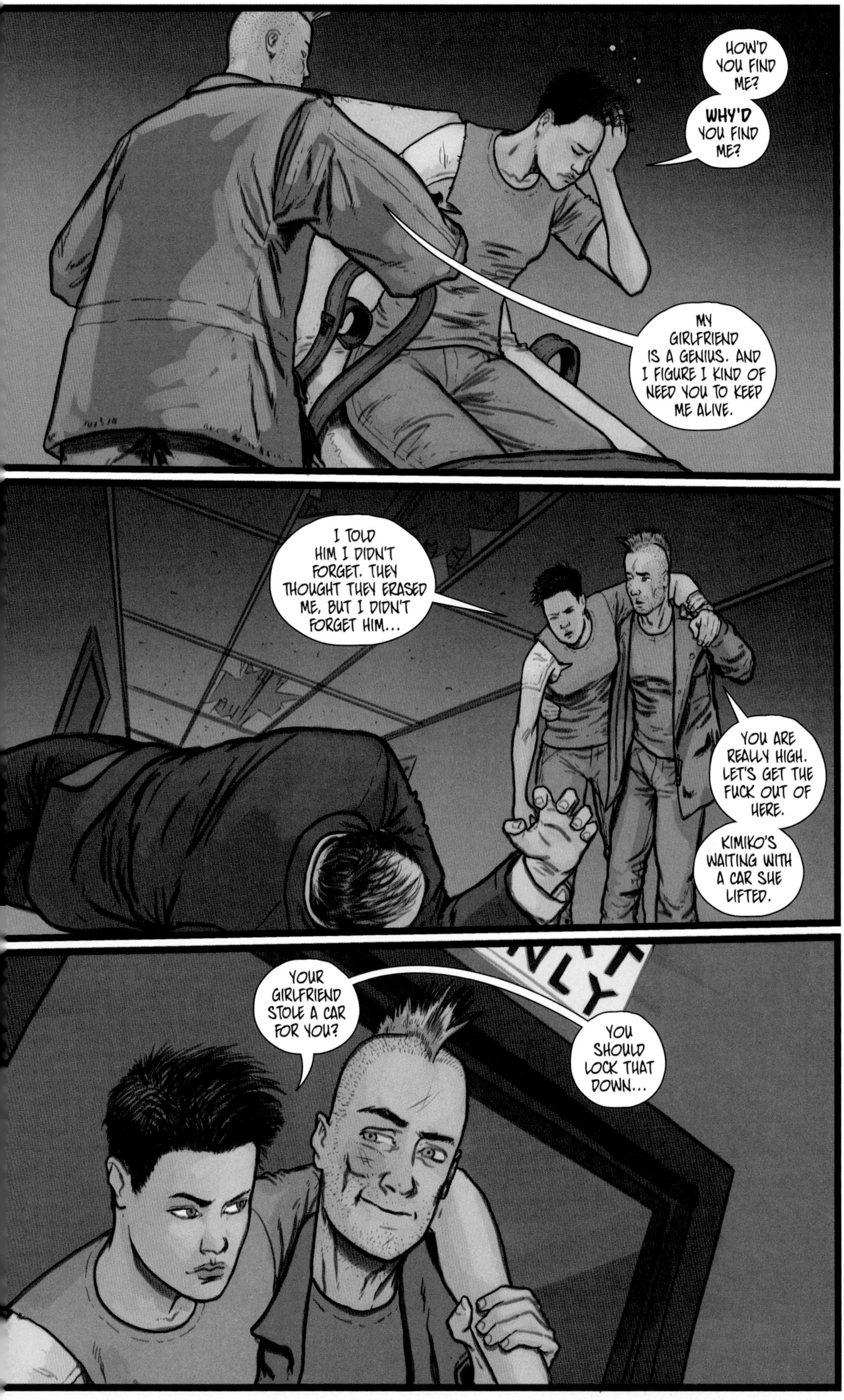
HOW'D YOU FIND ME?
WHY'D YOU FIND ME?
MY GIRLFRIEND IS A GENIUS. AND I FIGURE I KIND OF NEED YOU TO KEEP ME ALIVE.
I TOLD HIM I DIDN'T FORGET. THEY THOUGHT THEY ERASED ME, BUT I DIDN'T FORGET HIM...
YOU ARE REALLY HIGH. LET'S GET THE FUCK OUT OF HERE.
KIMIKO'S WAITING WITH A CAR SHE LIFTED.
YOUR GIRLFRIEND STOLE A CAR FOR YOU?
YOU SHOULD LOCK THAT DOWN...

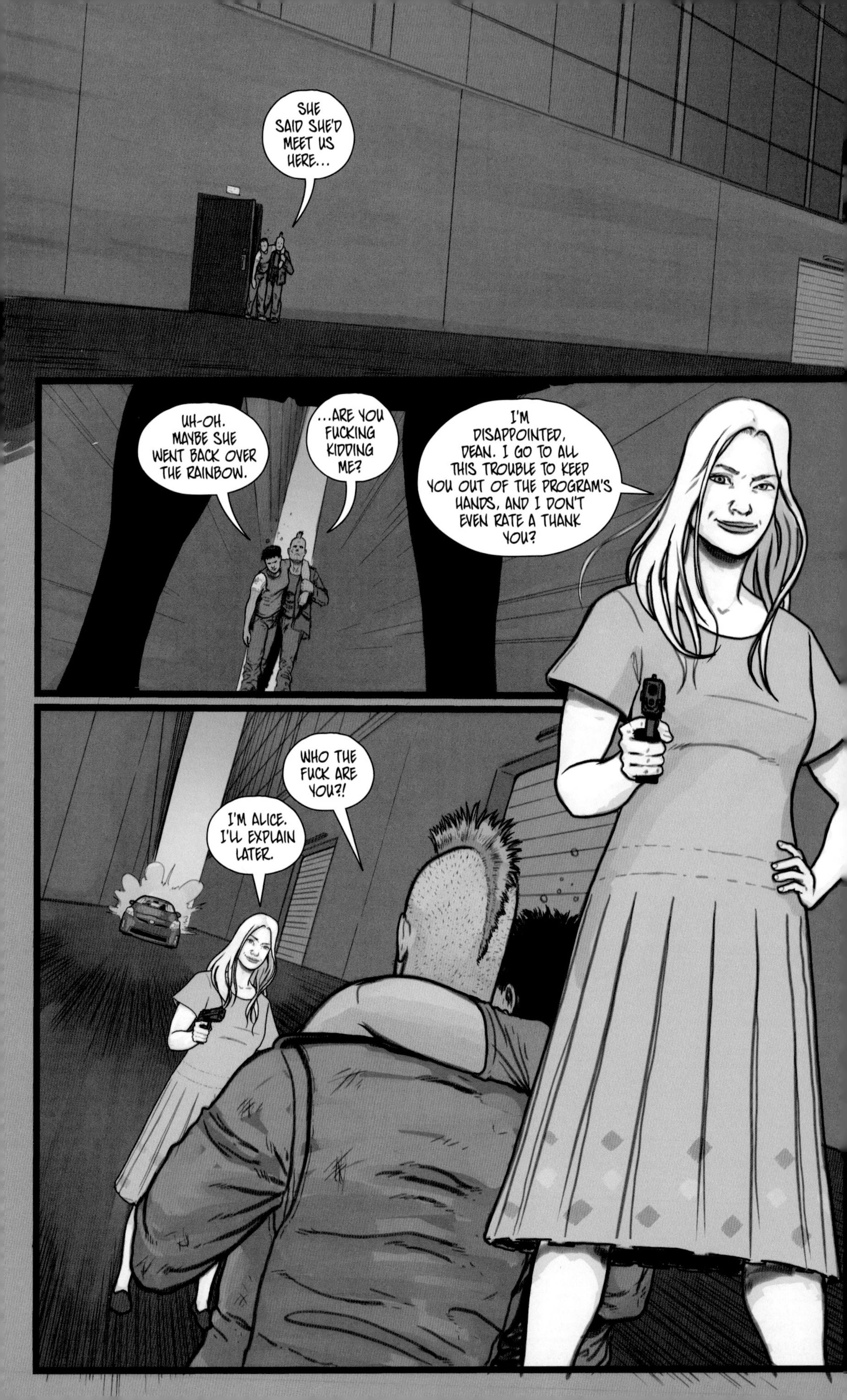
SHE SAID SHE'D MEET US HERE...
UH-OH. MAYBE SHE WENT BACK OVER THE RAINBOW.
...ARE YOU FUCKING KIDDING ME?
I'M DISAPPOINTED, DEAN. I GO TO ALL THIS TROUBLE TO KEEP YOU OUT OF THE PROGRAM'S HANDS, AND I DON'T EVEN RATE A THANK YOU?
WHO THE FUCK ARE YOU?!
I'M ALICE. I'LL EXPLAIN LATER.

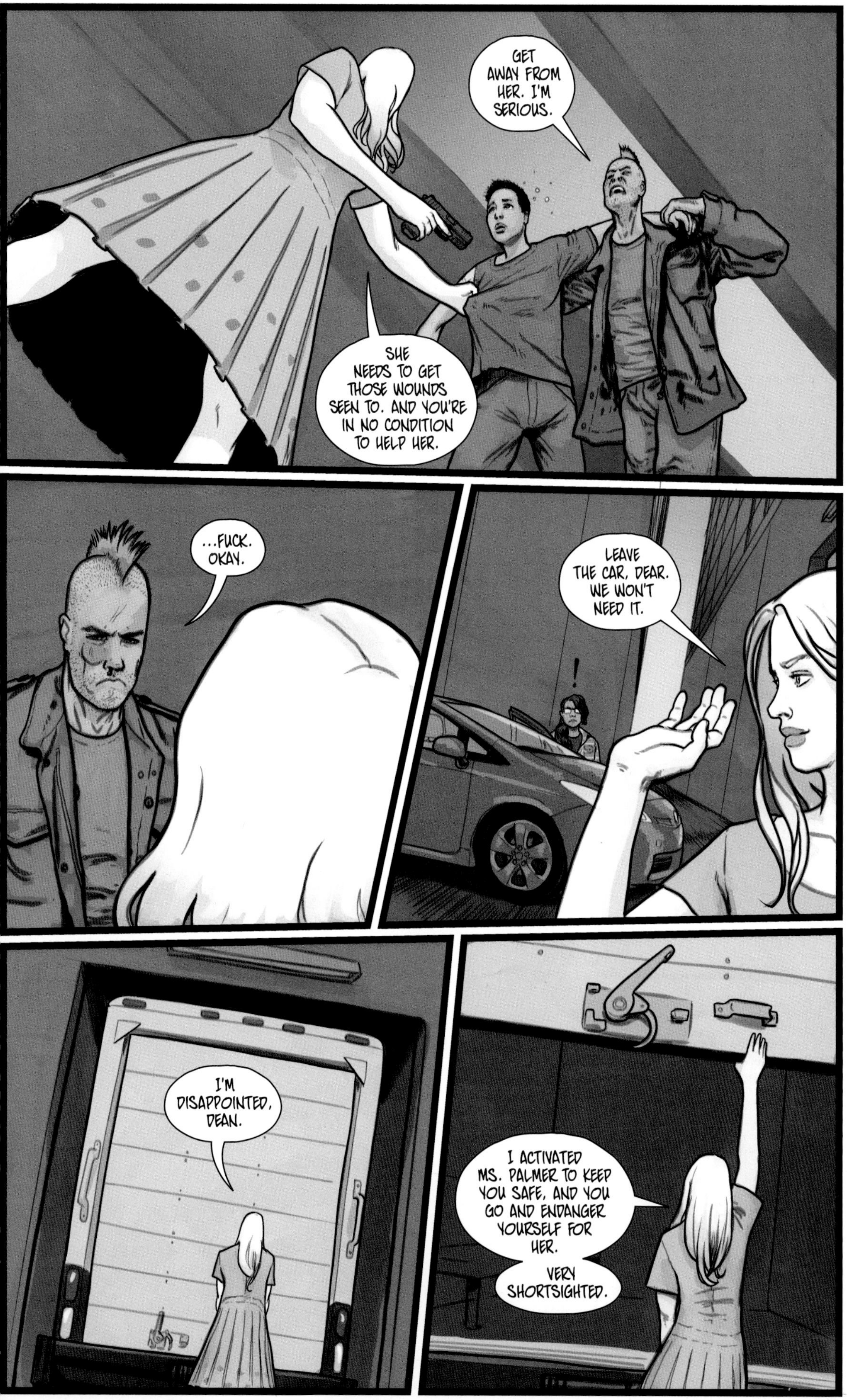
GET AWAY FROM HER. I'M SERIOUS.
SHE NEEDS TO GET THOSE WOUNDS SEEN TO. AND YOU'RE IN NO CONDITION TO HELP HER.
...FUCK. OKAY.
LEAVE THE CAR, DEAR. WE WON'T NEED IT.
!
I'M DISAPPOINTED, DEAN.
I ACTIVATED MS. PALMER TO KEEP YOU SAFE, AND YOU GO AND ENDANGER YOURSELF FOR HER.
VERY SHORTSIGHTED.

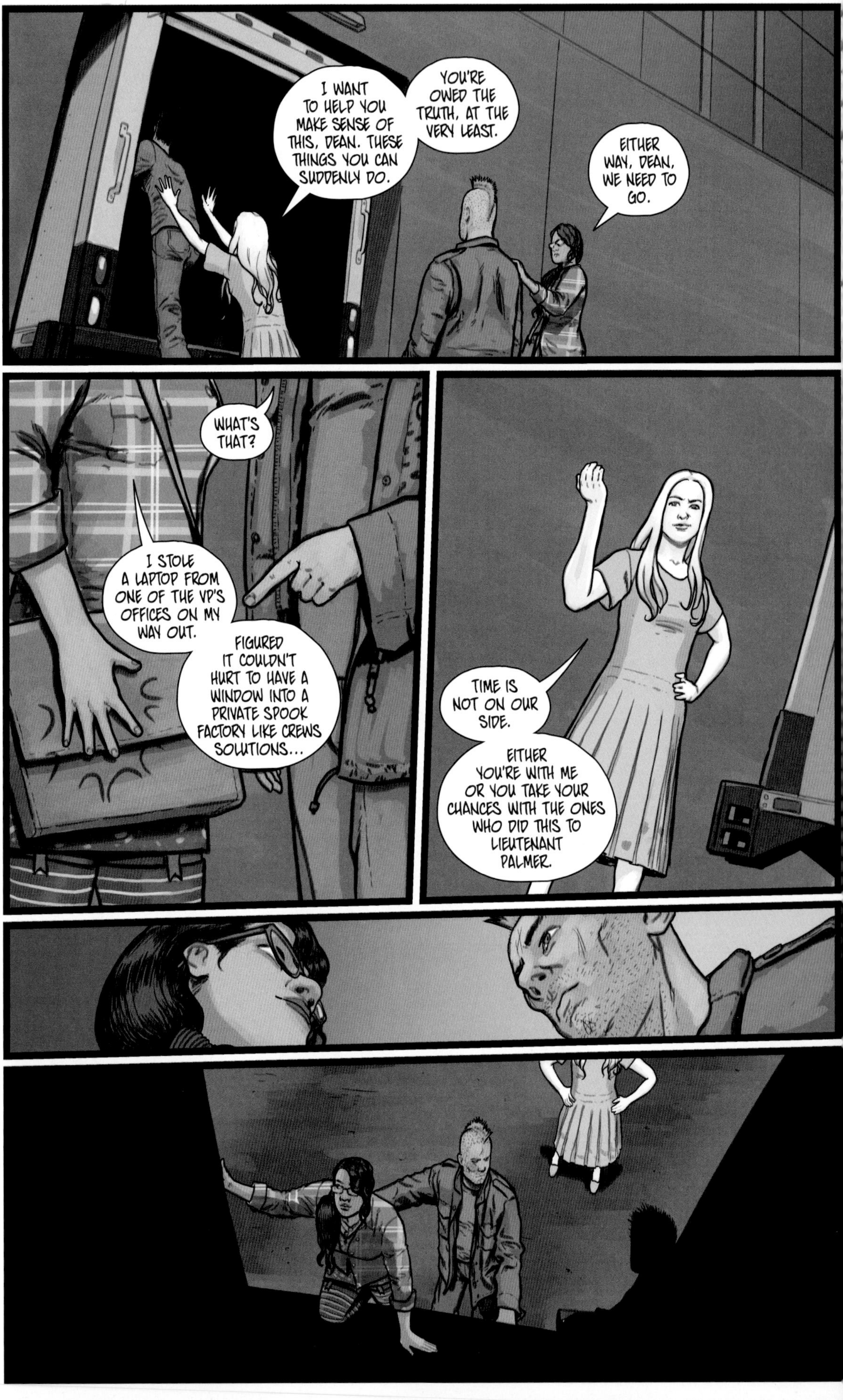
I WANT TO HELP YOU MAKE SENSE OF THIS, DEAN. THESE THINGS YOU CAN SUDDENLY DO.
YOU'RE OWED THE TRUTH, AT THE VERY LEAST.
EITHER WAY, DEAN, WE NEED TO GO.
WHAT'S THAT?
I STOLE A LAPTOP FROM ONE OF THE VP'S OFFICES ON MY WAY OUT.
FIGURED IT COULDN'T HURT TO HAVE A WINDOW INTO A PRIVATE SPOOK FACTORY LIKE CREWS SOLUTIONS...
TIME IS NOT ON OUR SIDE.
EITHER YOU'RE WITH ME OR YOU TAKE YOUR CHANCES WITH THE ONES WHO DID THIS TO LIEUTENANT PALMER.

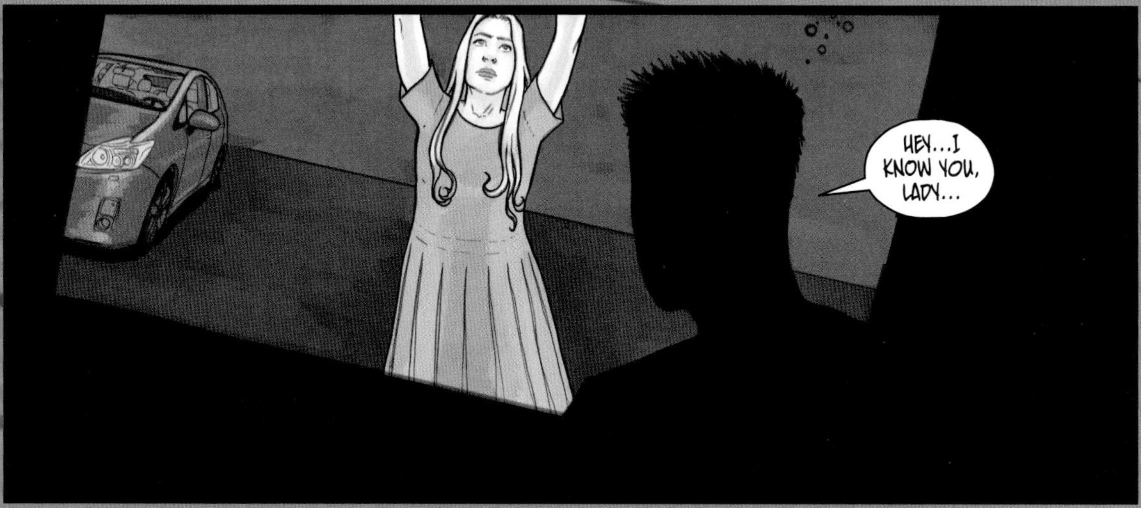
HEY...I KNOW YOU, LADY...

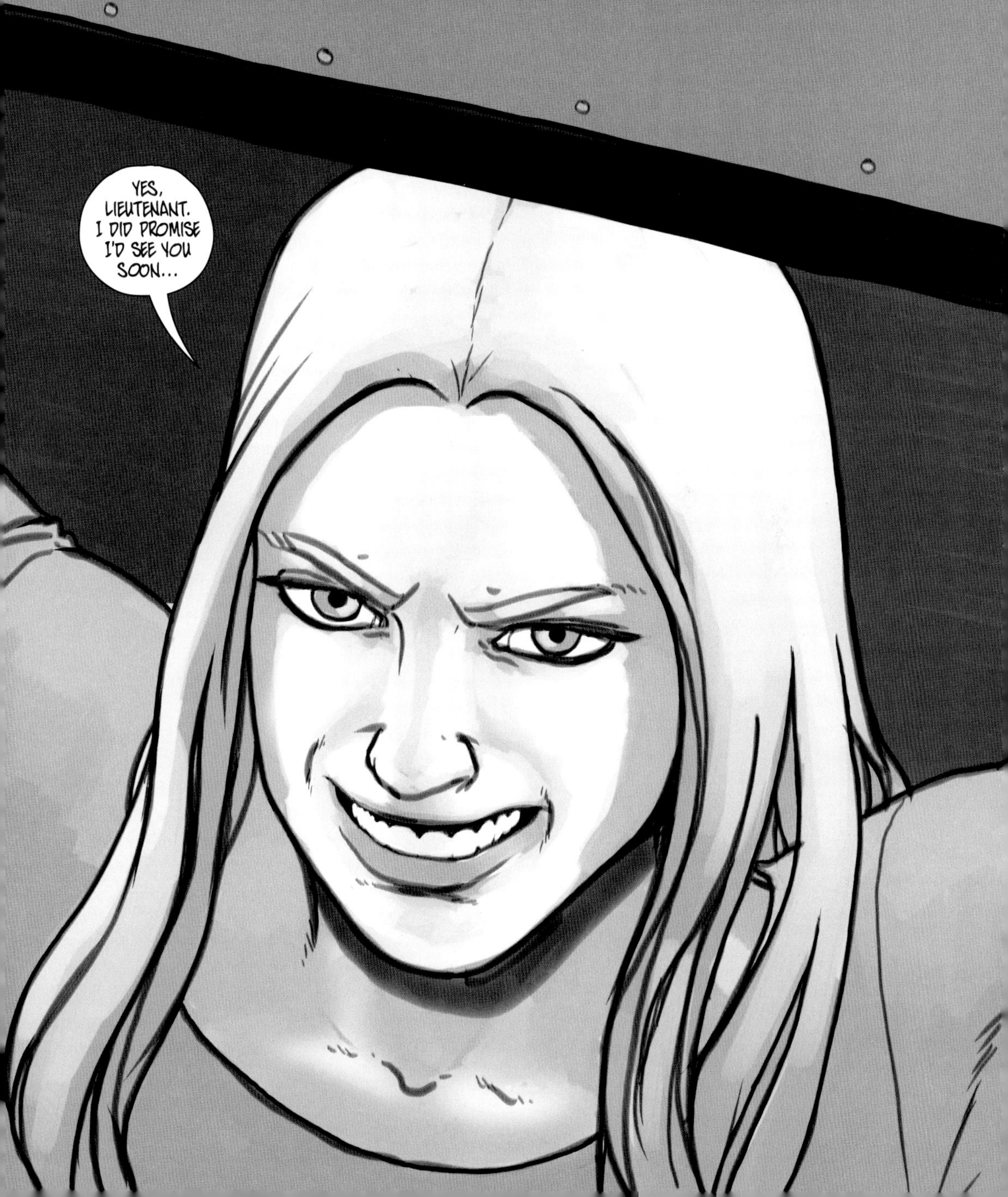
YES, LIEUTENANT. I DID PROMISE I'D SEE YOU SOON...

CHAPTER THREE

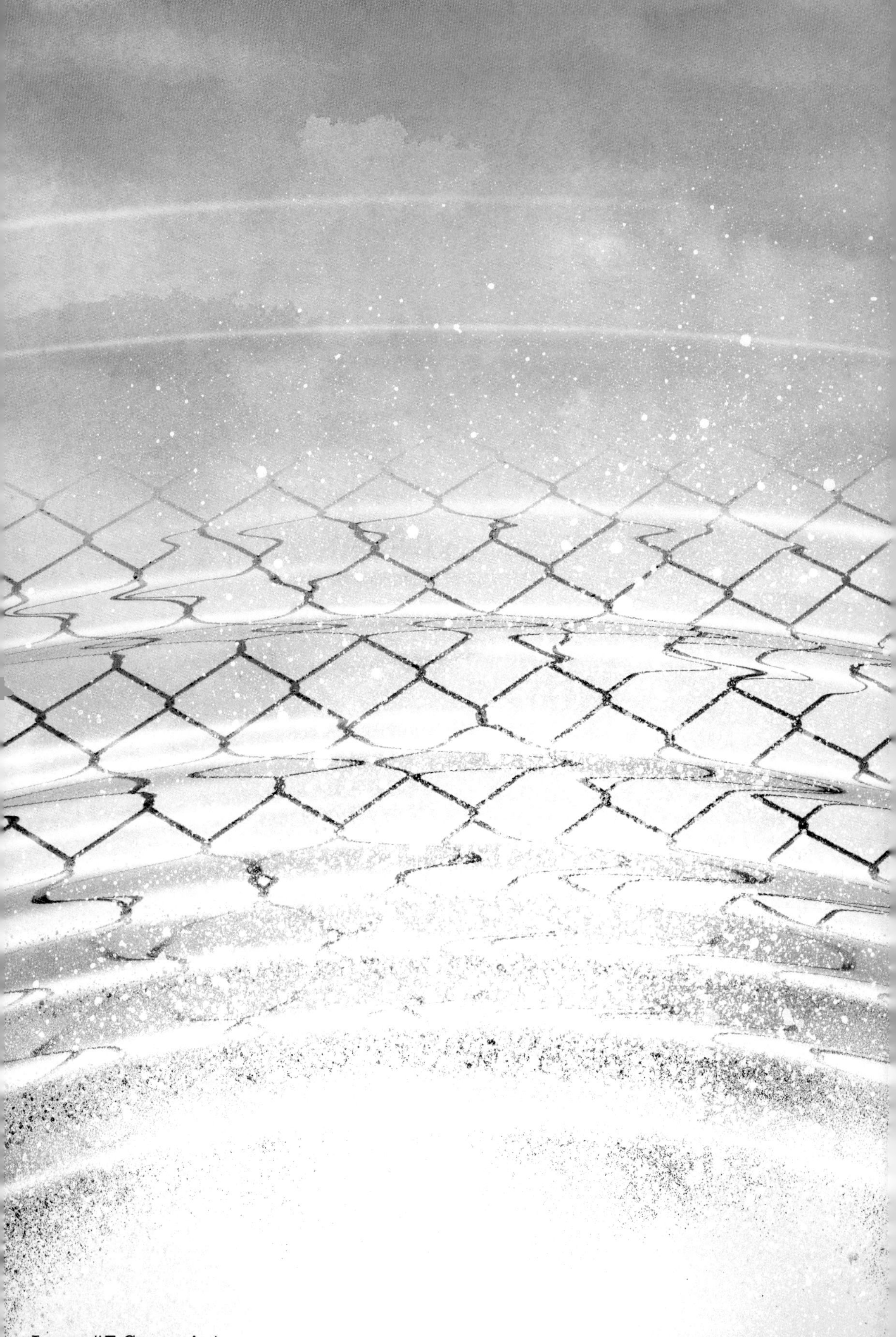

Issue #3 Cover Art

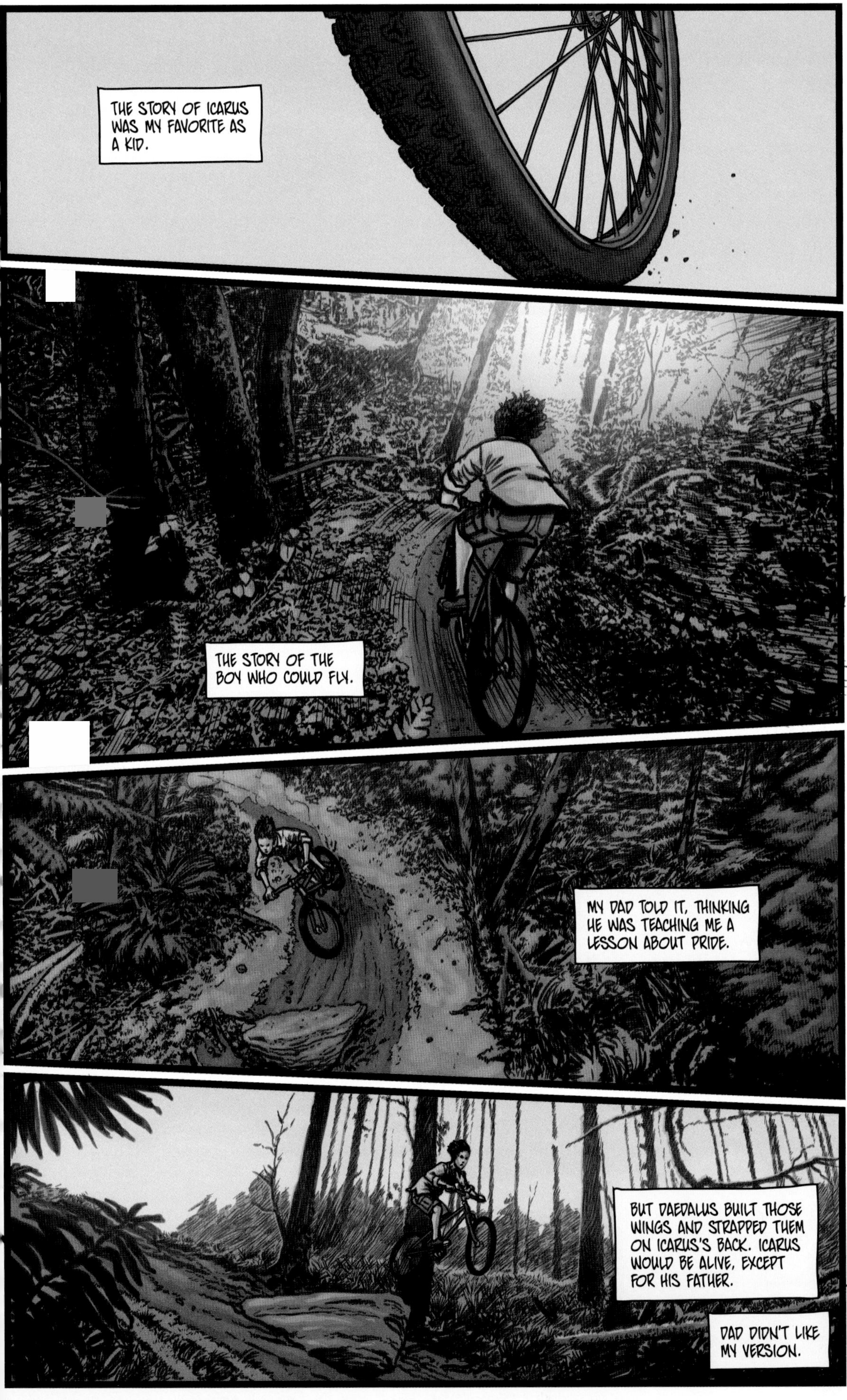
THE STORY OF ICARUS WAS MY FAVORITE AS A KID.
THE STORY OF THE BOY WHO COULD FLY.
MY DAD TOLD IT, THINKING HE WAS TEACHING ME A LESSON ABOUT PRIDE.
BUT DAEDALUS BUILT THOSE WINGS AND STRAPPED THEM ON ICARUS'S BACK. ICARUS WOULD BE ALIVE, EXCEPT FOR HIS FATHER.
DAD DIDN'T LIKE MY VERSION.

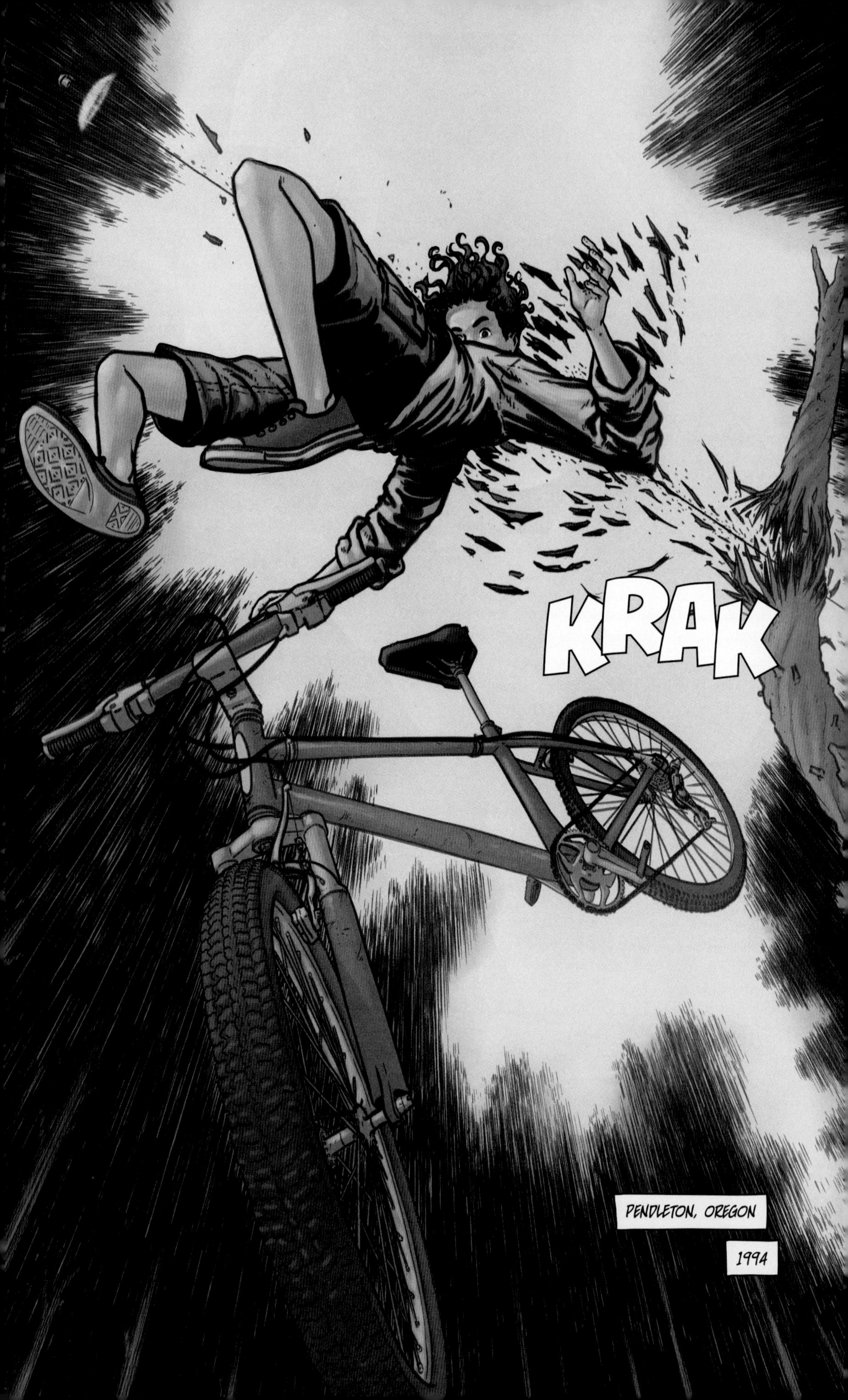
KRAK
PENDLETON, OREGON
1994

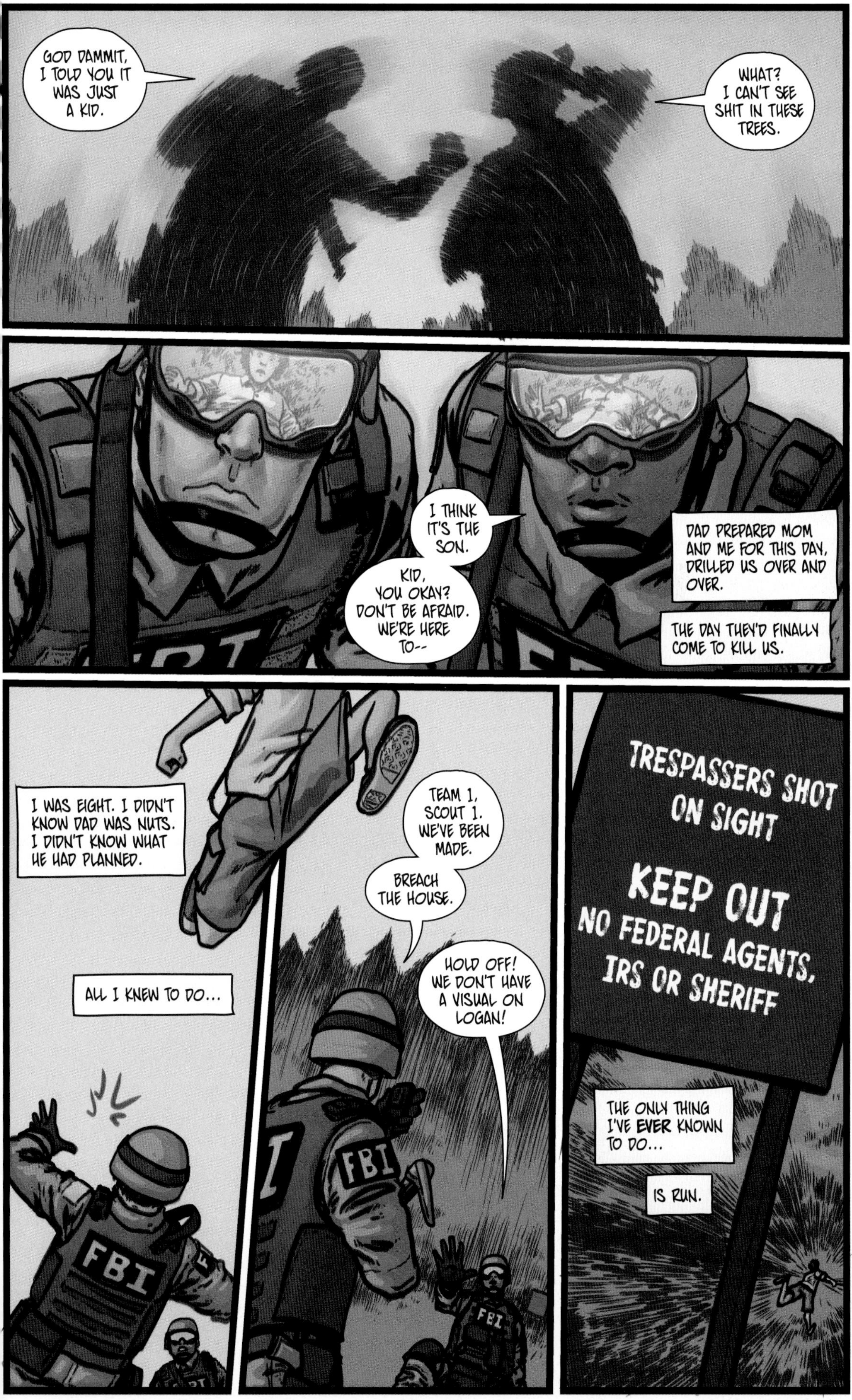
GOD DAMMIT, I TOLD YOU IT WAS JUST A KID.
WHAT? I CAN'T SEE SHIT IN THESE TREES.
I THINK IT'S THE SON.
KID, YOU OKAY? DON'T BE AFRAID. WE'RE HERE TO--
DAD PREPARED MOM AND ME FOR THIS DAY, DRILLED US OVER AND OVER.
THE DAY THEY'D FINALLY COME TO KILL US.
I WAS EIGHT. I DIDN'T KNOW DAD WAS NUTS. I DIDN'T KNOW WHAT HE HAD PLANNED.
ALL I KNEW TO DO...
TEAM 1, SCOUT 1. WE'VE BEEN MADE.
BREACH THE HOUSE.
HOLD OFF! WE DON'T HAVE A VISUAL ON LOGAN!
FBI
FBI
FBI
TRESPASSERS SHOT ON SIGHT
KEEP OUT
NO FEDERAL AGENTS, IRS OR SHERIFF
THE ONLY THING I'VE **EVER** KNOWN TO DO...
IS RUN.

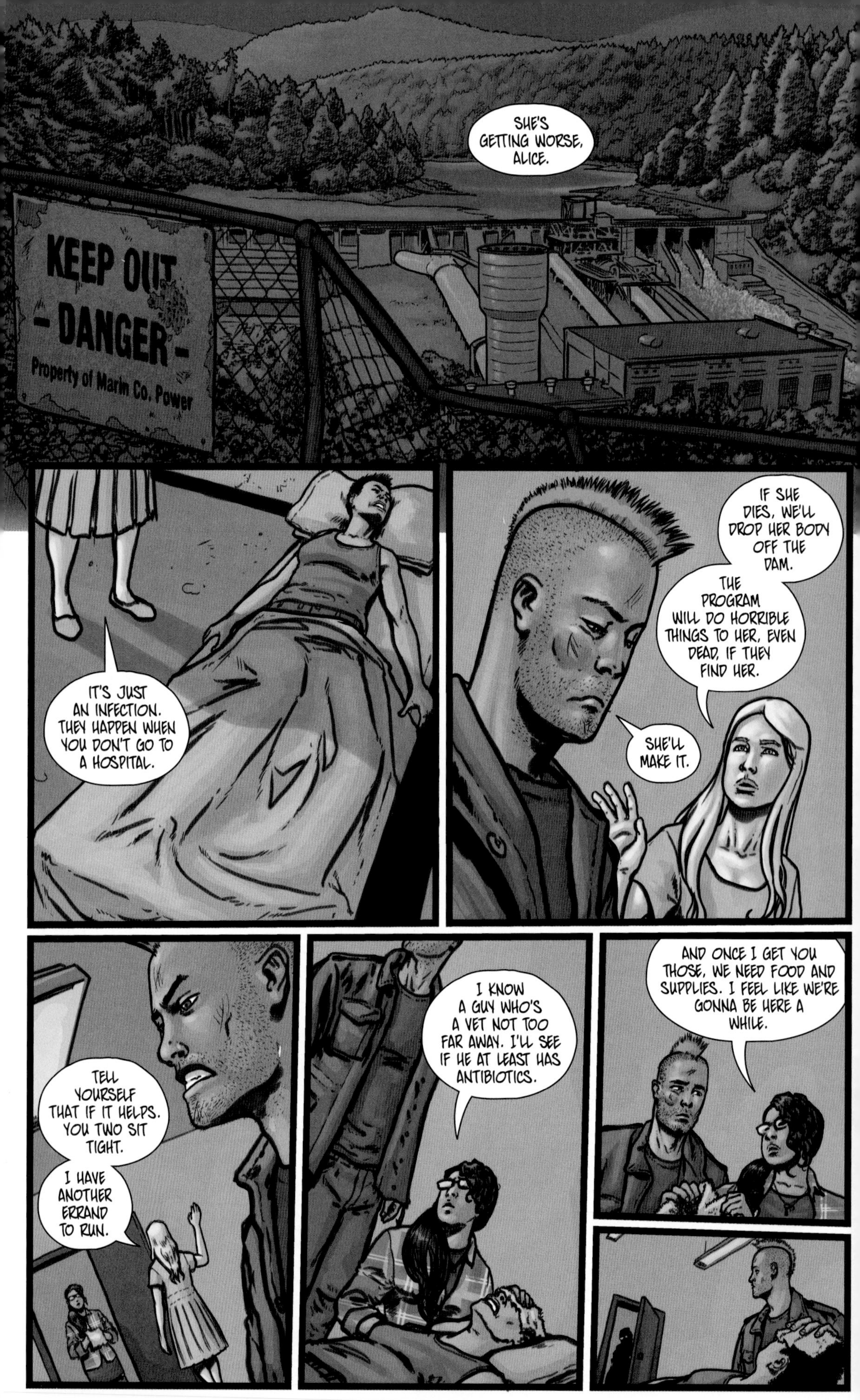
SHE'S GETTING WORSE, ALICE.
KEEP OUT
- DANGER -
Property of Marin Co. Power
IT'S JUST AN INFECTION. THEY HAPPEN WHEN YOU DON'T GO TO A HOSPITAL.
IF SHE DIES, WE'LL DROP HER BODY OFF THE DAM.
THE PROGRAM WILL DO HORRIBLE THINGS TO HER, EVEN DEAD, IF THEY FIND HER.
SHE'LL MAKE IT.
TELL YOURSELF THAT IF IT HELPS. YOU TWO SIT TIGHT.
I HAVE ANOTHER ERRAND TO RUN.
I KNOW A GUY WHO'S A VET NOT TOO FAR AWAY. I'LL SEE IF HE AT LEAST HAS ANTIBIOTICS.
AND ONCE I GET YOU THOSE, WE NEED FOOD AND SUPPLIES. I FEEL LIKE WE'RE GONNA BE HERE A WHILE.

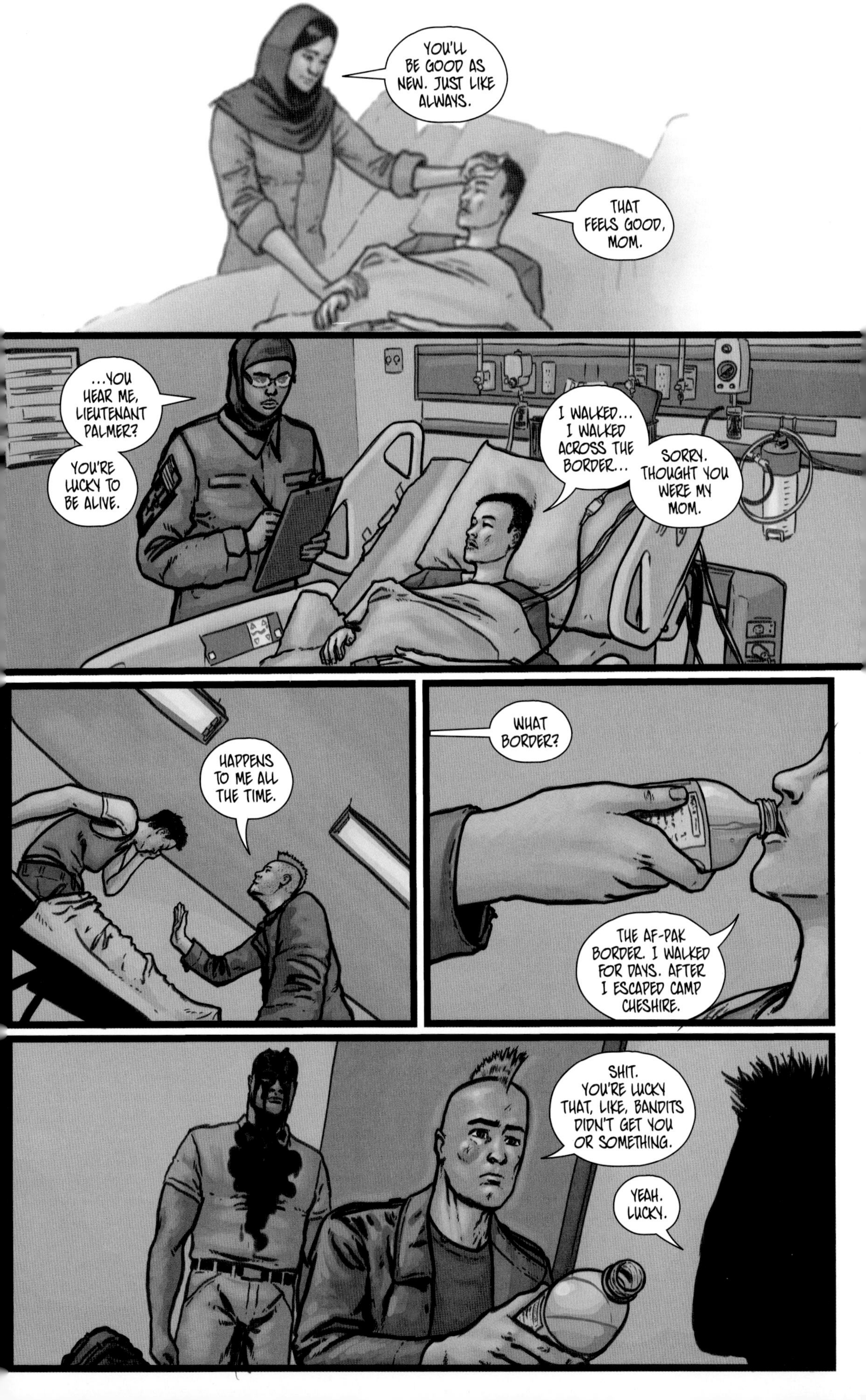
YOU'LL BE GOOD AS NEW. JUST LIKE ALWAYS.
THAT FEELS GOOD, MOM.
...YOU HEAR ME, LIEUTENANT PALMER?
YOU'RE LUCKY TO BE ALIVE.
I WALKED... I WALKED ACROSS THE BORDER...
SORRY. THOUGHT YOU WERE MY MOM.
HAPPENS TO ME ALL THE TIME.
WHAT BORDER?
THE AF-PAK BORDER. I WALKED FOR DAYS. AFTER I ESCAPED CAMP CHESHIRE.
SHIT. YOU'RE LUCKY THAT, LIKE, BANDITS DIDN'T GET YOU OR SOMETHING.
YEAH. LUCKY.

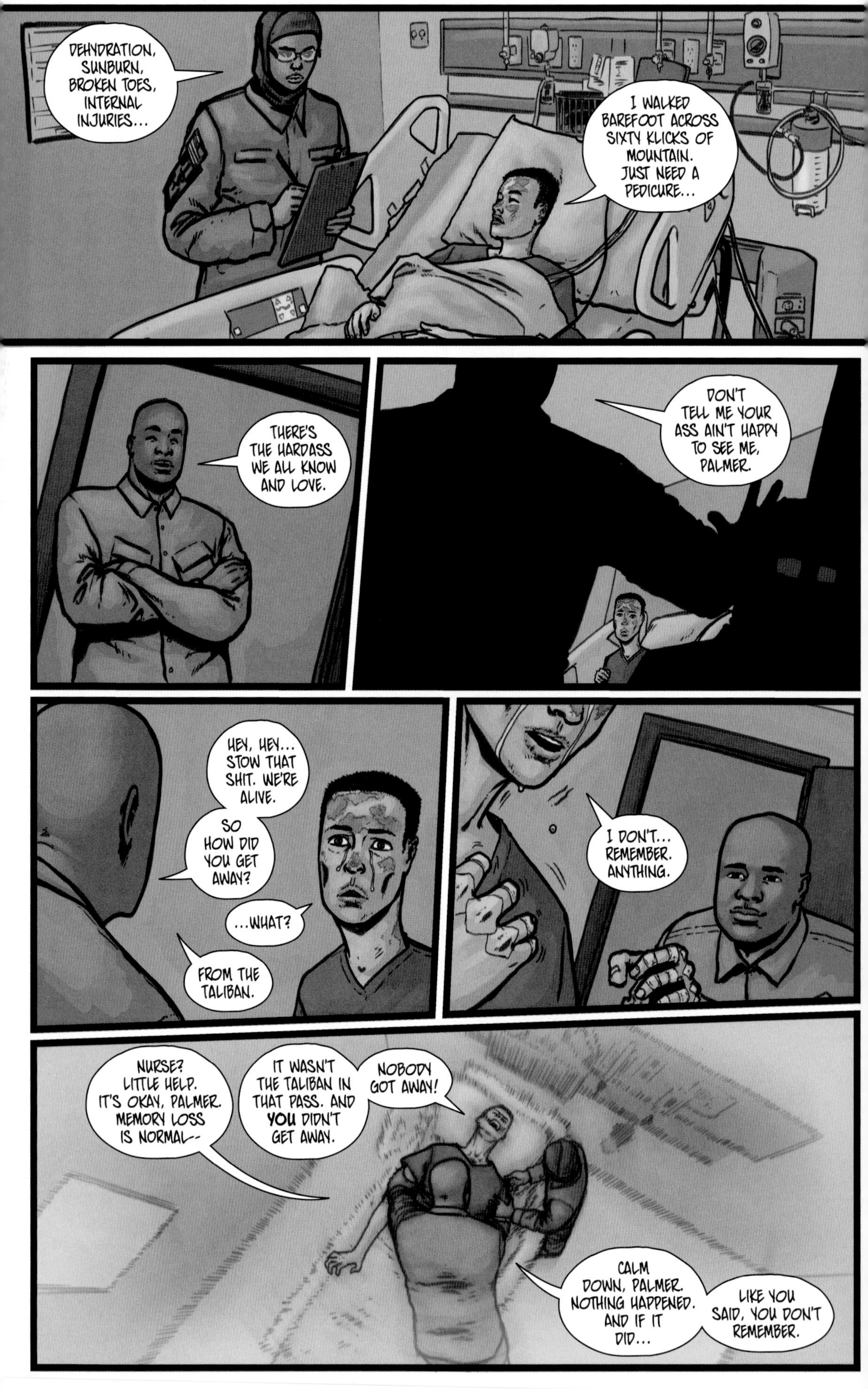
DEHYDRATION, SUNBURN, BROKEN TOES, INTERNAL INJURIES...
I WALKED BAREFOOT ACROSS SIXTY KLICKS OF MOUNTAIN. JUST NEED A PEDICURE...
THERE'S THE HARDASS WE ALL KNOW AND LOVE.
DON'T TELL ME YOUR ASS AIN'T HAPPY TO SEE ME, PALMER.
HEY, HEY... STOW THAT SHIT. WE'RE ALIVE.
SO HOW DID YOU GET AWAY?
...WHAT?
FROM THE TALIBAN.
I DON'T... REMEMBER. ANYTHING.
NURSE? LITTLE HELP. IT'S OKAY, PALMER. MEMORY LOSS IS NORMAL--
IT WASN'T THE TALIBAN IN THAT PASS. AND YOU DIDN'T GET AWAY.
NOBODY GOT AWAY!
CALM DOWN, PALMER. NOTHING HAPPENED. AND IF IT DID...
LIKE YOU SAID, YOU DON'T REMEMBER.

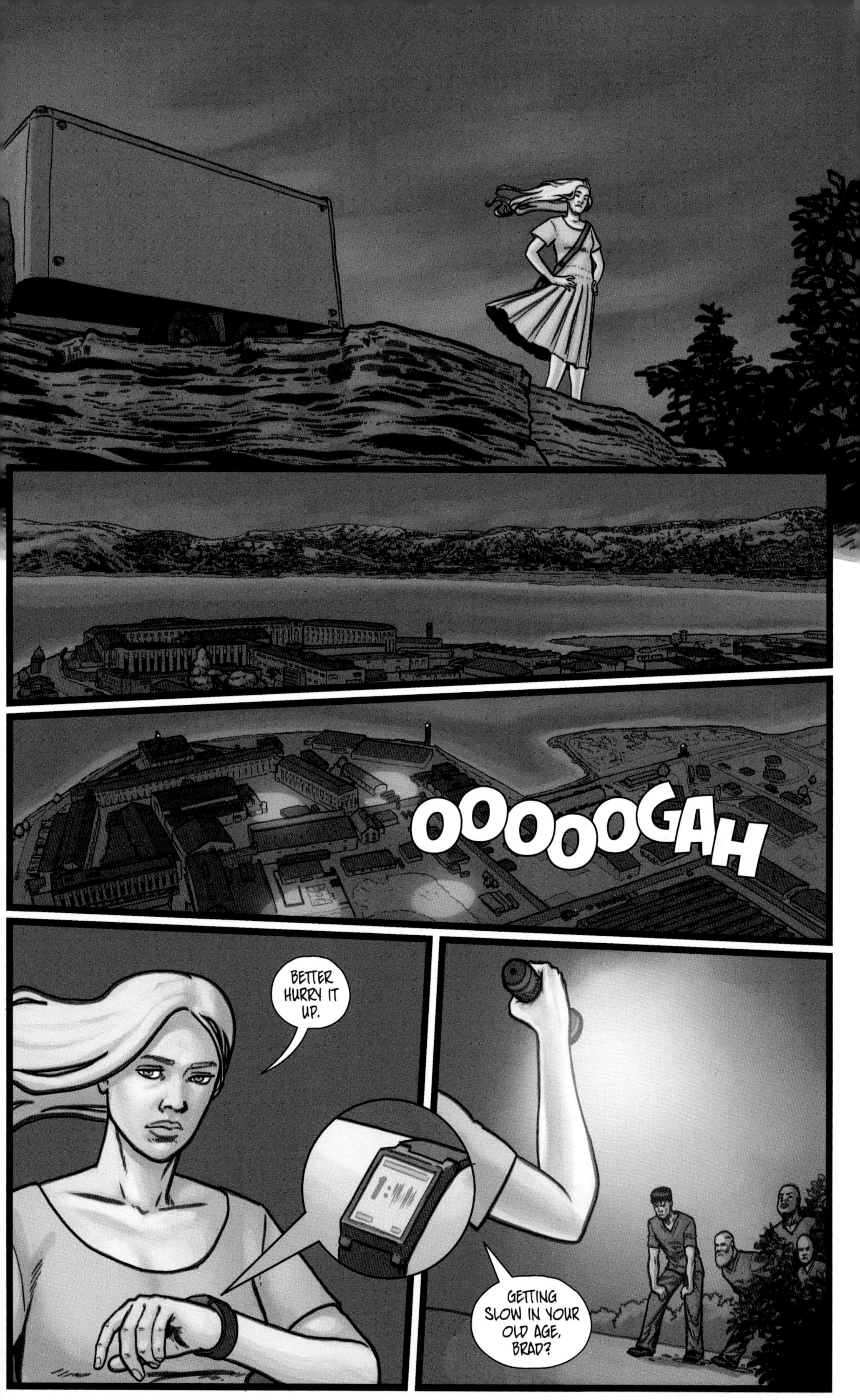
OOOOOOGAH
BETTER HURRY IT UP.
GETTING SLOW IN YOUR OLD AGE, BRAD?

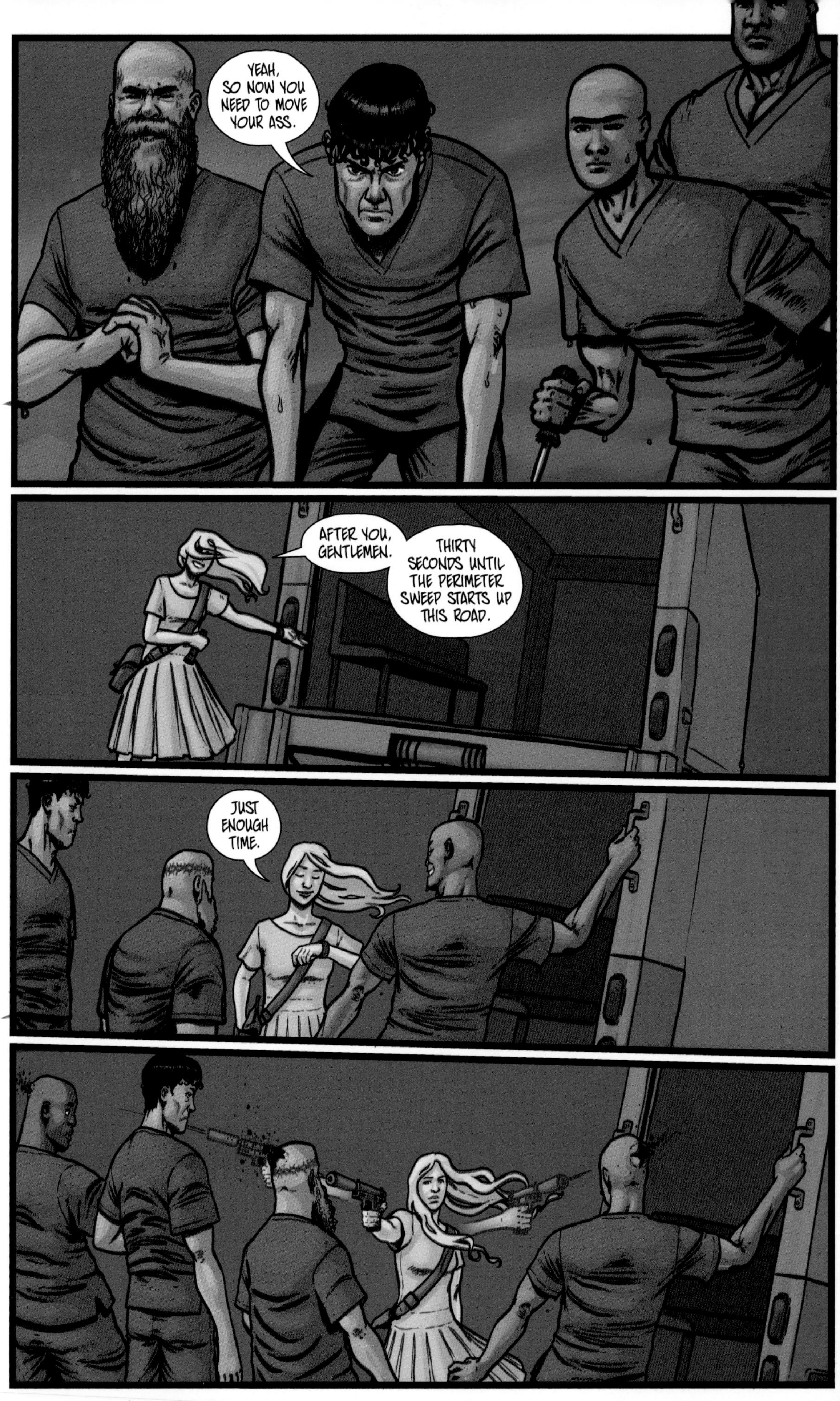
YEAH, SO NOW YOU NEED TO MOVE YOUR ASS.
AFTER YOU, GENTLEMEN.
THIRTY SECONDS UNTIL THE PERIMETER SWEEP STARTS UP THIS ROAD.
JUST ENOUGH TIME.

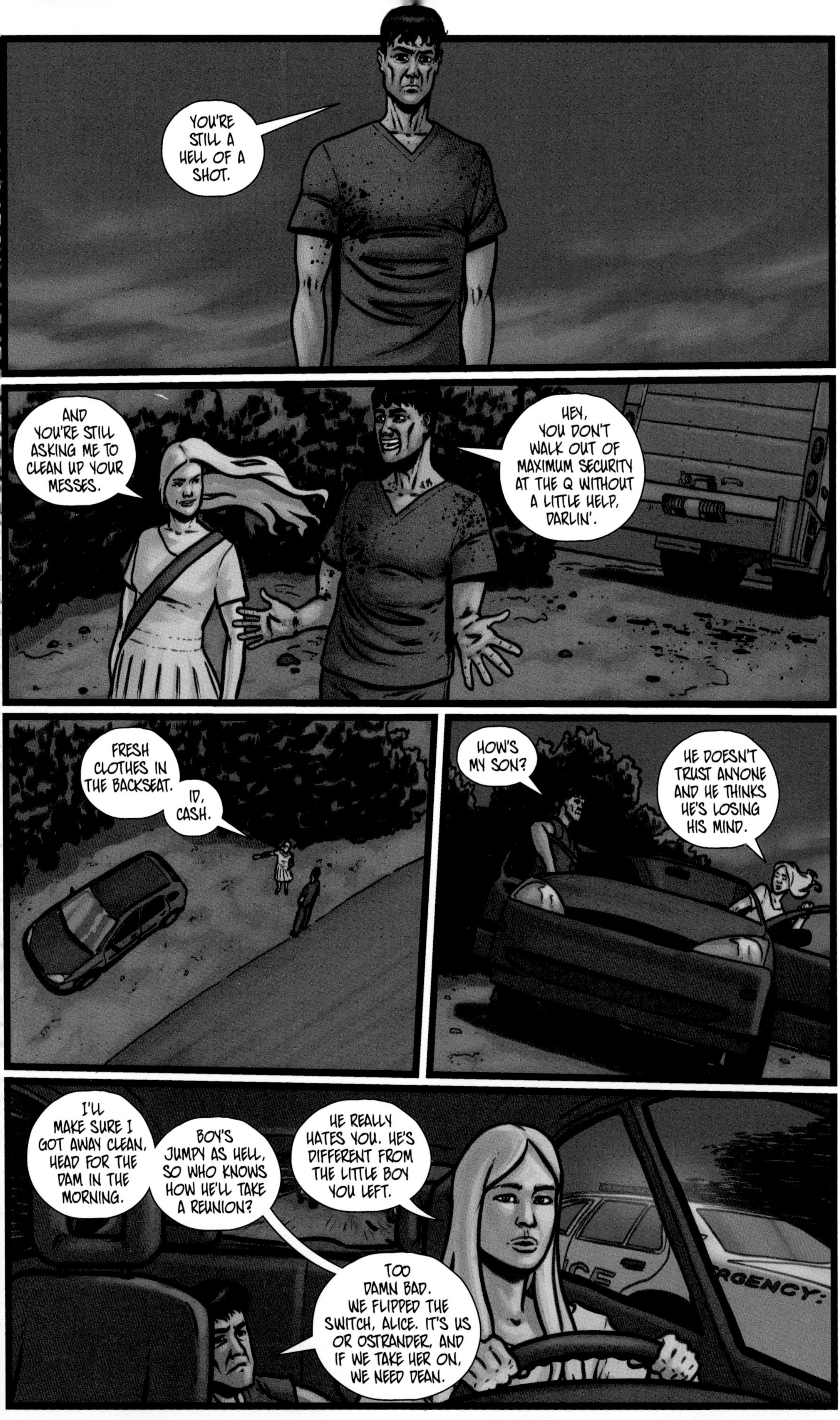
YOU'RE STILL A HELL OF A SHOT.
AND YOU'RE STILL ASKING ME TO CLEAN UP YOUR MESSES.
HEY, YOU DON'T WALK OUT OF MAXIMUM SECURITY AT THE Q WITHOUT A LITTLE HELP, DARLIN'.
FRESH CLOTHES IN THE BACKSEAT.
ID, CASH.
HOW'S MY SON?
HE DOESN'T TRUST ANYONE AND HE THINKS HE'S LOSING HIS MIND.
I'LL MAKE SURE I GOT AWAY CLEAN, HEAD FOR THE DAM IN THE MORNING.
BOY'S JUMPY AS HELL, SO WHO KNOWS HOW HE'LL TAKE A REUNION?
HE REALLY HATES YOU. HE'S DIFFERENT FROM THE LITTLE BOY YOU LEFT.
TOO DAMN BAD. WE FLIPPED THE SWITCH, ALICE. IT'S US OR OSTRANDER, AND IF WE TAKE HER ON, WE NEED DEAN.
ICE
RGENCY

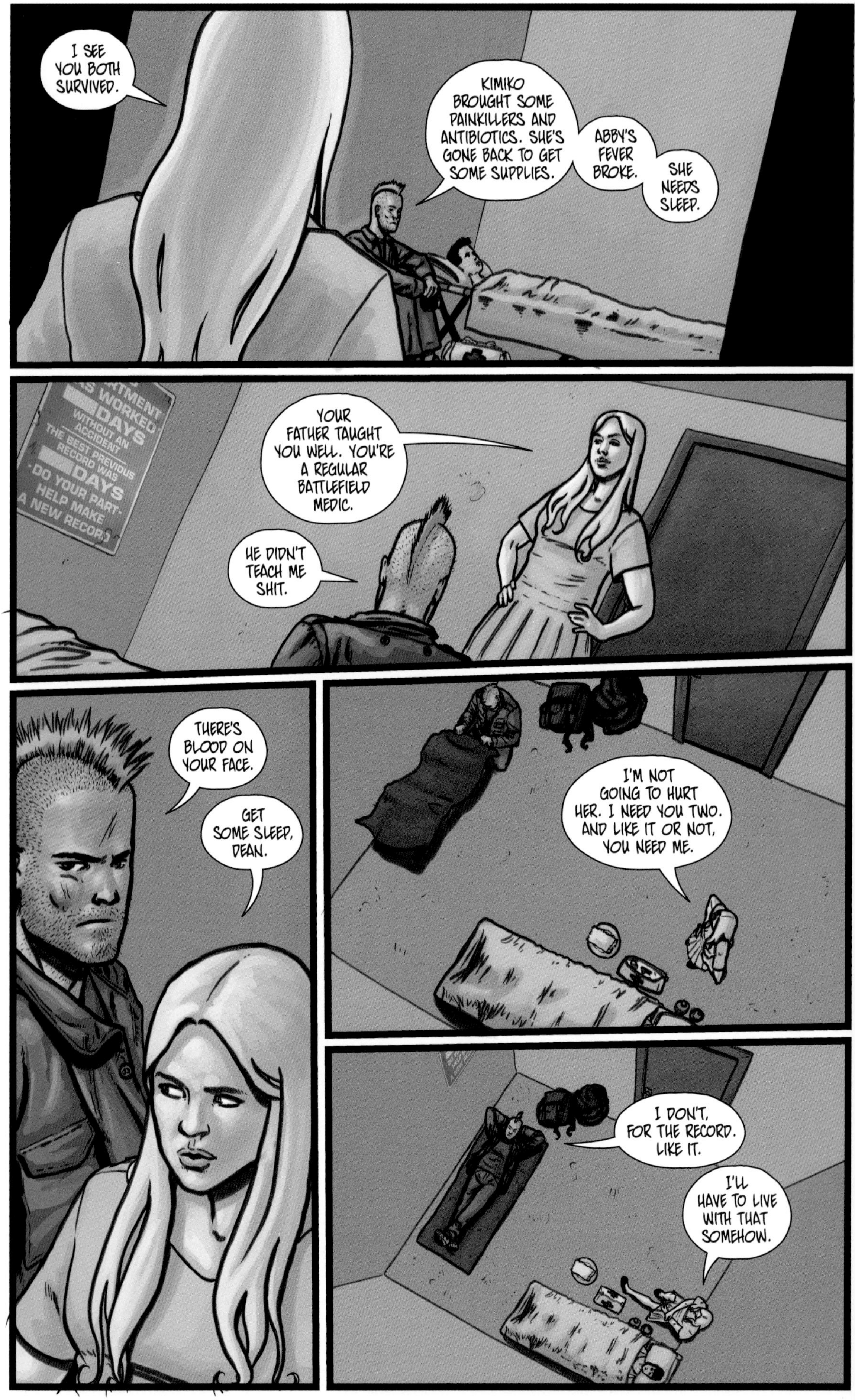
I SEE YOU BOTH SURVIVED.
KIMIKO BROUGHT SOME PAINKILLERS AND ANTIBIOTICS. SHE'S GONE BACK TO GET SOME SUPPLIES.
ABBY'S FEVER BROKE.
SHE NEEDS SLEEP.
YOUR FATHER TAUGHT YOU WELL. YOU'RE A REGULAR BATTLEFIELD MEDIC.
HE DIDN'T TEACH ME SHIT.
THERE'S BLOOD ON YOUR FACE.
GET SOME SLEEP, DEAN.
I'M NOT GOING TO HURT HER. I NEED YOU TWO. AND LIKE IT OR NOT, YOU NEED ME.
I DON'T, FOR THE RECORD. LIKE IT.
I'LL HAVE TO LIVE WITH THAT SOMEHOW.

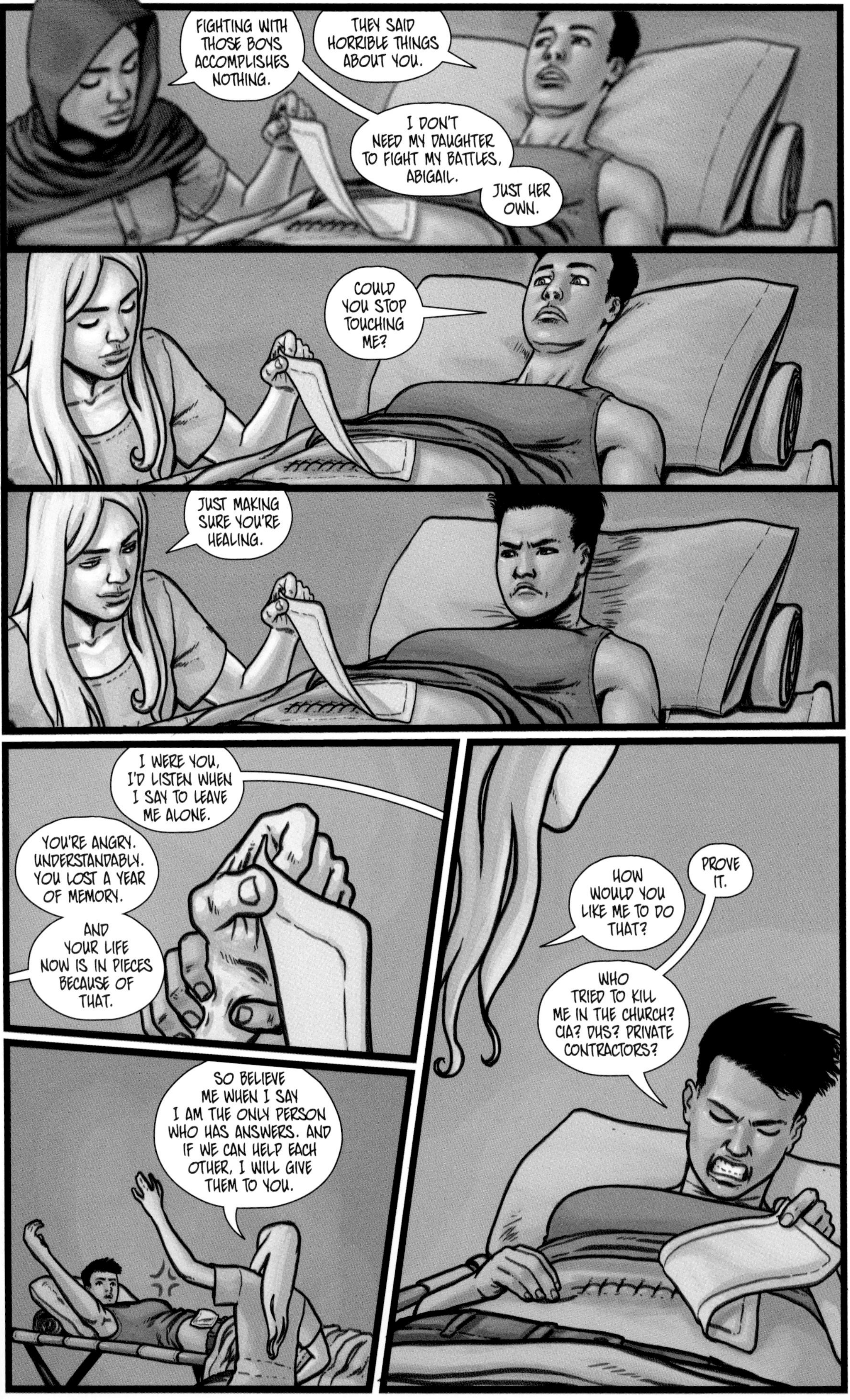
FIGHTING WITH THOSE BOYS ACCOMPLISHES NOTHING.
THEY SAID HORRIBLE THINGS ABOUT YOU.
I DON'T NEED MY DAUGHTER TO FIGHT MY BATTLES, ABIGAIL.
JUST HER OWN.
COULD YOU STOP TOUCHING ME?
JUST MAKING SURE YOU'RE HEALING.
I WERE YOU, I'D LISTEN WHEN I SAY TO LEAVE ME ALONE.
YOU'RE ANGRY. UNDERSTANDABLY. YOU LOST A YEAR OF MEMORY.
AND YOUR LIFE NOW IS IN PIECES BECAUSE OF THAT.
SO BELIEVE ME WHEN I SAY I AM THE ONLY PERSON WHO HAS ANSWERS. AND IF WE CAN HELP EACH OTHER, I WILL GIVE THEM TO YOU.
PROVE IT.
HOW WOULD YOU LIKE ME TO DO THAT?
WHO TRIED TO KILL ME IN THE CHURCH? CIA? DHS? PRIVATE CONTRACTORS?

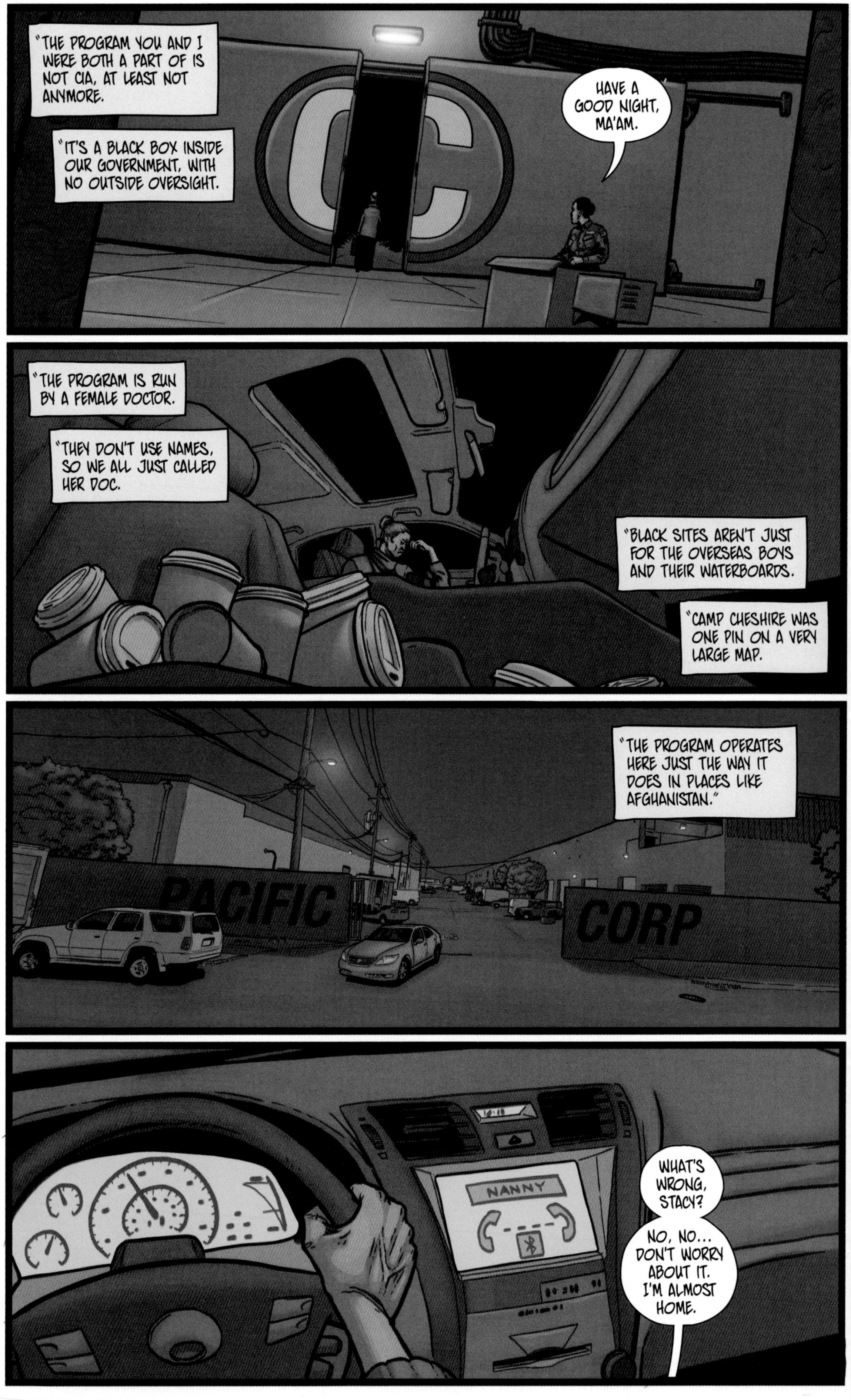
"THE PROGRAM YOU AND I WERE BOTH A PART OF IS NOT CIA, AT LEAST NOT ANYMORE.
"IT'S A BLACK BOX INSIDE OUR GOVERNMENT, WITH NO OUTSIDE OVERSIGHT.
HAVE A GOOD NIGHT, MA'AM.
"THE PROGRAM IS RUN BY A FEMALE DOCTOR.
"THEY DON'T USE NAMES, SO WE ALL JUST CALLED HER DOC.
"BLACK SITES AREN'T JUST FOR THE OVERSEAS BOYS AND THEIR WATERBOARDS.
"CAMP CHESHIRE WAS ONE PIN ON A VERY LARGE MAP.
"THE PROGRAM OPERATES HERE JUST THE WAY IT DOES IN PLACES LIKE AFGHANISTAN."
PACIFIC
CORP
NANNY
WHAT'S WRONG, STACY?
NO, NO... DON'T WORRY ABOUT IT. I'M ALMOST HOME.

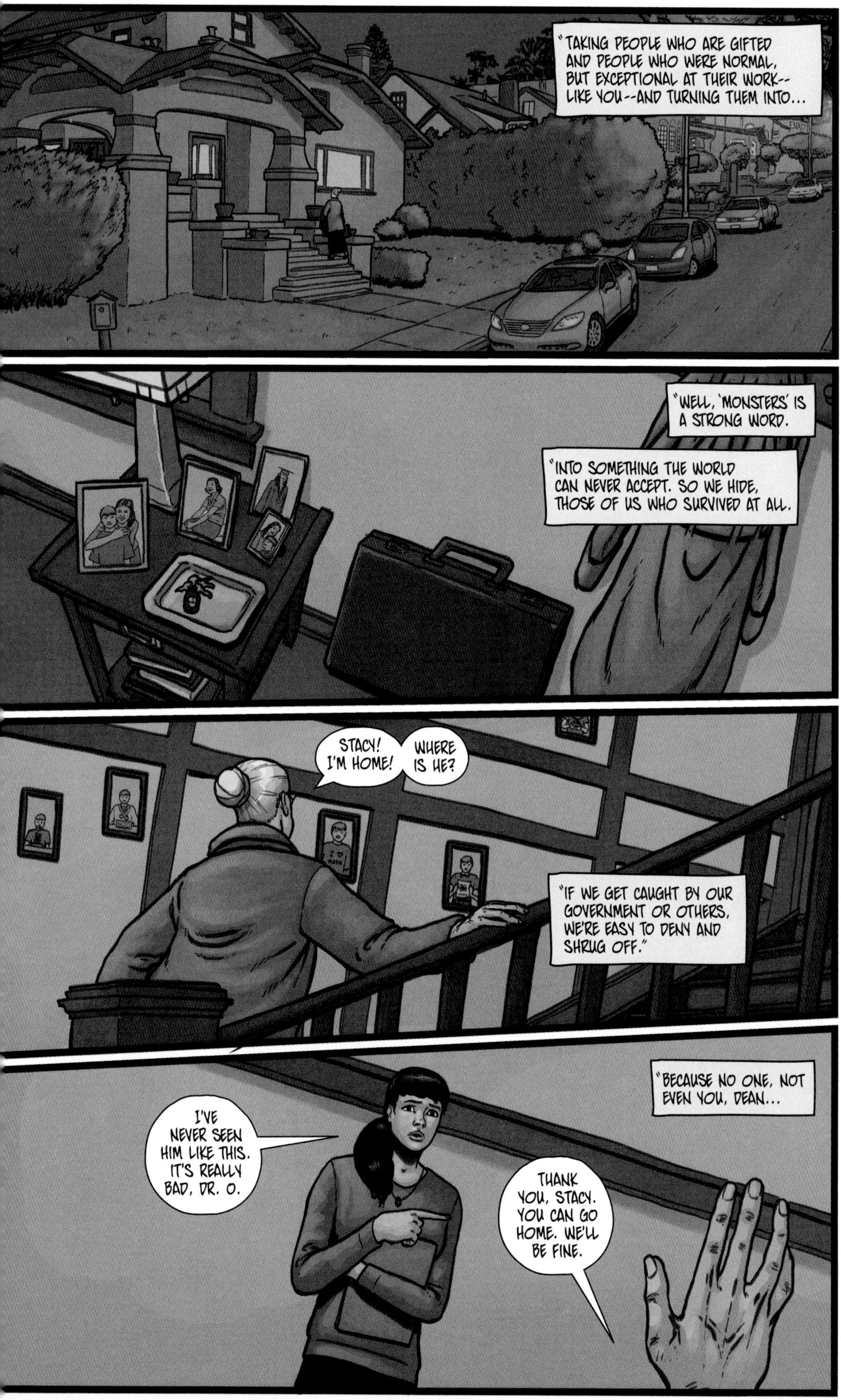
"TAKING PEOPLE WHO ARE GIFTED AND PEOPLE WHO WERE NORMAL, BUT EXCEPTIONAL AT THEIR WORK-- LIKE YOU--AND TURNING THEM INTO...
"WELL, 'MONSTERS' IS A STRONG WORD.
"INTO SOMETHING THE WORLD CAN NEVER ACCEPT. SO WE HIDE, THOSE OF US WHO SURVIVED AT ALL.
STACY! I'M HOME!
WHERE IS HE?
"IF WE GET CAUGHT BY OUR GOVERNMENT OR OTHERS, WE'RE EASY TO DENY AND SHRUG OFF."
"BECAUSE NO ONE, NOT EVEN YOU, DEAN...
I'VE NEVER SEEN HIM LIKE THIS. IT'S REALLY BAD, DR. O.
THANK YOU, STACY. YOU CAN GO HOME. WE'LL BE FINE.

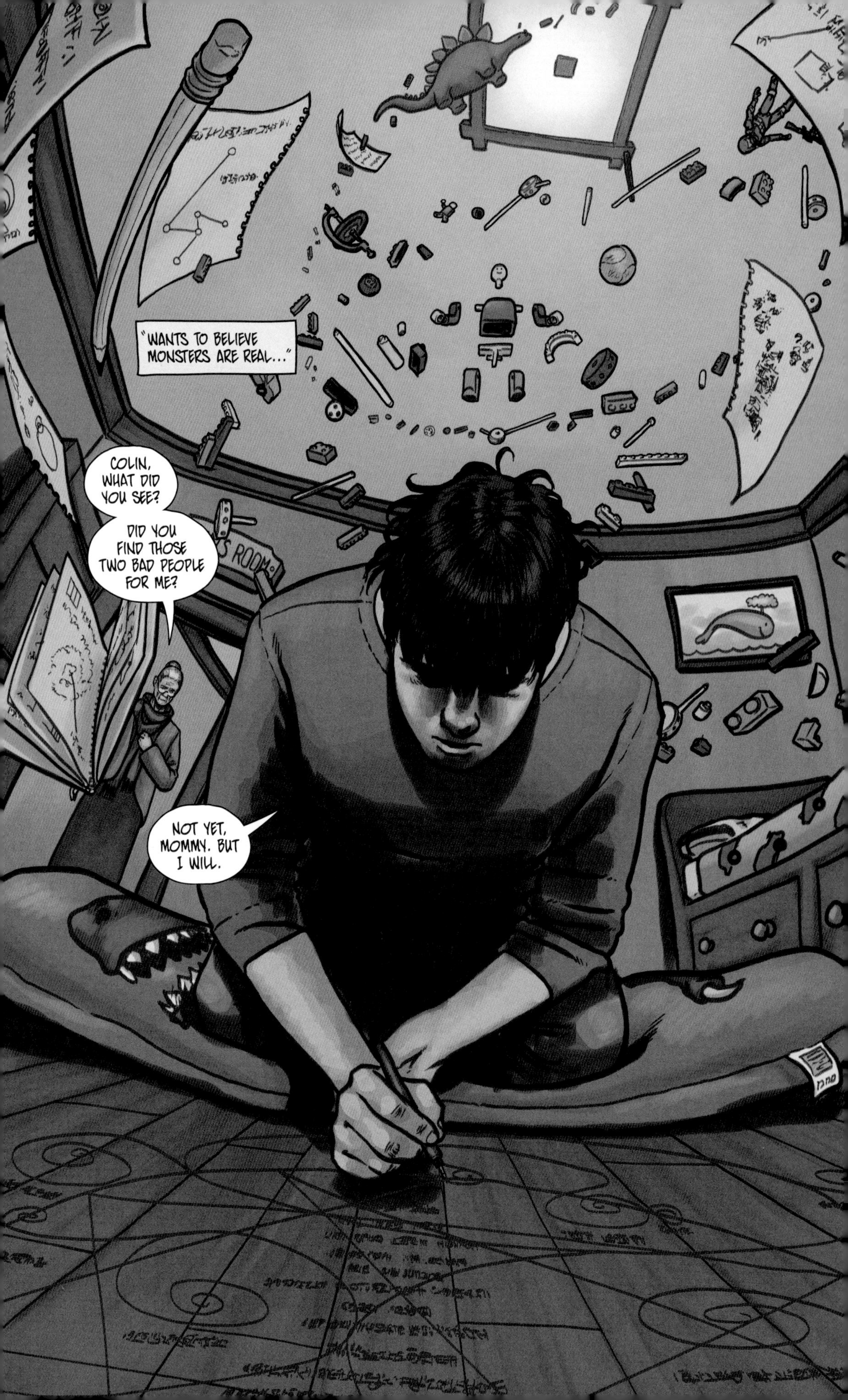
"WANTS TO BELIEVE MONSTERS ARE REAL..."
COLIN, WHAT DID YOU SEE?
DID YOU FIND THOSE TWO BAD PEOPLE FOR ME?
NOT YET, MOMMY. BUT I WILL.

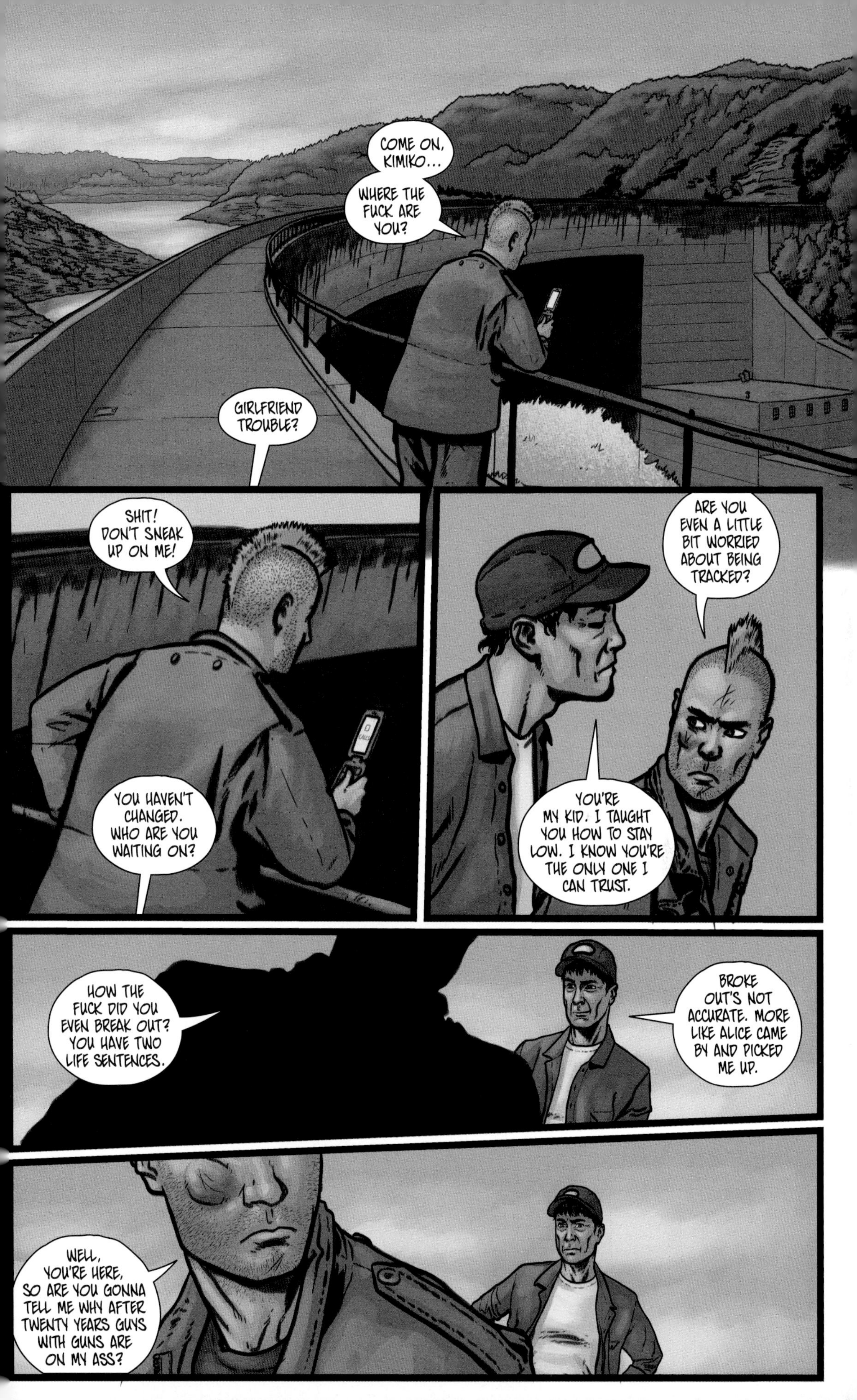
COME ON, KIMIKO...
WHERE THE FUCK ARE YOU?
GIRLFRIEND TROUBLE?
SHIT! DON'T SNEAK UP ON ME!
CALL
YOU HAVEN'T CHANGED. WHO ARE YOU WAITING ON?
ARE YOU EVEN A LITTLE BIT WORRIED ABOUT BEING TRACKED?
YOU'RE MY KID. I TAUGHT YOU HOW TO STAY LOW. I KNOW YOU'RE THE ONLY ONE I CAN TRUST.
HOW THE FUCK DID YOU EVEN BREAK OUT? YOU HAVE TWO LIFE SENTENCES.
BROKE OUT'S NOT ACCURATE. MORE LIKE ALICE CAME BY AND PICKED ME UP.
WELL, YOU'RE HERE, SO ARE YOU GONNA TELL ME WHY AFTER TWENTY YEARS GUYS WITH GUNS ARE ON MY ASS?

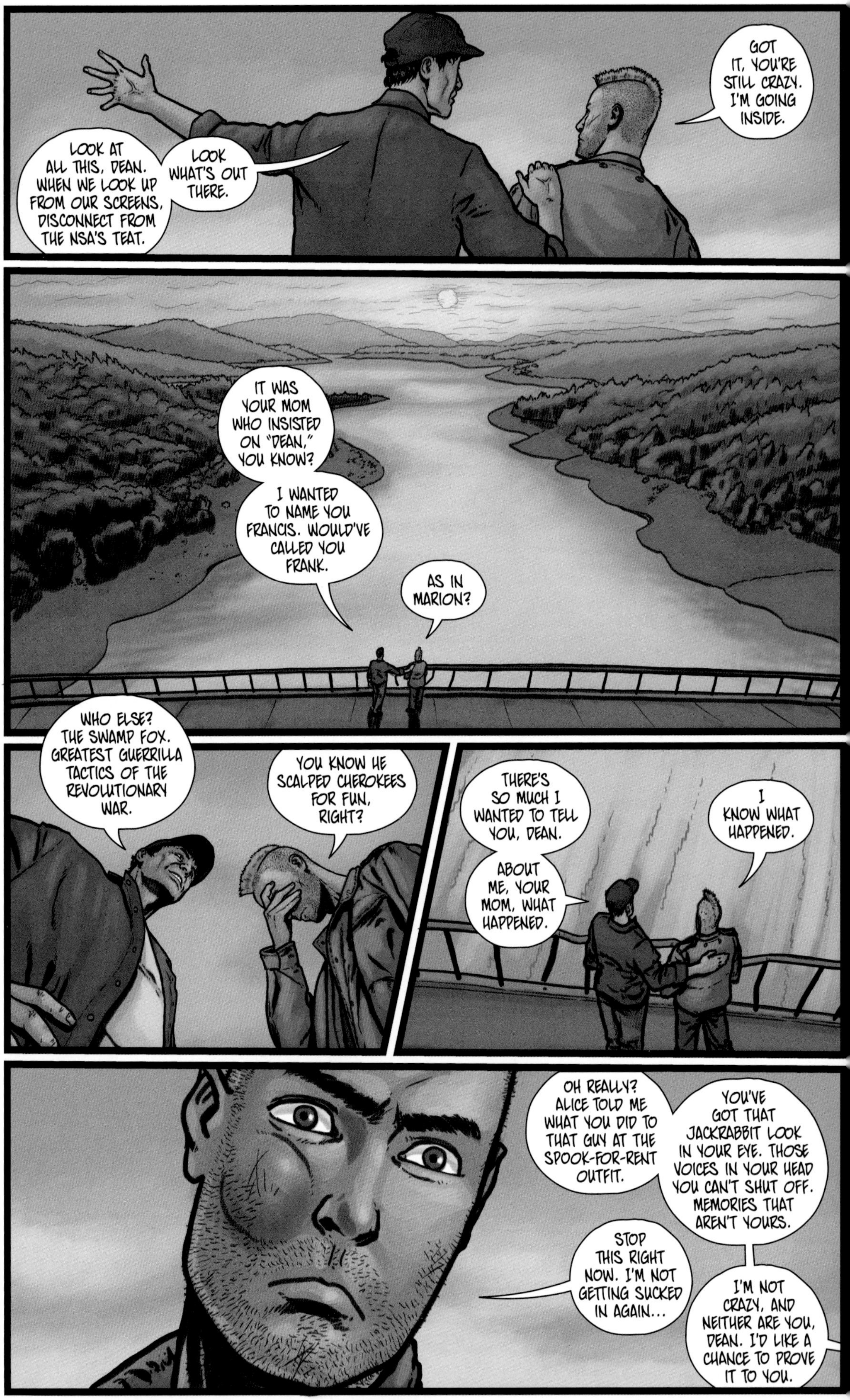
LOOK AT ALL THIS, DEAN. WHEN WE LOOK UP FROM OUR SCREENS, DISCONNECT FROM THE NSA'S TEAT.
LOOK WHAT'S OUT THERE.
GOT IT, YOU'RE STILL CRAZY. I'M GOING INSIDE.
IT WAS YOUR MOM WHO INSISTED ON "DEAN," YOU KNOW?
I WANTED TO NAME YOU FRANCIS. WOULD'VE CALLED YOU FRANK.
AS IN MARION?
WHO ELSE? THE SWAMP FOX. GREATEST GUERRILLA TACTICS OF THE REVOLUTIONARY WAR.
YOU KNOW HE SCALPED CHEROKEES FOR FUN, RIGHT?
THERE'S SO MUCH I WANTED TO TELL YOU, DEAN.
ABOUT ME, YOUR MOM, WHAT HAPPENED.
I KNOW WHAT HAPPENED.
OH REALLY? ALICE TOLD ME WHAT YOU DID TO THAT GUY AT THE SPOOK-FOR-RENT OUTFIT.
YOU'VE GOT THAT JACKRABBIT LOOK IN YOUR EYE. THOSE VOICES IN YOUR HEAD YOU CAN'T SHUT OFF. MEMORIES THAT AREN'T YOURS.
STOP THIS RIGHT NOW. I'M NOT GETTING SUCKED IN AGAIN...
I'M NOT CRAZY, AND NEITHER ARE YOU, DEAN. I'D LIKE A CHANCE TO PROVE IT TO YOU.

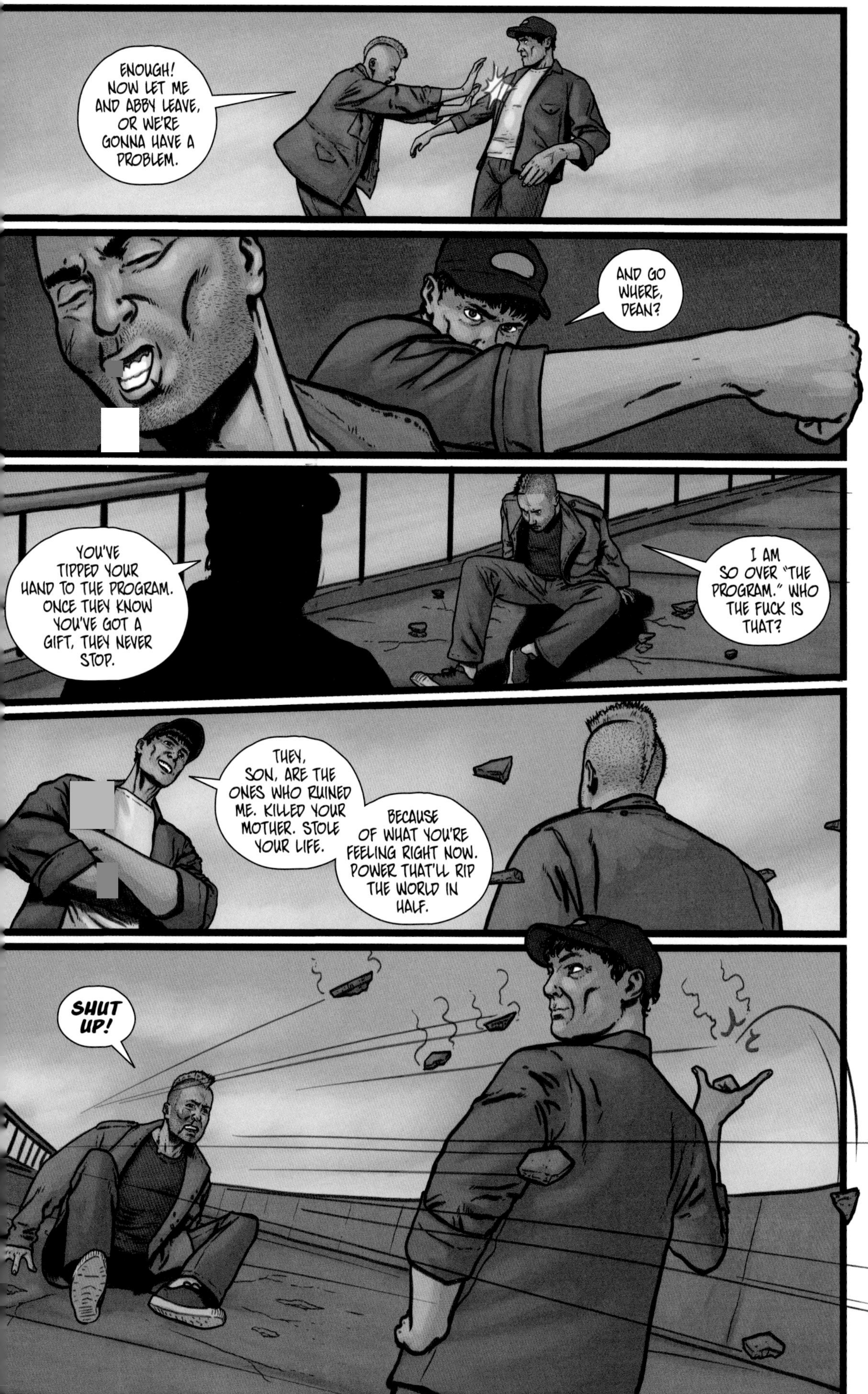
ENOUGH! NOW LET ME AND ABBY LEAVE, OR WE'RE GONNA HAVE A PROBLEM.
AND GO WHERE, DEAN?
YOU'VE TIPPED YOUR HAND TO THE PROGRAM. ONCE THEY KNOW YOU'VE GOT A GIFT, THEY NEVER STOP.
I AM SO OVER "THE PROGRAM." WHO THE FUCK IS THAT?
THEY, SON, ARE THE ONES WHO RUINED ME. KILLED YOUR MOTHER. STOLE YOUR LIFE.
BECAUSE OF WHAT YOU'RE FEELING RIGHT NOW. POWER THAT'LL RIP THE WORLD IN HALF.
SHUT UP!

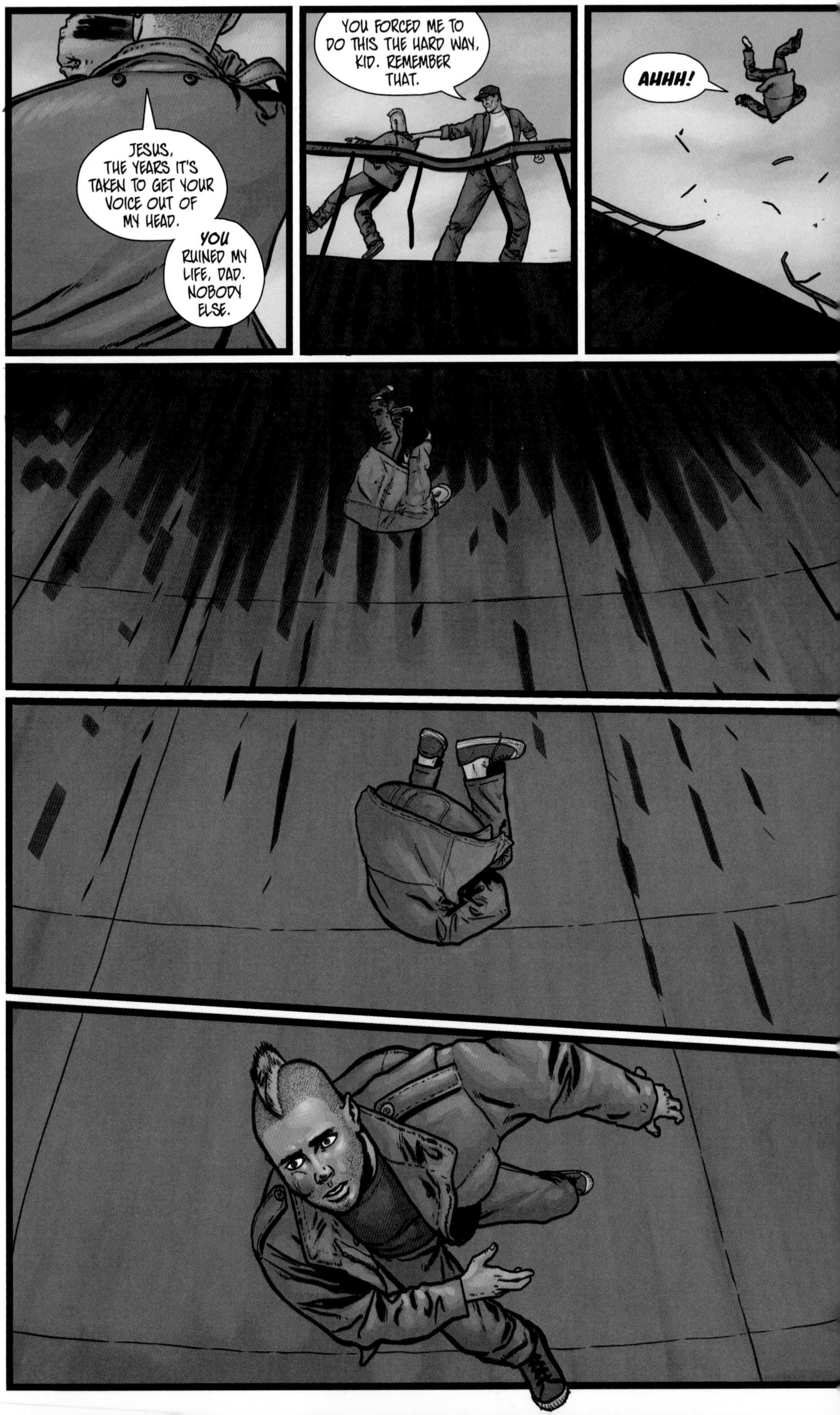
JESUS, THE YEARS IT'S TAKEN TO GET YOUR VOICE OUT OF MY HEAD.
YOU RUINED MY LIFE, DAD. NOBODY ELSE.
YOU FORCED ME TO DO THIS THE HARD WAY, KID. REMEMBER THAT.
AHHH!

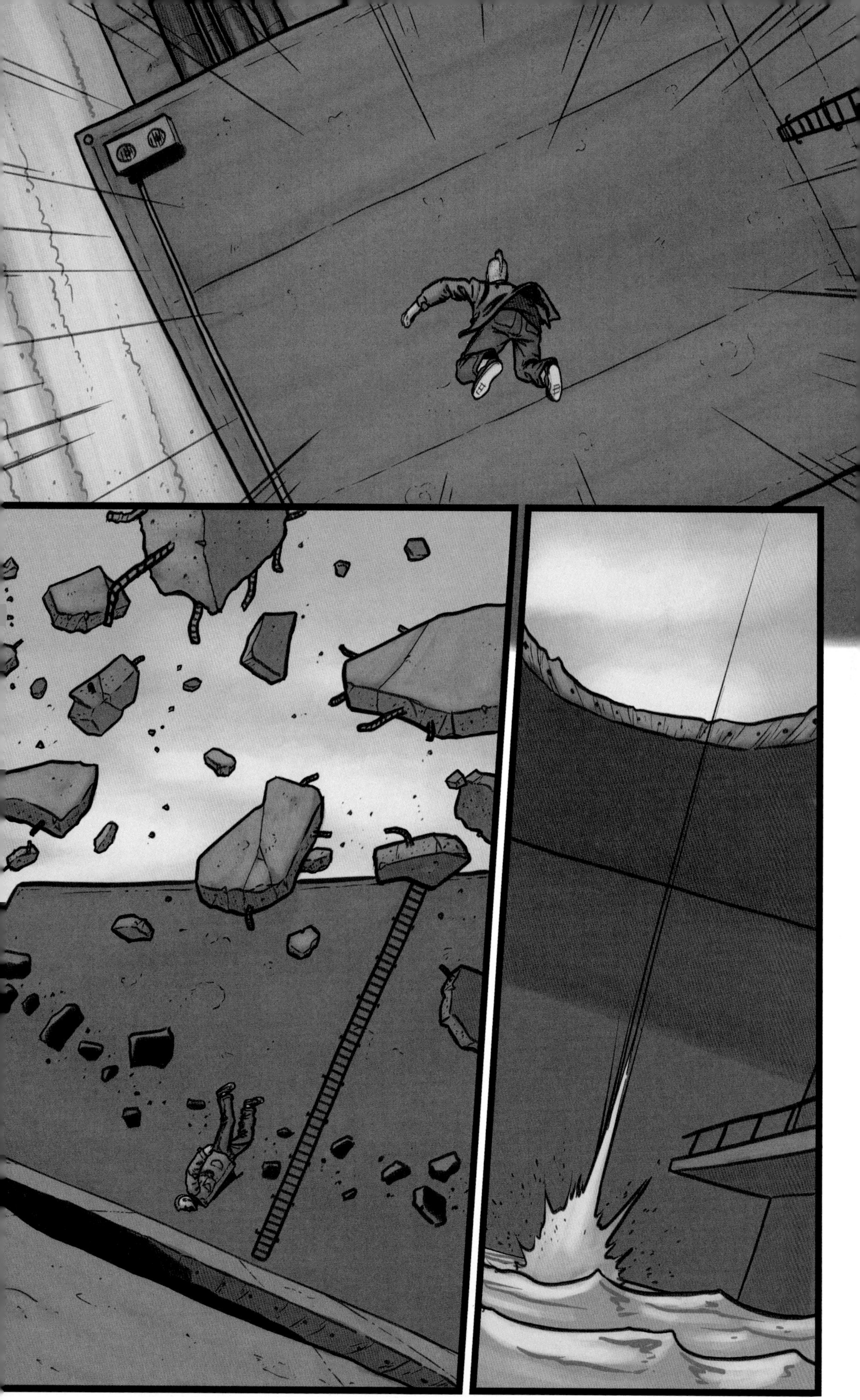

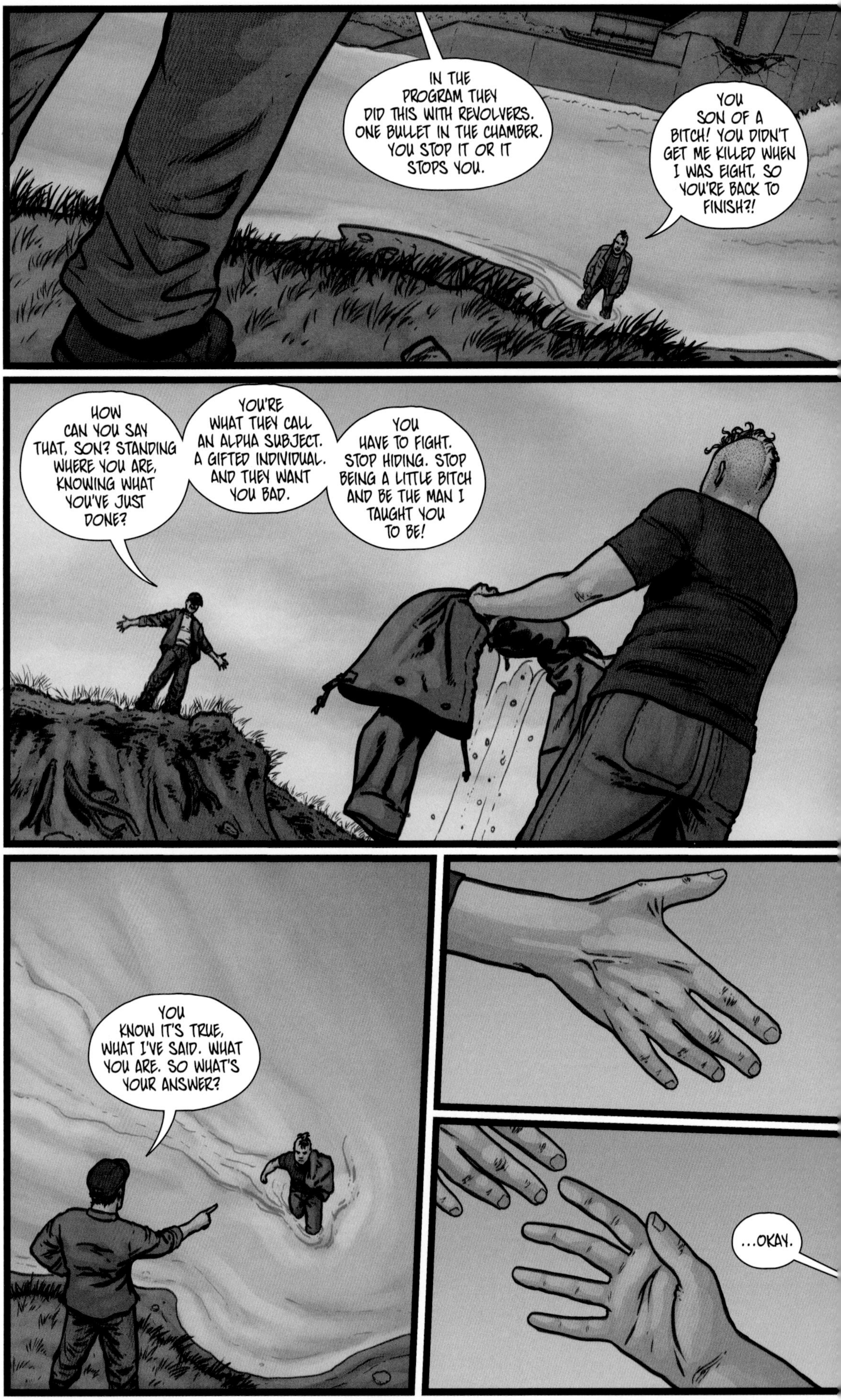
IN THE PROGRAM THEY DID THIS WITH REVOLVERS. ONE BULLET IN THE CHAMBER. YOU STOP IT OR IT STOPS YOU.
YOU SON OF A BITCH! YOU DIDN'T GET ME KILLED WHEN I WAS EIGHT, SO YOU'RE BACK TO FINISH?!
HOW CAN YOU SAY THAT, SON? STANDING WHERE YOU ARE, KNOWING WHAT YOU'VE JUST DONE?
YOU'RE WHAT THEY CALL AN ALPHA SUBJECT. A GIFTED INDIVIDUAL. AND THEY WANT YOU BAD.
YOU HAVE TO FIGHT. STOP HIDING. STOP BEING A LITTLE BITCH AND BE THE MAN I TAUGHT YOU TO BE!
YOU KNOW IT'S TRUE, WHAT I'VE SAID. WHAT YOU ARE. SO WHAT'S YOUR ANSWER?
...OKAY.

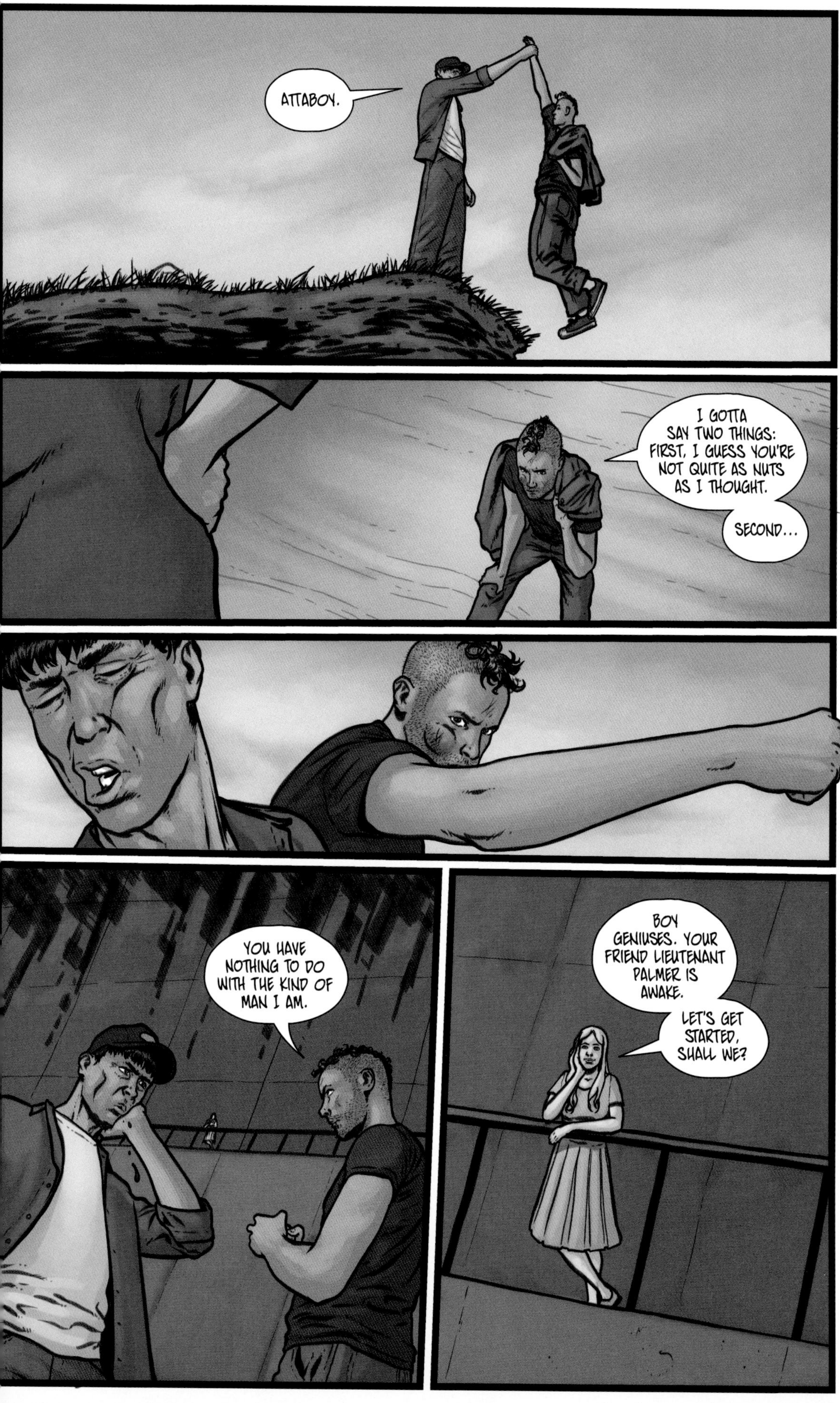
ATTABOY.
I GOTTA SAY TWO THINGS: FIRST, I GUESS YOU'RE NOT QUITE AS NUTS AS I THOUGHT.
SECOND...
YOU HAVE NOTHING TO DO WITH THE KIND OF MAN I AM.
BOY GENIUSES. YOUR FRIEND LIEUTENANT PALMER IS AWAKE.
LET'S GET STARTED, SHALL WE?

CHAPTER FOUR

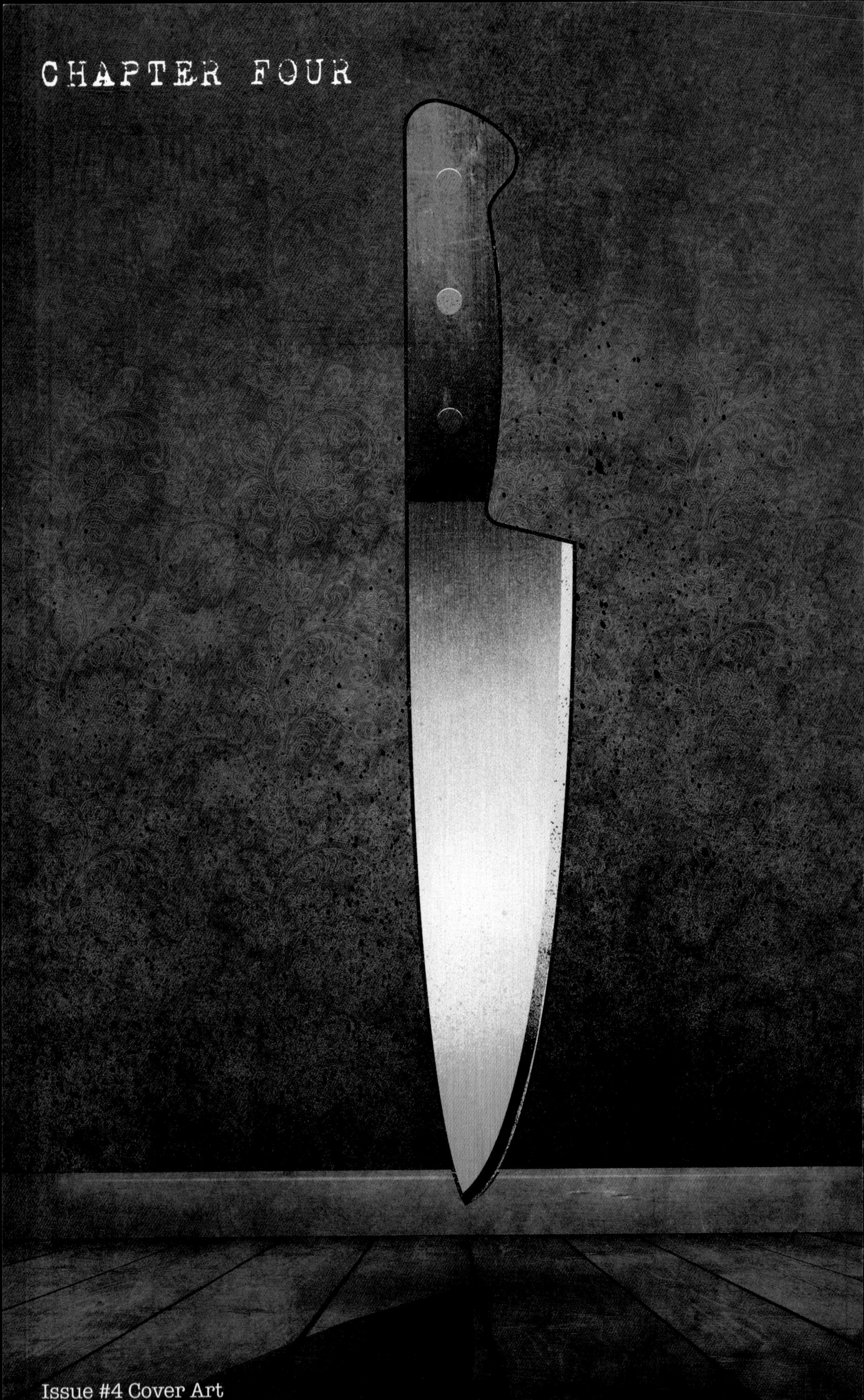

Issue #4 Cover Art

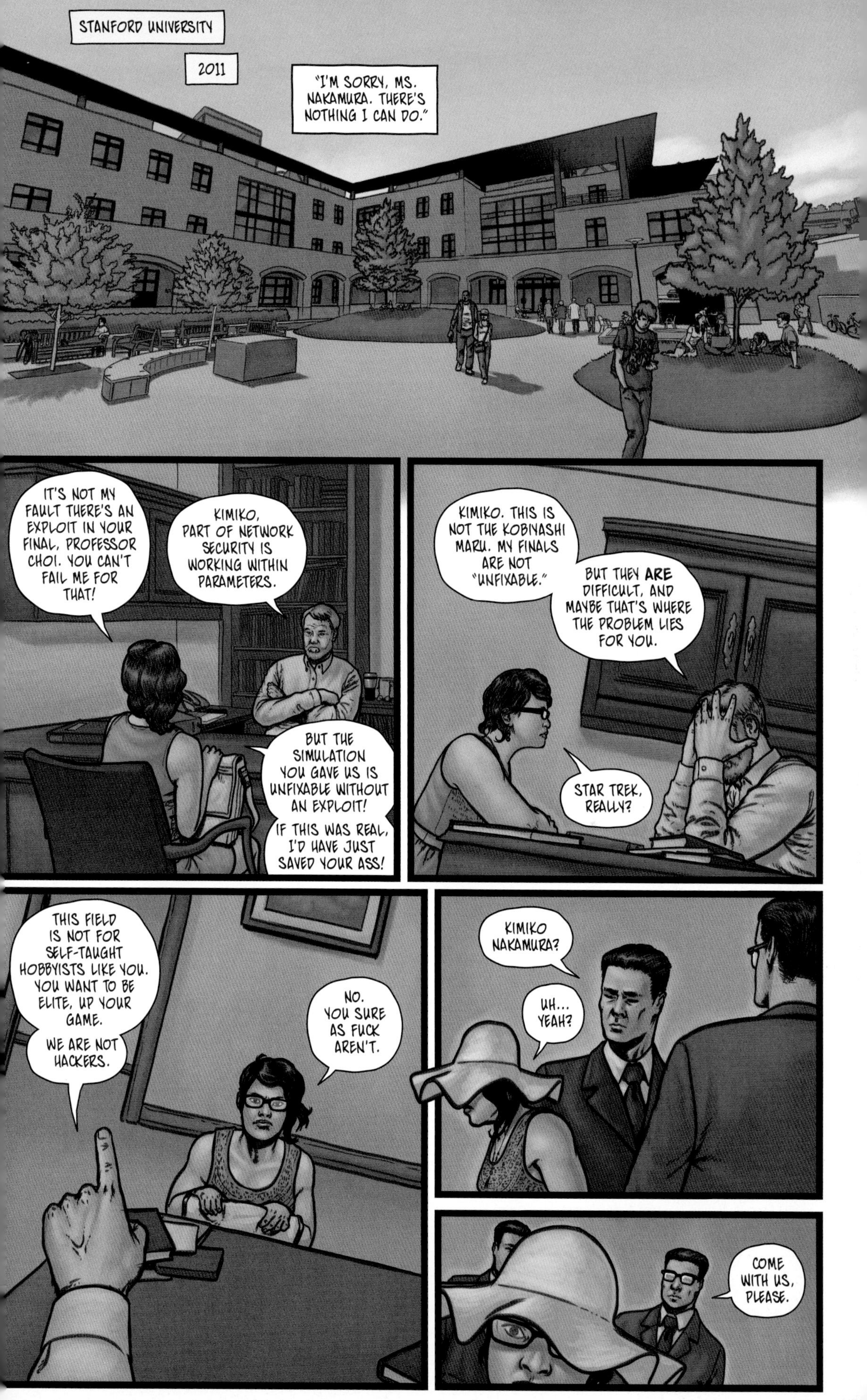
STANFORD UNIVERSITY
2011
"I'M SORRY, MS. NAKAMURA. THERE'S NOTHING I CAN DO."
IT'S NOT MY FAULT THERE'S AN EXPLOIT IN YOUR FINAL, PROFESSOR CHOI. YOU CAN'T FAIL ME FOR THAT!
KIMIKO, PART OF NETWORK SECURITY IS WORKING WITHIN PARAMETERS.
BUT THE SIMULATION YOU GAVE US IS UNFIXABLE WITHOUT AN EXPLOIT!
IF THIS WAS REAL, I'D HAVE JUST SAVED YOUR ASS!
KIMIKO. THIS IS NOT THE KOBIYASHI MARU. MY FINALS ARE NOT "UNFIXABLE."
BUT THEY **ARE** DIFFICULT, AND MAYBE THAT'S WHERE THE PROBLEM LIES FOR YOU.
STAR TREK, REALLY?
THIS FIELD IS NOT FOR SELF-TAUGHT HOBBYISTS LIKE YOU. YOU WANT TO BE ELITE, UP YOUR GAME.
WE ARE NOT HACKERS.
NO. YOU SURE AS FUCK AREN'T.
KIMIKO NAKAMURA?
UH... YEAH?
COME WITH US, PLEASE.

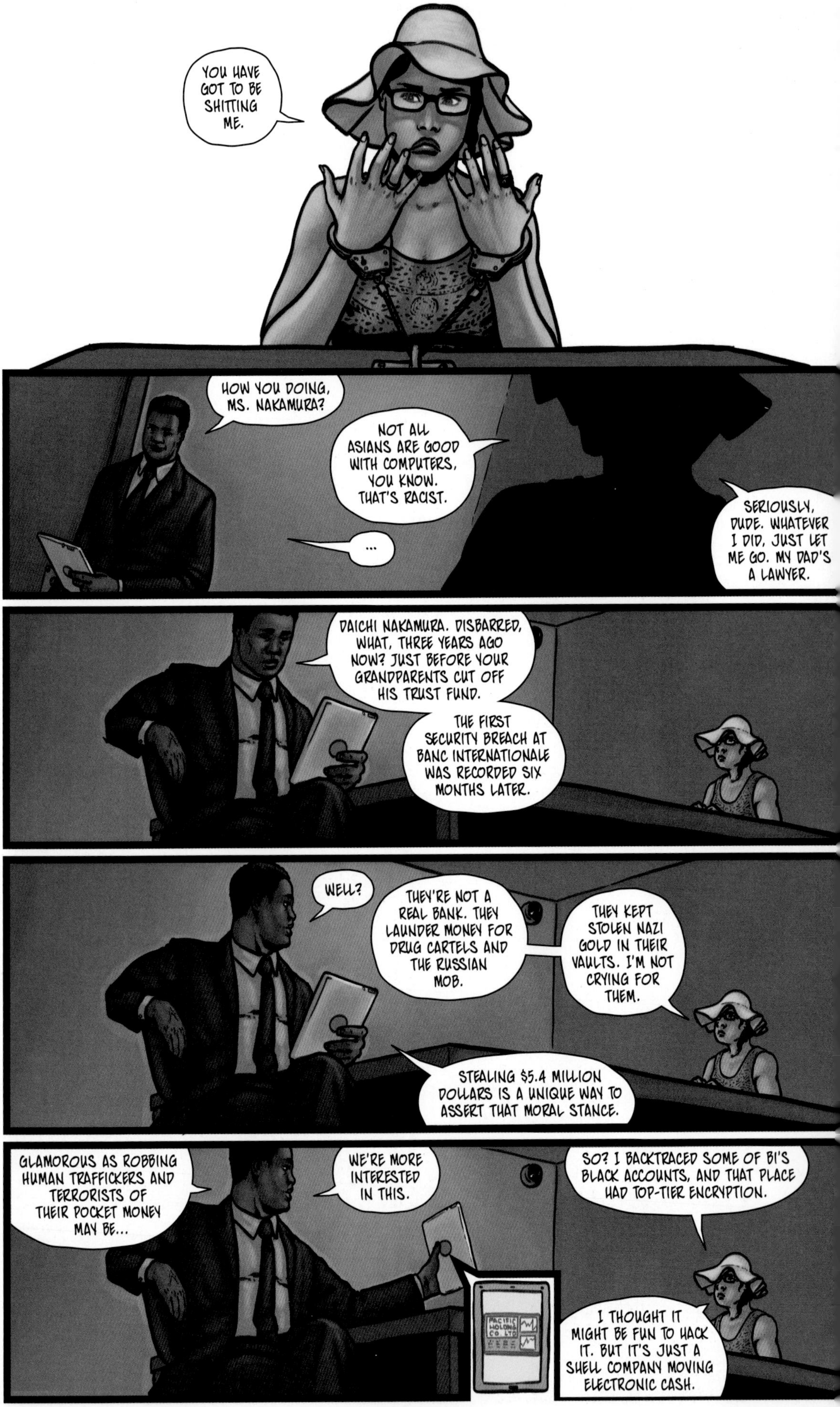
YOU HAVE GOT TO BE SHITTING ME.
HOW YOU DOING, MS. NAKAMURA?
NOT ALL ASIANS ARE GOOD WITH COMPUTERS, YOU KNOW. THAT'S RACIST.
...
SERIOUSLY, DUDE. WHATEVER I DID, JUST LET ME GO. MY DAD'S A LAWYER.
DAICHI NAKAMURA. DISBARRED, WHAT, THREE YEARS AGO NOW? JUST BEFORE YOUR GRANDPARENTS CUT OFF HIS TRUST FUND.
THE FIRST SECURITY BREACH AT BANC INTERNATIONALE WAS RECORDED SIX MONTHS LATER.
WELL?
THEY'RE NOT A REAL BANK. THEY LAUNDER MONEY FOR DRUG CARTELS AND THE RUSSIAN MOB.
THEY KEPT STOLEN NAZI GOLD IN THEIR VAULTS. I'M NOT CRYING FOR THEM.
STEALING $5.4 MILLION DOLLARS IS A UNIQUE WAY TO ASSERT THAT MORAL STANCE.
GLAMOROUS AS ROBBING HUMAN TRAFFICKERS AND TERRORISTS OF THEIR POCKET MONEY MAY BE...
WE'RE MORE INTERESTED IN THIS.
SO? I BACKTRACED SOME OF BI'S BLACK ACCOUNTS, AND THAT PLACE HAD TOP-TIER ENCRYPTION.
I THOUGHT IT MIGHT BE FUN TO HACK IT. BUT IT'S JUST A SHELL COMPANY MOVING ELECTRONIC CASH.

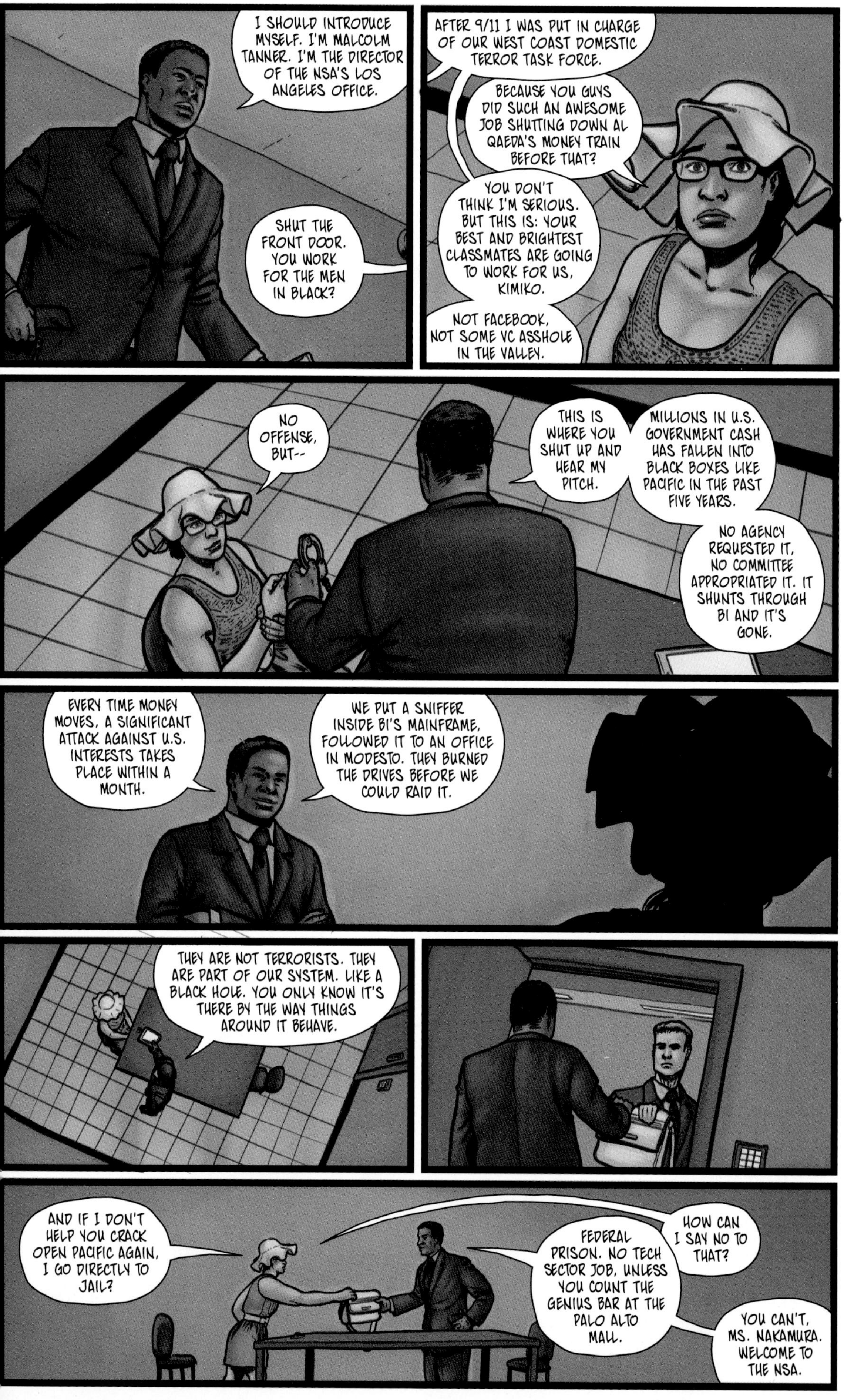
I SHOULD INTRODUCE MYSELF. I'M MALCOLM TANNER. I'M THE DIRECTOR OF THE NSA'S LOS ANGELES OFFICE.
SHUT THE FRONT DOOR. YOU WORK FOR THE MEN IN BLACK?
AFTER 9/11 I WAS PUT IN CHARGE OF OUR WEST COAST DOMESTIC TERROR TASK FORCE.
BECAUSE YOU GUYS DID SUCH AN AWESOME JOB SHUTTING DOWN AL QAEDA'S MONEY TRAIN BEFORE THAT?
YOU DON'T THINK I'M SERIOUS. BUT THIS IS: YOUR BEST AND BRIGHTEST CLASSMATES ARE GOING TO WORK FOR US, KIMIKO.
NOT FACEBOOK, NOT SOME VC ASSHOLE IN THE VALLEY.
NO OFFENSE, BUT--
THIS IS WHERE YOU SHUT UP AND HEAR MY PITCH.
MILLIONS IN U.S. GOVERNMENT CASH HAS FALLEN INTO BLACK BOXES LIKE PACIFIC IN THE PAST FIVE YEARS.
NO AGENCY REQUESTED IT, NO COMMITTEE APPROPRIATED IT. IT SHUNTS THROUGH BI AND IT'S GONE.
EVERY TIME MONEY MOVES, A SIGNIFICANT ATTACK AGAINST U.S. INTERESTS TAKES PLACE WITHIN A MONTH.
WE PUT A SNIFFER INSIDE BI'S MAINFRAME, FOLLOWED IT TO AN OFFICE IN MODESTO. THEY BURNED THE DRIVES BEFORE WE COULD RAID IT.
THEY ARE NOT TERRORISTS. THEY ARE PART OF OUR SYSTEM. LIKE A BLACK HOLE. YOU ONLY KNOW IT'S THERE BY THE WAY THINGS AROUND IT BEHAVE.
AND IF I DON'T HELP YOU CRACK OPEN PACIFIC AGAIN, I GO DIRECTLY TO JAIL?
FEDERAL PRISON. NO TECH SECTOR JOB, UNLESS YOU COUNT THE GENIUS BAR AT THE PALO ALTO MALL.
HOW CAN I SAY NO TO THAT?
YOU CAN'T, MS. NAKAMURA. WELCOME TO THE NSA.

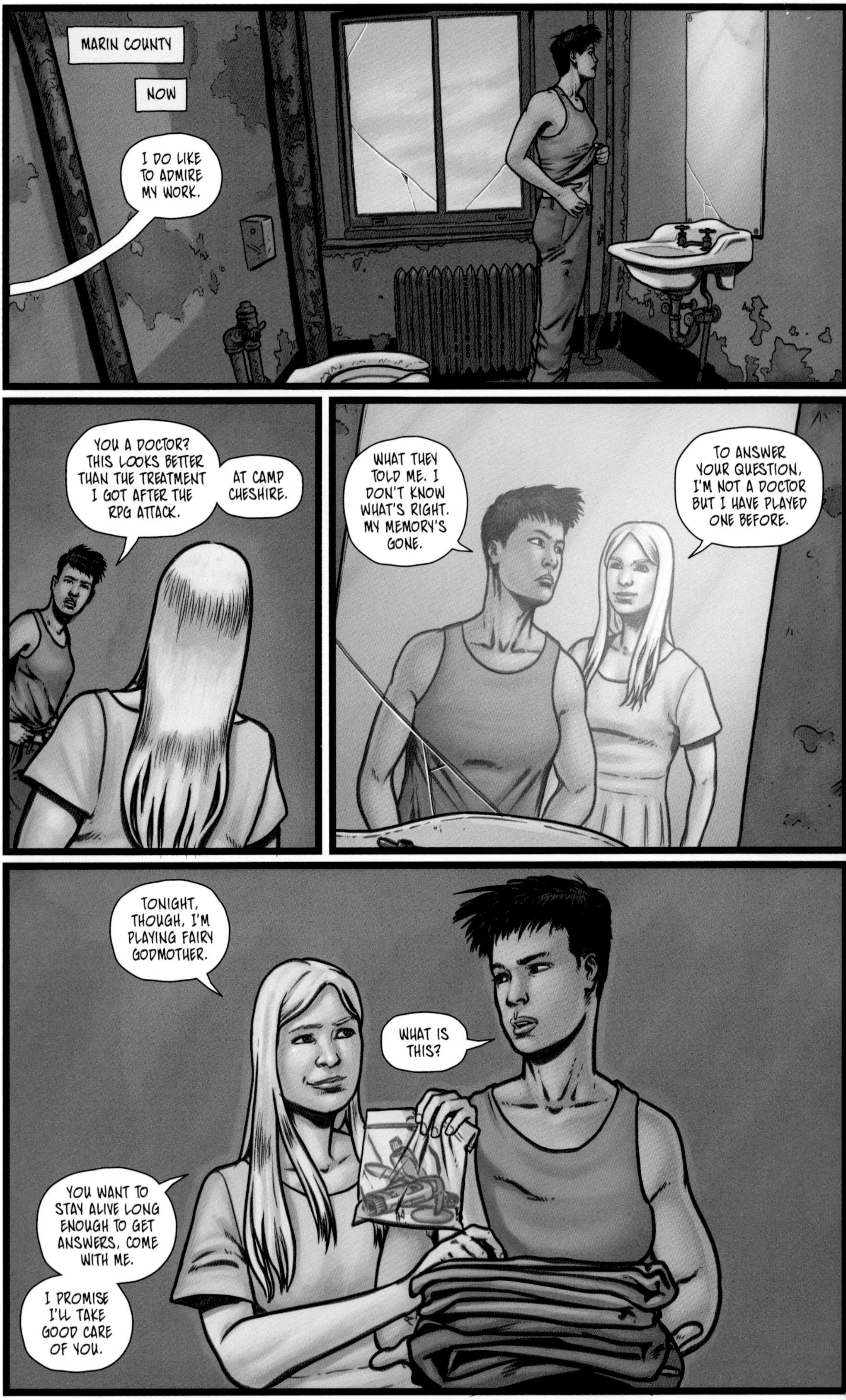
MARIN COUNTY
NOW
I DO LIKE TO ADMIRE MY WORK.
YOU A DOCTOR? THIS LOOKS BETTER THAN THE TREATMENT I GOT AFTER THE RPG ATTACK.
AT CAMP CHESHIRE.
WHAT THEY TOLD ME. I DON'T KNOW WHAT'S RIGHT. MY MEMORY'S GONE.
TO ANSWER YOUR QUESTION, I'M NOT A DOCTOR BUT I HAVE PLAYED ONE BEFORE.
TONIGHT, THOUGH, I'M PLAYING FAIRY GODMOTHER.
WHAT IS THIS?
YOU WANT TO STAY ALIVE LONG ENOUGH TO GET ANSWERS, COME WITH ME.
I PROMISE I'LL TAKE GOOD CARE OF YOU.

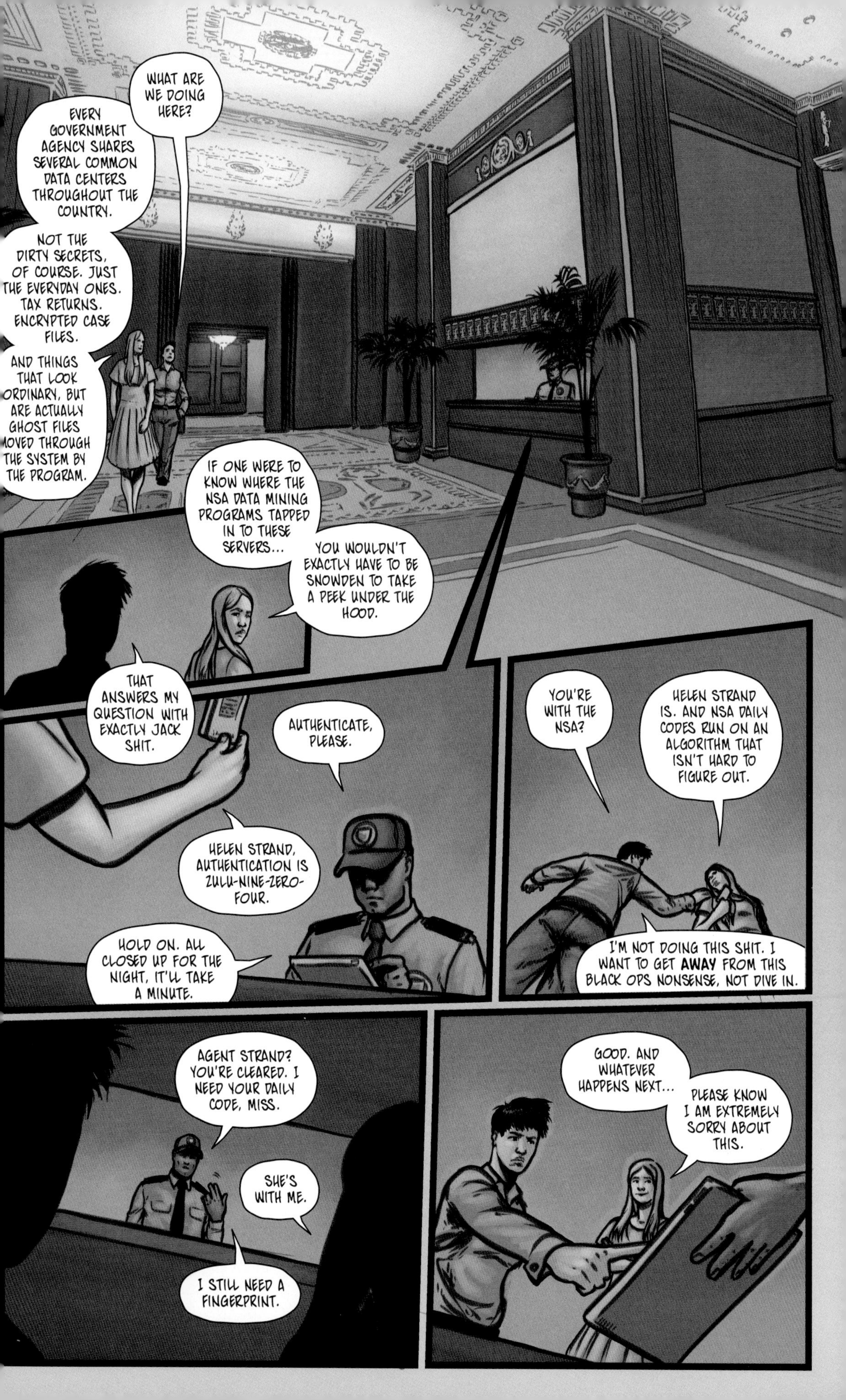
WHAT ARE WE DOING HERE?
EVERY GOVERNMENT AGENCY SHARES SEVERAL COMMON DATA CENTERS THROUGHOUT THE COUNTRY.
NOT THE DIRTY SECRETS, OF COURSE. JUST THE EVERYDAY ONES. TAX RETURNS. ENCRYPTED CASE FILES.
AND THINGS THAT LOOK ORDINARY, BUT ARE ACTUALLY GHOST FILES MOVED THROUGH THE SYSTEM BY THE PROGRAM.
IF ONE WERE TO KNOW WHERE THE NSA DATA MINING PROGRAMS TAPPED IN TO THESE SERVERS...
YOU WOULDN'T EXACTLY HAVE TO BE SNOWDEN TO TAKE A PEEK UNDER THE HOOD.
THAT ANSWERS MY QUESTION WITH EXACTLY JACK SHIT.
AUTHENTICATE, PLEASE.
HELEN STRAND, AUTHENTICATION IS ZULU-NINE-ZERO-FOUR.
HOLD ON. ALL CLOSED UP FOR THE NIGHT, IT'LL TAKE A MINUTE.
YOU'RE WITH THE NSA?
HELEN STRAND IS. AND NSA DAILY CODES RUN ON AN ALGORITHM THAT ISN'T HARD TO FIGURE OUT.
I'M NOT DOING THIS SHIT. I WANT TO GET **AWAY** FROM THIS BLACK OPS NONSENSE, NOT DIVE IN.
AGENT STRAND? YOU'RE CLEARED. I NEED YOUR DAILY CODE, MISS.
SHE'S WITH ME.
I STILL NEED A FINGERPRINT.
GOOD. AND WHATEVER HAPPENS NEXT...
PLEASE KNOW I AM EXTREMELY SORRY ABOUT THIS.

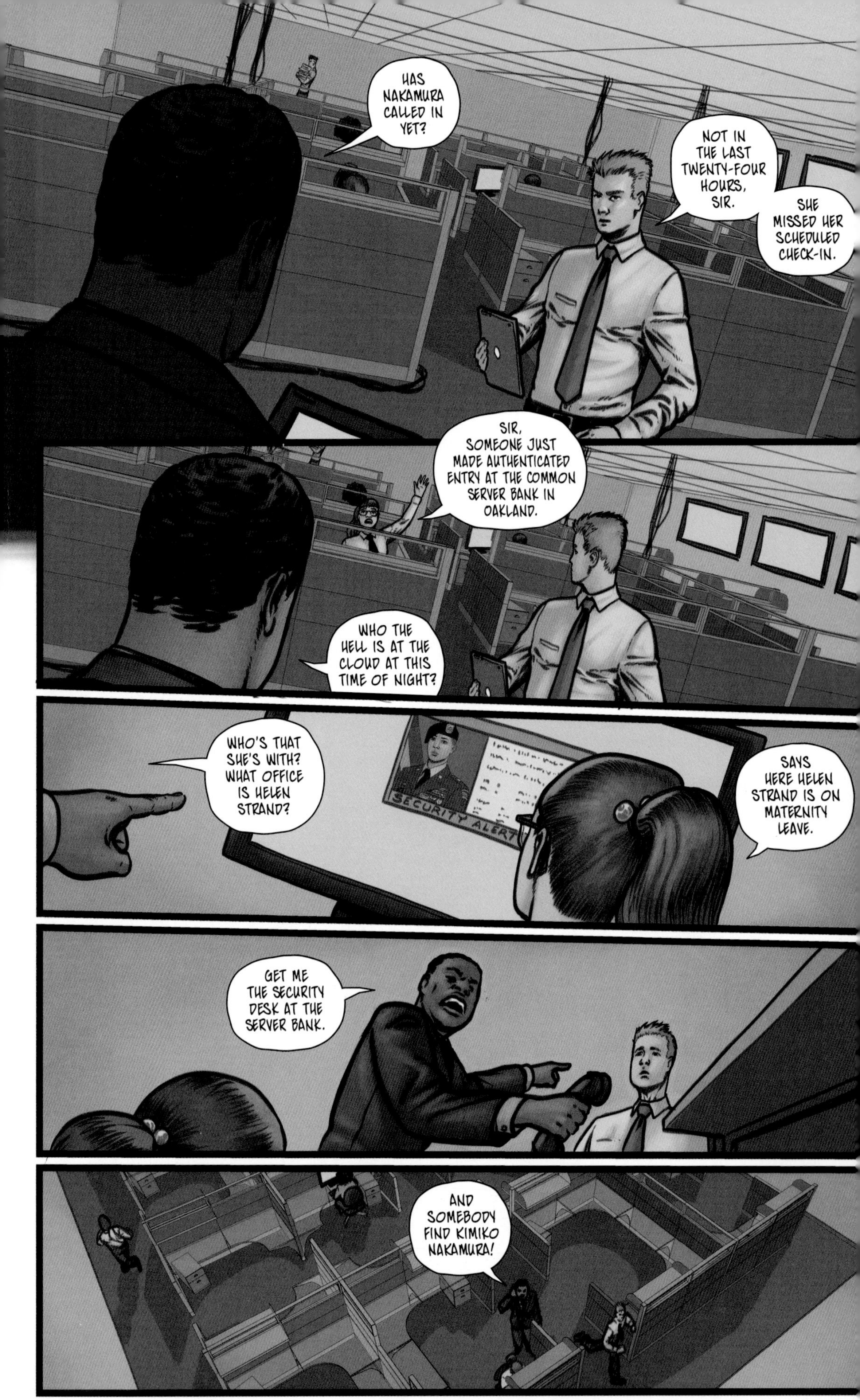
HAS NAKAMURA CALLED IN YET?
NOT IN THE LAST TWENTY-FOUR HOURS, SIR.
SHE MISSED HER SCHEDULED CHECK-IN.
SIR, SOMEONE JUST MADE AUTHENTICATED ENTRY AT THE COMMON SERVER BANK IN OAKLAND.
WHO THE HELL IS AT THE CLOUD AT THIS TIME OF NIGHT?
WHO'S THAT SHE'S WITH? WHAT OFFICE IS HELEN STRAND?
SECURITY ALERT
SAYS HERE HELEN STRAND IS ON MATERNITY LEAVE.
GET ME THE SECURITY DESK AT THE SERVER BANK.
AND SOMEBODY FIND KIMIKO NAKAMURA!

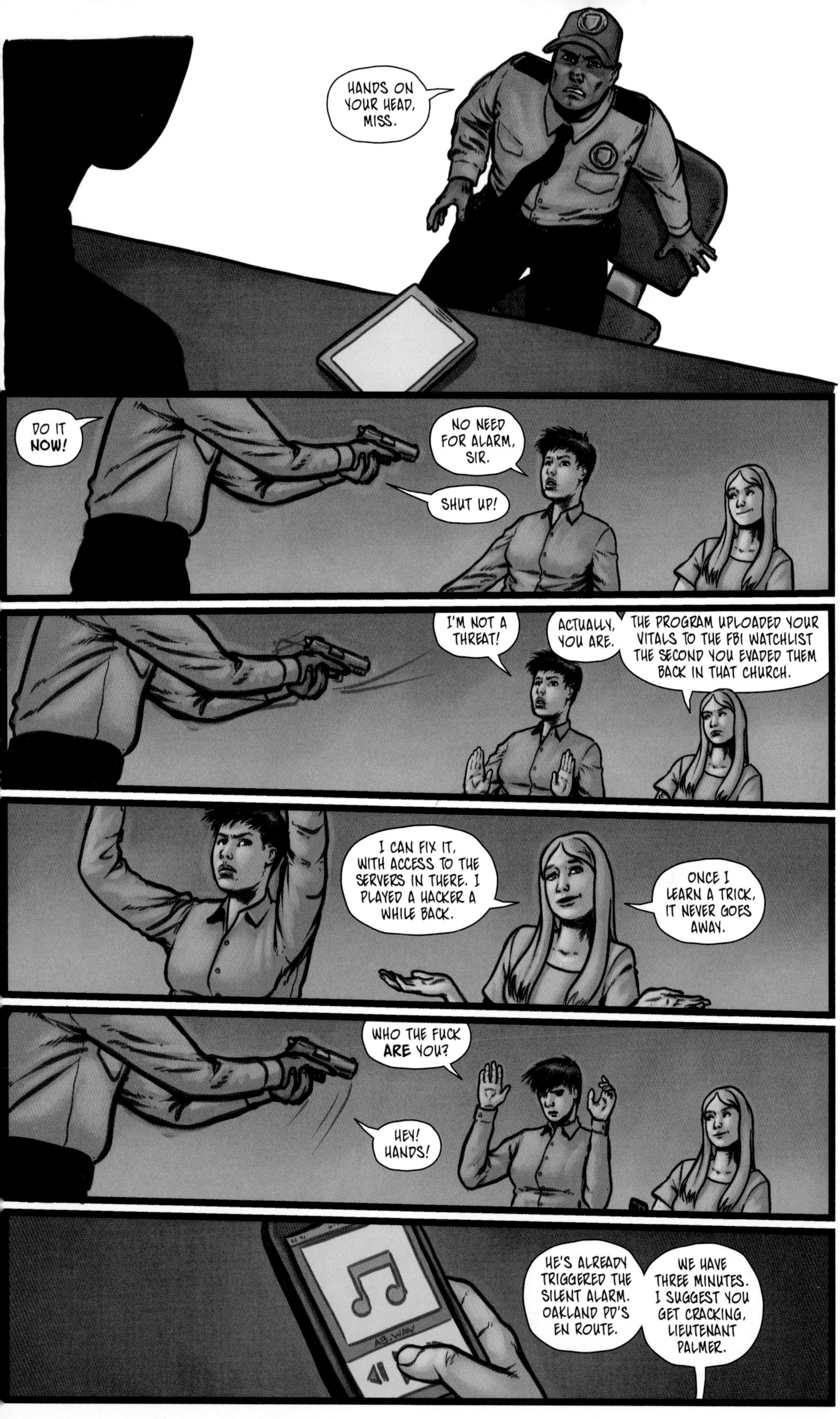
HANDS ON YOUR HEAD, MISS.
DO IT **NOW!**
NO NEED FOR ALARM, SIR.
SHUT UP!
I'M NOT A THREAT!
ACTUALLY, YOU ARE.
THE PROGRAM UPLOADED YOUR VITALS TO THE FBI WATCHLIST THE SECOND YOU EVADED THEM BACK IN THAT CHURCH.
I CAN FIX IT, WITH ACCESS TO THE SERVERS IN THERE. I PLAYED A HACKER A WHILE BACK.
ONCE I LEARN A TRICK, IT NEVER GOES AWAY.
WHO THE FUCK **ARE** YOU?
HEY! HANDS!
HE'S ALREADY TRIGGERED THE SILENT ALARM. OAKLAND PD'S EN ROUTE.
WE HAVE THREE MINUTES. I SUGGEST YOU GET CRACKING, LIEUTENANT PALMER.

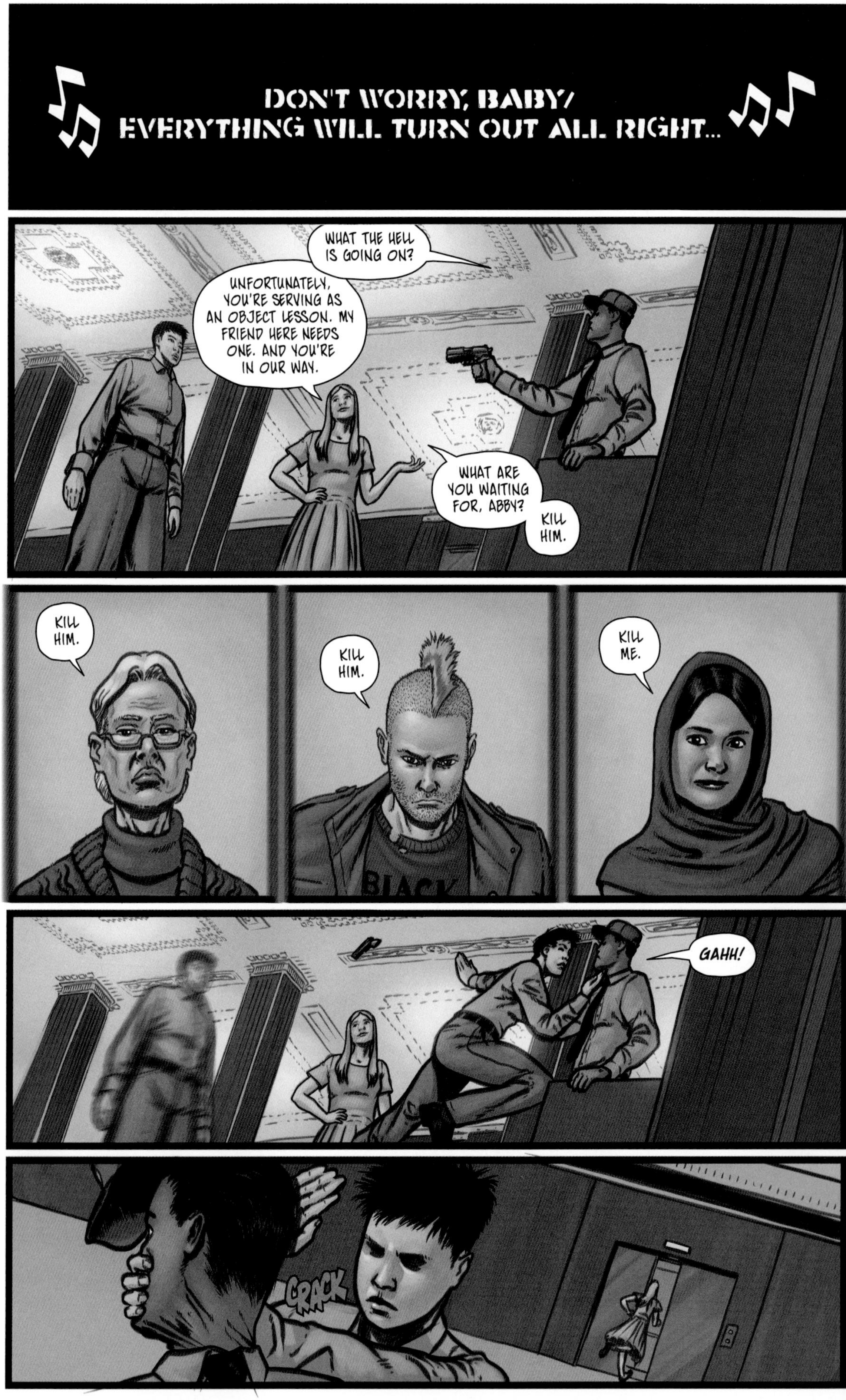
DON'T WORRY, BABY/
EVERYTHING WILL TURN OUT ALL RIGHT...
WHAT THE HELL IS GOING ON?
UNFORTUNATELY, YOU'RE SERVING AS AN OBJECT LESSON. MY FRIEND HERE NEEDS ONE. AND YOU'RE IN OUR WAY.
WHAT ARE YOU WAITING FOR, ABBY?
KILL HIM.
KILL HIM.
KILL HIM.
KILL ME.
GAHH!
CRACK

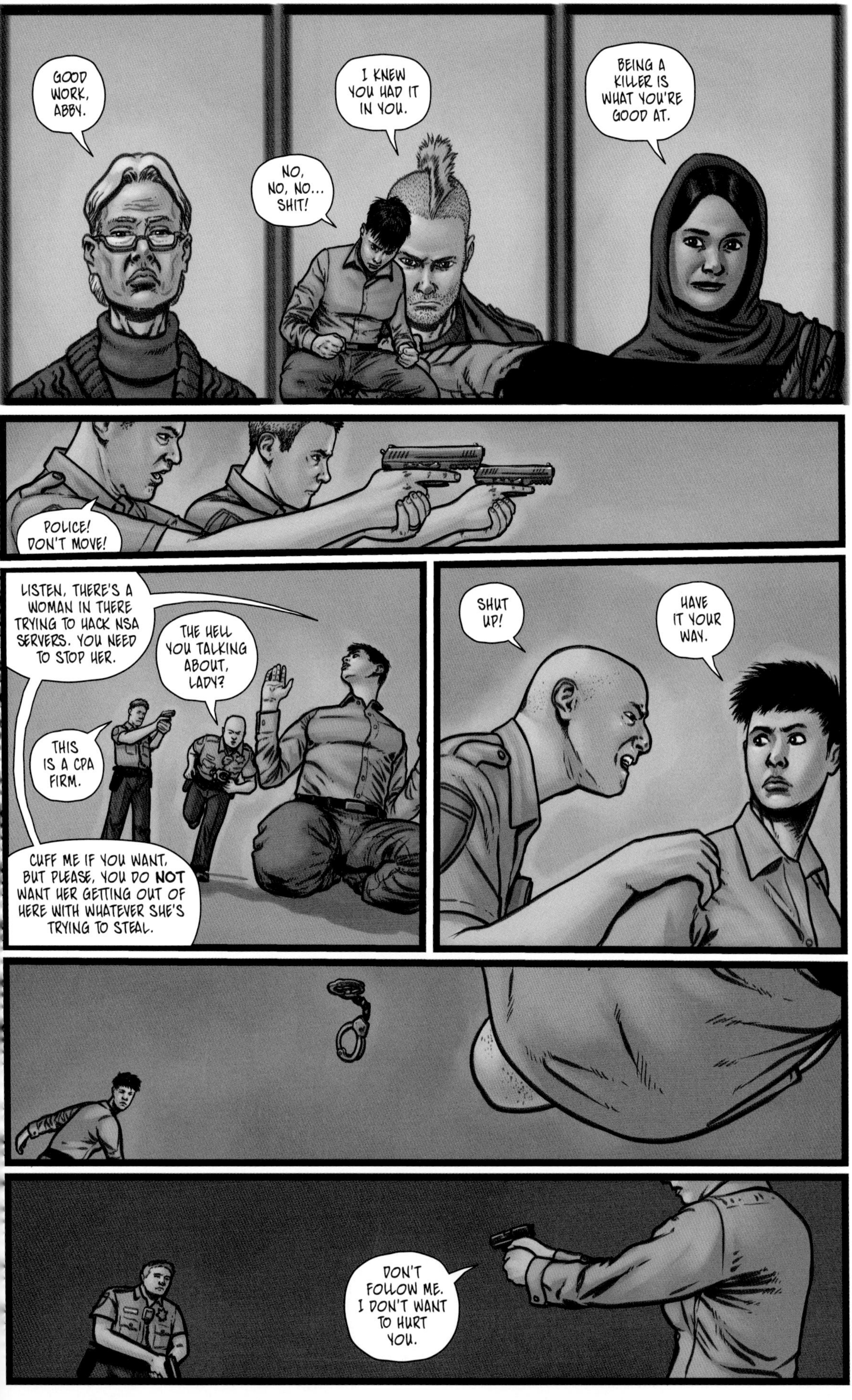
GOOD WORK, ABBY.
I KNEW YOU HAD IT IN YOU.
NO, NO, NO... SHIT!
BEING A KILLER IS WHAT YOU'RE GOOD AT.
POLICE! DON'T MOVE!
LISTEN, THERE'S A WOMAN IN THERE TRYING TO HACK NSA SERVERS. YOU NEED TO STOP HER.
THE HELL YOU TALKING ABOUT, LADY?
THIS IS A CPA FIRM.
CUFF ME IF YOU WANT, BUT PLEASE, YOU DO **NOT** WANT HER GETTING OUT OF HERE WITH WHATEVER SHE'S TRYING TO STEAL.
SHUT UP!
HAVE IT YOUR WAY.
DON'T FOLLOW ME. I DON'T WANT TO HURT YOU.

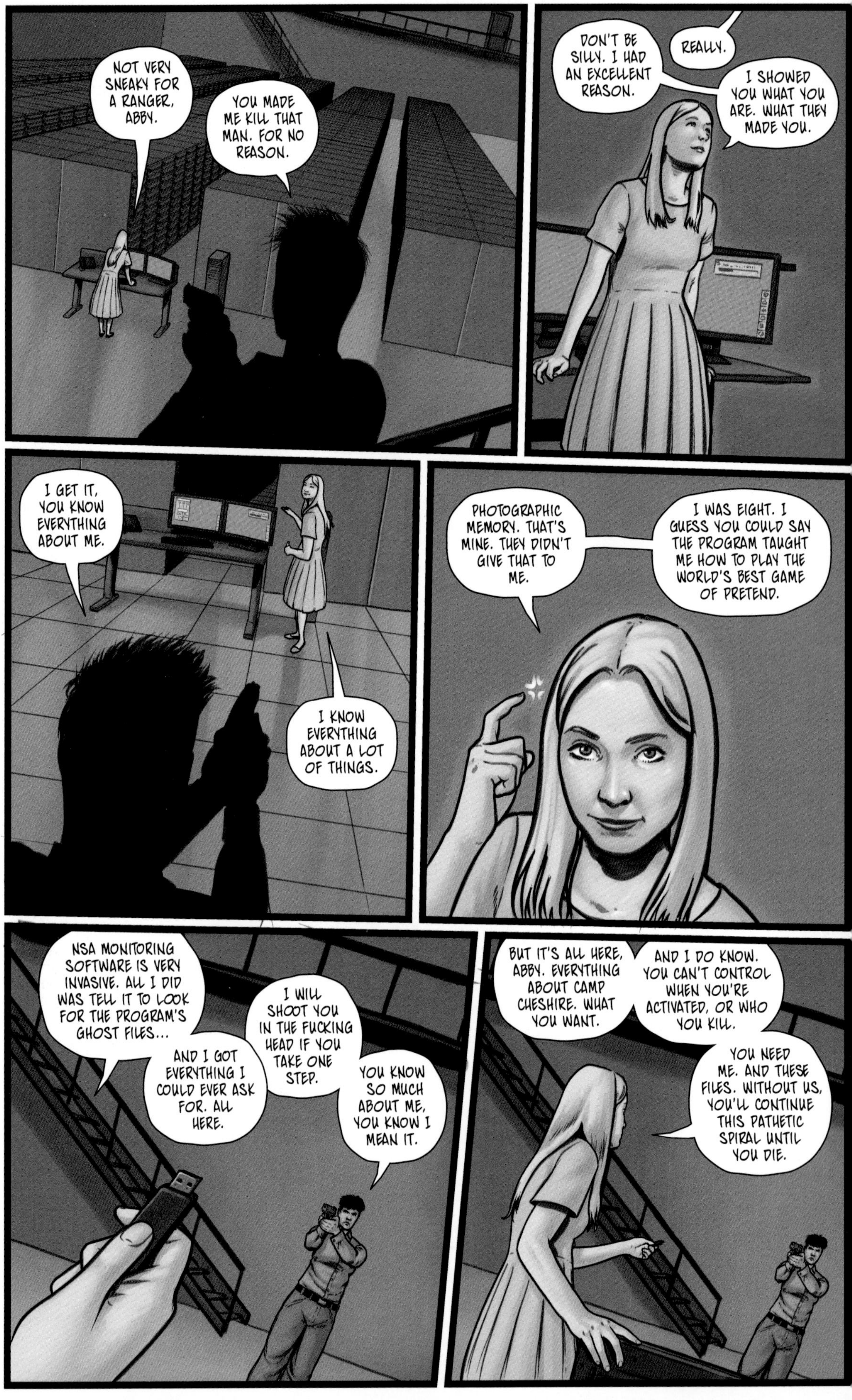

NOT VERY SNEAKY FOR A RANGER, ABBY.
YOU MADE ME KILL THAT MAN. FOR NO REASON.
DON'T BE SILLY. I HAD AN EXCELLENT REASON.
REALLY.
I SHOWED YOU WHAT YOU ARE. WHAT THEY MADE YOU.
I GET IT, YOU KNOW EVERYTHING ABOUT ME.
I KNOW EVERYTHING ABOUT A LOT OF THINGS.
PHOTOGRAPHIC MEMORY. THAT'S MINE. THEY DIDN'T GIVE THAT TO ME.
I WAS EIGHT. I GUESS YOU COULD SAY THE PROGRAM TAUGHT ME HOW TO PLAY THE WORLD'S BEST GAME OF PRETEND.
NSA MONITORING SOFTWARE IS VERY INVASIVE. ALL I DID WAS TELL IT TO LOOK FOR THE PROGRAM'S GHOST FILES...
AND I GOT EVERYTHING I COULD EVER ASK FOR. ALL HERE.
I WILL SHOOT YOU IN THE FUCKING HEAD IF YOU TAKE ONE STEP.
YOU KNOW SO MUCH ABOUT ME, YOU KNOW I MEAN IT.
BUT IT'S ALL HERE, ABBY. EVERYTHING ABOUT CAMP CHESHIRE. WHAT YOU WANT.
AND I DO KNOW. YOU CAN'T CONTROL WHEN YOU'RE ACTIVATED, OR WHO YOU KILL.
YOU NEED ME. AND THESE FILES. WITHOUT US, YOU'LL CONTINUE THIS PATHETIC SPIRAL UNTIL YOU DIE.

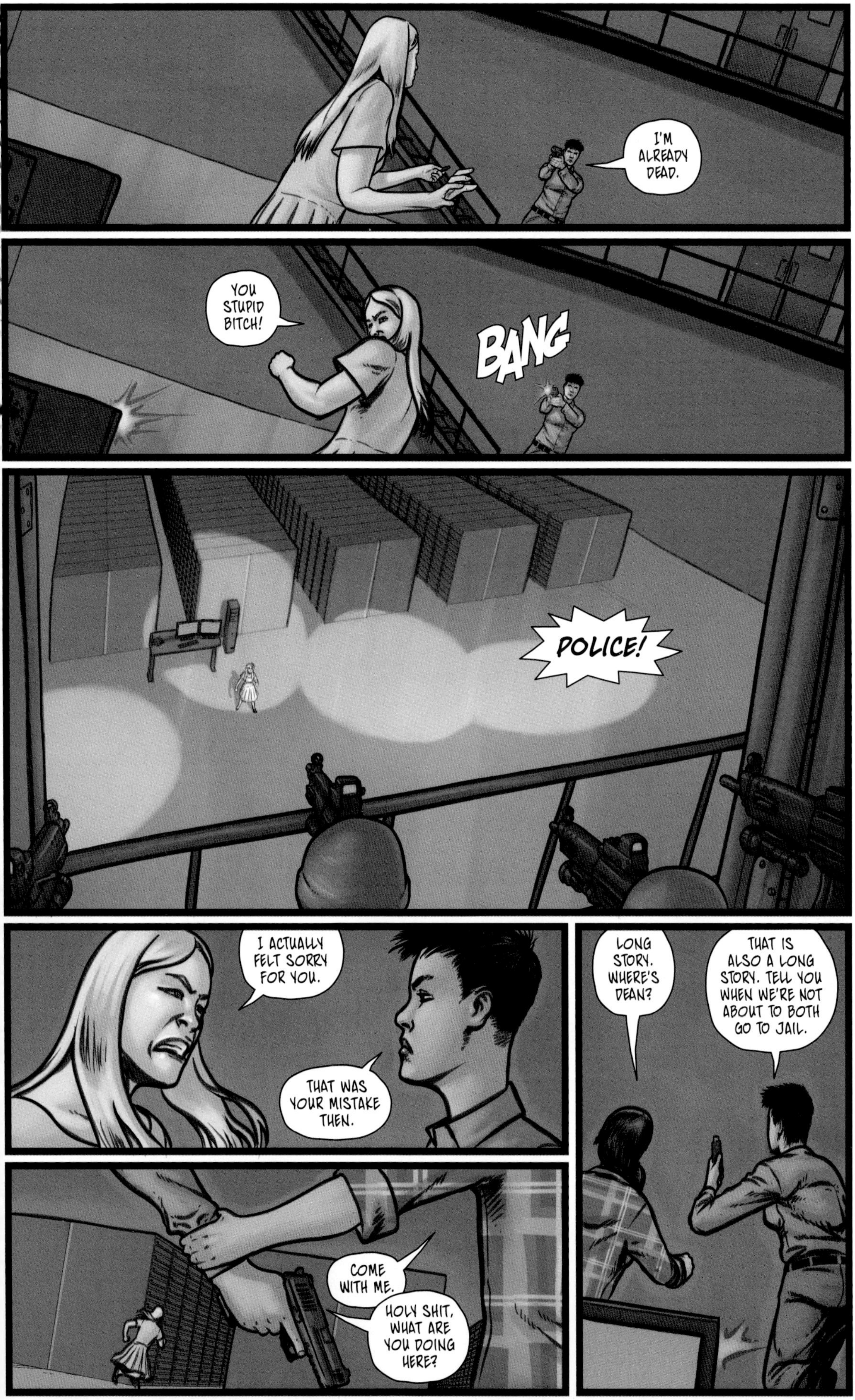
I'M ALREADY DEAD.
YOU STUPID BITCH!
BANG
POLICE!
I ACTUALLY FELT SORRY FOR YOU.
THAT WAS YOUR MISTAKE THEN.
COME WITH ME.
HOLY SHIT, WHAT ARE YOU DOING HERE?
LONG STORY. WHERE'S DEAN?
THAT IS ALSO A LONG STORY. TELL YOU WHEN WE'RE NOT ABOUT TO BOTH GO TO JAIL.

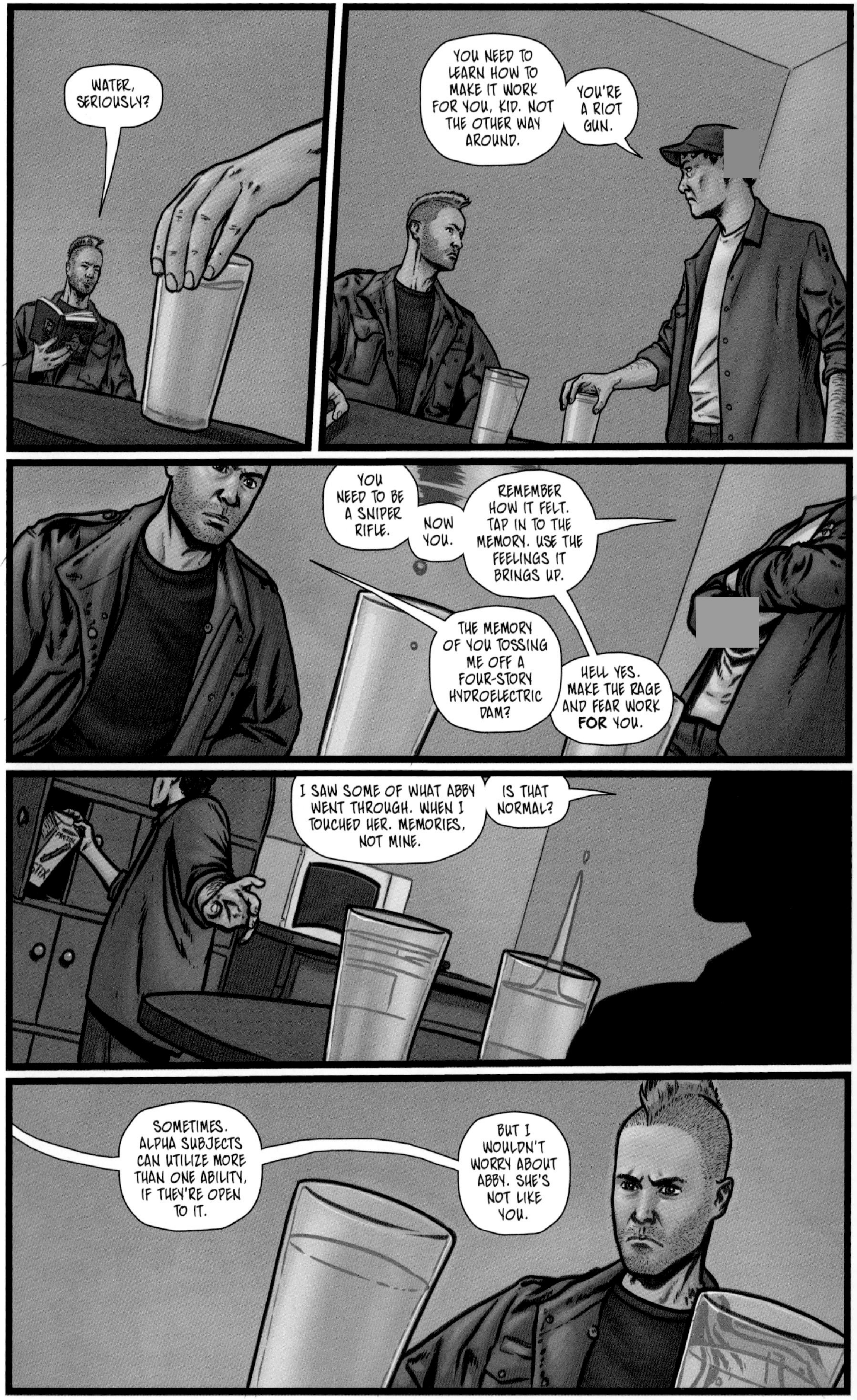
WATER, SERIOUSLY?
YOU NEED TO LEARN HOW TO MAKE IT WORK FOR YOU, KID. NOT THE OTHER WAY AROUND.
YOU'RE A RIOT GUN.
YOU NEED TO BE A SNIPER RIFLE.
NOW YOU.
REMEMBER HOW IT FELT. TAP IN TO THE MEMORY. USE THE FEELINGS IT BRINGS UP.
THE MEMORY OF YOU TOSSING ME OFF A FOUR-STORY HYDROELECTRIC DAM?
HELL YES. MAKE THE RAGE AND FEAR WORK **FOR** YOU.
I SAW SOME OF WHAT ABBY WENT THROUGH. WHEN I TOUCHED HER. MEMORIES, NOT MINE.
IS THAT NORMAL?
SOMETIMES. ALPHA SUBJECTS CAN UTILIZE MORE THAN ONE ABILITY, IF THEY'RE OPEN TO IT.
BUT I WOULDN'T WORRY ABOUT ABBY. SHE'S NOT LIKE YOU.

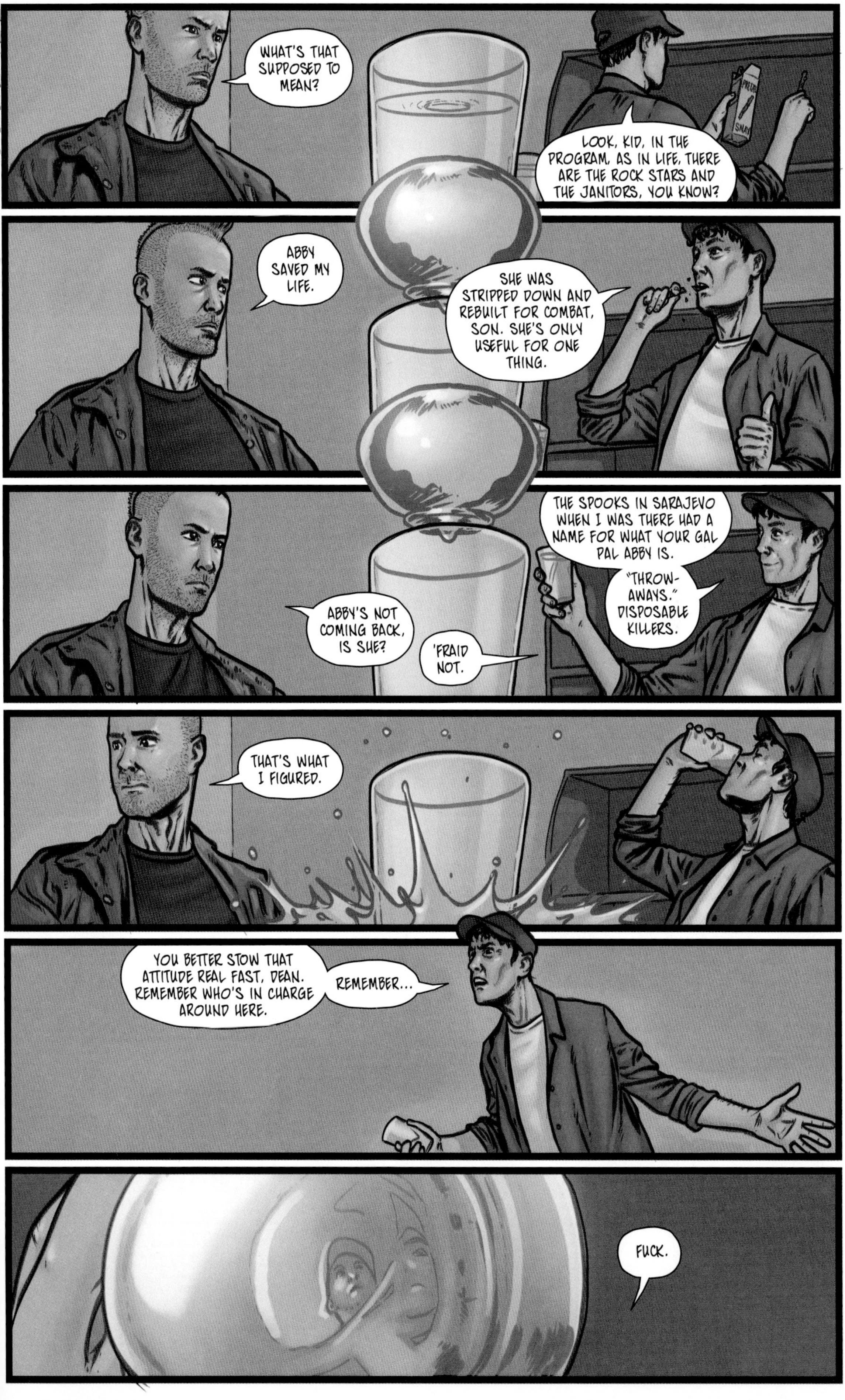
WHAT'S THAT SUPPOSED TO MEAN?
LOOK, KID, IN THE PROGRAM, AS IN LIFE, THERE ARE THE ROCK STARS AND THE JANITORS, YOU KNOW?
ABBY SAVED MY LIFE.
SHE WAS STRIPPED DOWN AND REBUILT FOR COMBAT, SON. SHE'S ONLY USEFUL FOR ONE THING.
THE SPOOKS IN SARAJEVO WHEN I WAS THERE HAD A NAME FOR WHAT YOUR GAL PAL ABBY IS.
"THROW-AWAYS." DISPOSABLE KILLERS.
ABBY'S NOT COMING BACK, IS SHE?
'FRAID NOT.
THAT'S WHAT I FIGURED.
YOU BETTER STOW THAT ATTITUDE REAL FAST, DEAN. REMEMBER WHO'S IN CHARGE AROUND HERE.
REMEMBER...
FUCK.

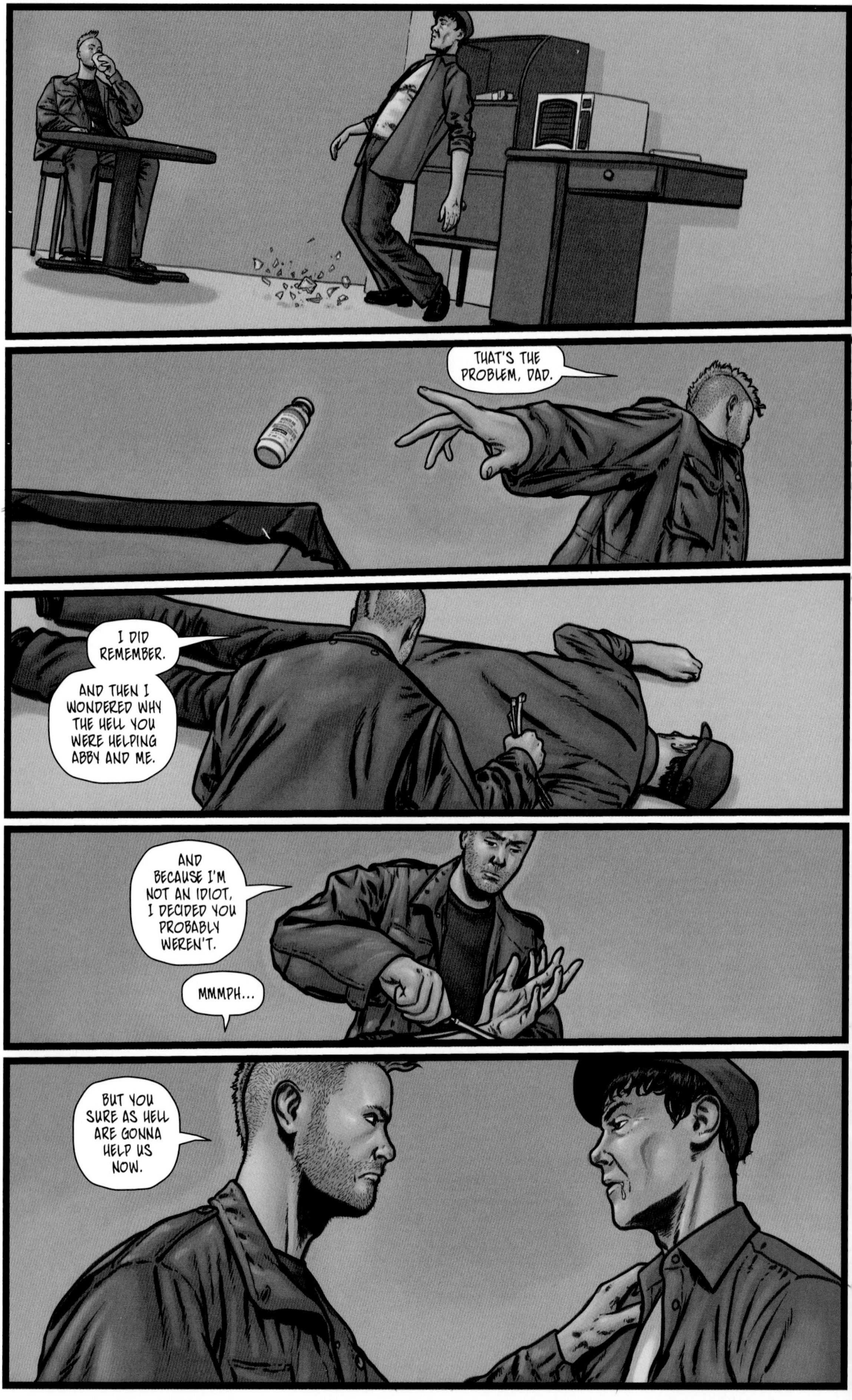
THAT'S THE PROBLEM, DAD.
I DID REMEMBER.
AND THEN I WONDERED WHY THE HELL YOU WERE HELPING ABBY AND ME.
AND BECAUSE I'M NOT AN IDIOT, I DECIDED YOU PROBABLY WEREN'T.
MMMPH...
BUT YOU SURE AS HELL ARE GONNA HELP US NOW.

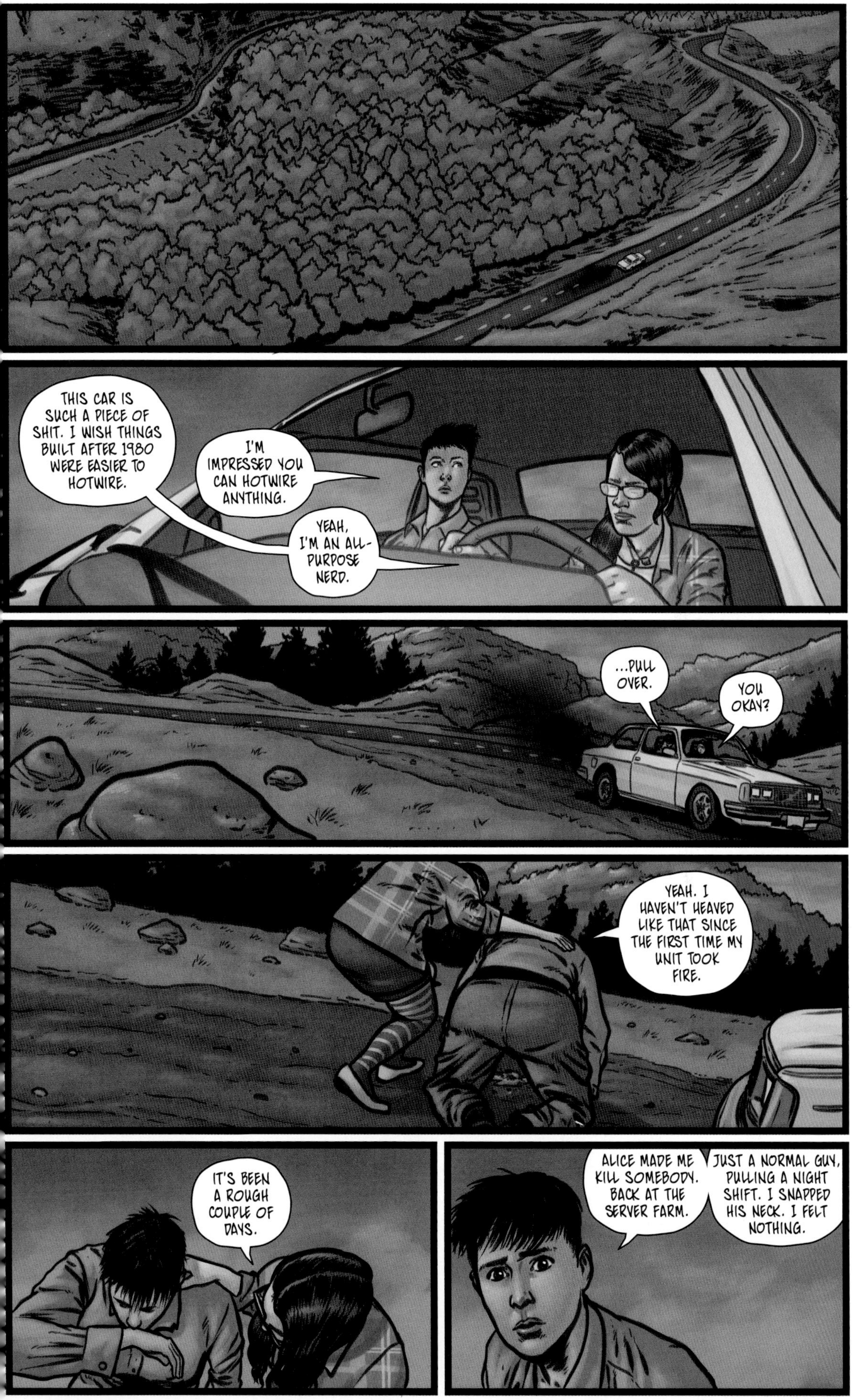
THIS CAR IS SUCH A PIECE OF SHIT. I WISH THINGS BUILT AFTER 1980 WERE EASIER TO HOTWIRE.
I'M IMPRESSED YOU CAN HOTWIRE ANYTHING.
YEAH, I'M AN ALL-PURPOSE NERD.
...PULL OVER.
YOU OKAY?
YEAH. I HAVEN'T HEAVED LIKE THAT SINCE THE FIRST TIME MY UNIT TOOK FIRE.
IT'S BEEN A ROUGH COUPLE OF DAYS.
ALICE MADE ME KILL SOMEBODY. BACK AT THE SERVER FARM.
JUST A NORMAL GUY, PULLING A NIGHT SHIFT. I SNAPPED HIS NECK. I FELT NOTHING.

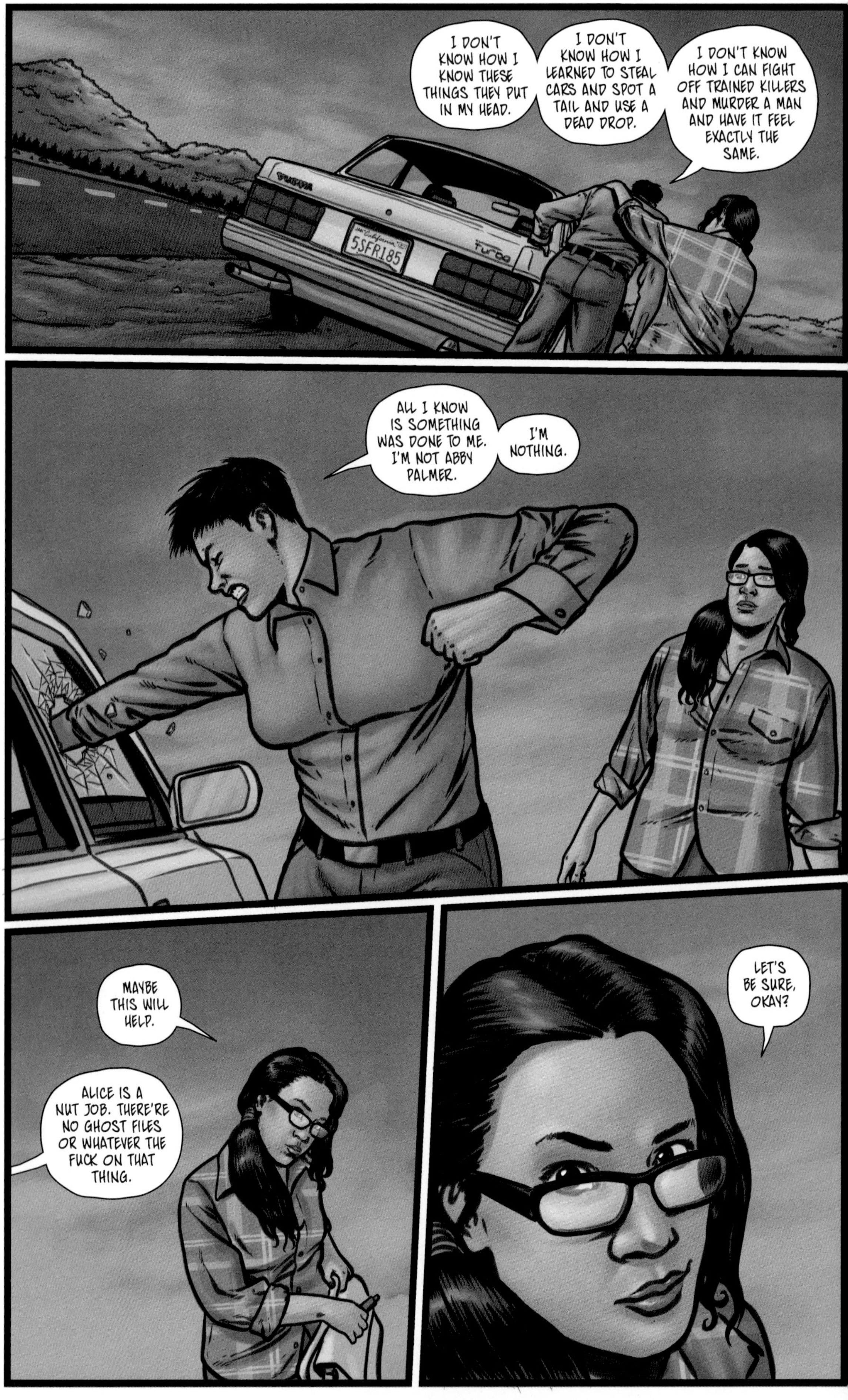
I DON'T KNOW HOW I KNOW THESE THINGS THEY PUT IN MY HEAD.
I DON'T KNOW HOW I LEARNED TO STEAL CARS AND SPOT A TAIL AND USE A DEAD DROP.
I DON'T KNOW HOW I CAN FIGHT OFF TRAINED KILLERS AND MURDER A MAN AND HAVE IT FEEL EXACTLY THE SAME.
5SFR185
ALL I KNOW IS SOMETHING WAS DONE TO ME. I'M NOT ABBY PALMER.
I'M NOTHING.
MAYBE THIS WILL HELP.
ALICE IS A NUT JOB. THERE'RE NO GHOST FILES OR WHATEVER THE FUCK ON THAT THING.
LET'S BE SURE, OKAY?

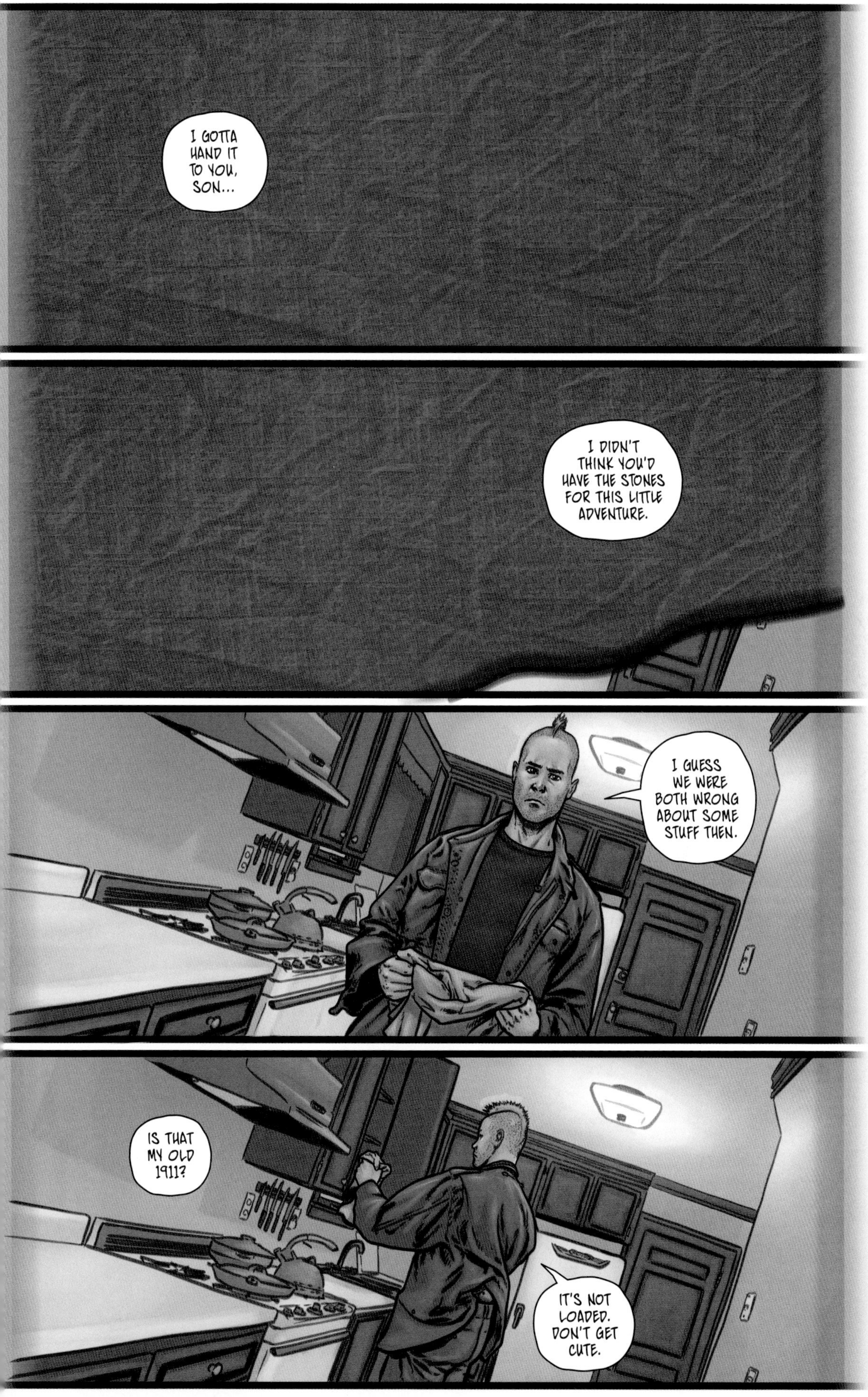
I GOTTA HAND IT TO YOU, SON...
I DIDN'T THINK YOU'D HAVE THE STONES FOR THIS LITTLE ADVENTURE.
I GUESS WE WERE BOTH WRONG ABOUT SOME STUFF THEN.
IS THAT MY OLD 1911?
IT'S NOT LOADED. DON'T GET CUTE.

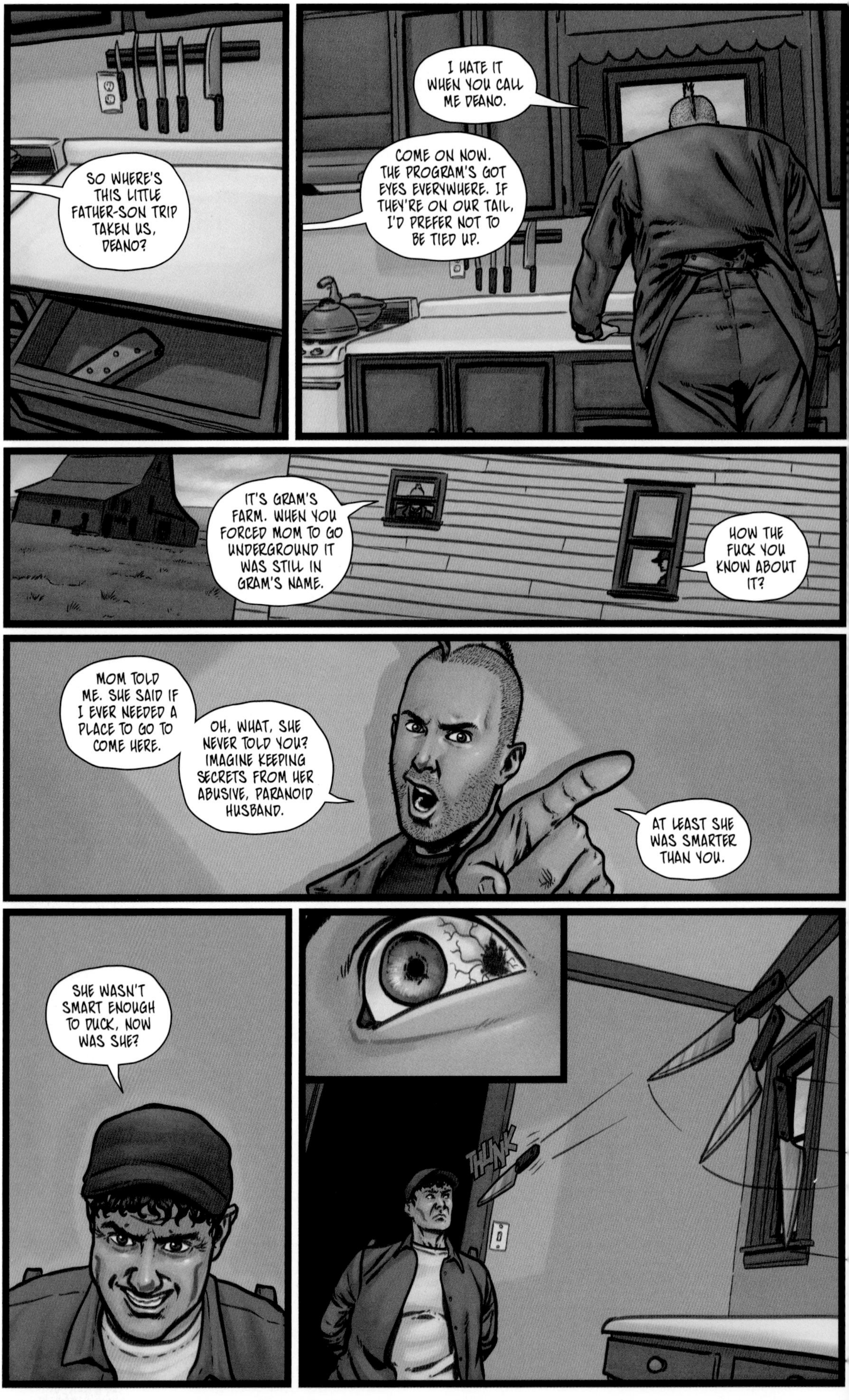
SO WHERE'S THIS LITTLE FATHER-SON TRIP TAKEN US, DEANO?
I HATE IT WHEN YOU CALL ME DEANO.
COME ON NOW. THE PROGRAM'S GOT EYES EVERYWHERE. IF THEY'RE ON OUR TAIL, I'D PREFER NOT TO BE TIED UP.
IT'S GRAM'S FARM. WHEN YOU FORCED MOM TO GO UNDERGROUND IT WAS STILL IN GRAM'S NAME.
HOW THE FUCK YOU KNOW ABOUT IT?
MOM TOLD ME. SHE SAID IF I EVER NEEDED A PLACE TO GO TO COME HERE.
OH, WHAT, SHE NEVER TOLD YOU? IMAGINE KEEPING SECRETS FROM HER ABUSIVE, PARANOID HUSBAND.
AT LEAST SHE WAS SMARTER THAN YOU.
SHE WASN'T SMART ENOUGH TO DUCK, NOW WAS SHE?
THUNK

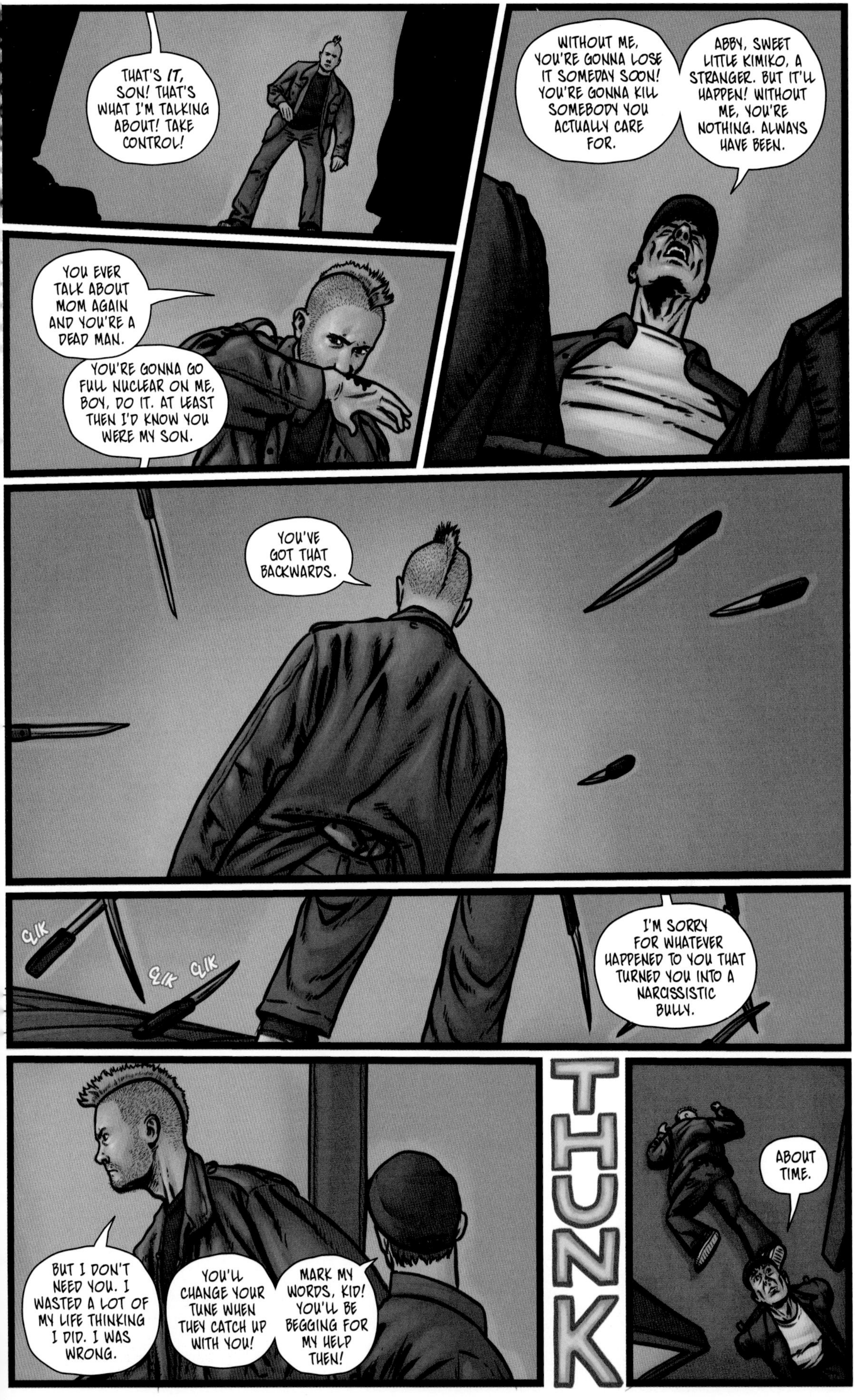
THAT'S IT, SON! THAT'S WHAT I'M TALKING ABOUT! TAKE CONTROL!
WITHOUT ME, YOU'RE GONNA LOSE IT SOMEDAY SOON! YOU'RE GONNA KILL SOMEBODY YOU ACTUALLY CARE FOR.
ABBY, SWEET LITTLE KIMIKO, A STRANGER. BUT IT'LL HAPPEN! WITHOUT ME, YOU'RE NOTHING. ALWAYS HAVE BEEN.
YOU EVER TALK ABOUT MOM AGAIN AND YOU'RE A DEAD MAN.
YOU'RE GONNA GO FULL NUCLEAR ON ME, BOY, DO IT. AT LEAST THEN I'D KNOW YOU WERE MY SON.
YOU'VE GOT THAT BACKWARDS.
CLIK
CLIK
CLIK
I'M SORRY FOR WHATEVER HAPPENED TO YOU THAT TURNED YOU INTO A NARCISSISTIC BULLY.
BUT I DON'T NEED YOU. I WASTED A LOT OF MY LIFE THINKING I DID. I WAS WRONG.
YOU'LL CHANGE YOUR TUNE WHEN THEY CATCH UP WITH YOU!
MARK MY WORDS, KID! YOU'LL BE BEGGING FOR MY HELP THEN!
THUNK
ABOUT TIME.

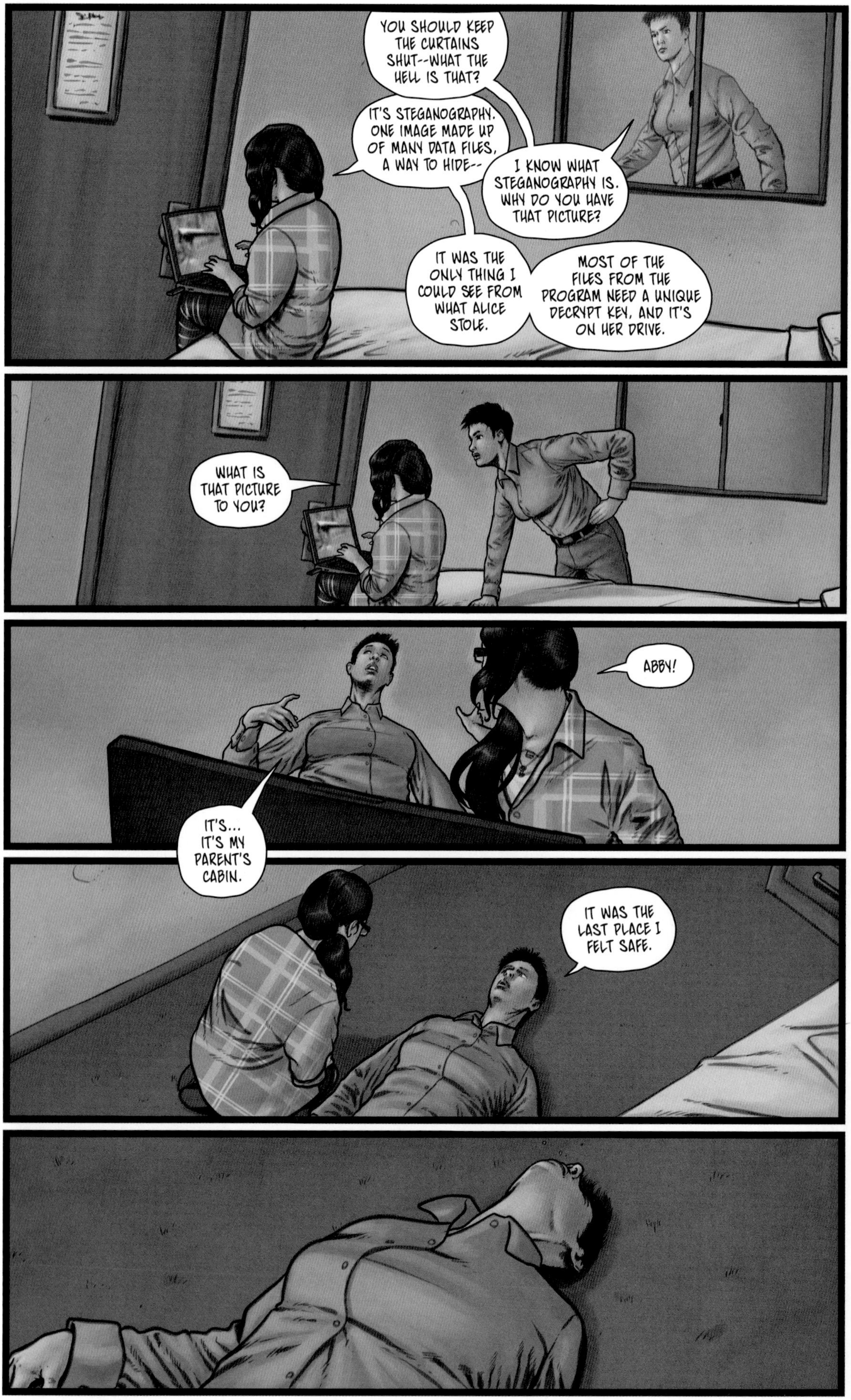
YOU SHOULD KEEP THE CURTAINS SHUT--WHAT THE HELL IS THAT?
IT'S STEGANOGRAPHY. ONE IMAGE MADE UP OF MANY DATA FILES, A WAY TO HIDE--
I KNOW WHAT STEGANOGRAPHY IS. WHY DO YOU HAVE THAT PICTURE?
IT WAS THE ONLY THING I COULD SEE FROM WHAT ALICE STOLE.
MOST OF THE FILES FROM THE PROGRAM NEED A UNIQUE DECRYPT KEY, AND IT'S ON HER DRIVE.
WHAT IS THAT PICTURE TO YOU?
ABBY!
IT'S... IT'S MY PARENT'S CABIN.
IT WAS THE LAST PLACE I FELT SAFE.

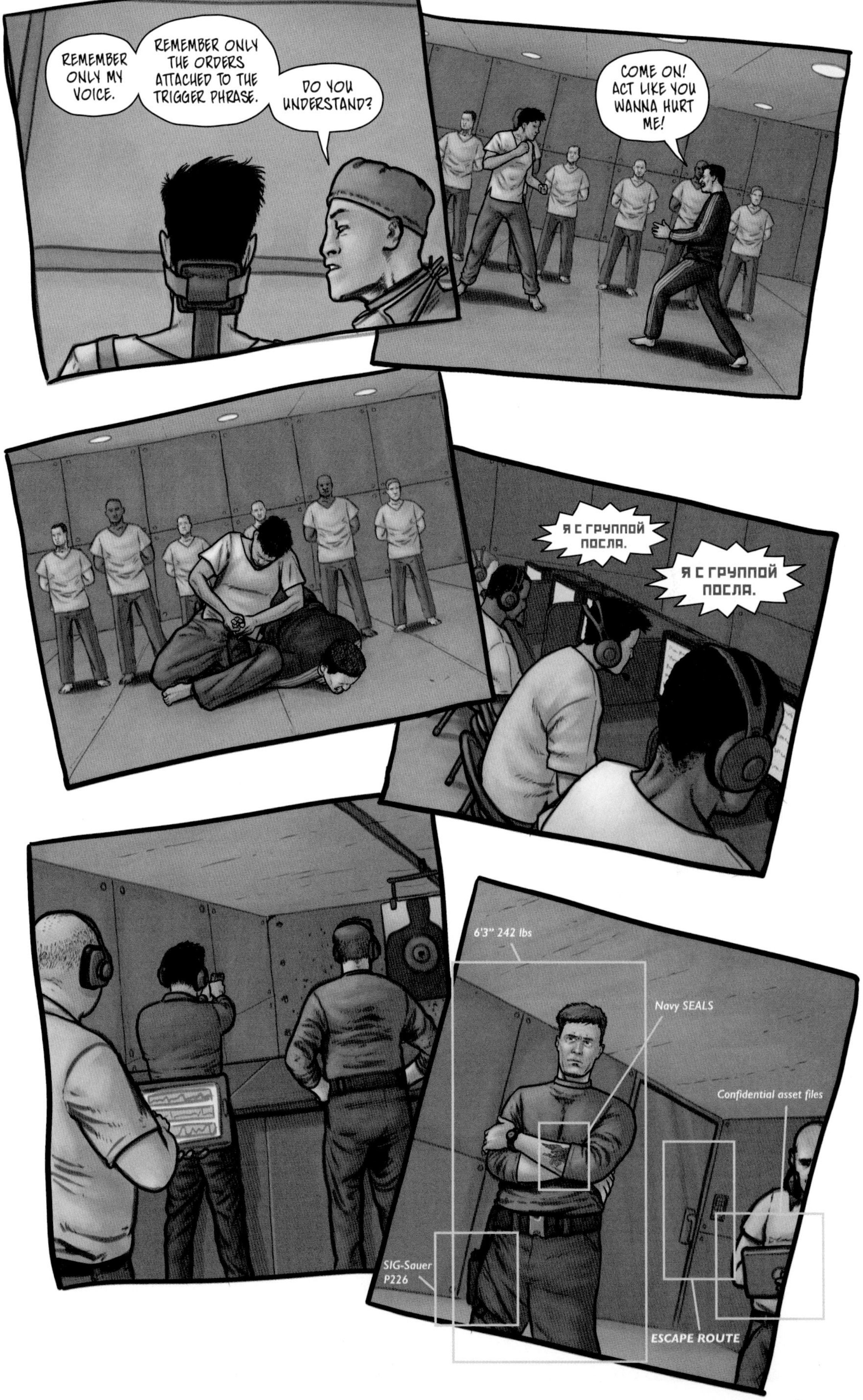
REMEMBER ONLY MY VOICE.
REMEMBER ONLY THE ORDERS ATTACHED TO THE TRIGGER PHRASE.
DO YOU UNDERSTAND?
COME ON! ACT LIKE YOU WANNA HURT ME!
Я С ГРУППОЙ ПОСЛА.
Я С ГРУППОЙ ПОСЛА.
6'3" 242 lbs
Navy SEALS
Confidential asset files
SIG-Sauer P226
ESCAPE ROUTE

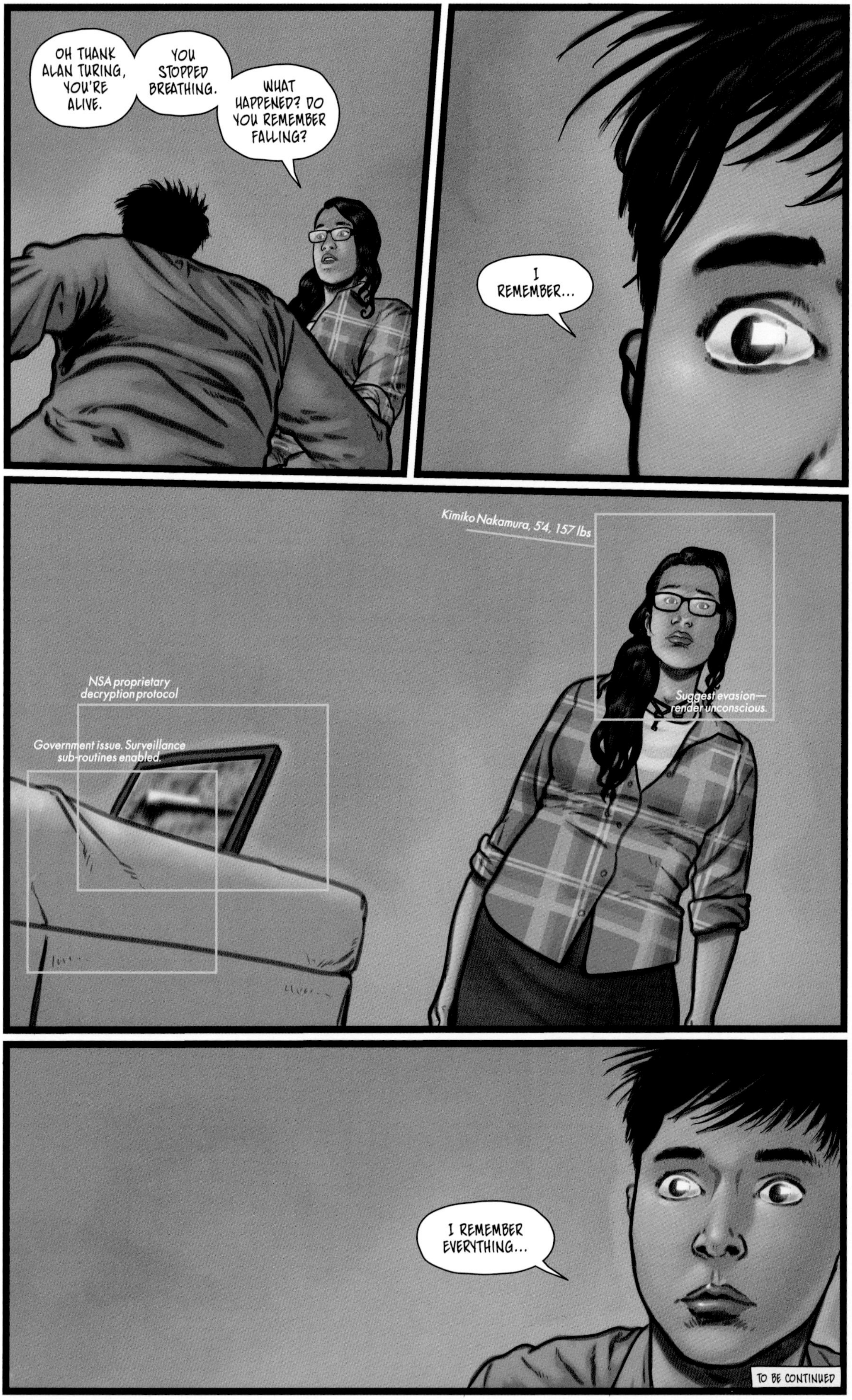
OH THANK ALAN TURING, YOU'RE ALIVE.
YOU STOPPED BREATHING.
WHAT HAPPENED? DO YOU REMEMBER FALLING?
I REMEMBER...
Kimiko Nakamura, 5'4, 157 lbs
Suggest evasion— render unconscious.
NSA proprietary decryption protocol
Government issue. Surveillance sub-routines enabled.
I REMEMBER EVERYTHING...
TO BE CONTINUED

EXTRAS

—Character Designs

—Image Expo 2016 Poster

—San Diego Comic-Con 2016 Exclusive Variant

—Issue #1, Pages 5-7, Script to Story

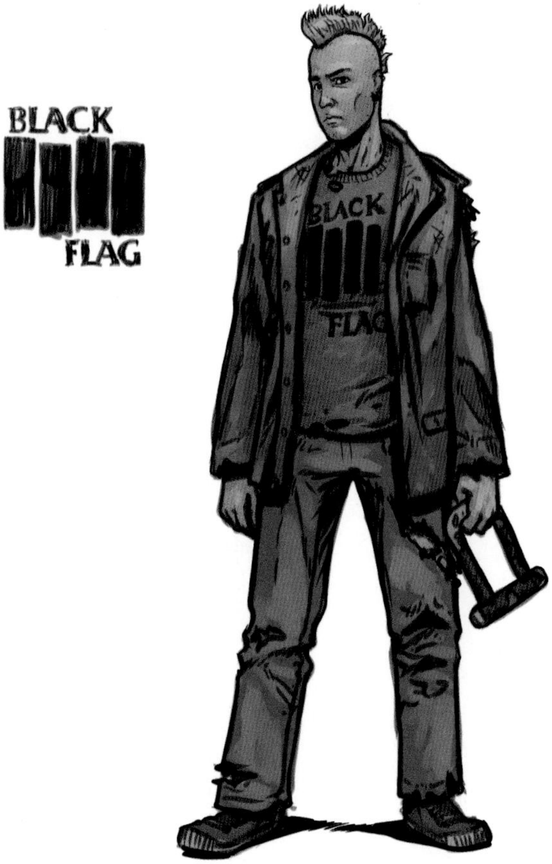
BLACK
FLAG
BLACK
FLAG

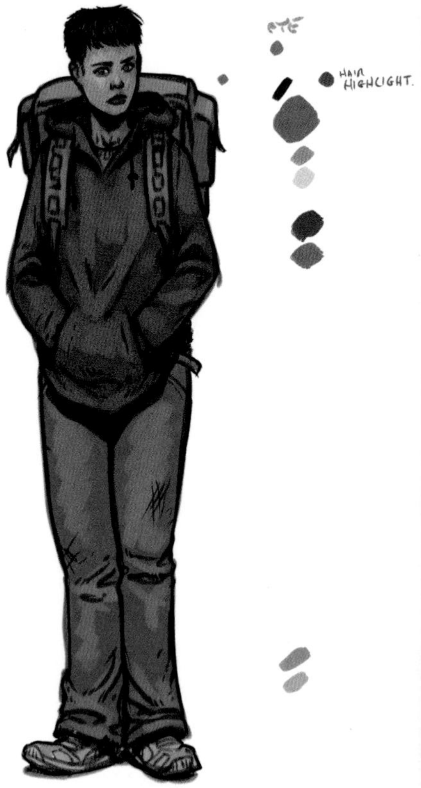
EYE
HAIR
HIGHLIGHT.

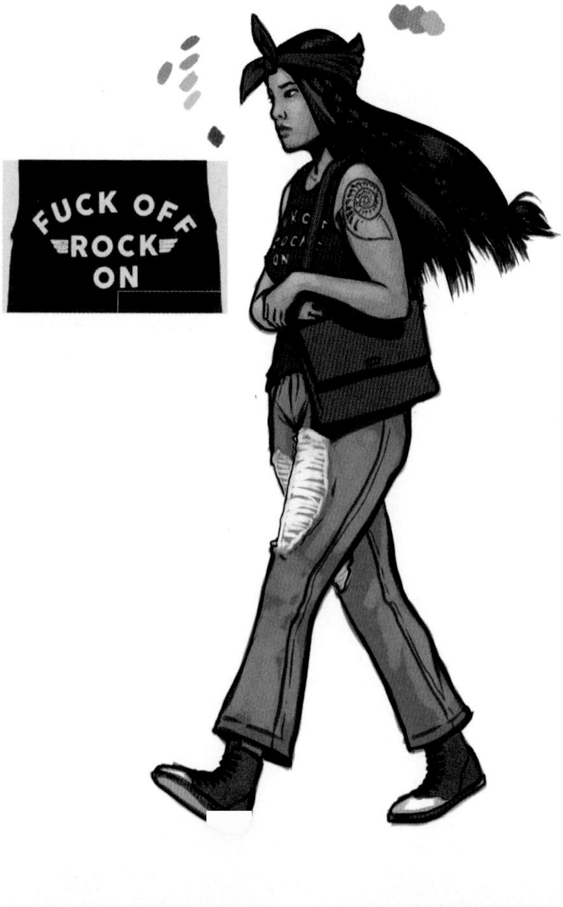
FUCK OFF
ROCK
ON

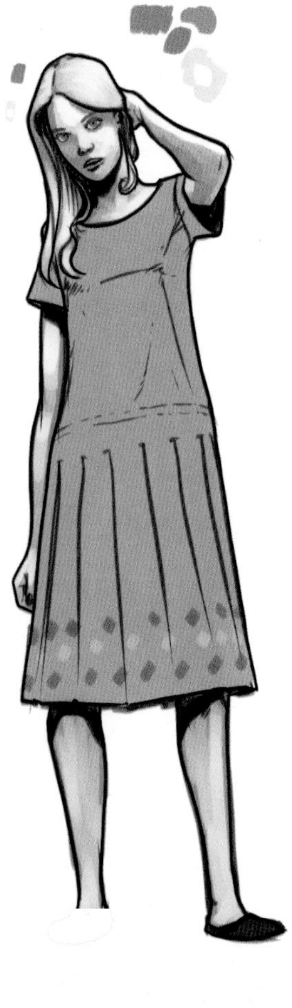

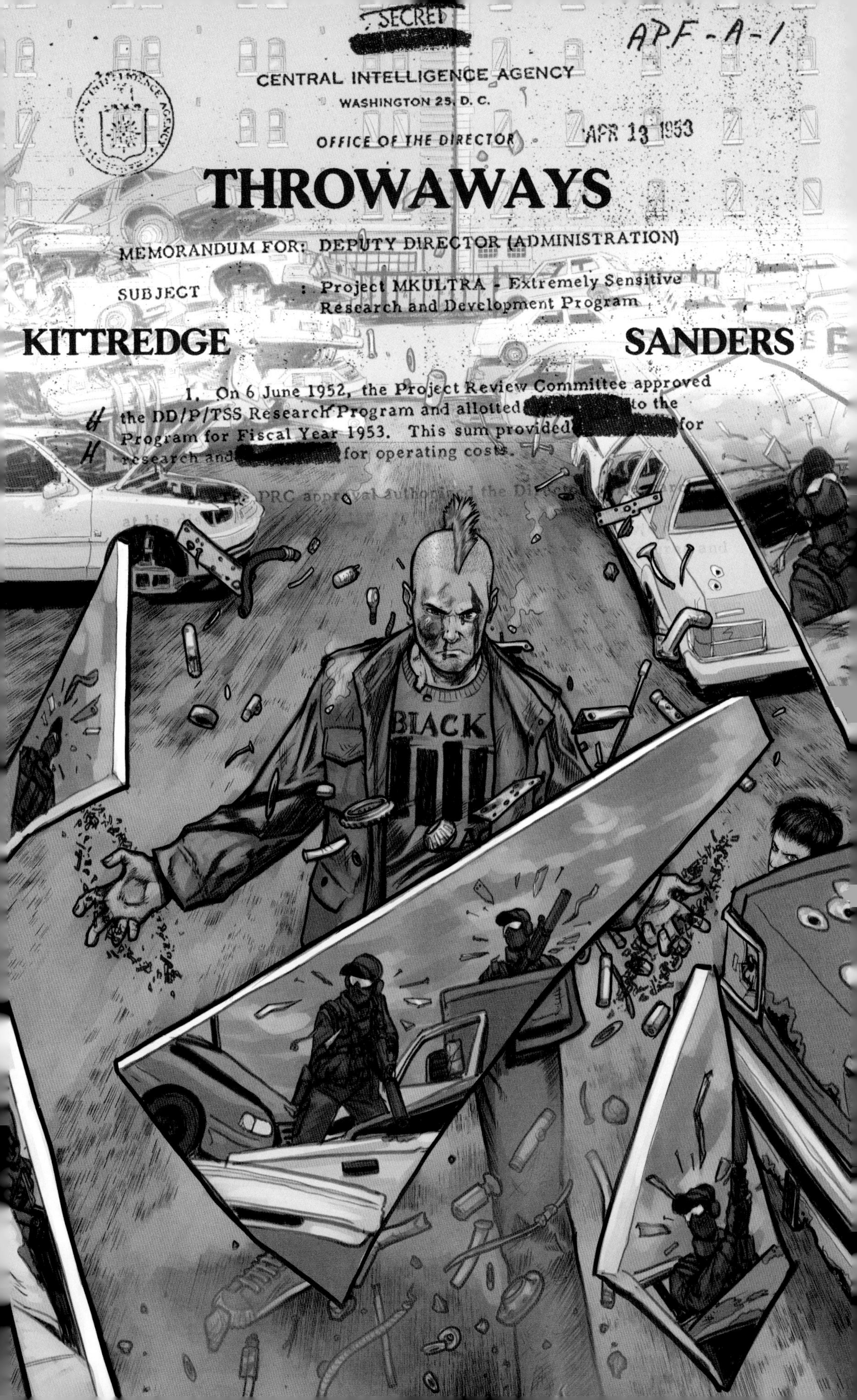
SECRET
[redacted]
APF-A-1
CENTRAL INTELLIGENCE AGENCY
WASHINGTON 25, D. C.
OFFICE OF THE DIRECTOR
APR 13 1953
THROWAWAYS
MEMORANDUM FOR: DEPUTY DIRECTOR (ADMINISTRATION)
SUBJECT : Project MKULTRA - Extremely Sensitive Research and Development Program
KITTREDGE
SANDERS
1. On 6 June 1952, the Project Review Committee approved the DD/P/TSS Research Program and allotted [redacted] to the Program for Fiscal Year 1953. This sum provided [redacted] for research and [redacted] for operating costs.
BLACK

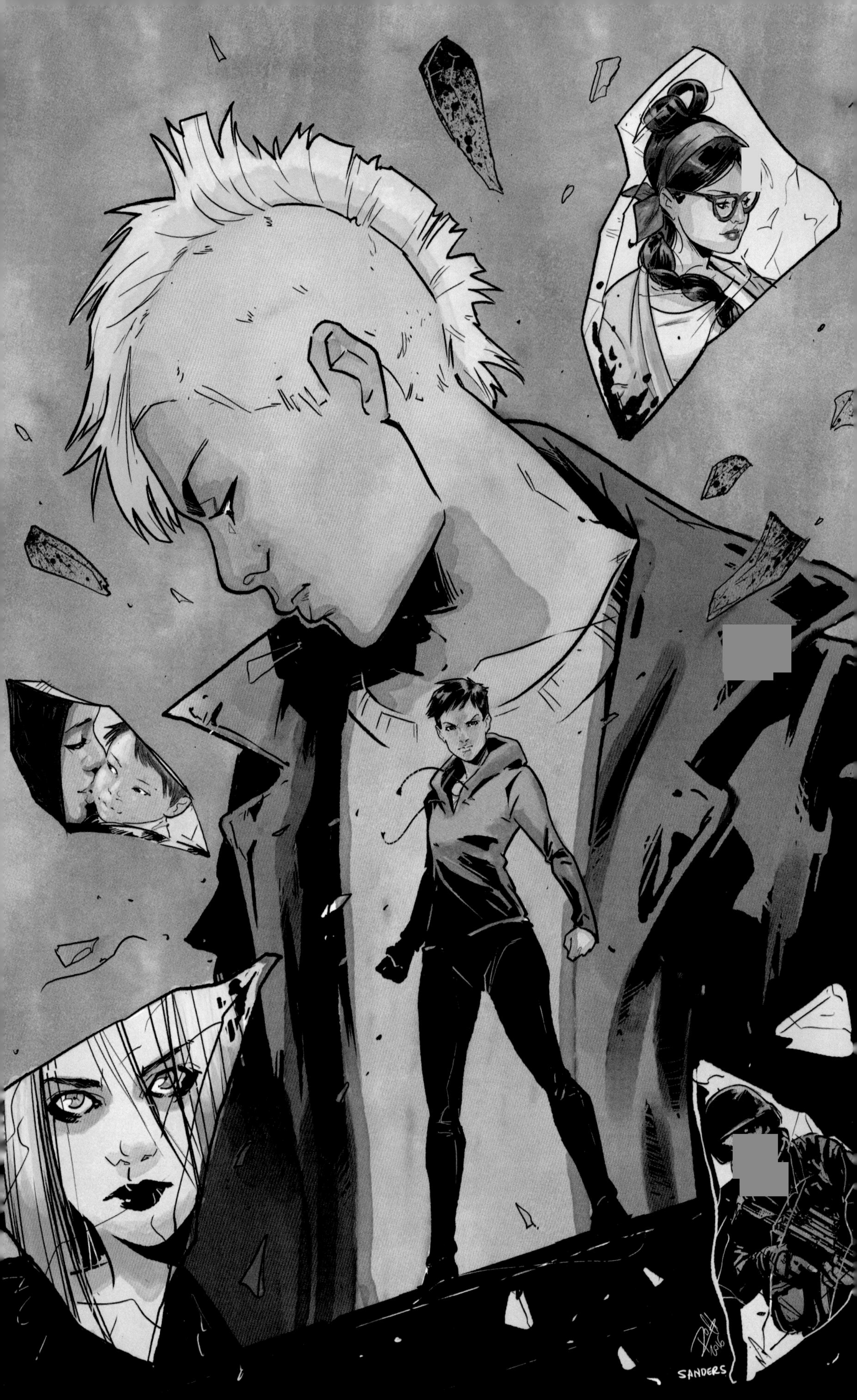
SANDERS

SCRIPT TO STORY

There's often a lot of changes that happen as part of the process of collaboration in comics. We thought you might find these pages to be an interesting behind-the-scenes peek.

PAGE 5

Panel 1
Charles stares ahead for just a moment, the phone sliding from his grasp, as Hanson looks on with concern.

HANSON
Captain Crandall? Everything five by five?

Panel 2
Charles stands, still staring, a gun coming from under his shirt.

HANSON
What are you--

Panel 3
Charles shoots Hanson directly between the eyes. The poor gunny is knocked backwards off his chair, blood and brains flying.

SFX
BLAM!

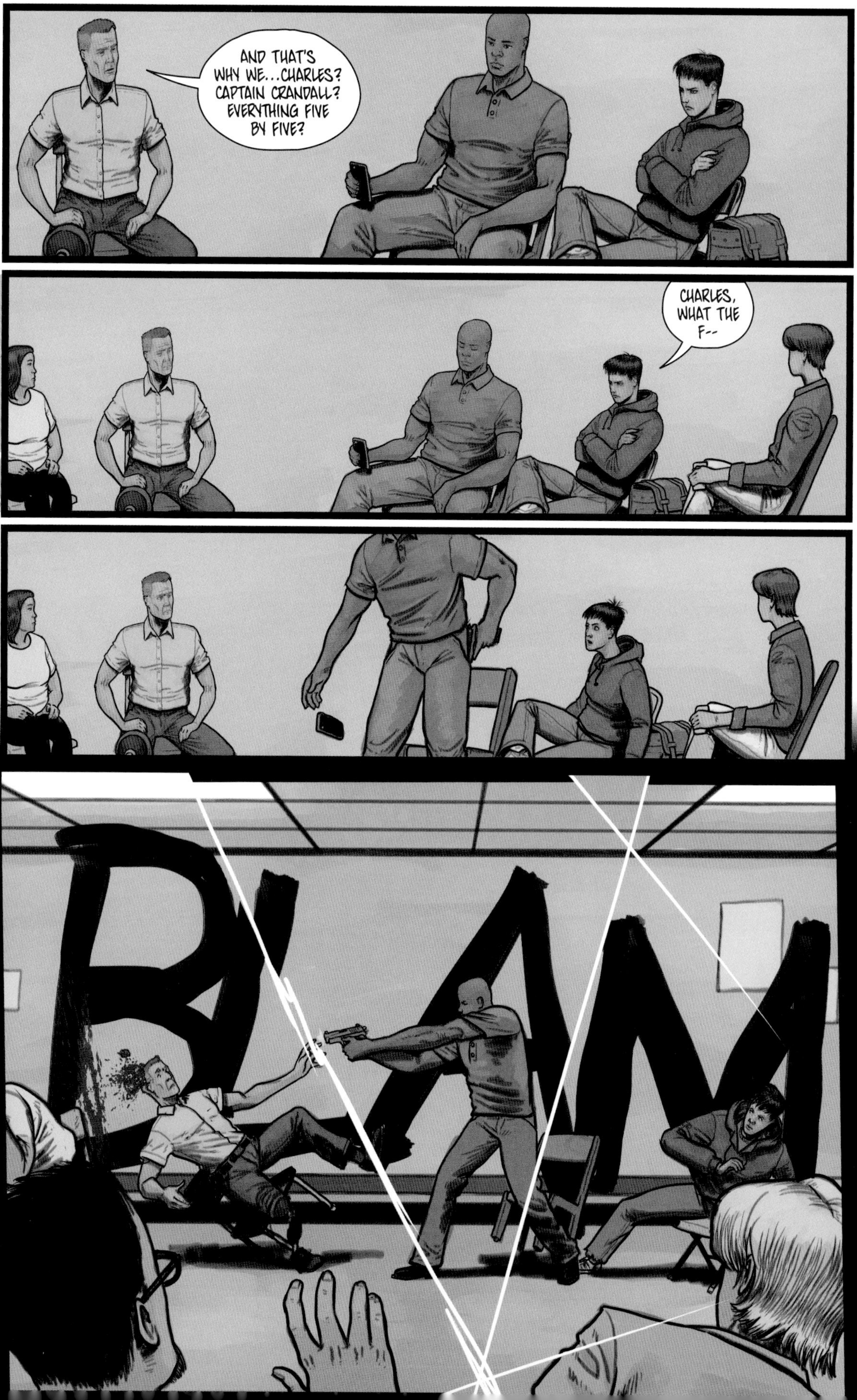
AND THAT'S WHY WE...CHARLES? CAPTAIN CRANDALL? EVERYTHING FIVE BY FIVE?
CHARLES, WHAT THE F--
BLAM

PAGE 6

Panels 1-4
No copy. With precision and calmness, Charles aims and executes four more members of the group—everyone except Abby, who cowers behind a chair.

SFX:
BLAM
BLAM
BLAM

Panel 6
Charles raises the gun and aims at Abby, who is on her knees and one hand, the other held up in supplication. A pool of blood creeps close to her splayed hand.

CHARLES
Stop staring at me.

ABBY
You're gonna have to look at me, Charles. Just do it already.

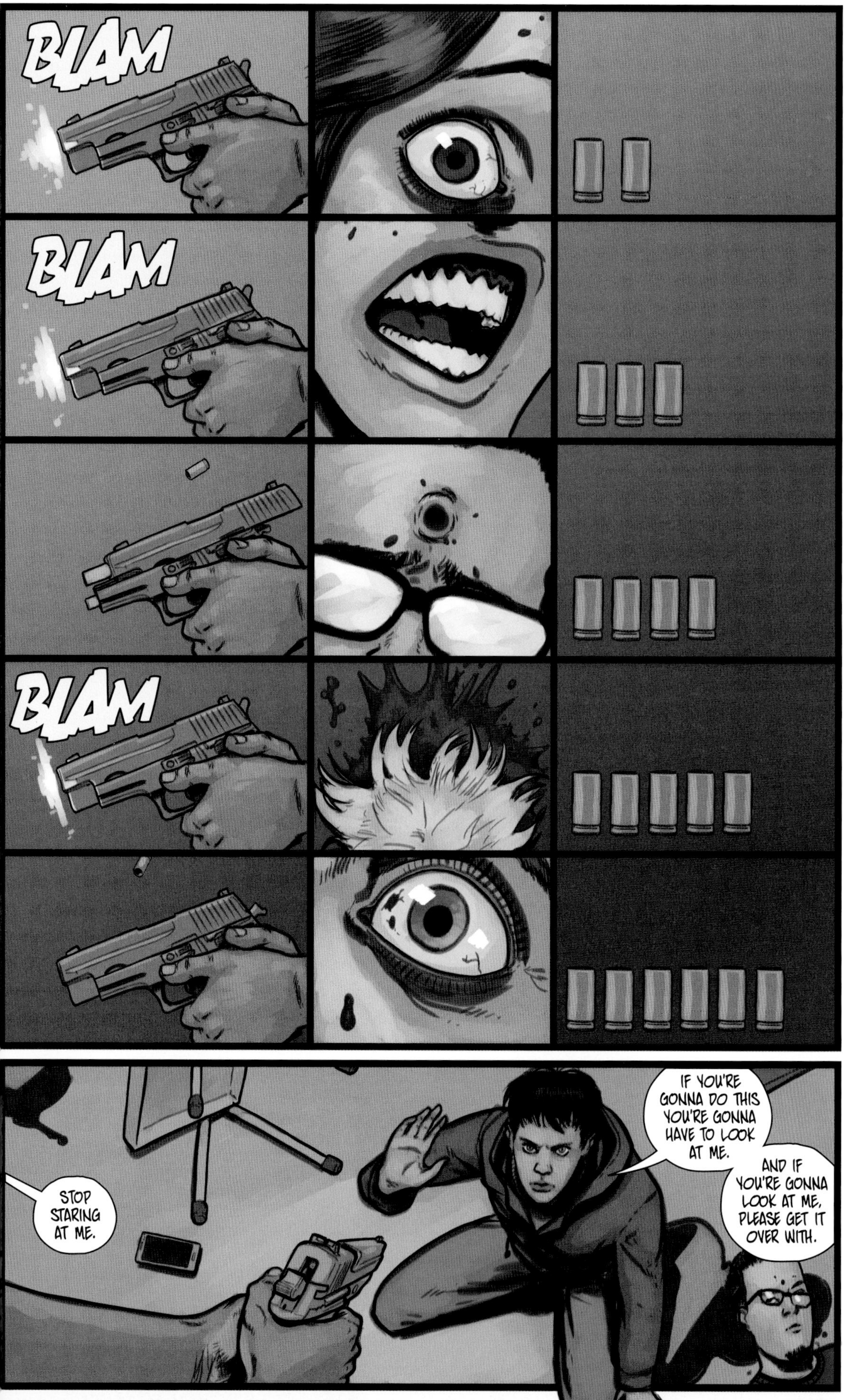
BLAM
BLAM
BLAM
STOP STARING AT ME.
IF YOU'RE GONNA DO THIS YOU'RE GONNA HAVE TO LOOK AT ME.
AND IF YOU'RE GONNA LOOK AT ME, PLEASE GET IT OVER WITH.

Panel 1
Charles squeezes the trigger. The gun jams. Abby is still caught in a reflexive flinch although she's true to her word—she doesn't look away.

SFX
Clik

Panel 2
Charles clears the jammed round as Abby spies his phone, still bright with a text message, on the floor a few feet away.

CHARLES
Abby...

Panel 3
Abby freezes in mid-grab for the phone as Charles jams the gun tightly under his own chin rather than aiming at her again. A few tears of desperation work down his face.

ABBY
Charles, this isn't--

CHARLES
Don't tell Jada I was scared.

Panel 4
We don't see Charles shoot himself, just Abby's reaction to it. Pure agony rips her apart as the brilliant flash of the gunshot lights up the frame.

SFX
BANG

Panel 5
Abby scrambles for the phone again as Charles's fallen body lies in the foreground of the shot, gun just slightly beyond his fingers. She's in shock, pale and also crying, but she's still moving, like the soldier buried inside the traumatized shell was trained to do.

ABBY
Shit, Charles! Shit, shit, shit... What'd you do that for?!

Panel 6 (small.)
Abby has the phone, moving to dial 911, but on the screen is a text, a single word in caps. As she stares the phone begins to ring.

TEXT:
ECHO.

SFX
brrrrRRRRRING...brrrrRRRRRING...

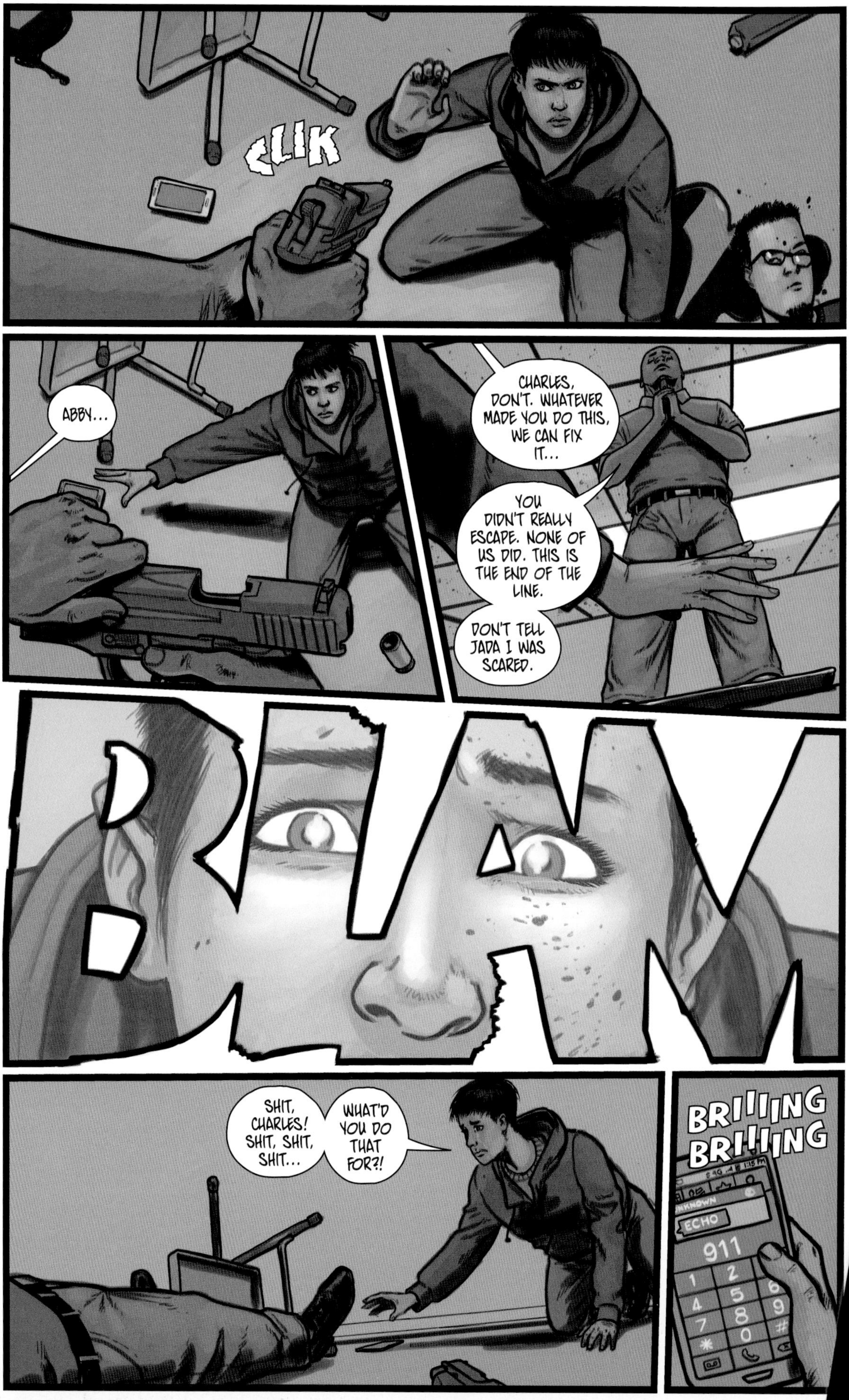
CLIK
ABBY...
CHARLES, DON'T. WHATEVER MADE YOU DO THIS, WE CAN FIX IT...
YOU DIDN'T REALLY ESCAPE. NONE OF US DID. THIS IS THE END OF THE LINE.
DON'T TELL JADA I WAS SCARED.
BLAM
SHIT, CHARLES! SHIT, SHIT, SHIT...
WHAT'D YOU DO THAT FOR?!
BRIIIING
BRIIIING
ECHO
911